"A wild and weird collection of fantasy stori[es ...] sense of fun. Highly recommended!"
—*New York Times* be[stselling] author of *V-Wars* [and ... Jud]ger series

"Plenty of adventures that end with a twist that leave you shaking your head in pleased surprise."
—Jody Lynn Nye, author of *View from the Imperium* and *Dragon's Deal*

"Whole-hearted adventure, swashbuckling fun, daring heroics and plenty of humor. Prepare to be thrilled and amazed!"
—Gail Z. Martin, author of *Scourge* and *The Chronicles of the Necromancer*

"From the ridiculous to the sublime to the downright heartfelt and—at some instances—mildly terrifying, Ventrella's collection promises you that in Fortannis, anything and everything is up for grabs."
—Tee Morris, author of the *Ministry of Peculiar Occurrences* series

"Heroic tales are side by side with character studies, with workaday people just trying to get by in a fantasy realm, with tragedy and comedy."
—Ryk Spoor, author of the *Balanced Sword* trilogy

"Fortannis is a complex world. This richness gives its authors plenty of room to move around."
—Allen L. Wold, author of *The Planet Masters* and *Jewels of the Dragon*

Want bards? Check. Elves? Check. Betrayal? Love? Sacrifice? Humor? Got 'em all."
—Peter Prellwitz, author of the *Shards Universe*

Other Books by Michael A. Ventrella

Terin Ostler and the Arch Enemies
Terin Ostler and the War of the Words
Terin Ostler and the Axes of Evil
Terin Ostler and the Zombie King (and other stories)
Bloodsuckers: A Vampire Runs for President
Big Stick
Skeptic Soup

Anthologies edited by Michael
Tales of Fortannis
Baker Street Irregulars (with Jonathan Maberry)
Baker Street Irregulars: The Game is Afoot! (with Jonathan Maberry)
Release the Virgins!
Across the Universe (with Randee Dawn)
Three Time Travelers Walk Into…
The Eye of Argon and the Further Adventures of Grignr the Barbarian

Books edited by Michael
It's a Wonderful Death (by Derek Beebe)

Nonfiction
Long Title: Looking For the Good Times: Examining the Monkees Songs (with Mark Arnold)
Headquarters: The Monkees Solo Years (with Mark Arnold)
How to Argue the Constitution with a Conservative
The Beatles on the Charts

Tales of Fortannis
edited by
Michael A. Ventrella

FANTASTIC
BOOKS

Collection © 2024
(This page continues on page 255 for individual story copyrights.)

This novel is a work of fiction. All the characters, organizations, and events portrayed in it are likewise fictional, and any resemblance to real people, organizations, or events is purely coincidental.

All rights reserved. Printed in the United States of America. No part of this publication may be reproduced, stored in a retrieval system, or transmitted in any form or by any means, digital, electronic, mechanical, photocopying, recording, or otherwise, or conveyed via the internet or a website without prior written permission of the publisher, except in the case of brief quotations embodied in critical articles and reviews.

Fantastic Books
1380 East 17 Street, Suite 2233
Brooklyn, New York 11230
www.FantasticBooks.biz

ISBN: 978-1-5154-5829-6

First Edition, 2024

Contents

Introduction by Michael A. Ventrella. 7
The Mystery of the Dead Cat in the Darkness by Bernie Mojzes. 9
Hidden Bouquet by Derek Beebe. 24
The Lost by Miles Lizak. 33
The Vacarran Corsair by Jesse Grabowski. 52
A Charming Encounter by Tera Fulbright. 65
Hoarfrost by Susan Bianculli. 74
The Curse of the Dwarven Necromancer by W. Adam Clarke. 87
The Dragon in the Kettle by Christine L. Hardy. 104
Bartleby Goes Adventuring by Jesse Hendrix. 119
Unscarred by Mike Strauss. 139
The Otherside Alliance by Jon Cory. 151
Chalric Hill by Henry "The Mad" Hart. 177
A Matter of Death and Life by Mark Mensch. 196
The Mutiny of Broken Things by Beth Patterson. 212
Greenpool by Sarah Stegall. 226
Garg the Good by Dominic Bowers-Mason. 246
About the Authors. 250

Introduction
Michael A. Ventrella

Welcome to the magical world of Fortannis—a place where adventure awaits to waylay you around every corner.

It's a land where humans mingle with stubborn dwarves, mysterious elves, and feathered biata to battle against shape-shifting gryphons, necromantic zombies, and silly goblins. It's a land where things are never as they seem, where good and evil are not always clear-cut, and where the strong do not always prevail.

In Fortannis, one can learn magic by summoning the power of the flow of order in the world, to tie yourself to the living cycle of all around you. Or, if your inclinations are darker, you can be tempted by the flow of chaos and entropy, which allows you to create undead abominations and cast substantially more powerful spells (in exchange for the corruption of your soul and the destruction of the land around you).

Fortannis was originally created years ago for a live action role-playing game called the Alliance. The game has chapters all over the US and Canada, where players experience the adventures it provides. A dozen or so years ago, I began writing novels set in this world (although I admittedly ignored most of the rules of the game). Knowledge of the game is not necessary for your enjoyment of these books or the stories in this collection.

The three novels I wrote in the land of Fortannis have recently been reissued as *Terin Ostler and the Arch Enemies*, *Terin Ostler and the War of the Words*, and *Terin Ostler and the Axes of Evil*. There were also a bunch of short stories that I had written that feature Terin Ostler and the gang that have been compiled into the collection *Terin Ostler and the Zombie King (and other stories)*. Derek Beebe also wrote a novel in the world of Fortannis which takes place after the Terin Ostler novels and features Terin and his fellow squires as well, called *It's a Wonderful Death*.

While all this was going on, I also edited a series of five Fortannis anthologies with short stories written by other authors. The book you currently are reading features the best stories from those collections.

I am very proud of the stories collected here. There are grand adventures, humorous contrivances, and strong morality tales. You'll meet clever con artists, suspicious spies, and pompous nobles. There are unexpected twists and turns and danger lurking on every page.

Happy adventuring!

The Mystery of the Dead Cat in the Darkness
Bernie Mojzes

Normally, finding a dead cat is a bad thing, especially when it's nailed to your front door. But there are worse things.

Being poor, unemployable, and shunned by society, for three.

Being suddenly but discretely wealthy, but still unemployable and shunned by society, for another.

If you're reading this now, then you probably already know some of my earlier adventures: you've either read my own (entirely true, and almost unbiased) accounts, or were at least subjected to the lurid revisionism of the local bards and broadsheets. "The Ballad of Maris Goselin" is only slightly less offensive than the fabrications printed in the *Ashbury Times*. If you can't be bothered to do basic research, well, don't look to me to fill you in. I've done my part, and paid my dues. Suffice to say, my last job earned me enough money that I never needed to work again. Which I suppose is good, if dull, because it's not like clients were lining up at my door.

Except for the cat. And that didn't really count as "lining up." More like just hanging around.

Which is exactly what my own life consisted of at that point. Hanging around and waiting for something to happen to break through the daily monotony of dining (alone) in Ashbury's finest restaurants and then drinking myself stupid until it was late enough to go to sleep.

Can there be anything worse than boredom?

I examined the cat. It wasn't terribly large, but showed no signs of being feral; its coat was glossy and well-groomed, a calico, and it wore a worked leather collar with a bell. A large spike had been driven through its chest and into my oak door. Blood stained and matted the fur beneath the wound, and discolored the wood below.

Very curious, and I decided I'd begin my investigation immediately upon recovering from my hangover the following afternoon. In the meantime, it wouldn't do to have a cat hanging from my door. What would my neighbors say? They already hated and feared me. I would, I decided, put it in a canvas sack and store it in the basement until the morning. I reached for the cat.

And learned exactly what is worse than boredom.

As I carefully tugged the dead cat off the nail, it hissed and spat, and raked a sharp claw across my cheek. I dropped it and jumped back, gracefully catching my heel on a cobblestone, and sprawled on my back.

The last I saw of the dead cat, it was racing into an alley.

There was no way I'd be able to catch it, so I went inside, poured myself a glass of wine, and collapsed on the bed. And I don't remember much else.

I awoke with the expected pounding hangover and a face full of bees. Which, in hindsight, should have been a clue that something was wrong. But at that moment, the bees were only an annoying and dangerous impediment to getting my face over a briefly empty chamber pot.

I managed to scoop them away with no loss of life, and afterward, spent the remainder of the day sheltering in the quietest, darkest, coolest place in my humble abode, with cool compresses against both the back of my neck and my forehead.

The sun had crept low enough that his insufferable gaze intruded through my windows into even the darkest depths of my home, my hangover refuge, when I heard something crashing against my door. It was as if a stone giant had come calling. I pressed my wrists against my ears to block the sound, and rolled over.

The sound came again.

"Go away," I said. Perhaps. I'm not certain that I actually moved my mouth. This was the worst hangover I'd ever had. My head pounded, and felt like it had been stuffed with cotton, stretching my skin painfully. My kidneys hurt. Everything hurt.

Again, that insufferable crashing against the door. I remember wondering how long the wood could possibly withstand the abuse. I managed to reach the door before the timbers splintered, throwing it open with what I hoped was a suitably impressive display of force.

"If you touch my house again," I said, "I will kill you, and everyone in your family."

"I should hope not," said Sir Edwin, for that was who had been torturing my ears. "I think my wife would be rather put out by being killed."

I tried to get my eyes open enough to see him. It was at that moment that the air filled with bees, clearly come to protect me in my moment of distress. I remember hoping they wouldn't hurt Sir Edwin too badly. And then I remember realizing that, no, I didn't actually care, as long as he went away.

"What are you doing here?"

"I followed the bees, now, didn't I?" Sir Edwin sounded pleased with himself. I couldn't tell if he was preening; I still couldn't get my eyes open properly.

And I still might have killed him, but the bees corroborated his story, so I settled for just thinking bad thoughts. The bad thoughts swirled around my head like bats caught in a sudden storm. In fact, everything was swirling around, both inside and out of my head.

"You look terrible," Edwin said.

I considered telling him to fuck off, but decided to collapse instead.

Worst hangover ever.

Where Sir Edwin managed to find a whole bathtub's worth of ice in the middle of summer (and what it cost him), I still don't know. I also didn't know where he dredged up the sorry excuse for a healer whose countenance hovered over my face when I awoke. She was an antique, a septuagenarian at the very least, with a single tooth protruding at an unlikely angle from her wrinkled face. Her hair clearly hadn't seen blade or comb since she was a child; there were twigs and leaves caught up in the matted tangles, and between blinks of my eyes, a brown-whiskered face shoved strands of white hair out of its way to peer down at me from atop her head.

The image sent shivers through my body. No, it wasn't the image. It was the fact that I was sitting in a tub of ice water.

I tried to get up, but the healer put a withered hand against my chest, and with her mighty, twig-like arm, pushed me back down.

"Need to get your temperature down," the crone said. The rat in her hair nodded in agreement. "So stay put until I say otherwise."

Given that the monumental effort needed to lift my body was far beyond what little strength I had—most of which had left me after my first attempt to stand—my nodded assent was unnecessary. Still, it seemed only polite.

She harumphed, but accepted my promise. I watched her shuffle away, and then things got a bit hazy.

Next thing I knew, strong hands were gripping me under my arms and hauling me out of the tub. I considered threatening my assailant's life, but it seemed too much trouble. Far easier to just let him lay me atop my kitchen table and towel me dry.

I blinked my eyes, trying to get them to focus. When they did, I realized it was Sir Edwin. His hands felt hot on my skin through the towel, and then even hotter when he held my wrists fast and leaned his body across my thighs, effectively restraining me. I tested it. I'm pretty sure if I was in full health, I could have squirmed away, but as it was, I was helpless.

"If only your wife could see us now," I said. "I'm sure she'll want to hear all about this little adventure. Especially since she's barely forgiven you for the last time."

The crone hobbled up and scowled into my face. She wrapped her fingers into my hair and tugged a bit harder than necessary to hold my head immobile, and then she jabbed a knobby finger into my cheek.

The pain was indescribable. I tried my best to describe it with my screams, but I'm sure I did an inadequate job.

The crone, on the other hand, seemed unimpressed with my vocabulary, and continued to poke and prod at my cheek. She leaned in close and sniffed. She pinched and squeezed, and I learned that what I'd earlier thought was pain was really just mild discomfort.

"Oh," Sir Edwin said. "I forgot to make introductions. Lady Goselin, I'd like you to meet Laura's grandmother, Larissa."

I have an unfailing ability to impress new acquaintances. Usually negatively.

"Ah. Um." It was difficult to speak between screams, but I did my best. "It's a pleasure to meet you."

"It's gone septic," Larissa said. "You're going to die."

A wound gone septic is not necessarily a death sentence, especially not with the miracle of modern magic. Even before proper curative spells were perfected, there were healing balms and charms that could draw the poison from all but the worst infections, and in extreme cases, there were surgeries to excise or amputate the affected area.

Larissa, it turned out, was no minor hedge witch, despite her somewhat hedge-like appearance. She was a professor emeritus at the Royal College of Healing Arts. Which explained her bedside manner.

She had performed all the greater healings while I was unconscious, and all it had done was slow the progression of the illness. It was only her knowledge of ancient and discredited techniques—old wives' remedies that had been "proven" by the medical authorities to have no beneficial effects, such as ice to reduce fever, and herbal medicines that worked on a purely physiological basis—that had brought me to anything resembling a state of coherence.

"It's a magical affliction," she explained, "but it's not constructed like any spell I've ever seen. It's a crazy tangle that shouldn't work, by any of the rules of magic I have ever seen, and nothing that I know has worked to counter it. This was no accident. Do you have any enemies who might want to do you harm?"

Sir Edwin kindly laughed out loud, since I was feeling too weak to do it myself. "Only half of Ashbury," he said.

"Used to be three quarters," I said. "I've been slacking."

I closed my eyes and tried to visualize the spell infecting my cheek, and more. It had gotten into the bone, I could tell. Yes, I could see it: sickly green and yellow tendrils of magic, red, and black—the color of pus, of infection, of fever, of necrosis—twisted and tangled around my body, permeating my flesh and bones.

"I recognize this," I said. "But the only person I've ever seen use magic like this is in the deepest cell under the Duke's castle. Edwin knows who I'm talking about."

Nine months earlier, I had—with the help of an insane man named Brian, two guards named Ned and Buckminster, and our very own Sir Edwin—defeated a plot in which an evil mage sought to make himself a doppleganger of the Duke, and his partner into the Duchess. This looked like his magic.

"You need to convince him to remove the spell," Larissa said. "Or kill him. That should dissipate it."

"Can you get me into the dungeons?" I asked Sir Edwin.

He shook his head. "It's not him. The villain died last month, of a fever."

"Then I need to see his lover. Partner. What was her name? Melissa something?"

"Malena," Sir Edwin said. "Malena Bane. And you can't. She's gone. The Duke decided that she was just a pawn, and harmless. After Tomas died, he set her free."

To say I spoke freely of the Duke's naiveté is, perhaps, an understatement. By the time I had finished my monologue, several bottles of not-inexpensive wine lay smashed on the floor and my bees swarmed through the house in a confused rage. Sir Edwin cowered within my wardrobe. Larissa did not. She stood and waited, lips pursed, until I came into range, and then slapped me.

I'd like to think that in the heat of the moment, she simply forgot the magically festering wound on my cheek. That she would have realized that it would have been kinder to disembowel me with a rusty scythe, and done so.

It took everything I had to calm the bees. Not because I cared at that moment what happened to Larissa, but because I love my bees, and didn't want any unnecessary deaths. Larissa may have deserved to be stung by a hundred bees, but she wasn't a threat, and those bees didn't deserve to die from my anger.

"Screw it," I said. "I can see how this spell is put together. I can pull it apart."

"No, you mustn't!" For the first time, genuine concern flashed across Larissa's face. Or perhaps it was fear.

"I've taken apart spells like this before," I said. "You just have to find the right thread and the whole thing unravels."

"It's a trap," Larissa said. "The spell that's making you sick is just a container for another spell. Pull it apart, and you'll loose the sickness as a plague over all of Ashbury."

I had thought nothing she said could dissuade me from tearing this wretched spell off me. I was wrong.

Malena Bane had been escorted to the city gates and told not to come back. Though nobody reported having seen her since, clearly she'd ignored that advice, just as she'd ignored the rules that said you can't imprison people and take their place, and then start torturing and killing everyone who might have a problem with that.

In a city the size of Ashbury, finding her at all would be a feat; finding her quickly was nearer to an impossibility. Unless you were me. I had a hundred thousand pairs of eyes at my disposal. The only problem was that they were only good during the day, and I'd wasted away the daylight almost dying. If Larissa's ministrations could keep me alive another twenty-four hours, I had no doubt my bees could find Malena Bane.

But while Malena wasn't the least of my problems, she also wasn't the worst of them. Somewhere out there was a dead cat, and whatever was going on with me was tied closely to that cat. I could feel the ghost of the thread of malignant energy tethering us together. And so, with a strip of willow bark between my teeth—which almost overpowered the taste of the other foul concoctions Larissa had required I gag down—and a flask of sweet cream in my pocket, I set off into the dark of night.

Sir Edwin tried to accompany me, but I knew his presence would only distract. For this, I needed to be alone.

This was no systematic search. Nor was it random. I opened my eyes only as much as needed to keep from tumbling over curbs or stepping in front of carriages. Instead, I felt for that wisp of death that linked me to the cat and followed, through streets and alleys, behind heaps of trash and down drainage tunnels. Over fences, or under them, or through them if need be. I tried to conserve my strength as much as possible.

Once, I was accosted by four roughs in the alley behind a tavern where the dead cat had hidden. One of them joked about wanting to get into my purse, in a way that made it clear that it wasn't my purse that was on his mind, but when he grabbed me and felt the heat of my fever, he released me quickly. Nobody wants to play with plague.

I held on to him, pulling him close to stare into his eyes.

"Come on, then," I said. "Come die with me."

He pushed me away roughly. But not before I learned his face. If I lived through this, I would come back here some night.

Big if. The tussle took more from me than I expected. I crawled away, following the dead cat's trail. I heard the men's jeers only vaguely; they didn't matter, as long as they didn't stop me.

What mattered was the cat, and the cat wasn't far away. I found her at the end of the alley, hiding behind a broken water barrel. She looked worse than I remembered, some of the fur coming out in patches; whatever affliction I suffered was but an echo of the rot and decay which ravaged the poor dead cat.

I wasn't suffering from some illness that would eventually kill me; I was suffering from death itself. I despaired then. How do you cure that? There were only two ways to save myself: find some way to bring a dead cat back to life, or unravel the spell and loose death and decay on the whole city.

The cat cowered away from me, ready to run. I knew I'd be hard-pressed to catch a skittish cat when in the best of health. In the shape I was in now… even a dead cat could outrun me.

I put a small bowl down and poured some cream for the dead cat, pushed the bowl close to the barrel and stepped back. I spoke gentle nonsense to the creature. The cat took nearly twenty minutes to approach the bowl, and another five before she dared to taste it. It was nearly dawn when she consented to let me pet her. She was cold to the touch.

She arched her ragged body against my hand and vibrated. It should have been a purr, but the air escaped through the hole in her chest with a moist, rumbling hiss.

When I stood, she twined between my legs, smearing the cream that leaked from her body onto my clothes.

"Come on, then," I told her, "let's go home."

The cobblestones were warming under the morning sun when we arrived at my door, and my friends were humming and buzzing happily as they emerged from the hive on my roof and prepared to embark on their daily rounds. The effects of willow bark had worn off, and I ached as my fever spiked. The dead cat followed on unsteady legs, keeping as much to the shadows as she could.

My front door was ruined. The heavy, iron spike was still jammed in the splintered wood, and the cat's viscera still stained the surface. It was dried and had started to peel. Worse, it had started to stink.

I worked the spike free, further damaging the wood. I was about to toss it into the street when I saw the dead cat cowering away from it, back arched and fur raised. That meant something, though my fevered mind couldn't think what it might be. I wrapped the spike in a handkerchief and shoved it into my belt pouch. Once it was out of sight, the cat relaxed, and rubbed her cold body against my legs.

When I pulled the door open, she ran inside. I heard hissing, and Sir Edwin's startled shout, and a sudden rearrangement of furniture. I found Sir Edwin standing on a chair, looking as pale as I felt, blade pointed at the dead cat.

I scooped her up and rubbed behind her ears. She purred, and leaked pinkish cream on my shirt.

"That's an abomination," Larissa said, making a warding gesture. Her rat, which had been—I think—helping her sort twigs out of a bowl of dried herbs, squeaked and ran up her arm to hide in her hair. "A necromantic abomination. You could be jailed for this. We all could be."

"I think I'll call her Thana," I said, placing the dead cat on my bed.

"You're delirious," Larissa said. "You need to get some sleep, and let me tend you. And while you sleep, I'll do what I can to banish this thing back to the grave, where it belongs. You'll feel better when you're rested."

I certainly couldn't feel worse. And I wanted nothing more than to lie down. It was a struggle just to care whether I ever woke up again. But I couldn't afford to do that. Not yet.

"No graves, no banishing. Help me get to the roof." The ladder was more than I could manage by myself.

Larissa crossed her arms, and Sir Edwin shook his head. The rat poked his little face out of Larissa's hair and shook his head as well.

"Edwin. Just five minutes to talk to my bees. Then I'll rest."

"Five minutes?" He shifted on his chair.

I nodded. "And then rest. I promise."

I dreamed in hexagons. Fragmentary images in yellow and blue and violet, and colors deeper than violet that I have never seen with my own eyes. Hundreds of faces, thousands, as my bees searched the city.

Sir Edwin woke me a few hours past noon.

"Something's wrong with the bees," he said. "They're angry."

They weren't. They were excited. They'd found what I'd asked them to find—that singular, special flower that the Duke in his wisdom had deemed "harmless"—and they had begun to swarm into my home, eager to lead me to it.

"They found her," I said. "I need to go."

I collected what I needed: dagger, sword, a poisoned knife… I tried to think what else I might need, but my mind was foggy, and my strength started to fail me before I'd even finished dressing.

Larissa handed me a glass of greenish-brown liquid; I swallowed it without asking what it was. She gave me a couple of small leaves, each about the size of my thumb, to chew. My mouth went numb almost immediately, which would normally have bothered me, but at the moment, it only meant that I wouldn't have to taste the willow bark she gave me next.

I felt somewhat more energetic, almost like I wasn't dying.

Larissa gave me more of the leaves. "Use them when you need them," she said. "Not before."

"Yes, ma'am." I put them into my belt pouch, next to the iron spike.

I scooped up Thana, wrapped in a towel to shield her from the light, and Sir Edwin and I went out into the glare of the afternoon sun, following the bees.

Freedom had not treated Malena Bane kindly. She had found refuge in a crowded tenement in the Rail District.

"Where are we?" Sir Edwin asked. He glanced around nervously, like a shipwrecked sailor landing in a foreign and hostile land. His hand strayed to the hilt of his sword, and stayed there.

"Ferris Street," I said. There was no sign, of course. The Rail District lay just south of the Docks, and adjacent to the slaughterhouses, and derived its name from the rails that ran live animals from the docks and dead ones back. Once the slaughterhouses built their own docks to bypass the rail tax, there wasn't much left but the people. When I was still just a girl, the duke—the former duke—vowed to clean up the city. The guard swept through and arrested hundreds of whores and pickpockets, drunks and gamblers. They put cobbles down atop the mud and whitewashed the walls. They put up signs for streets, and for the few businesses they hadn't closed down.

A week later, Rail District struck back. They hammered the metal of the signs into weapons and used the cobbles to smash in the bars of the prison in Ashbury's largest jail break in history, before burning it to the ground.

So now, the streets are mud again, and there are no signs, and you won't find that prison break in any of the books.

Sir Edwin wrinkled his nose. Possibly against the odor. "This is unbelievable. In Ashbury! Its very existence is an affront to decency. It should be razed to the ground."

I didn't have the energy to argue. The effects of the mouth-numbing leaves were starting to wear off.

"However, it is fitting that our quarry is to be found surrounded by the worst dregs of humanity."

"I grew up here," I said.

"What?" Sir Edwin stopped in his tracks. "Here? In one of these... I hesitate to call them buildings."

"No." I pointed down an alleyway. "Down there. There's shade in the summer, and there's always a trash heap. Enough to keep a fire going in the winter, and attract rats for food."

"I don't understand."

I spun to face him, anger overcoming the sudden dizziness. "You have no idea how hard it is to change your position in life. Look at you. No matter how stupidly you live your life, you haven't managed to become destitute. The people here work hard, when they can find work, and harder when they can't. They do work that would kill you, working at the docks, or the slaughterhouses, shoveling coal or shit or breaking rock to turn into the cobbles that pave your street, and what do they get for it? They get old and sick and die, and then they get blamed for not working hard enough to live a good life. Do you have any idea what your friend 'Lady' Maris Goselin did to get out of that trap?"

I pushed him, and tried to pretend that I hadn't actually forced myself to take a step back. Thana hissed in her towel.

"Go home, Sir Edwin, where it's safe."

I braced myself, and pushed him again, and this time he was the one that stepped back.

"Maris, I'm sorry. I wasn't thinking." Sir Edwin reached for me, but I slapped his hand away.

"Don't touch me!" And now, finally, my friends clued in to my anger and swarmed up between us, forcing the bastard back, away, and down the street before I called them back.

The confrontation with Sir Edwin had exhausted me. I fished more leaves from my pouch and jammed them into my mouth, leaned against a sun-warmed brick wall until that false sense of well-being percolated through my body.

The bees had shown me her window, on the third floor of a grimy tenement. If I was healthy, it would have been no difficulty to scale the wall. I wasn't, and I had to settle for the stairs. That was hard enough.

The lock on her door gave its secrets without difficulty, despite my jittery hands. Thana tried to trip me as I pushed the door open, and slipped through the crack before I could.

Malena Bane sat on her filthy mattress, facing me. She had never been pretty, except for the one brief, shining moment when she had looked like the Duchess. But now, she was gaunt. Her bones showed through her cheeks, and her clothes hung off her emaciated frame. There was nothing that hinted of food in her room, and I wondered when she had last eaten.

Suddenly, I no longer wanted to kill her.

"You're more resourceful than I expected," she said. "But it won't help you. If there's one thing you taught me, it was to prepare for the unexpected."

I closed my eyes and let myself see the threads of her magic. They wound around me like poisoned brambles, and coiled around her like dense armor. It would deflect anything foreign. Any blade I struck her with would shatter. My bare hands would suffer a similar fate, and my magic would slide off her like water on wax. In time, I could pick apart her defensive spells. But time was what I didn't have; I would be dead before the sun set, I knew, or I would give in to the temptation to save myself, and damn the city.

I closed the door, and sat next to her on the bed. Fleas hopped away from me. Thana jumped into my lap.

"You were always the real wizard," I said. "Not him."

"Tomas," she said. Grief and loss welled up, drowning the hatred and madness in her eyes.

I wondered what she'd have made of the smirk on Tomas' lips when he struck the Duchess, knowing that every blow would be reflected on Malena's body. Would it surprise her if I told her? Would she even be able to hear it?

I'd been with a man like Tomas, a soldier whose love promised a life without whoring, back when that's how I made my living. A man whose persistent, cruel mockery made me almost believe, the first time he hit me, that I surely deserved it.

Almost.

Instead, I jammed a knife through his femoral artery and watched him bleed out.

A hundred moments like this were what separated my life from Malena Bane's. And thousands of moments of pure chance, pure dumb luck.

Nothing I could say now would change her course. The madness had settled too deeply in her mind, so deeply entwined with her magic that I couldn't tell which had given rise to which. But I had to try.

"I can help you," I said. "I know where you've been. I know how hard it is. It doesn't have to be this way."

Her face tightened, and she stood, spinning to face me with a knife drawn. "What do you know? How could you possibly imagine what my life has been like?"

She threw down the blade.

"You don't get to die quickly. I'm going to watch you die like Tomas did. I'll hold you in my arms like I held him. I'll cradle you as you scream in pain because a little scratch went unattended, and the magic-proof cell you put us in kept me from healing him. And when you're gone, I'll find the guards who watched without helping, and everyone else, and I will not stop until they are all dead."

"I understand," I said, because I did.

And I flung Thana into Malena Bane's face.

Malena's defenses protected her from foreign assault. But the dead cat was her magic. Thana's claws dug into Malena's flesh, distracting her for the few seconds I needed to find the iron spike, also imbued with Malena's magic, and jam it into the poor girl's throat.

It felt like I was killing myself.

Thana ran under the bed as Malena fell back onto the mattress. She clutched at her throat. Her mouth worked, but no sound came out.

I knelt at her side, and brushed the hair from her eyes.

"I'm sorry," I said. "For everything. We can end this now, together." I placed her dagger into her hand, and helped her press the tip against my ribs, aimed at my heart.

Her lips moved. Closer, they said.

I leaned in, and the blade moved up to my throat, and then to my cheek. She drew a line of red across my face, under my eye, parallel to the festering wound left by Thana's claws.

I kissed her forehead, and when she was gone, I closed her eyes.

The fever was already fading, and the infected cat scratch was cooling, but I felt worse than when I climbed the tenement stairs. I fetched Thana's cold, stiff corpse from under the bed and clutched her close, rocking softly next to Malena's body.

The door creaked as it opened.

Sir Edwin, of course. Nobody else in the Rail District smelled of such fine perfumes.

"It's over, then," he said. "You didn't need me."

Of course I did. He was the only friend I had left, the only one I hadn't already driven away, or abandoned, but I'd poisoned even that. Only his knightly sense of duty brought him back.

"Give Larissa my thanks," I said. "And I'll pay for her services promptly."

He put a hand on my shoulder. "Let's get you home."

I flinched away. "I can't. Not now. Not yet."

He crouched next to me, put a hand on my forehead, tilted my head into the grimy light to examine my wounds. Then he nodded.

"When you're ready, then," he said.

I listened to his footsteps down the stairs, until he was gone.

The problem was, I wasn't sure where home was any more. I had run so hard and fast and far to get away from this place that I'd lost who I was, and thought myself the better for it. It was only when I was alone with Malena that I realized I hadn't been angry with Edwin. I'd only lashed out at him because I couldn't bear to lay blame where it belonged.

Edwin gave voice to the words I had been thinking. The worst dregs of humanity. Of course it was his fault.

I needed to find who I was, if I was ever to be whole.

I sat with Malena and Thana through the night, remembering pieces of my life I had worked hard to erase.

And in the morning when I stumbled into my house, my friends were waiting.

Malena Bane's real name was Kiema, according to those who remembered her, and that's what we put on her grave, and on the sign Edwin painted over the door: "Kiema Memorial Clinic & Shelter."

When Larissa came to see the building I'd bought on Ferris Street, she declared it a disgrace. Barely adequate. Her nose wrinkled in disgust at the rodent droppings and the boldness of the cockroaches—which is odd for someone with a rat living in her hair, I think—but her eyes shone with the challenge of it.

"It's a crazy idea," she said. "It's not going to make the Rail District a paradise."

I shrugged and gestured toward the door. "If you're having second thoughts, I can find other healers."

"Hrmph." Larissa jabbed a finger at my still-tender cheek—scarred not from a dead cat's claws but from Malena's knife, her final gift, which I had refused to let Larissa heal. "To work for someone stubborn and pig-headed as you are? Doubtful." Her rat stared at me from the back of her hair, chittering in agreement, as she went to inspect what would become the examination rooms.

For once, I didn't try to stifle the grin on my face.

"Well, there's something I'm not used to seeing," said Sir Edwin, who was coming down the stairs from the second floor, wiping his grimy hands on his trousers. A toolbelt hung from his waist, in place of his sword. It looked good on him, though I doubted he'd recognize that as a compliment. He laughed at my gestured response.

"How's it look upstairs?" I asked.

"It'll need some changes to make it defensible. Nothing major."

"But it'll work?"

"Laura says it will. She's the expert."

Had I known before that Sir Edwin's wife volunteered in the women's home where she and her mother had once spent three months in hiding? Had I bothered to learn anything about her other than how to annoy her?

I've made a career of knowing everything about everybody that can be used against them, or against someone else. How to push people away. I still marvel at how much I didn't see.

Maybe it was about time I started.

Hidden Bouquet
Derek Beebe

My dear Terin,
    And Darlissa. And Rendal. And Leander.
    Am I forgetting anyone?

It's your old friend, or brief acquaintance, depending on how fondly you remember me, Elmeki! Yes, I'm still alive. I'm even more shocked than you are. I've been Duke of the Hidden Kingdom for an inexplicable twelve months now. I don't know how I've managed it.

I hope this letter finds you well, or indeed, finds you at all. It's not like we send a lot of messages all the way to Ashbury very often. I wouldn't be surprised if my honeyed words were currently sitting at the bottom of an ocean trench somewhere, unread and unloved. Oh well.

Anyway, assuming you *are* reading this, things have been going as well as could be expected. I've only had three assassination attempts, and none of them got very close to succeeding. And we've only had two armed rebellions, both of which we managed to put down relatively quickly. I got an arrow stuck in my arm a couple months ago, but it's healing up nicely thanks to those potions Leander was kind enough to leave with me.

Speaking of potions, that leads me to the story I wanted to tell you. Don't worry, it's not boring. At least I hope not.

Our tale begins a few weeks ago, with me and General Roque traveling to the distant city of Goolwa far in the eastern reaches of the Hidden Kingdom. Roque's turned out all right, by the way. The months with me seem to have rounded off his rough edges. He still has a sharp tongue, but I'm vaguely confident he hasn't been behind any of the various attempts to kill and or overthrow me. So there's that.

Let me paint a picture for you. Roque and I rode at the head of our caravan of wagons. Goolwa, unlike most of the Kingdom, is not an arid desert, but a scrabbly patch of greenery on a river *next* to an arid desert. Our wagons were covered from a recent sandstorm, and our tempers were not the brightest, so the gorgeous green city before us came off looking a little smug, quite frankly. The buildings all looked brand new and towered five stories up; nothing compared to my own Karratha, of course, but impressive for the boondocks.

Next to me, Roque sneezed, creating a small puff of dust and sand mimicking his entire body. The poor bastard had gotten sick a day out of the city. For a battle-hardened general, he was surprisingly a bit of a baby about it. "You can count me out of any fancy dinners once we get there," he said. "I just want to lie in a soft bed and sleep."

"I didn't bring you all this way to sleep, General," I said. "You're supposed to make sure my head stays on my shoulders."

He snuffled wetly. "Seeing as how my head would be in the same danger as yours, I wouldn't worry about it. That's what all the large intimidating soldiers are for."

"Appearances are important, which is why you'll be making one."

He grumbled mightily, but didn't contradict me. Amazing what a few months had done.

As our caravan approached the city, a dozen soldiers on horseback thundered up to us and blocked the road. We dutifully ground to a halt.

"Halt!" their captain shouted. "What is your business in Goolwa?"

I stood up from my seat, trying to brush off as much sand as I could. "I am Elmeki, Duke of the Hidden Kingdom. I have come to treat with your lord and master."

I looked closer at him. This was not my first such encounter, but I still found it disconcerting. He appeared to me as a man-sized shadow sitting atop a horse, with no details visible within that black shape. Now, I realize this may sound a tad hypocritical to you all, since we've *always* looked that way to you, but it's still new for me!

Goolwa was far enough away from Karratha that when Jabiru exploded, they were not affected. They still retain their veil as Hidden Folk, and for those of us in Jabiru's vicinity who lost our own, they appear to us the same as they would to a foreigner. Which, of course, was the reason we had come.

The captain tilted his head in what I'm sure was a conceited sneer. "We do not allow Unhidden Folk within these walls."

We hadn't had a proper war since Jabiru, but the stage was certainly set for one. Only this time it was for a new reason, an incredibly silly one if you ask me. The Hidden Folk in the far reaches of the country, who still maintained their veil from the Jabiru juice running in their veins, had gone and decided the "Un" Hidden Folk were impure and inferior. They wanted to form their own kingdom separate from mine, seeing as how I and everyone else in Karratha were Unhidden.

I rolled my eyes mightily. "This is a lot of unnecessary posturing, don't you think? I've already arranged this meeting, weeks ago, through messengers."

The captain ignored me and plodded on. This must have all been written out beforehand. "We've heard rumors of Hidden Folk becoming infected by the Unhidden and dying. That you carry some disease within you. Perhaps it's not magic at all that has rendered you inferior, but a malady of the body."

Roque unfortunately chose that moment to sneeze loudly. All the Hidden guards turned to stare at him. "It's just a head cold!" he shouted irritably.

"Look," I said. "I haven't heard a single word of anyone getting infected by anyone. These are just vicious lies concocted to cement your amusing little rebellion here. I'm the Duke of the Hidden Kingdom, and you *will* grant me entry to your cesspool of a city."

The captain grumbled. "You may be permitted to enter, but you will be kept to a single road to the palace. You will be seated far away from any of the Hidden, and must leave the city boundaries when your business is done."

"Lovely!" I said brightly. "I didn't want to sleep here anyway. I can smell the place from here."

Our caravan entered the city under heavy escort. The Goolwan guards gave us a wide berth, and the city streets stood empty where we passed. I saw the huddled and shadowy masses watching us from a clear block away. I couldn't tell, but I'd bet you they wore cloth masks over their faces. It was a shame to see so many hoodwinked by this foolishness.

They led us to a respectable sized palace (not as big as my own, of course!) on the edge of the river. As a matter of fact, it looked like a pale imitation of Karratha itself, with onion domes and everything. Only much smaller and cheaper. We Hidden Folk are not known for our ingenuity in architecture, alas.

We disembarked from our wagons in the palace courtyard.

"You may only take ten men with you," the captain said.

"That doesn't sound very fair," I said. "What if this is a trap?"

"Then I hope you all have wings."

I pulled Roque aside once he was done blowing his nose into a cloth. "Am I in mortal peril, General?"

"I thought the Doomsayer said you would die in Karratha," he said.

"*Die*, yes. Maiming and torture is still an option anywhere."

He shrugged. "I'm going in with you, so it must be safe."

I looked around uncertainly. "This would be a very poor situation to finally get to say I told you so."

Their guards led our guards through ornate—though not as nice—hallways into the main dining hall, which surprisingly was as large as my own. Must have really thrown off the building's planners. The Lord of Goolwa, Bartnil, sat on a golden throne at the far end of the room at the foot of a long table filled with Hidden Folk. At least fifty guards lined the walls. A long table for us sat at the entrance of the hall with a wide empty space between the two parties.

"Greetings, Lord Bartnil!" I said brightly. "Thank you for your glorious hospitality. I truly feel like I'm back home."

"Are you a leper there, as well?" Bartnil responded from across the room.

"Only symbolically, I assure you. We're all as healthy as can be." I shot a quick glance at Roque. "And I've brought you a gift."

I motioned to two of my men who awkwardly carried in a heavy wooden crate wrapped in cloth. They lugged it into the empty center of the room and dropped it with a loud thud. Glass bottles tinkled inside.

"The finest wine in my cellar, which believe me is saying something." I gestured to the men who pulled the cloth away to reveal the crate underneath. "And knowing your silly fears of sickness, I've kept the entire thing wrapped and untouched by our filthy little hands."

Bartnil whispered to his men, and two came forward with the greatest of hesitation to examine the crate. They opened it to reveal a series of dusty old bottles packed in straw. One of them apparently knew something because he read the print on the bottle and looked back with surprise to Bartnil.

"Very well," Bartnil said reluctantly. "We thank you for your gift." A bottle was brought to him. "Hmm. Let's open this now, shall we? I'll look forward to trying it… after my tester has tasted it first. And you, Duke Elmeki."

I grinned. "I was hoping you'd share. I think I'm going to need to be inebriated to get through this night."

They opened the bottle and poured out glasses. Bartnil's poison tester took a long draught and nothing happened. Before any of the Goolwans took a sip, they brought glasses over to us. As they placed them on the table, Roque sneezed, rendering the hushed murmurs on the other end of the room into sudden silence.

"It's just a head cold," he said loudly, his voice echoing off the stone walls.

"Really, Lord Bartnil," I projected across the room. "Spreading these false reports of illnesses? If you're going to insult me, at least say something about my nose."

Bartnil stood up in his golden chair. I could spy the points of a crown sticking out of his shadowy head. "I received them. I did not create them. And they have come from multiple sources."

I patted the wooden table with my hands. "I guess you'll be burning this table once we're done, then?"

"And the dishes."

I shook my head and took a long drink of the wine. It was indeed delicious. "What a waste of good cutlery. You can't keep a lie going forever, you know. Eventually the truth gets out. People talk."

"Not when they're at war with each other."

The Goolwan guards shifted on their feet, ready to spring into action. My own men did the same.

"There's no need for that," I said. "I have no interest in fighting a war with anyone."

Bartnil tilted his head in amusement. "Are you surrendering to me, Duke Elmeki?"

I waved my hand around in the air. "I prefer to think of it as a cowardly compromise. Looking at all these armed guards of yours staring at me menacingly, I suddenly feel inspired to grant you a certain degree of latitude you wouldn't have had before…"

"You bloody coward," Roque muttered under his breath.

I laughed awkwardly and patted his shoulder. "Now, now, General, we're all friends here. No one wants to horrifically disembowel anyone. Isn't that right, Bartnil?"

Bartnil settled back into his throne and tilted his head. "We shall see. Tell me more of this 'latitude'."

The servers brought my wine over to the Goolwan nobles. I watched carefully as Bartnil took a hesitating sip, and then a longer one.

"Goolwa is far removed from Karratha," I said. "I have little actual interest in ruling these far-flung provinces, but I must maintain the appearance of control, you understand."

Bartnil swirled the wine in his glass. "I'm listening."

I took a long gulp myself. "I'm prepared to let you do whatever you want within your own borders, as long as you claim to maintain fealty to me and drop this talk of racial purity and plague. You can have everything you want without a single drop of blood spilled, Hidden or Unhidden." I stopped and looked around abruptly. "Where's the food, by the way? I'm starving."

Bartnil let out an exasperated sigh and motioned for the servers to bring out the dishes. I tore into a leg of some animal. Not sure of what, really...

"I have a counter offer for you," Bartnil said. I could tell he was building up a proper head of steam. "I will take my independence from you. And I will lead a revolution of the *true* Hidden Folk against the unclean such as yourself and your witless lackeys. You will be herded away into the Wastelands, where we will be safe from your *impurity* and *infection*. The Hidden Kingdom will be cleansed of the Unhidden, and made a safe place for the pure once again!"

I nodded thoughtfully, pretending to consider his words carefully. "I see. I see. You *do* realize the 'purity' you're talking about is the result of an evil creature's blood running in your veins, right? Your veil is just the mark of Jabiru, the Great Devourer. That's, ah, not a good thing. If anything, I would say that I'm the pure one, and *you're* the gamey beef in the stew. The only thing I've lost in the process is my direction-finding power, and quite frankly it wasn't that useful very often."

"More unclean lies," Bartnil spat. He actually spat. On the table. One of the servers hurried forward to wipe it up. This is the sort of thing you have deal with out in the sticks. "We are as we have been for untold generations! It is you and yours who have changed. Who are *new*. Wrong."

I laughed nervously. "I'm as terrified of change as much as the next man—"

"Man?" Bartnil interrupted. "How old are you?"

I made a show of looking offended. "I have all my grown up hair, if that's what you're getting at. Does it really matter? I'm the one in charge here."

"For the moment." The Goolwan side of the room chuckled haughtily.

I looked around at them. "Maybe this is just a regional difference, but where I come from, we treat our guests a lot nicer than this."

Bartnil gestured to his guards. "Ah, but you are not my guests. You are my prisoners."

The large intimidating shadow men moved forward. My own guards rushed up from the back wall to form a defensive line in front of my table.

I anxiously climbed onto the table, kicking aside the food, and waved my hands around desperately. "Wait! Wait! No fighting, please!"

Bartnil raised his right hand, and his soldiers paused in the middle of the room. "Do I have your surrender, then?"

How long had it been now? I should have been counting in my head the whole time. "Well, if you *really* feel that strongly about it… Let me get this straight. Your entire rebellion here is based on the fact that you're pure and I'm not?"

"If you want to be simple about it," he said through (presumably) clenched teeth.

"Because me losing my veil, and my evil Jabiru blood, has rendered me less than human?"

"Are you surrendering or not?"

I was running out of things to say. And normally I'm so good at patter. "Surely you realize if you kill us, my Generals will declare war on you. They're all Unhidden too, you know. Karratha and its surrounding region is the most populous part of the Kingdom. You'd be outnumbered."

Bartnil waved his hand at me dismissively. "Kill them."

I held up my hands. "Okay, okay! I surrender! Let's discuss terms. Maybe get a scribe or two in here to write something really flowery—"

A young man screamed in horror at the far corner of the chamber. The poison tester. Finally!

Bartnil turned his head away from me. "What is the meaning of this?"

The tester ran up to him in a mad panic. I could now see his body clearly. He was no longer Hidden. "They've poisoned me, My Lord! Some evil spell! I cannot see you! You are veiled to me!"

Bartnil reared back in disgust. "You're… you've become Unhidden! It's poison!" Their direction-finding power also let them sense whether someone was still veiled or not—either way, a Hidden Person would not see a shadow in the place of a man.

I held up one finger politely. "It's a *cure*, actually."

Bartnil spun to face me. "What did you do to him?!"

"I cured him of his impurity. My foreign friend Leander, he left a bunch of elixirs with me. Bottled spells to remove Jabiru's influence from the Hidden Folk. Basically recreating the effect that happened to everyone in Karratha when Jabiru exploded." I cupped my hands to shout to the panicked taster. "You're welcome, by the way!"

Bartnil pointed at the tester. "Guards! Seize him! Take him away! Don't let him touch us."

"Ah, it's too late for that, I'm afraid. You see, we all drank the wine."

"What?!" he snarled.

I shrugged innocently. "I put the elixir in the wine. Does nothing to me, of course. I'm already cured. But for you lot…?" As if on cue, Bartnil suddenly became visible to me, followed by the rest of them. I waved at him. "Hello, Lord Bartnil! I can see you now!"

Bartnil cried out in despair.

I strolled along the top of the table, making a proper mess of things. "The effect *is*, of course, permanent. You're all Unhidden now, just like us." I made a show of suddenly realizing something. "Oh! That's not good, is it? You just spent the past several months drumming up your own people into a frenzied paranoia against the Unhidden. Telling them we're—and by 'we' I'm including *you*—all inferior and diseased and unclean…" I clapped my hands together. "They're not going to be very happy with you, are they?"

Bartnil took a few halting steps towards me with his fists balled up. "Change me back! Or I'll kill you!"

I help out my hands sheepishly. "Sorry. You can't re-infect someone once they're cured. You're stuck this way now."

Bartnil looked uncertainly at the still Hidden guards surrounding him. They shifted uncomfortably on their feet and looked to one another. "Kill him!" he finally barked.

Before they could move, I spoke up. "I wouldn't do that if I were you."

"Why not?" he snapped.

"The news isn't all bad," I said brightly. "In spite of your atrocious hospitality, I'm prepared to help you out. I am the Duke of the Hidden

Kingdom, after all. We can work together to dispel these ignorant fears against the Unhidden, and thusly ensure your head stays on those finely embroidered shoulders of yours."

The rest of the table guests were visible now. They spoke in frantic hushed tones with one another.

"Take the offer, My Lord, *please!*" one of the women screeched.

"Don't worry," I said. "I'm prepared to overlook this little homicidal misunderstanding. This *is* the Hidden Kingdom, after all."

Bartnil scanned his fellow nobles with rising fear. He finally looked up to me. "Very well, *Duke*. You win. I shall do as you ask."

"Excellent! Our first priority is to spread the word that there is no disease. The Unhidden are uninfected."

Roque sneezed loudly.

"Shut up, you," I hissed.

So that's the end of my amusing little anecdote. Bartnil turned around his propaganda machine with astonishing swiftness and became the champion of the Unhidden cause overnight. Things have settled down since then. There's still some grumbling from the 'true' Hidden Folk, but now it's just worthless griping from the periphery.

All the same though, I would beg good, sweet, noble, finely feathered Leander to please send me as much of that elixir as quickly as he possibly can. I may need to convert some more upstarts. Hurry, before someone else tries to kill me!

Hugs and kisses, Duke Elmeki of the Hidden Kingdom

P.S. I kept my word and put statues of Beryl and Chryseim in every city. You should see the one in Karratha. It's *huge*! I put it right in the city square behind the Great Gate, so everyone entering Karratha is reminded of the brave people who saved their lives. I've also hired a scribe to put her story into a book. He's a bit garbage, but not I'm not paying him very much, so there you go. I'll spread copies of this book throughout the land. The life, and death, of Beryl Truesword will never be forgotten in the Hidden Kingdom. We will always remember her name.

The Lost
Miles Lizak

"The biata people are set apart from the other races of Fortannis by their innate mental ability, a sixth sense of sorts, which allows them not only to read the thoughts and memories of other beings, but to manipulate them. Many theorize that these abilities are tied to ancient artifacts called Homestones, nodes of psychic power to which all biata minds are tethered from birth and which contain their memories long after their deaths. Whatever its source, this mental power is a double-edged sword. Like any tool, it can be used for good or ill, but there is always an element of danger. When one mind meets another, whether they are willingly joined or one is pried open by force, neither can emerge unchanged."
—Sage Uriel Bevington, "On Species of the Realm," pg. 134

Gray streaks of rain pattered against the slate roof of the hall and ran in rivulets down the window, through which the afternoon cast its dull, cool light. The light spread in soft pools with soft shadows across books neatly piled or lined up soldier-like on shelves, stacks of parchment, a heavy chest, and a wash basin. The chaise lounge (that may have been richly upholstered once upon a time) and its matching armchair stood in the center of the room, vacant and sleepy, protected from the draughts of the ancient place by a wide, faded weaving on the outward facing wall. But the wind made it through all the same, sending a bundle of dust and quill shavings skittering across the floor and into a corner. While in the street below, the steady autumn rain began to overflow the gutters and people pulled cloaks around their shoulders and hoods up over their ears, Rorick Del'mora sat hunched over his oaken writing desk and an antique tome, squinting at the swoops and turns of the ancient biata language in which it was written. His master had assigned him the project of translating *Applied Principles of Nhostir Medicine on Age-Demented Minds*, an atrociously pedantic text about memory alteration and retrieval written by a long-winded traditionalist nearly a millennium ago. For the sake of the initiates who would come after him and have to read it, Rorick was trying to trim the monstrosity down and make it a bit more interesting, which was turning out to be more difficult than he expected.

He set down his quill and rubbed his eyes with his fingertips, sending starbursts of light twisting against the dark insides of his eyelids, the reverse-shadows of the lines upon lines of text he had already translated into the Common Tongue. At least he felt no sign of one of the headaches that had been plaguing him for the past few months; he had learned to work through them, and they seemed to be tapering off.

A mouse scratched its way along somewhere inside the wall behind him. He really should get a cat. Stretching his neck and rolling his shoulders back, Rorick adjusted his position in his chair, picked up his quill, and set back to work. No sooner had he set pen to parchment than the bell outside his chamber door rang with an anxious clamor.

He set his quill down again, closed the tome and, standing behind his desk, bade his visitor enter.

A broad-shouldered biata peered around the door. He looked to be around Rorick's age, but nearly a head shorter, with a mess of dark blonde hair. His form was stout and he bore the rounded features characteristic of the lower rings of the city, but he carried himself as a man modestly aware of his own handsomeness. Deep orange plumage speckled with brown and dark red sprung in tufts from his brows and in pinfeathers at his temples, highlighting the grey-blue of his eyes. His wide hands were clawless and calloused, bearing the tiny burns and scars in the webbing between fingers that bespoke an alchemist. Something about the man seemed strangely familiar. His eyes widened as they met Rorick's.

"Can I help you?" Rorick asked, pointedly.

The man stepped inside, one hand on the half-opened door, as if to make a quick escape if it became necessary.

"Master Torvick was indisposed." His voice was deeper than Rorick would have expected, "They told me I'd be seeing you instead."

"I see."

"Is that a problem?"

"Of course not. Please, take a seat." He indicated the lounge chair with an open palm as he stepped out from behind his desk. The man obeyed, settling into the divot that had been worn into the chaise by countless patients before him. Rorick lowered himself into the arm chair across from it. "Is this your first time seeking counsel with a Nohstir?"

The biata looked down at his hands. He nodded. "Is it true? That the oaths you take…?"

"Forbid us from breaking the confidence of our patients? Yes, that is our oath."

"So." He looked up at Rorick with the usual kind of caution that accompanied the question. "Nothing I say will leave this room?"

"Even if you told me you were a Thessi spy and guilty of high treason."

"Would you believe me if I told you that?"

"That would be irrelevant."

The biata paused.

"Let's start with the basics, shall we?" Rorick folded his hands in his lap, the way he had often watched Master Torvick do. "What should I call you?"

"My name is Arin. Arin Krayn."

"Why have you come here today, Arin?"

"I recently… lost a close friend."

"I see. Those in mourning often come to the Nohstir to ease their grief. When did your friend pass on?"

"He's not dead, not exactly. But he was lost ten moons ago."

Rorick nodded stoically. Denial and delusion were not uncommon in such cases, where the truth was painful.

"I see. And what were the circumstances of his… loss?"

"It's rather a long story."

"We have as much time as you need."

In the moment of silence that followed, Arin opened his mouth and closed it again, as though wrestling with himself over whether or not to speak. But he set his jaw, looked up at Rorick, and began.

"Jeziah Lovak and I… had been friends for as long as I could remember. My father took him in as a child when his parents died in the Thessi wars. They had served on the same ship as my mother. Jeziah and I were practically brothers. There were no secrets between us. We worked in my father's cookhouse, where he would make stews, rice, and flatbread, and pack them into pails to be delivered to customers throughout the city. It was up to us to make the deliveries, navigating the crowded streets with piles of lunch pails balanced on our heads. Jeziah hated crowds, but he braved them because he thought he owed it to my father… But I don't suppose that matters.

"What does matter is that Jeziah wasn't meant for pail-running or sweeping a hearth. He had a talent. You never would have thought it by the look of him—he had always been scrawny, pale… soft-spoken. But his mind's power was… unbelievable. He was intelligent, yes, but it was more than that. When he had a nightmare, everyone in the house would wake up screaming. We used to meld minds all the time—it was our secret language—and he would read a week's worth of memories in the blink of an eye.

"Looking back on it, his power should have terrified me. I'm sure it terrified my father.

"The day he came of age, Jeziah got a letter, delivered by hawk and sealed with fine wax. It was an invitation—though when he read it to me, it seemed worded more like a demand—for him to attend an academy in the upper ring of the city, an academy which trained mentalists and only accepted those of great natural ability."

Rorick raised one feathered eyebrow. He recognized in Arin's story the Ellorek Academy, where those selected to become Nhostir were trained, where he had studied.

"You must have missed Jeziah very much when he left for this academy."

"He never left. My father forbade him from going. He seemed frightened, and threw the letter into the fire."

"Hmm." Rorick's professional composure allowed him to express his surprise only with a raised eyebrow and a slight tilt of the head. He had never heard of anyone turning down an invitation to the academy. It was generally unheard of, even among the Nohstir graduates. But Arin only shrugged.

"Jeziah did not protest. He told me it would pain him too much to leave the city and the family that he knew and loved… but I could never shake the feeling that it was something more. That he knew something about that place that I didn't. Call it intuition.

"But at that point, my father was getting on in years. My whole life, I had watched him labor for long days over a hot fire and remain poor as ever. My father was a man who valued honest work. Jeziah and I promised each other that we wouldn't make the same mistake.

"Father grew old, as fathers do. He expected us to take over his kitchens, but Jeziah and I had greater ambitions. Well-practiced at slipping through the streets and with an intimate knowledge of the city only a pail-runner could have, we started a business of our own, one that would take advantage of Jeziah's natural talents.

"We started with small jobs—the location of a savings treasury, a password, a key, the face of a euphoria dealer… I had learned a bit of alchemy over the years, and that helped. When we found a target, I would shadow them, find out where they slept. After that, it was easy to slip into their house at night and gas them unconscious long enough for Jeziah to do his part."

"You stole secrets." Rorick leaned forward on his elbows.

"We did more than that." A nostalgic grin broke out across Arin's face. "We stole memories, spied on pieces of lives after the fact. I'll never forget the way Jeziah looked, hunched over a target in the moonlight, fingertips at their temples, the whites of his eyes showing beneath his eyelids as he flipped through their memories like the pages of a book.

"We were quite the team. I got him in, he extracted the information, and I sold it. Before too long, word got around to the right people, and we had a very profitable business on our hands. We took jobs from thieves, suspicious wives, merchants looking to sabotage the competition, even politicians. Once a Countess who had her daughter's pet hound killed paid us ten gold crowns to implant a memory in the girl, a memory of the poor beast running away.

"It all began when we were approached by Glendara Norrick—not her real name, of course, but that was the one she gave us. Jeziah and I were walking to the market when her curtained wagon nearly ran us down. A high orc in armor jumped down. He didn't seem to speak the common tongue, but he made it clear we were to get in the carriage. We didn't dare disobey. The heavy drapes closed behind us, and we blinked as our eyes adjusted to the dark. Even in the dark she cut an intimidating figure—a mass of silver-specked braids fell around her shoulders, decorated with beads, some of which I could have sworn were human knuckle bones. She wore a deep green robe with a roc in flight embroidered on the shoulder. One clawed hand rested on her knee.

"'Well met, boys,' she began, "Forgive me for plucking you off the streets, but I prefer to conduct business on the road. You see, you two are going to do a job for me. You will be paid handsomely, of course.' She quoted a figure ten times our usual fee. Something in the back of my mind didn't much appreciate her making demands of us, but my better sense kept me quiet. She named our target: Owen Temar. I recognized the name, anyone in the city's underground would have. He was the head of a crime organization that he had built from the ground up into one of the most feared in the city. Or, he had been, anyway. He'd been caught in a fire while he slept and burned to death. There were plenty of suspicions, but to my knowledge, no one was ever accused.

"'Here is a list of the information I want from him.' She handed me a scroll of parchment, with a long list of business dealings, passcodes, and contacts scrawled in cramped handwriting. I looked back up at her.

"'But… Temar died more than two moons ago, my lady. He's burned and buried, isn't he?'

"'Yes,' she didn't look at me. "The old bastard had an eidetic memory—didn't keep a single written record. All in his head. He did it for his own protection: If an underling were to kill him, they would lose everything, investments, contacts, secrets of the trade…"

"'But if he's dead, there is no way for us to access his memories. I'm sorry, but…'

"'What happens to a biata's memories when he dies?' she interrupted. We stared dumbly. 'That wasn't a rhetorical question.'

"'They… they are transferred to the Homestone, to become part of it.' Jeziah answered. 'The collective memory of the biata people. *What is remembered is not lost.*' He quoted the traditional Nhostir funeral words. 'You can't seriously be suggesting…'

"'Do you think I'm simple, boy?' she hissed, 'I know you were accepted into the Academy, and I know about the manticore incident. The Nhostir would love to get their hands on you. It was no small trick, finding you two. If I didn't know you could do the job, I wouldn't have bothered.'"

Rorick paused his mental note taking, his brow furrowed.

"This woman wanted you to read memories out of a Homestone? That's impossible."

Arin locked eyes with him. The strange intensity in his gaze caught Rorick off-guard. He was telling the truth, at least as far as he knew.

"Not for Jeziah." The words fell like stones. There was a moment of silence.

"All right..." Rorick surrendered with a nod, grateful for the chance to break eye contact. "Please continue."

After a moment's consideration, he did. "Well, with a pile of gold on one hand, and that orc bodyguard on the footman's rail, what could we do? We accepted the job. Now, security around the Homestone is nearly watertight... as a Nhostir, I'm sure you know that. You conduct the very funeral rites of memory transfer that we were there to violate."

Rorick nodded, slightly stung. It was true that the Nhostir were responsible for those rites, but he had never been allowed to conduct them himself. He was more than ready, but for some reason his masters kept denying him that honor. But that was beside the point.

"But there are cracks in any system, especially where mortal greed is involved. Glendara gave us a map of the hematite caverns where the Homestone stands, and told us about a little-known route into the main chamber, a tunnel which was supposedly sealed off. She had managed to have it opened again (she didn't say how, and we didn't ask), and gave us the time, in the hours before dawn, when the cavern would be unwatched. It would take Jeziah several sessions with the stone to unearth all the information, and Glendara assured us we would have as many nights as we needed (within reason, of course), although she could only promise an hour or so at a time.

"She offered us half up front, provided we would begin that night. Of course, we agreed, and she dumped us back into the street to begin our meager preparations.

"That night found us deep beneath the heart of the city, first crawling, then walking, then crawling again, Jeziah behind me, through the tunnels on Glendara's map. The tunnel had been created in the early days of the city by silver miners, who had accidentally knocked through to the system of hematite caves where dwelled the Homestone. Every miner involved either disappeared or suffered an unexplained bout of amnesia shortly thereafter. The support beams they had left were rotting in places and growing mushrooms in others. As they passed in and out of our circle of torch light, I wondered if we'd even make it to the Homestone. We went deeper, and the tunnel walls grew closer. We could hear the rush of water somewhere overhead, like the breath of some giant beast. The dull echo of our footsteps was oddly reassuring—I think silence would have driven us mad. In the guts of that terrible darkness, our footfalls reminded us that we were real.

"When we stepped out into the grand chamber, I felt my breath leave me. The veins of silver in the walls of the rough-hewn cavern glimmered in the torchlight. Beneath our feet was a sea of small stones, from pebbles to chunks the size of fists, winking up at us like pearls. As I stepped over them, my stomach turned. I felt a stab of guilt—each of these stones had once held a lifetime of memories, now empty as dry bones. It was as if we were robbing a mass grave. Jeziah paused at the edge of the cave, his eyes wide. I called back to him, but he just stood there, entranced.

"In the center of the chamber it stood, a boulder of lustrous grey stone, taller than a man and three times as wide, looming over us. The Homestone. It was the most beautiful and terrible thing I have ever seen—or ever will see, I imagine.

"'Do you hear that?' Jeziah said, with a furtive glance around the cave. I heard nothing.

"Eventually, I goaded him into following me, and we made our way over the mound of rocks towards the Homestone. Jeziah kept looking around for the source of whatever voices I could not hear, but we carried on. After what felt like a great climb but, which was really only a few meters, we stood in front of it, feeling awfully small. I looked to Jeziah. His jaw was set.

"'Remember what we're looking for,' I told him, more for my benefit than his. He said nothing, but closed his eyes, centered himself, and reached out. As soon as his fingertips touched the polished surface of the stone, he was thrown back, tumbling into the hematite gravel, cradling his head. I ran to him, nearly dropping the precious torch as I scrambled to pick him up.

"'This is ridiculous,' I told him. 'Let's go. We'll return what she paid us, we'll...' But he shook his head fiercely.

"'No,' he insisted, 'I can do this. I've seen it now. I can do it, Arin... Help me up.' I did, and said nothing more as I lead him back to the Homestone."

Without realizing it, Rorick had inched up to the edge of his seat. But as Arin spoke, Rorick became aware of a dull pain boring into the base of his skull. It was an inopportune time for a headache, but it would pass eventually—they always did.

"Kneeling at its side, Jeziah gripped the stone with his fingertips." Arin, looking somewhere over Rorick's left shoulder, raised his hands to imitate his friend's grip on the Homestone. "Suddenly, his body tensed. His eyes snapped open, unseeing. Veins stood out at his temple, and his knuckles went white. Cold sweat ran into his eyes. I could do nothing but watch, my form as tense as his, as Jeziah's mind entered the Homestone.

"I had no way of knowing how much time had passed, but after what felt like a thousand years, I heard the distant sounding of the dawn trumpet echo through the tunnels from the great hall above us. Our time was up. I shook Jeziah out of his trance, but he was weak—he could barely stand. Supporting him with one arm and holding the torch in my other hand, we made my our back out through the narrow tunnels into the light of the breaking dawn.

"By the time we reached the exit, Jeziah had stopped muttering under his breath and was walking on his own. It would be another few hours before he was truly himself again, but we couldn't afford to wait that long. As soon as we reached our rooms, I shoved quill and parchment into his hands. Dazed and slumped in his chair, he kept falling forward over the table, so I had to hold him up and strike him awake more than once. I should never have been so harsh with him—I should have let him sleep, should have taken care of him. He had just done the impossible. But I wanted to see the results. Slowly, so slowly, his nose inches away from the parchment, he began to write. I leaned in over his shoulder, but he barked at me to go away. I didn't know what to say; that kind of aggression wasn't like Jeziah at all. So I said nothing and watched from a distance.

"An anxious hour later, Jeziah slumped over onto the desk, asleep. I leapt up and snatched the parchment out from underneath him, bringing it over to the window's light to examine it. My heart sank as I read it. The words on the parchment were little more than gibberish. It was a page of streaming thought and random memory, descriptions, ideas, regrets, and dreams. I read it twice over, but there was nothing even remotely related to Owen Temar or his organization.

"I shook the paper in Jeziah's face, demanding to know what was going on.

"'There is so much to go through...' he murmured, still half asleep. 'I'll find him, though. I'll get him tonight...'

"But we didn't go back that night, or the night after that. Jeziah came down with a fever, and it was three days before he was well enough to go out again. But he did go out again, shivering beside me as we again worked our way through the tunnels to the Homestone. The heat of his palms fogged the surface of the stone as he poured himself into it. He seemed half asleep as I dragged him away when our time was up and back through the tunnels. Again I pulled out a quill and parchment and held them out to him, but Jeziah simply shook his head. Again Temar eluded us.

"Knowing that we could not afford to wait, we went back the next night. And the next. And the next.

"With each failure, the knot of dread in the pit of my stomach twisted and grew. Jeziah grew paler, he had headaches that he tried to hide from me. I knew, but offered him no aid. My sleep was fraught with nightmares of being hunted and torn apart by wolves with Glendara Norrick's face, but I began to suspect that Jeziah wasn't sleeping at all. He had never been talkative, but as those days went on, he hardly spoke at all, except to discuss the job. In hindsight, it was my fault. As the days and nights passed, my nerves grew worse and worse—and anger is always a comfortable replacement for fear. Whenever my friend did speak, I was liable to snap some sharp insult at him. But each night, he would pace the length of the room until it was time to go, chewing on the nails of his left hand. When the hour struck, Jeziah would practically drag me out of our room, his pace quick and his eyes bright with purpose. I had to struggle to keep up with him, almost jogging through the tunnels as I held our torch aloft. Each night I had to shake him harder to wake him from the Homestone trance. Despite his determination and my terror, two weeks passed and still we had nothing.

"One morning, when we got back to our room after another night of failure, I rounded on him.

"'This is taking too damn long,' I spat, clutching the list that Glendara had written us. 'That Norrick woman will skin us alive! You need to stop mucking about in there and get what we need!'

"'I'm not m...' he murmured, as though only hearing me from a great distance.

"'Then what *are* you doing?!' I interrupted. 'Whatever it is, it's not working. She's not going to keep buying us time in the cavern if we aren't getting results.' That at least seemed to get his attention. He looked up at me.

"'Tell her I'm working on it,' he said, 'I just need more time.'

"'I *have* told her that, but she's starting to suspect that something's wrong.'

"'Nothing is wrong,' he replied in a monotone.

"'Don't you understand? If we don't get her what she wants, we're as good as dead. You said you could do this. We're in too deep to back out now.

"'I can do it. I need more time with the stone.'

"'We're running out of that, Jez!'

"'If she wants the information, she'll *give me more time*!' He was on his feet, hands curled into fists, his jaw clenched. I opened my mouth to counter, instinctually moving to square off with him, but something stopped me. I saw the pallor in his cheeks, the heavy circles under his eyes, the way his hands shook slightly, even then. He said nothing.

"'Look…' I sighed, 'I'm sorry. Take a night of rest. We can try again tomorrow night.'

"Jeziah protested, but I insisted. He didn't really seem to have the energy to argue. I made sure he washed, ate a crust of bread, and got into bed before I lay down on my own mattress. As soon as my head hit the pillow, I fell into a heavy, dreamless sleep.

"I was awoken by the light of dawn pouring through the window that I had carelessly forgotten to shut. I rolled over, blinking away sleep, and looked over at Jeziah's bed. It was empty.

"My heart jumped into my throat as I shot out of bed, calling his name. I had only just thrown back Jeziah's cold blankets when the door opened behind me. I whirled around to find Jeziah standing in the doorway, looking guilty. I could have struck him.

"'Where have you been?' I snapped.

"'I was… fetching water.' Jeziah was a miserable liar. The water pail was sitting in the far corner of the room, untouched.

"'You went out to the Homestone without me, didn't you?' After a long moment, he nodded, shame-faced. I grit my teeth, feeling anger rising in me again, but I swallowed it for his sake. 'I know you're trying to prove your dedication to this job,' I continued after a long, steadying breath, 'but…'

"Jeziah's gaze flickered and fell to the far corner of the room. We could never keep secrets from each other. I could read his face like a book. In that moment, the realization came crashing down over me.

"'You're not…?' I stammered, 'You don't care about Owen Temar or his information at all. Have you even been…?'

"'I'm sorry, Arin,' he murmured at the ground.

"'What is wrong with you?!'

"'You don't understand,' he cried, looking up at me, 'The stone… It's… it's… everything. It has shown me so much. I need to get back. I need it, Arin.'

"'I can't believe this… How could you?!' I felt heat rising in my chest, my voice growing louder, 'You're going to get us both killed!'

"'No, you don't understand! I am nothing, we are nothing compared to what it contains. In the stone, I can live countless lives. Lives more beautiful, more exciting, more real than mine. I am alive there!'

"'Those are the memories of the dead, Jeziah. I should never have let you do this…'

"'No, finding the stone is the best thing that could have happened.' Desperate tears were welling in Jeziah's eyes. 'If only you could see it, Arin…'

"His eyes were wild. There was something in them that made me take a step away from him, shaking my head.

"'You're mad.'

"'Let me show you.'

"I drew back, but before I knew what was happening, Jeziah's fingertips clamped my temples, his eyes boring into mine.

"What I glimpsed there, inside Jeziah's mind, I cannot possibly describe. It was only a glimpse, for I wrenched myself free after half a moment. What I saw was like sunlight reflected in a mirror—blinding, but only hinting at the intensity of the original, for it had been filtered through Jeziah's memory. I think that is the only thing that prevented me from going mad that day. It happened all at once, in sickening, vivid color.

"Hundreds of thousands of lives—their love, hatred, and fear. I fought and died in a thousand wars. I saw agony and ecstasy. I was ten generations of farmers tilling the same field. Cities rose and fell as I watched. I stood before a hundred thousand hearth fires and house fires and funeral pyres and I felt the ashes in my eyes. I was a hundred thousand sets of lovers. I forgot most of what I saw the very instant that I saw it. But I will always remember the lens through which I watched: Jeziah's utter awe, his sense of soaring freedom, of being one with all those minds, a drop and the ocean at once. Nor will I forget the sudden, crushing loneliness that closed around me the instant it was gone. It was like stepping from a dark cave into daylight and suddenly being plunged back into darkness.

"I vaguely remember pushing Jeziah away and staggering out of the house. I ran. I must have kept running. The next thing I knew, I was walking along the docks on the far side of the city, exhausted to the last inch. Night was falling. The fishermen were packing the last of the day's catch and tying the final knots in their moorings. I considered finding a quiet corner and giving in to sleep, but I remembered Jeziah, and I turned towards home.

"I had wandered far, and even on the most direct route it was well into the night by the time I rounded the corner onto our street. The embers in the blacksmith's forge caught a scrap of fuel and spit up a small flame as I passed. A white moth flew over my shoulder and into the red glow. It reached the fire, hovered for a moment in the smoke, and then burned itself to ash. I kept walking.

"I was almost home, and wistfully imagining falling into my bed, when a towering figure stepped out of the shadows in front of me, blocking my path. I froze in my tracks. I looked over my shoulder, but another figure blocked the way I had come. Suddenly wide awake, I darted to the side, but before I had taken two steps a fist caught me in the gut, knocking the air from my lungs and doubling me over. The next instant they were both upon me, dragging me into the shadows with a hand clamped over my mouth. I struggled. The hand on my face drew away long enough for me to take a sharp inhale before my head snapped sideways under the dizzying impact of a fist. I collapsed onto the cobblestones. My attackers—a tall biata with dark feathers and an orc I recognized as the footman of Glendara Norrick's carriage—stood over me.

"I would rather not relive the details… but they made it clear that Glendara was unhappy with us. She wanted the information by the next nightfall, or her money back in full, plus what she'd wasted on bribes for the project—a sum we couldn't possibly hope to pay. The last thing I remember was the orc laughing while the biata raised a club over his shoulder.

"I woke up to the first light of dawn breaking over the street and the taste of blood in my mouth. My whole body ached; it felt like someone was driving a nail into each of my temples.

"Jeziah. At the thought of Jeziah alone back at the house I leapt to my feet (or tried to—I stumbled over my own legs and nearly fell on my face). Pain stabbed at my ribs as I staggered towards home. I finally reached the door and threw it open, breathing hard. Everything was quiet. Jeziah's bed was empty."

The door of Rorick's chambers rattled, and he jumped, snapped away from that empty house and the freshly beaten Arin. The real Arin gave a frightened glance towards the door. Again the handle shook from the other side. Rorick gave a small huff of annoyance and pressed two fingers to his aching temple. The bell was unhooked, signaling that he was with a patient. Surely they could see that. After another tentative rattle, footsteps retreated down the hall and the door stood quietly.

"I apologize for the interruption…" he sighed. "Please, continue. The dawn came and you found that Jeziah was gone. Had he been taken by Glendara's men?"

Arin shook his head, finally looking away from the door.

"That's what I thought at first, but no… there was no sign of a struggle. He must have left willingly, before the men had reached the house that night. That was why they were waiting for me in the street. No, I knew at once where Jeziah had gone.

"My body ached terribly and there was still blood caked to the side of my face and the corners of my mouth, but I didn't care. I ran outside, down the back roads, each breath stabbing me in the sides as I moved as fast as I could towards the caverns of the Homestone. I scrambled over rocks and through the tunnels—I hadn't thought to bring a torch, so I groped my way through the dark. At long last, there was a flicker of firelight from ahead. I chased it until the main chamber opened in front of me. The torch propped up among the smaller hematite stones was burning low. Even in the half light, there was no mistaking the figure hunched at the base of the Homestone.

"'Jeziah!' I called out to him, but he gave no answer, no sign that he had heard me. I clambered over the stones until I could see the beads of cold sweat running down the back of his neck. I grasped his shoulders and shook him, but he was stiff as a corpse. But he was warm, I reassured myself, he had a pulse. His eyes were wide and unblinking, staring into somewhere I could not perceive.

"Footsteps. Slowly descending. I looked up in horror at the corridor leading to the halls above. A distant glimmer of torchlight reflected off of the flagstones.

"'Jeziah!' I hissed his name into his ear. I struck him across the face. Once, twice. I shook him again. Still nothing. The footsteps were drawing closer. The murmur of voices echoed out into the cavern. Again and again I tried, but…"

Arin trailed off, biting his lower lip. "I'm sorry."

Rorick leaned closer to his patient, offering a small smile that he hoped was comforting. "You need not apologize. It—"

He was interrupted by another rattle at the door, more forceful this time. Rorick sighed through his teeth, feeling more than a little irked by now. The dull pounding of his headache wasn't helping matters. Whoever was outside the door began knocking frantically.

"Excuse me for a moment," he said, pushing himself reluctantly out of his chair. Arin started.

"Wait!"

"This will just be a moment," Rorick assured him as he made his way to the chamber door. He unlatched it, a bit more forcefully than was necessary. "I truly am sorry for the interrupt—"

The door refused to open. He tried the handle again, but it remained stubbornly and firmly shut.

"You won't have any luck there, I'm afraid," Arin's voice came slow and steady from the couch behind him. "I treated the edges of the door with alchemical paste. It's sealed shut. They're going to have to break it down."

"What is the meaning of this?!" Rorick rounded on him, glaring, trying to bring anger to take the place of fear. "You know that assaulting a Nhostir carries the penalty of—"

Arin shook his head, unintimidated.

"I'm not going to hurt you. And Master Torvick is only drugged—he'll regain consciousness in a few minutes."

"You will release me at once."

"Please, hear me out. There's not much left to tell."

Something doleful and sincere in the other man's gaze gave Rorick pause. He stood for a long moment, before slowly, deliberately, making his way back to his chair. Arin took a long breath before he continued.

"I couldn't break Jeziah away from the stone. I ducked back into the side tunnel before the guards could reach the cavern, but he… There were three of them—two guards and an elder in Nhostir robes. I heard the moment when they saw him; they halted, dumbstruck for a moment before shouting and running forward. Crouching in the dark tunnel only yards away, I dared not breathe.

"I heard a sharp intake of breath and a sickening thud. Jeziah fell backwards, rolling down the hill of hematite pebbles a few feet before coming to rest. My heart stopped for an instant before I saw that his chest still rose and fell. Only unconscious, then.

"I strained to listen, my chest heaving. I heard the crunch of gravel as the guards knelt to examine him.

"'Surely he wasn't…' a guard gasped.

"'Melding with a Homestone?' An elderly voice—the Nhostir master—spoke with a hint of amusement. 'He should be dead.'

"'Take him to the dungeons.'

"'No…' the master said, after a moment's pause. 'Take him to the cells beneath the Nhostir halls. I'll take charge of him from there. Such a man should do more than rot in a dungeon.'

"'As you wish, Master.'

"And that was that. I could do nothing but watch from my hiding place as they carried Jeziah away."

Muffled voices came from the far side of the door. The handle shook again. Rorick glanced to the door then back to Arin, who was looking at him as though he expected some kind of reaction.

"That's it?" Rorick asked. "That's the last you saw of Jeziah?"

"Not exactly."

"That's the second time you've said that." Rorick spat, too exasperated to care about patient protocol. Arin wasn't a patient anymore, after all. "What do you mean? You drugged a Nhostir master, you held me captive just so that you could tell me a story that ends in 'not exactly'?"

A low thud resounded through the chamber, and the door shook on its hinges. Arin stared at him.

"This is madness! If that is all you wanted, you've done it," Rorick realized he was shouting and didn't care. Something in the back of his head blared a high-pitched note. "I've listened. Now release me at once!"

"Don't you see it?"

"See what?!"

Another thud, and a crack as something splintered. Arin leapt to his feet and Rorick followed suit, noting the tension in the other man's shoulders, the way his hands had curled into fists. Arin was trembling.

"Your name is not Rorick Delmora," he said, "You never studied at the Ellorek Academy. You've been with the Nhostir for less than a year."

"What?" He felt the blood drain from his face. The room suddenly grew cold.

"You are Jeziah Lovak, you're the best friend I've ever had," he nearly shouted, "and you're a fool if you think I'd let them take you from me!"

The door fell in with a crash. There was a shout and a flash of light as a spell shot from the doorway and caught Arin square in the chest. It was all distant, as though Rorick was observing the scene from underwater. Arin lay sprawled and unconscious on the floor. The room began spinning on some oblique axis. His skull felt as though it were being split open. Piece by piece, memories came rushing back to him like a cascade of rock-falls into an avalanche. He felt a warm trickle of blood drip from his left nostril, but made no effort to stop it.

Rorick—no, Jeziah—was vaguely aware of a cluster of people bursting into the room with spells at the ready. Their footsteps echoed in his head, far too loud, along with the pounding of blood in his ears.

The guards parted to make way for a biata with sunken cheeks and blue feathers flecked with grey on his brows, his thin lips twisted into a frown. Jeziah could not decide if what he felt was relief or terror, but his hands shook with whatever it was. The guards rushed towards Arin's prone form, but the elder turned towards Jeziah.

"Ah, my poor child." Master Torvick shook his head, his features softening into something pitying, regretful. "I should have known this day would come. Removing your connection to this man was the most difficult part of your re-programming. It nearly destroyed the whole operation."

"M-master," he stammered, "I remember…"

"Yes, it should be coming back to you now." Torvick stepped closer, and something made Jeziah flinch away. "It was necessary, you understand. I'm sure you do. It was this or sending you to your death. After all you'd seen… Your mind was on the verge of collapse anyway. What we did was a mercy."

"I don't understand." The word broke in his throat.

Torvick sighed. "Rorick Delmora is a constructed personality, with a lifetime of memories built into you by the Nhostir Order. Jeziah Lovak can never be fully erased, but he can be entirely suppressed as long as there isn't…" he glanced in Arin's direction, "…strong interference."

Jeziah could not bring himself to meet Master Torvick's eyes. As he looked at Arin's unconscious form, his vision began to blur. He remembered running through the city streets with him to deliver food, staying up late watching the dying embers in the hearthfire, laughing over ale and stories of successful heists… Something in his chest twisted into knots.

"Please, don't hurt him," he begged, his voice weak. "I'll do whatever you like. I'll cooperate. But let him go."

"Heh… That was the one condition you gave the first time, when we discovered his involvement through your memories." Master Torvick looked up at him, trying to catch his gaze. "Fear not—no harm will come to him. You are too valuable to us to be crippled by grief. But we cannot allow this sort of thing to happen again. You understand." Streaks of silent tears burned into Jeziah's cheeks.

"What happens now?"

"Your memory of today will have to be wiped," Torvick said, giving a small, pitying smile, "and your old memories suppressed again." Jeziah reluctantly allowed him to place a hand on his shoulder. "It will be a painful process, but you will not remember it. And when it's over, you will return to your work as Rorick Delmora, and continue your life among the Nhostir."

Jeziah felt his breath hitch in his throat.

"Yes, Master."

"Now rest, my child. This will all be over soon." Master Torvick raised his hand, his fingertips brushed his apprentice's temple, and Jeziah knew no more.

Pale sunlight wound its way through the cracks in the shutters to fall in long streaks across the dusty loft of an inn on the southern side of the river. It was the thin, grey light of a morning after rain. The wind whispered over the thatched roof while the city outside began to wake. A late flock of geese squawked overhead, and Arin Krayn stirred on his straw mattress. He winced as the light fell across his eyelids. His head ached.

His eyes still closed, Arin searched for memories of the previous day. It felt like a habit, though he wouldn't have been able to explain it if he tried. Yes, there they were—it had been an average day. Working in the kitchens. Going to the nearby tavern for a lonely measure of rum, which conveniently explained the headache.

He opened his eyes and rolled over onto his back. Blinking sleep out of his eyes, he watched the dust that swirled in the lines of sunlight that split the air. He had almost worked up the power to sit up and drag himself through another day like the last, when he noticed something scratched into the ceiling directly above his head. As he squinted up at the scratches, they formed words.

Second board to the left.

He lay there for a long moment, reading it over again. He reached up and brushed the scratches. They were slightly weathered, splinterless and smooth. Second board to the left. Arin sat up. As if drawn by muscle memory, he reached towards the left side of his mattress. He counted two boards over and leaned down. The floorboard gave way under his hand as he pressed it. Arin felt his heart skip a beat. He dug his fingernails into the side of the board and pried it up. The puff of dust he expected never came, but lifting the board away revealed a bundle of papers folded and tied in twine. He brushed them with his fingertips, as if to make sure they were really there. They were material, at least. He picked them up, untied them, and carefully unfolded them. They were covered with handwriting— familiar handwriting. *His* handwriting. His pulse quickened as he read the first line. The ache in his head grew stronger, stronger, then snapped.

"Jeziah Lovak and I had been best friends for as long as I can remember..."

He looked over the edge of the papers. In the hiding place beneath the loose floorboard there sat a quill and a small bottle of ink. Beside them was another scrap of paper—a hastily-drawn map of the Nhostir halls. At the top, a note was scrawled in Arin's own handwriting:

Bring him home.

The Vacarran Corsair
Jesse Grabowski

"What are ye goin' ta spend yer loot on, mate?" asked a tanned, leathery faced man in his thirties.

The other man couldn't easily come up with an answer. He hadn't actually given it much thought yet. He was one of the newer additions to the ship's crew, and he had only just completed his second raid. He wanted to fit in though. He was younger than most of them, but he was also faster and a better fighter than most of them, earning him instant respect.

"Women and drink!" he lied, trying to fit in.

"Atta boy! Me too! Follow me and I'll show ye a good joint," the other promised, and slapped him on the back. "Morrin Lorant, ye goin' ta make a fierce pirate cap'n one day!"

The corsair then plodded along the streets of Dockside, eager to find his favorite watering hole.

The thought was amusing, but not what Morrin wanted. He once imagined apprenticing to a ship builder, but wasn't so sure any more. He had had the opportunity two years ago, but declined it. He was now a young man of twenty, and thought himself a bit too old to be anyone's apprentice. The truth of it was he was good at fighting, and not much else.

Morrin followed the corsair through the streets of Dockside, a town well known for its corruption and dangerous neighborhoods. Rumor had it that the magistrate and most of the town guard were in the pockets of the local thieves' guild. Along the way to the tavern, he couldn't help but notice many children on the street begging for money. Some were missing a leg, a hand, an eye...

It seemed very bizarre to him that all of them were in this state. He normally would never give his money to beggars, but after seeing corner after corner of children thus afflicted, he gave in to one sitting just outside the tavern who was missing a leg from the knee down.

"Here ya go, lad," Morrin said, as he dropped two silver pieces into the kid's makeshift wicker basket. This was a lot for such a donation. It was probably more than the kid would make in a month. A weak, feeble smile and an inaudible, "Thank you," was all the child could reply. It broke his heart, but he felt good about giving his money to a child in need.

He looked up at the sign above the tavern. The Crow's Nest. "How appropriate," he muttered.

Upon entering the tavern, the crew ran to the bar and ordered drinks.

A young woman walked up to Morrin with a smile on her face. She was a bit on the short side, even with the heeled boots she was wearing. As she got closer, Morrin noticed that the heavy makeup revealed a much younger woman. She got very close to him and whispered in his ear, "Would you like to have some fun, stranger?"

"Isn't it past your bedtime, little girl?" he replied.

She recoiled with a bit of confusion. "Little girl? Do you want to have fun with me or not?"

"You are very pretty, but you are very young. See me in about five years." Morrin slowly sipped an ale and looked away.

She seemed to almost tear up, and Morrin thought that was rather odd for a woman in her profession. She gave him a dirty look and stormed out of the tavern.

Morrin absorbed the sights around him. There were a few bards on a very small, wooden stage playing various drinking songs. People dancing and singing filled the floor. An unfamiliar dice game dominated one table, and a card game occupied another.

Many of his shipmates occupied their time kissing strange women and ordering more drinks.

Morrin thought of his mother. He often wondered how she managed to keep a roof over their heads and food on the table after his father left. He tried to dismiss the thought as he was faced with the apparent answer. His mother, now in her late thirties, was alone at home, in dire need of coin. He felt guilty about leaving her for a life on the seas. He knew he wouldn't stay with this for long, and one day, he'd return with his ill-gotten gains.

In the back of the tavern, a very well-dressed man sat with several beautiful, scantily clad women. In addition to a rather large hat with a purple feather in it, the man also wore a lot of gaudy jewelry.

From the advice Morrin had been given about Dockside, you hide all of your valuables, keep one hand on your weapon, and another on your purse. Yet, here was this man defying all of that.

During the evening as Morrin's eyes made their way naturally across the room, he noticed wenches bringing this man food and drinks many times, tending to his every need. All the while, he never paid them.

Morrin's drink was empty. He fought through the crowd to get to the bar, ordered another drink, and looked over.

The well-dressed man stood up and bid his company farewell. Two armed men in black leather armor showed up at the door, made eye contact with him, and nodded in his direction. As he left his table, the room parted for him. The music didn't stop, but the dancing did until he was safely clear of the floor. When he reached the tavern door, the armored men drew their swords and turned to leave. The man turned around, tipped his hat to the bartender, and with a smile, departed. The dancing recommenced, and once again the room became packed and difficult to navigate.

The bartender returned to Morrin with his ale. "Who was that?"

"No idea."

Morrin knew it was an obvious lie, and he slipped him three extra copper pieces for the drink. The elderly bartender leaned in and whispered, "That's Alotovar Daniels."

"Is he nobility?"

The tavern worker let out a small chuckle. "Hardly. If ya don't know 'im, it's best ye ferget the name, lad." He went back to work, serving the thirsty and now rowdy crowd.

Morrin wondered some more over his next drink, and was thinking about offering a few more coppers to appease his curiosity, but something about the fear in the tavern keeper's eyes told him that he probably wouldn't get any more information that way.

After a good night's rest in a warm bed, many of the crew came downstairs to nurse their hangovers. The captain instructed the men to have fun, but if they wanted to return to the open seas with him, they had better be on board by sunrise the following morning.

Morrin wondered what he would do to pass the time. Some of his shipmates headed off to buy new weapons, wine, ale, and the like, but he wasn't interested in those things. The captain provided for his food and shelter, and he preferred to save his money and return home with as much of it as he could.

He decided he would leave the Crow's Nest and see the sights of Dockside. It wasn't as dangerous during the day. As soon as he took one step outside, he noticed the same legless kid he saw yesterday begging in the streets again. He approached, and the kid shook his basket towards Morrin.

"Hey kid. Back so soon?"

The kid looked up and recognized Morrin and his generosity from the previous day. "Oh, it's you. Yea, this 'ere is my corner."

"Your corner, eh? But didn't I give you enough money yesterday to last you for a long time? Why would you come back so soon?"

"I 'ave to. Times are hard. I 'ave to eat," he said. He looked a bit nervous, and held out his basket for more coins.

"I gave you enough to eat for two months, and judging by the looks of you, you haven't had a good meal since half past never," Morrin said with a tone of authority. "What's your story, kid?"

"I 'ave to go now," he replied, as he picked up his crutches, placed his basket on his head as a hat, and hobbled away.

Morrin had nothing better to do with his time, so he decided to follow the kid and see where he wandered off to.

The kid lead him through the streets, past several market streets and storefronts, and eventually made his way to a large, stone wall that encompassed the entirety of the street. It was about ten feet high and was clearly the outer wall of a compound with a courtyard inside. From far away, a visible tower stood above it all, dark, brown, dirty stones made up the facade. Someone opened an iron gate and the kid made his way inside. Morrin got a bit closer, but couldn't see any signs as to indicate what this place could be. As he approached the gate, one of the armed men from the night before stood sentry and said, "Get lost."

"My apologies. I didn't mean to offend. I am new here, and was curious what this place is," Morrin said with a forced level of respect.

"None of yer business. Ask another question and I'll remove your head from your shoulders. Now get lost!"

Morrin backed away slowly and carefully and accidently bumped someone in the street behind him. As he turned around startled, he looked down to see an old man lying on the street with an empty basket, its contents of assorted vegetables now rolling along.

"I am so sorry! Are you okay?" Morrin assisted the man back up on his feet. He then gathered the produce from the street, replaced the items in the basket, and handed the basket back to the old man, who looked completely amazed and astonished at this act of good manners.

"You are clearly not from Dockside, young man." He dusted off his brown robes. "What brings you here?"

"Ah well, we um... I am part of a crew on a merchant vessel, just stopping in to resupply and things. Sorry again about that. There was a thug behind the gate and he kind of threatened me and I just wasn't paying attention."

"Ah yes... that place," the old man said with a bit of derision in his voice.

"You know of it? What is it?"

"Know it? I used to work there. Walk and talk, friend. We aren't safe here."

The old man lead Morrin a few streets away before he would open his mouth. Even then, he still whispered. "Aye, I used to work there. I am a healer and a good one, too. My name is Dannijer. Dannijer the Caring they used to call me. I was fired when the new owner... took over." He said those words as if they conveyed a different meaning and he was just giving Morrin a euphemism. "Do you like vegetable soup? Come join an old man and I'll tell you some more."

Morrin introduced himself, nodded in agreement, and followed Dannijer to his humble dwelling a few blocks away. Once inside, Dannijer set to cooking and preparing. Morrin feigned assistance, but really didn't know his way around a kitchen. "So what was that place?"

"What was it? Heh." He chuckled with pride. "It was one of the finest institutions of learning in Dockside is what it was. It was an orphanage, but unlike any other. We prepared the children for the outside world. We taught them how to read and write and how to make a way for themselves in the world, earning honest wages through a trade. We were able to get them apprenticeships, and give them a chance where fate did not. We taught them morality in a town devoid of it. I devoted my life to it, until... until this bastard took over." He looked embarrassed at the profanity he used in Morrin's presence. Tears welled up in the old man's eyes as he cut the vegetables. Anger soon followed, and the speed of his knife carelessly slipped and cut his finger.

Morrin handed him a cloth. "So what has it become now?"

"Now? Now he uses it to force the orphans to the streets to beg for money to give to him so he can get wealthy off of their misery."

Morrin was appalled to hear of such abuse. Even for a Vaccarran Corsair, this was hard to accept.

"That's horrible."

"You don't even know the horror. Have you seen the orphans?"

"Yes, I have. I followed one from the tavern there, but I noticed many of them are maimed in some way."

"And how do you think they got that way?" the old man asked, eyebrows raised.

"You don't mean… you can't mean… he does that to them?"

"Yes. Well, he has his butcher do that to the children to garner more sympathy from the passersby."

Morrin thought he was harder than this, but something pulled at him inside. Disgust and rage began to fill him. He had killed men out at sea, but this was different. This was cruelty at its ugliest. "What sick bastard would do something like this? How did he come to own the place?"

"His name is Alotovar Daniels. It is very mysterious how things came to be. Rumors say he won it from my master in a gambling bet, others say he killed him and took the deed to the estate by force. Whichever is true, my master was never seen or heard from again. Shortly thereafter, my services were no longer needed."

"Have you gone to the town guard, the sheriff, the magistrate?"

"You haven't a clue about Dockside. They all turn a blind eye towards him. He pays them off and they leave him alone. All criminal activity operates this way in Dockside!"

Morrin was vaguely familiar with pay offs. In fact, the captain alluded to paying off the dock master, who knew full well that they were Vaccarran Corsairs, enemies to the duchy, and not truly a mere merchant vessel.

"What can we do, then?" Morrin asked the defeated old man.

"We can't do anything. You should just get back on your ship. You can't get involved or you'll go missing, too," He stirred the chopped vegetables in the broth.

Morrin stared at his hands for many long seconds. "I've never done anything good in my life," he finally said. "In fact, I've done a few bad things along the way. Let me try to help. Please."

"What are you proposing? You alone will storm the compound and kill Alotovar and his thugs?" The impossibility hung in the air a few seconds with the silence.

"I could climb the wall in the middle of the night, sneak in, kill him, give you the deed to the place, and end the suffering once and for all," Morrin offered, even though it did sound quite ridiculous as he heard his mouth say those things.

"You would do that for the children you don't even know?"

"I would do that to rid the world of evil like him."

The old man shook his head, and with a slight smile said, "If you're willing to risk your neck, at least let me draw you a map of the place. Also, the guard in the courtyard carries the key to the main building, but leave him to me."

"You're coming with me?"

"Yes, you will need a distraction to get over the wall. I have a few tricks up my sleeve," the old man said, with a spark in his eye.

Morrin had to pass the time until nightfall. He studied the map as best he could, and went over the plan several times with Dannijer. He sharpened his short sword and dagger, all the while thinking about the lawlessness in the town and how evil such as this man was allowed to thrive here, in the shadow of the capital city of Ashbury and under the blind eyes of the Ashban nobility.

Several hours later, they both made their way to the orphanage from separate directions.

Morrin hid across the street under a wagon and watched as the old man approached the gate, appearing to be a beggar. Morrin took this sign and crawled his way to the wall.

"Alms for the poor," Dannijer asked humbly to the gate guard.

"Go away, old man, or I'll run you through. Hey, wait. I know you! Aren't you—"

Before the guard could finish, Dannijer threw sand in his face and whispered a sleep spell. The guard fell to the ground and began to softly snore.

Morrin grabbed the keys from the unconscious guard and climbed over the wall. He made his way to the main compound, unlocked the door, and slipped inside.

Once inside the main hall, he tried to remember the map the old man had drawn for him. He prepared himself mentally for the assassination.

He had never killed a defenseless, sleeping person before. This time, he would make an exception.

He heard crying coming from one of the rooms. The door was slightly ajar, and Morrin glanced in.

A large, bald, grotesquely fat figure stood over a small child. He carried a whip in one hand and a large pouch in the other. "This is all you made today, you little worthless maggot?" With that, he cracked the whip on the child.

Heart bursting in his chest, Morrin grabbed his short sword—but thought better of it. If he caused a ruckus here, he might miss his opportunity for Alotovar.

Morrin made a mental note of this room's location, and said to himself, "Hang in there, kid."

He continued down the hallway, up a set of stairs, out into another corridor, and then heard voices coming. Unsure of what to do or where to go, he tried a random door in the hall.

Upon entering, he saw several occupied beds. A faint candle on a nearby night stand provided the only light. The voices outside of the room grew louder and seemed to pause right in front of the door to finish their conversation.

With one hand on his sword, Morrin waited a few minutes for them to finish and leave.

One of the sleeping people behind him stirred in their sleep and Morrin caught a faint whiff of familiar perfume. Careful to remain quiet, he examined the young girl, stains on her cheeks from crying herself to sleep. Without makeup, she was barely recognizable, but Morrin understood now.

With a renewed sense of purpose, Morrin peeked into the corridor and continued his way to the third floor and then to the master bedroom. The old man had done an excellent job with the map.

Morrin found the door and tested it slowly. It was locked. He tried the key from earlier, but it didn't fit.

He sighed. It had been a long time since he'd picked a lock, and wasn't sure he still knew how.

He reached into his boot and pulled out a few rusty picks. The salt air had not been kind to them while at sea. He chose one that appeared to be the correct size and gave it a shot.

He turned the pick and it snapped off inside the lock. It made a considerable noise and he waited to see if anyone heard the sound. No one stirred within the room. He pulled out another pick, attempted to remove the remnants of the first failure, and gave the new tool a go.

Success. The door was now unlocked.

Morrin put his picks away and drew his sword and dagger. He readied himself for the assassination, and slowly and quietly opened the door.

Morrin squinted and his eyes tried to adjust to the dark of the room. He wasn't sure if anyone was even in the bed. He made his way closer, weapons raised and ready to strike, and then realized the bed was empty.

Morrin stood in utter disbelief, and then contemplated his next move. Could he have been one of those voices he heard on the second floor? Or were they just the guards?

Not wanting to get caught, he resolved to leave. He was just about out of the building when he remembered the room where he saw the fat whip master tormenting the children. Morrin thought about the good he could have done if he had killed Alotovar, but at least if he killed this one, he wouldn't be around to torment the kids any longer.

Morrin made it to the door that was ajar and saw him again. It was so late at night and the whip master kept the kids up to harass them and torment them for his sheer amusement. Morrin wanted to kill him, but how could he do it in front of the kids? He hadn't thought about that on his way here.

Morrin closed the door, knocked on it, and waited.

"Who dares disturb me while I'm having fun?"

Morrin waited for the door to open so he could plunge his dagger into the other's chest. However, the bastard only repeated it without opening the door. "Who dares disturb me?"

"Err… Alotovar says he can't sleep with you making all the kids cry. Leave them alone and let them go to bed!"

"How dare you!"

As the door opened, Morrin inserted his dagger into the whip master's fat, blubbery chest, and pulled him out into the hallway. The corpse fell to the floor with a loud thud. He closed the door and waited to see if anyone came running to inspect. Silence.

Now what? Should I help the kids in this room escape? Where will they go? Is it enough to rid them of him?

Then it hit him. He had to be at the ship at sunrise. With all of his sneaking around and staying still and quiet, he had completely lost track of time.

He desperately tried to find a window. It was not yet light out. He returned to the hallway where the corpse lay, and struggled to roll the heavy man away from the door. He dragged him down a hallway and around a bend, to where the kids wouldn't see. He then returned to the room, entered, and the kids cowered in fear.

Putting his index finger to his lips, he quietly shushed them. "If you want to escape and leave this life behind, follow me, and Dannijer the Caring will take care of you."

At the mere mention of the old man's name, hope glimmered in a stray eye or two. Slowly, the kids followed Morrin out of the main building and through the courtyard to where Dannijer waited with the still-sleeping guard.

"Is it done?" Dannijer asked.

"No, I couldn't find him anywhere. I took care of his whip master though. Can you hide these kids and take care of them?"

The old man stuck out his chin. "And what about the rest?"

Morrin knew there were more rooms inside with many more orphans who needed rescuing, especially the girls.

"I can't, Dannijer. I did what I could. I'm sorry. I have to get back to the ship or I'll be stranded here. I am a Vaccarran Corsair. If I'm discovered, I'm dead."

"Ohh. A pirate. Well, then." Dannijer stood, eyes blinking. "I guess I should be thankful you did this much."

The old man hung his head in defeat. He motioned for the kids to follow him, as most were already hugging his robes. "Good luck to you, Morrin. Safe travels. Thank you for trying." Dannijer and several children scurried away into the night, until the sound of light snoring at his feet was all that Morrin heard.

Morrin just stood there. Still.

He thought about the ship leaving him here, and he began walking through the quiet streets towards the docks. He looked up at the sky. It was just starting to turn a light indigo. He thought about the children still within the walls.

He remembered his own childhood, growing up with his mother—poor, but free. He thought about how these children would never know freedom. What would Alotovar do with them when they become useless adults, no longer needy child beggars?

I still have time, he thought. He sprinted back to the orphanage, thinking himself insane. Insane, but determined.

He climbed the wall, crossed the courtyard, and went back inside the main building.

He remembered some important rooms on the map, and ran there hastily. The office was first. Morrin opened the door and it revealed no one.

He then ran to the treasury. The door was locked, but he picked this lock, too. He opened the door, and a glorious sight met his eyes. There were a few chests of coins spread about the room. He quickly deduced that this is where Alotovar must be storing his hoard of greed. On a desk were a few piles of gold coins that appeared to have been recently counted. Above the desk, nailed to a wall, was the deed for the orphanage. Morrin contemplated taking it and running it over to Dannijer, but he knew if Dannijer contested Alotovar, he'd go missing in the night like his previous master had.

He left the treasury and decided to go back to the master bedroom. He had to pass the whip master's corpse on the way back up, but it was gone.

A swelling erupted in the pit of Morrin's stomach. He couldn't still be alive.

After examining the floor, it appeared someone had dragged him to another room. Before Morrin could soak it all in, the door to that room opened, and two guards saw him.

"Intruder! Surrender yourself!" the guards shouted as they drew their weapons. Morrin threw his dagger into the throat of the first guard, who fell to the ground gurgling.

The surviving guard charged Morrin, thrusting with a long sword. Without his dagger to block, Morrin barely evaded the thrust with a side-step. He slashed out and ripped the guard's bicep.

With his other hand, the guard punched Morrin square in the face. Morrin fell back, dazed. He blinked to find the guard wheeling around to come at Morrin again with his sword. Morrin instinctively raised his sword to block. The swords made a loud clang, and he knew more guards would soon be on their way.

He kicked the guard in the stomach, and the guard backed up a bit to recover. He crouched down and tried to withdraw his dagger from the other guard's throat. His aggressor jumped him, determined to tackle Morrin to the ground.

Morrin's sword flew from his hands as the guard tried to choke Morrin. Morrin tried desperately to dislodge the man's fingers from his throat. While Morrin was a more agile, dexterous fighter on his feet, this man was simply a strong brute.

Gasping for breath, he raised his hands and stuck his thumb in the man's eye while his right hand continued to seek the dagger somewhere nearby. The guard ignored the thumb in his eye and kept trying to squeeze the life from Morrin.

Morrin felt a nose, then the chin, and then felt the pommel of his dagger. He gripped it, and with all of his might wrenched it out of the throat of the dead guard and into the neck of the other. He heard a gurgling as he rolled the dying man off.

Morrin recovered his breath and gathered his weapons. He knew for sure that his time was limited now, as surely the whole place would be crawling soon with people. He charged up the stairs and made his way back to the master bedroom, but it was still empty and the door was still unlocked from when he had picked it. The tapestries on the wall depicted students learning, and several men in robes teaching them.

All the students in the tapestries still had their limbs.

At that somber thought, Morrin thought he felt a breeze near one tapestry in particular. He began looking behind the tapestries, but no one was hiding there. Then he felt it again. He followed where he thought it was coming from and it led him to a simple wall.

Closer examination revealed a loose brick. He touched the brick, heard a click, and the wall opened to reveal a secret chamber. Inside, he saw a seated man wearing a large hat with a purple feather who was covered in gaudy jewelry.

Morrin sprang into action. Before he could reach him, Alotovar slumped forward in his chair, hat falling to the ground. The purple feather danced its way out of the hatband and landed motionless on the floor.

Protruding from the man's back was a small dagger.

In the shadows, cowering behind the chair, a young girl cried. Devoid of makeup, she alternated between holding up her ripped clothes and wiping her eyes.

Morrin knelt next to her. "It's okay now. It's all going to be okay now."

He tried to sound convincing, but in reality, he knew how hard it would still be for her, and others like her, here in this building. "Don't be afraid. I'm here to help. You did the right thing. No one will ever know about this. I promise. Come with me. I will take you to Dannijer."

Morrin put his dagger in its sheath and held out a hand to her. She slowly accepted and lifted herself off the ground. As she got closer to him, she collapsed in his chest and continued sobbing.

He led her out of the room, away from that grisly sight, and into the corridor. They descended the stairs, neared the courtyard, and Morrin turned to her.

"Do you know the way to Dannijer's house?"

"Yes."

"Go to him. Tell him I killed Alotovar. Tell him I went back in after he left and finished the mission. Also, tell him the deed to the place is in the treasury. I have to get back to my ship. Go now. I still have something left to do here."

With that, the young girl gladly hurried to the front gate, quietly hopped over the sleeping guard, and ran off.

Half an hour later, Morrin was full of smiles. He felt a certain level of pride when he considered his adventure. As first light began to show and warm the faces of the crew, he sauntered off towards the docks, with the weight of a very large, jingling sack over his back.

He was a Vaccarran Corsair, after all.

A Charming Encounter
Tera Fulbright

It was almost evening and the city was quiet. At least it was until she walked in. A hobling of surpassing grace and beauty, which was wonder enough, but the fact she stomped into my little hole in the wall was beyond believable. Gals who look like that ain't lookin' for guys like me.

She was blond and her sideburns were nice and bushy. She wore a pretty green dress of some silky material and a bright white apron. Her hair was pulled up on top of her head, but I noticed she had several expensive ruby hair combs tucked in it. A large ruby necklace was nestled just below her neck. She stood expectantly over my desk and her bright blue eyes stared at me, waiting.

I blinked and rubbed my eyes.

"You looking for someone, miss?" I asked.

"I am looking for someone called Crites."

Crites was me. I lifted up my old hat to look at her. "Well, ya found him. What do you want?" I thought maybe if I was short with her she'd go away.

"I want you to steal something for me."

Coughing, I sat up and held out my hand with its two missing fingers in front of her. "I don't steal." I said flatly.

"Yes, yes... not anymore." She waved my objection away with a hand. "But you came recommended, and I pay well."

I leaned back into the wooden chair and rocked it back on two legs. Paying well would be good. I was already a month behind on rent, and there hadn't been much for a former thief turned good to do in the city lately. The guards seemed to be doing their jobs a bit too well. I ran my tongue across my teeth. "How well?"

"Twenty gold."

I nearly rocked out of my chair. Twenty gold would pay my rent for a year and leave me some nice spending money. I could buy some books and really clean up the place. But things like that don't fall in my lap. There had to be a catch.

"Look, Lady, I catch thieves and find missing things. I don't steal."

She lowered herself into the wooden chair across from my desk and crossed those long legs of hers. Most hobling women-folks lean a little to the plump side with good living, and she clearly lived well.

"It is a simple theft. I understand you were quite good in your prime."

"Hey, I'm still in my prime!" I said indignantly, as I brushed a messy lock of almost-grey hair out of my face. I ain't pretty, but I'm still good in a fight.

She raised an eyebrow, "Then this should be easy for you."

"Look, Lady, I…"

"Fifty gold."

Flames! That was a lot of money.

"How simple a theft?"

She smiled, and I suddenly had the feeling I'd been caught in a trap. Her smile had that look about it. Like the cat that got into the milk or a kid who raided the cookie jar.

"There is a girl. She is poor and works in a bakery on Legion Street. She wears a bracelet on her right wrist. The bracelet has a gryphon charm. I want that charm." I could hear the disdain in her voice.

"Why?"

She stood up so she was looking down on me. "I am not paying you to ask questions, Crites. You get me the charm, and I'll give you a nice easy reward." She swung her hips a little as she spoke.

I didn't like the idea of thieving again, but talk about easy money. It would be nice to add some cushions to the chairs, buy some new books, and have really good ale.

"Alright, ya got yourself a thief. Where do you want me to deliver the charm and who should I ask for?"

"Deliver it to The Cursed Cauldron and ask for… oh… 'Lady Masque' will do."

I nodded and stood up to shake her hand, but she looked down at my hand with its missing fingers, and turned on her heel and walked out.

Bother. If it weren't for that gold, I'd have let her keep the job and find someone else, but that was a lot of meals and rent. I might not be much to look at, but I can do the job. I sighed and stood up, pulling my hat back down over my eyes. Well, I'd been planning to head home anyway, but at least I could go check out the girl.

I wandered down the streets of Ashbury city to the aforementioned bakery on Legion Street. The fresh baked bread smell was incredibly enticing. I opened my pouch to stare at the few coppers left in the bottom. I'd been hoping to save them for ale, but a bit of bread wouldn't be amiss either.

Looking around the bakery, the walls on either side were filled with shelves of bread. Behind that counter, a young hobling girl stood on a stool. She smiled as I entered, "How can I help you this evening, sir?"

"Just a slice of that fresh bread I smell." I replied.

She nodded and hopped down with a graceful leap. A contrast she was to the Lady Masque. While the Lady Masque was all curves and plush, the girl was slightly thin… a bit underweight, I thought, which kept with Lady Masque's estimate of her wealth.

The girl handed me the bread with a "One copper, sir." On her wrist, plain as can be, there was a gold bracelet with a colorful gryphon charm.

I laughed as I handed her a copper. "I'm no sir, I'm Crites."

"Lily, sir… I mean, Crites."

"Hi, Lily. That's a beautiful bracelet." I said, nodding to her hand. "Don't you worry about losing it in the dough?"

Lily glanced at and put her hand over it protectively. "Oh no, this was my mother's bracelet. I always take it off when I mix the bread."

"Oh, is this your bakery?" I took a bite of the bread. It was good. Soft and warm. She'd slathered some fresh butter on it for me, and the creamy butter mixed with the bread to fill my mouth with joy. Man, it was almost worth giving up an ale. Almost.

"Oh, no. I just work here. Master Shields owns the store."

"Well, Lily, it was a pleasure to meet you. Thank you for the bread."

The next day, I hung out near the bakery for most of the morning. Around lunch, I saw Lily dart out the back and run down an alley. I followed her, keeping to the edges of the alley and staying just out of her sight by ducking into doors and behind trash.

When I found her, she was wrapped in the arms of another hobling. The two shared a couple kisses and bottle of wine and bread before they went their separate ways.

Ain't it sweet?

I followed Lily back to the bakery, and when it was clear that she wasn't going anywhere, decided to see if I couldn't scrounge up a meal.

The city streets were fairly crowded with folks returning from errands and lunches.

I watched with interest as a couple of ragamuffins picked the pockets of the less wary. They knew better than to try their luck with me… though they wouldn't find much in my pockets. Walking along the dusty street, I stopped at a meat cart and spent a couple copper to buy a small sausage and chunk of bread to wrap it in. It wasn't great, but it was something.

Staking out a spot in an alley, I tore into the sausage and bread. After eating, I pulled my hat low over my face and closed my eyes.

It didn't seem long before one of the guards came by and kicked me awake because night had fallen.

"No sleeping in the alleys!" He said gruffly.

I stood up and tipped my hat at him.

There wasn't much to do until the next morning, so I drug myself back to my flat and opened a book to read. I could see the stars in the sky from the holes in the roof. But at least it wasn't raining.

The next morning, I rose good and early. And of all the prophecies… it was a cold, gray day and the sun had barely begun to rise over the horizon. It was probably going to rain, which meant my flat would be cold and damp by the time I got back to it. I probably should have moved my bed.

Sneaking back to the bakery, I carefully let myself in the back and found a place to hide behind a shelf covered in pots and pans against a wall. All those years as a thief hadn't gone to waste yet. I had settled in just in time before Lily came in still pulling her hair back. She took the bracelet off and set it carefully on a high shelf on the rack against the wall and began to make bread.

I shook my head. Lady Masque wasn't kidding. This was beyond easy. I stood, careful not to knock any of the pots and pans, and picked up the bracelet. Palming it, I hid back into the shadows.

Once the bread was in the oven, Lily turned back to pick up her bracelet and didn't see it. She let out a cry of fear and started to remove the pots and pans. I huddled back even further into the darkness and just when I thought she was about to see me, I heard the door ring.

"By the Stars!" Lily cursed, and I watched her dash a tear away from her eyes. She rubbed her face with her apron and headed to the main room. I took advantage of the distraction and snuck back out the door.

A Charming Encounter

Once outside, I set the bracelet in the palm of my hand and looked at it—a very simple, plain gold strand, but the gryphon charm was something else. Brightly colored and intricately detailed. I noticed something on the button, and turned the charm over to read it. "The stars look down," were written in teeny tiny words.

Huh, what an interesting engraving. I shrugged and pocketed the whole thing. Worth an easy twenty gold to me. Correction, fifty gold!

Later that afternoon, I made my way across town to the Cursed Cauldron. From the outside, the tavern looked intimate, warm and cozy. Soft wooden planks and marble stones made up most of the building's outer structure. It was hard to see through the closed windows, but the loud voices from within could be heard outside.

Upon entering the tavern, I was surprised to find the man behind the bar was the same one Lily had been kissing.

My hackles went up. I'd felt this was a trap the minute Lady Masque smiled, and now I knew it was one. Though what form that trap took, I had yet to figure out.

I took a seat at the bar, doffed my hat and laid it on the chair beside me.

"Can I help you?" the barman asked.

"I was told I could get nice cheap ale here by… Lily?"

The man smiled and his face lit up. "Lily is a dear." He turned and poured me an ale, sliding it across the table.

As I reached into my pouch, he waved me off. "Any friend of Lily's is a friend of mine." I don't know that I'd call myself her friend, but if it gets me free ale, it's all right with me.

I nodded and took a sip of the ale. And nearly spit it right back out. That offal was more water than ale.

He saw the look on my face and leaned in conspiratorially. "Lady M waters the ale; it makes it last longer, and the humans take longer to get drunk and stupid, which means they spend more money."

I looked around the room and saw that it was, in addition to being a tavern, a gambling hall. Thick wooden beams supported the upper floor and the sconces attached to them. The walls were completely empty, besides the lighting, most likely because customers stumbled against the walls too often and knocked off anything on the walls.

The tavern itself was packed. Several long tables were occupied by what looked like couples, lone travelers and anybody else who enjoyed company. The other, smaller tables were also occupied by various gambling opportunities. Most of the bar stools were empty, mostly likely because the folks patronizing The Cauldron were more interested in gambling than ale. Pretty women of all races moved among the men, offering shoulder rubs, sitting on laps and giving long drawn-out kisses. Men and women gambled at cards, darts and dice and couple other games I couldn't figure out.

As I watched, Lady Masque herself came out from a back room. Today, she wore a bright red, low-cut gown that emphasized her assets, but still had a stark white apron tied over it. One of the patrons stood up and walked over to talk to her. She whispered a reply and pointed toward the back. The man walked into the back room.

She saw me and came over, glaring at the bartender, who quickly stepped away.

She leaned in close and whispered breathily. "Do you have the bracelet?" I could smell the scent of jasmine.

"Not yet."

Her hand hit my cheek faster than I could blink. "Then get out." She hissed. Her eyes flashed angrily. "I don't want you in here until you have that charm."

I stood up quickly, grabbed my hat and walked out before I said something I knew I would regret.

If I didn't know it was a trap before, that slap guaranteed it. I took out the bracelet and looked at it. It was just a simple charm.

Then I thought about Lily's tear-streaked face and the way her lover's face lit up in a smile when I mentioned her name. Something wasn't right, and I wasn't about to give the bracelet to that bitch until I knew what was really going on.

I still had some friends in the guild. Unfortunately, the best person to ask would have been Sarah, but I was pretty sure she was still not talking to me. The connections I did have confirmed to me that Lady Masque was not a nice person. I still didn't know exactly why she wanted the charm, but given some of the stories I heard, I couldn't imagine it was good. She had a reputation of getting what she wanted, whether that was men, women or coin. More rumors seemed to imply that she housed stolen items until they could be sold. As far as I knew, she wasn't tied to a guild, which meant she was runnin' independent. Ain't no guild that likes that.

A Charming Encounter

A few nights later, I walked into the bar, cocky and acting like I owned the place. I smiled at the bartender, took off my hat, waved it around and shouted. "Ale for everyone!"

The crowd jumped and rushed the bartender; I picked a likely drunk and stuck my foot out to trip him. He landed face first into some girl's lap, who pushed him to the ground. He came up swinging at me, but since I stood about two feet shorter than he expected, his swing went right over my head. I kicked his knee and he let out a cry. Soon everyone was hitting and fighting as the gambling hall went from calm to chaotic in seconds. I kept my eye on the back door, whence Lady Masque had come last time. When she charged out yelling and swinging a club, I let myself be pushed and prodded until I bumped up against her. She shoved me out of the way and continued to beat the tavern patrons into submission.

A few seconds later, the outside door slammed open and several guards came tromping in. A few swift kicks, hits of clubs and a couple guys thrown out the front door, and the room was soon settled back down. I found a corner booth and tucked myself into it, pulling my hat down low.

"What goes here?" One of the guards shouted. I'd worked with Darian before. Sometimes even the guards can't find a thief, so they ask for my help.

Lady Masque straightened her gown and slithered up to the guard. Looking up at him, she blinked those big blue eyes and smiled, "Oh nothing, Darian, just a little incident, but as you can see, things are all calm now."

Darian looked down at her. "Uh, huh." He turned back and shouted, "Come on in, Miss Lily."

Lily walked in and pointed straight at Lady Masque. "Her. It's her who stole my bracelet."

Lady Masque blanched and then recovered quickly. "Stole your bracelet? Child, I don't even know who you are. What is the meaning of this?"

"We've had an official charge lodged against you, Ma'am." He tapped his chest. "I need to search your premises."

She shrugged. "Sure. I've got nothing to hide."

Darian called a couple guys in, and they took time searching the various rooms. When they came out shaking their head, Darian looked at Lily.

"It's her. I know it's her. Maybe she's wearing it."

Lady Masque held up her hands which, while covered in bright colored rings, did not have a single bracelet.

"I don't see anything that matches your description on her, Lily." He turned back to Lady Masque and looked her up and down. "But, lady, if you wouldn't mind removing your apron and emptying the pockets."

Lady Masque shrugged and untied her apron. She stepped up to a table and emptied it out. Several gold, silver and copper pieces tumbled out.

At the same time, a golden bracelet with a brightly colored gryphon charm fell into the pile.

"There!" Lily shouted, "That's mine!"

Before Lady Masque could respond, Darian picked up the bracelet from the pile.

"How do you know that's hers?" Lady Masque said.

Now it was Lily's turn to smile, and while she didn't have quite the fierceness of Lady Masque's, it was one that promised revenge.

"Because it's engraved on the bottom, 'And the stars look down'."

Darian turned the charm over to see. His eyes widened slightly and he nodded. "Very well." He handed the bracelet to Lily. "Lady Masque, you are under arrest for the theft of Lily Newbow's bracelet."

"What?! You can't do that! Anyone could have given that to me," Lady Masque said.

One of the other guards stepped up and whispered something in Darian's ear.

"Oh, and you'll also be charged with possession of the other stolen items that were found secreted away in a back room."

Lady Masque shrieked and yelled as Darian placed his hand on her shoulder to escort her out.

As she left the room, I stood up. Lily looked over and caught my eye. "Thank you." She mouthed.

I winked, put my hat on and walked out the door. Outside, the stars above sparkled like thousands of tiny diamonds.

A few months after I'd helped Lily with the bracelet, I found her at my door. Things had been good for me, and I hoped to keep it that way.

"What do you want?" I grumbled.

A Charming Encounter

"I just wanted to say thank you."

I waved off her thanks. Didn't need it. But I was curious… "I have one question. Why you? Why that bracelet?"

Lily pulled out one of the now-cushioned chairs and sat down.

"Because it was my mother's and my mother is the only one who Lady Masque could never get the best of. She married my father, who Lady M wanted. And mother's tavern, at least until she died, was twice the one that Lady's M is.

"So… jealousy. All that over jealousy."

Dames.

Hoarfrost
Susan Bianculli

Galicia's black servant's skirts puddled about her knees as she knelt before the door to the castle's treasure room. The torches in their iron-banded wall sconces lit up the dead-end corridor to reveal that the door's large built-in lock had a smaller inner lock as well. It looked like both would need to be dealt with at the same time in order to open it. Galicia frowned darkly—in all her long experience, she'd never seen or even heard of such a device. To succeed in the unlocking she'd need two sets of different sized lockpicks and two sets of hands. The tools she had, but not the four hands.

Galicia Alienthal, ex-Master of the Thieves' Guild of Ashbury, ground her teeth. She was here because her and her itinerant bard husband's three-year-old son Aarlen had been snatched away by a mysterious force four nights ago. The note she'd found in place of him in the morning had said that if Galicia didn't recover Hoarfrost the Ice Sword from the Ducal Treasury before the last night of the full moon, she could expect to have Aarlen returned to her by the new moon.

In pieces.

Galicia narrowed her brown eyes at the impossible lock and ran one hand through her short greying hair in frustration. To get this far, she'd already spent three days and two nights scouting the castle grounds in the guise of a serving girl. But the servant she'd been replacing had let Galicia know in no uncertain terms when she'd arrived with this night's payment that their arrangement was over as of the morning bell. The serving girl's decision had forced the ex-Guild Master to make her move now, ready or not.

One of the torches on the wall above her flared brighter for a second, and the little burst of light revealed a slight movement around the strike plate. Galicia narrowed her eyes at it, and the wavering become more pronounced.

Magic is at work here; I'm sure of it, she thought.

Struck by inspiration, she closed her eyes to reach for the double device and felt only smooth steel beneath her fingertips. She opened her eyes and saw her pale fingers buried partially inside the smaller lock.

What sorcery is this? she wondered, mouth hanging open. *I've never before heard of magic that can make things appear to not be there! How can this be?*

But obviously, it was somehow possible. Galicia shut her eyes again to search around under the magic until she found the real keyhole. She gritted her teeth at the delay this caused because the Guard patrol was due soon. And if they saw a serving girl at the treasure chamber door with thieves' tools in her hands, they wouldn't bother with politely asking her why she was there.

As if her thoughts of the Guard were a summons, her ears caught a faint clang. The far cross-corridor door had been opened. Galicia hurriedly reached into her white apron pocket and took out her lockpicks to attack the real lock. She'd learned to pick locks under all kinds of circumstances, and she was relieved to find her hard-learned skills hadn't deserted her since her self-retirement. But despite her expertise, the mechanism was stiff.

Galicia sweated. There was no place to hide in the bare stone walls around her, and no time to escape out the corridor unseen. She either succeeded now, or failed. But failure wasn't an option; she didn't have years to sit in the gaol because Aarlen didn't have years to live. She redoubled her efforts and felt her lockpicks bend under the strain. The ex-Guild master cursed without sound. If her tools broke, they'd be useless; and the tramp of approaching feet meant she wouldn't have time to start over with her backup set. She shoved her picks hard and felt the tumblers slide into their unlocked positions.

Fast as sand through an hourglass, Galicia opened the door on hinges she'd pre-oiled and slipped inside, pulling the door not quite closed behind her. There was an eerie blue glow in the chamber, but she ignored it to dive under the nearest table in case the Guard checked on the door. She rolled up against the wall, pressed her back to it, and held her breath.

After Galicia had silently counted to one hundred with nothing happening, she crawled out from under the table. The peculiar glow lighting the treasury showed that the room was filled with sturdy wooden tables and shelves bearing gold coins, jewellery, and other precious things. But she only had eyes for the source of the cool blue-white illumination: a short sword displayed on a weapon stand in the middle of the room. A closer look at it revealed snowflakes etched in a crystalline pattern on the blade.

This must be Hoarfrost, Galicia thought. *And of course it has to be a sword that somehow glows. Is there no end to the wonders of extraordinary magic I'm being shown tonight? I certainly hope there is.*

She searched around the room for an accompanying sheath for the weapon, but came up empty-handed.

The ex-Guild Master frowned. *It would've been nice had I been told that not only would I have to deal with getting the sword out of the castle, but I'd have to do it while it's lit up like a novelty lantern.*

She took off her apron and held it up before the blade without touching it. The fabric wasn't quite big enough to wrap up the whole weapon more than a couple of times, but that didn't matter because the material wasn't thick enough to stop much of the light anyway. Galicia put her apron back on and took out flexible black leather gloves from another pocket, hoping they would provide her some protection against this strange magic if needed. She grasped the hilt with gloved hands and lifted it clear of its wooden support with surprising ease.

A tinkling, like icicles breaking, sounded through the room.

Galicia stopped dead, her heart skipping a beat. But as nothing else happened after that sound, she shrugged it off. She hefted the weapon in her hands—it was much lighter than she'd thought it would be from its size.

Experimentally, she swung the sharp-looking blade around and grinned. *Too bad I'm not a swordswoman, or let my enemies beware my wrath!*

But this thought reminded her of the unknown adversary she did have, and of her worries for Aarlen.

The icy tinkling sound came again, but slower this time. It sounded almost sympathetic.

Galicia stopped swinging the blade around and stared at it. The sound had come from the sword *and* in response to what she'd been thinking. Could this thing be reading her?

She smirked to herself for the whimsy. *Of course not. It's only an inanimate piece of sharpened metal, even if it is magical.*

The sword tinkled again, louder and faster, as if it was objecting to her thoughts.

Unnerved, the ex-Guild Master put the weapon back in its holder. She took a couple of calming breaths while reaching out to a nearby table to grab a couple of handfuls of loose gems and gold coins. Treasure could be useful to ensure any regular servant's blindness to her while she used their corridors to leave the castle. She stowed just those handfuls in her apron pockets. There was no need to be greedy, despite the abundance surrounding her; greed was how many an amateur thief fell into the hands of the Guard. And she was—had been—no amateur.

Now that she'd accomplished the first part of her mission, retrieving Hoarfrost, Galicia needed to achieve the second: getting out with it. She gingerly picked up the sword again. It was after midnight now, but the guard was always about. And when, not if, she was spotted because of the glowing weapon she was forced to carry, she didn't doubt it would be a race between her and a multitude of crossbow bolts and guards to escape.

She sighed internally. *I wish this thing was more like a normal, everyday sword. It would certainly help with escaping with it.*

The blade went out abruptly.

In the sudden resulting darkness she was blinded, but that didn't stop her from widening her eyes in surprise and dismay. The blackness had come directly after her wish. Galicia swung the weapon off her shoulder and held it in front of her, even though she couldn't see it.

Can you be—are you—alive? she mentally asked.

The sound of ice tinkling answered her.

Galicia sighed. Not only did it glow and was incredibly light, but it was somehow sentient and able to read thoughts.

Unparalleled magic upon unparalleled magic. No wonder the kidnapper wants this sword!

The tinkling happened again, but louder and harsher, as if Hoarfrost was arguing with her.

Hush! Galicia thought with fierceness. *If you're too loud, the guard will hear you, and then I'll be caught. And then* you *will remain in this treasury.*

The icy noise cut off as if the blade had been sheathed.

Can you glow just a little, so I can find my way to the door without bumping into anything?

A faint radiance that was just enough for her to see around her feet was her answer.

Perfect, thank you, she thought, pleased.

By its light, the ex-Guild Master made her way from the room and closed and locked the door behind her. After all, there was no need to immediately announce to the next noble who came here that someone else had come and gone from their treasury.

Extinguish yourself, please, Hoarfrost. We need to get you back to my home undetected.

Obligingly the sword stopped glowing again. Galicia walked softly to the cross-corridor with Hoarfrost resting on her shoulder.

"A-ha! I *knew* there was something off about that door when we passed it!" came a deep, unexpected voice.

Galicia froze. A burly male guard stepped around the corner and aimed a wicked looking crossbow straight at her. Her stomach dropped as she recognized whom it was.

Of all the members of the guard who could've caught me, it had to be Rolaan, she groaned to herself.

Rolaan first looked startled at seeing her, but then bared his teeth in a tight smile. "Well, well, well. If it isn't the ex-Guild Master herself. And dressed as a servant girl! My, my. I wonder what the Head Server will have to say about that!" His expression dropped into a sneer. "I knew it had to have all been a ruse, you quitting the Thieves' Guild four years ago. No thief can ever truly reform, I've always said. And here you are, proving me right."

Galicia reddened, but didn't say anything to upset the finger pressing on the trigger. She knew what he was like all too well. "Hair trigger" was a term that could've been invented for him, for both his temper and his delight in usually shooting at the first sign of opposition. He'd always claimed that a crossbow bolt to the leg unlocked tongues much faster than mere questions ever could, and he enjoyed proving it every chance he got.

"You'd been very careful all your years as Guild Master," he went on. "We could never pin anything on you, so we could never extend to you the hospitality of our dungeons. I'd wondered why you stepped down, because marrying that pitiful traveling song-maker wasn't a good enough reason to leave your office. But now I know why: you wanted to up your stakes, didn't you?"

Anger rose in Galicia, but she kept it off her face. There was no point in explaining the reasoning to him. Rolaan had been angry at her ever since she had turned him down as a suitor long ago, even before she'd found her career. She was convinced he'd become a guard specifically to harass her when he'd found out she'd become a ranking member of the

Thieves' Guild, even though he could never prove it in a court of law. Things had only gotten worse when he'd found out she'd stepped down from being Guild Master to marry Donal and when she later became pregnant with Donal's child. But as she'd become a strict law-abiding citizen upon her self-retirement, Rolaan could do nothing to her. This shared past, his present duties as a guard, and Donal being out of town all ensured that she would be arrested by Rolaan at the very least. Not even the loot in her pockets would sway him to look the other way.

"Well? Say something, Galicia!" Rolaan demanded.

"What do you want me to say?" she replied, fighting to stay calm.

He smiled, cruelness evident in his tooth-baring smile. "That you've been caught red-handed, that you deserve death, and that you wish to go down on your knees and beg me for mercy. I will, of course, after a suitable amount of time, grant you that mercy and allow you to be imprisoned for the rest of your life. With me as your gaoler."

A leer crept into the expression on his face and twisted it further. Galicia inhaled sharply as images of what that experience might be like flashed through her head.

Hoarfrost tinkled with an angry, icy harshness.

"What? What was that sound?" asked Rolaan, looking around defensively.

Galicia seized the moment to try to knock the crossbow out of his hands with the sword. But Hoarfrost burst into cool blue-white light instead, surprising and blinding her. Rolaan whipped his head back to stare at it, and Galicia, eyes squinting, cursed at herself for the lost opportunity.

"How…?" was all he managed to say before a shiny, swirling silver ray shot out from Hoarfrost's sharp tip and engulfed him.

Galicia's arms wobbled from the force of the beam and nearly made her drop the sword in shock, but she hung on. The cold radiated from the handle into her hands, and she was very glad that she'd put on her gloves before picking up the blade. If she'd had bare skin touching Hoarfrost now, her palms might have ended up stuck to the handle the way wet skin sticks to metal on a freezing winter's night. The cold, but not the light, abruptly cut off, and the ex-Guild Master blinked to regain her eyesight. Rolaan was oddly silent.

I guess there really is no end to the unusual magics around here, she thought. After a moment, she said tentatively out loud, "Rolaan?"

His skin glistened in the sword's light. Galicia reached out to touch him and discovered Hoarfrost had encased him in ice, turning him into a frozen sculpture.

Wow! You can do that? That's amazing, Hoarfrost, she thought, *but that's also a problem. He's too heavy for me to move and hide. We need to escape the castle quickly, before the next patrol comes along and finds him!*

She didn't waste time pitying what had happened to Rolaan, because her relief that he was gone from her life was too great. Galicia put out the nearest torch and reached to extinguish the next, but to her pleased surprise, Hoarfrost beat her to it with a puff of frost. Smiling for the first time in four nights, she ran on light feet down the corridor with the blade putting out the torches along the way.

At the corridor's end Galicia put her ear up to the iron door's keyhole. She already knew where it went—into a corridor just off the central castle courtyard. If she could get to the door leading to the serving passageways just down the hall, making her way to the outside grounds would be immeasurably easier.

By the way, thank you for saving me, she thought at Hoarfrost.

The blade pinged back softly once.

After a few minutes of not hearing anything, the ex-Guild Master looked at the lock with a professional eye and scoffed. Opening this lock would be as easy as opening her jewellery chest at home. She oiled the hinges before cracking both the lock and the door, and Hoarfrost turned itself off before she glided into the corridor. Turning right, Galicia stopped short and cursed silently. There was a new guard station down the hallway that hadn't been there yesterday. The Ducal Guard of Ashbury was clever—they changed internal stations on no set schedule and re-arranged patrol patterns often. She'd known this going in, which was why she'd spent time scouting as a serving girl; but time and circumstances had forced her hand. She'd hoped that her luck would hold on what she'd observed before going to the treasury, but it seemed that chance was not with her. She slipped back into the doorway behind her.

I don't suppose you can do anything magical to help out? she thought to the sword.

A very faint, sad-sounding tinkle was her answer. Galicia took that for a "no," and guessed that Hoarfrost needed recharging, or a rest, or whatever it was that a magical item like this needed to do in-between bouts of sorcery. The ex-Guild Master whipped off her apron and wrapped it around the blade loosely. She cradled it in her arms and tried to make Hoarfrost look like a bolt of fabric before stepping back into the hallway, but she knew with a sickening feeling that it would never pass even a cursory glance from anybody who walked by.

Can I make it to the next serving corridor without running into any new guard stations? Galicia wondered as she walked the opposite way from where she'd wanted to go.

Passing one of the long, low windows that looked out onto the open space in the castle's centre, it occurred to her that she could use the courtyard to get out. Climbing the trees there up to the castle roofs might throw off the pursuit that would happen when Rolaan was discovered. She walked with quiet feet to the nearest courtyard door and opened it. The fitful moonlight illuminating the garden allowed Galicia to slink into a covey of orange trees whose branches reached past the second story.

Getting up these should be easy enough, she decided after inspection, *and once I get up to the decorations on the upper lintels, those'll get me all the way to the roof itself. I hope.*

She couldn't climb with Hoarfrost in her arms, however, so she improvised a sling for it out of her apron and tied the bundle across her back. Then, picking up the sides of her skirts, she tucked them into the belt at her waist to free up her legs in preparation for climbing.

A brassy bell rang out to shatter the night's stillness.

Galicia gulped. *Hoarfrost! Rolaan's been found!*

Her heart pounded as points around the castle took up the alarm like a beehive awakening in anger. Fear of being caught made her almost fly up the tree trunks. The sounds of running feet came from everywhere, and harsh voices giving orders filled the air. She scrambled out of sight onto the roof just as a search party came out of a door on the balcony nearest the trees.

Galicia ran light as a cat to the closest chimney and crouched in its shadow to catch her breath. Torches flared in the courtyard she'd come from. She peeked around the chimney and watched them leave, and took the chance to flit straight out from the chimney to the outer roof of the castle that faced the city.

Peering over its edge made the ex-Guild Master smile in relief. It seemed luck was on her side again. There was a trellis of roses and ivy extending all the way from the ground to the roof in front of her. The famous trellis had been designed in the symbol of the duchy and had been filled with the plants that decorated the official seal. It could be seen easily from the main gate that led from the castle grounds to the city, letting her know exactly where she was. The only bad part was that there was no ground cover between it and the outer wall. If she went down the trellis and crossed the lawn, at some point she'd be seen. Then she'd have to dodge the guards *and* make sure she wasn't ventilated by their crossbow bolts while getting to her pre-prepared escape route over the rooftops of the city. But there was little choice now.

Galicia clambered down the trellis, both praising the ducal architect for its construction and cursing the royal gardener for its thorns. She was bleeding from a hundred scratches by the time she set foot on the grass, and it was just her misfortune that the guard broadened the search onto the smooth grassy grounds at that point. She fled quick as the wind towards the entrance barracks, hoping that the clouded moonlight would stay dark long enough for her to get away. But she was spotted when she was three-quarters of the way there by the gate guard, who sounded another brash alarm.

The hue and cry of the guard converging from all sides mixed with the whine of their bolts as the shafts fell in a lethal rain around her. Adrenaline helped Galicia dodge left and right in short bursts to avoid getting hit, and minus a few holes appearing in her skirts, she made it unscathed to the barracks. She shimmied up the garrison building using their windows, then dodged both bolts and grasping hands as she scaled the outer wall from the garrison roof by using their chimney. The ex-Guild Master laughed in pure relief as she made good her escape over the wall.

Though the Ashbury City Watch took up the alarm from the gate guard, Galicia had the advantage in the city proper and made full use of it. She flitted through several rooftop way stations of the Thieves' Guild to ditch the extra loot and her serving girl outfit. Only then did she make a break for the merchant-class building she owned, where she disarmed her own security traps handily and slid in through her bedroom window.

As she stepped down from her bed to the floor, a throat cleared itself in the bedroom doorway. Galicia stood for an instant as frozen as if Hoarfrost had kissed her with its ice breath.

Someone's found out what I've done!

She sprang for the window to escape with her bounty—she could not lose Hoarfrost now. The window slammed shut by a sharp gust of wind before her fingers touched the latch. Galicia stopped short and turned slowly around. A cloaked and cowled figure stood in her bedroom doorway. The mystical symbols done in silver thread that decorated the midnight blue fabric proclaimed the presence of a powerful mage. Emotions whirled through her—anger, anxiety, fear. She shoved them all down with a firm hand as she took a deep breath.

"I presume you are the mysterious force who has my son?" Galicia asked as evenly as she could manage.

"I am," a kind masculine voice responded as his hands lowered the cowl to reveal a young, bearded man. He smiled disarmingly at her.

"Where is Aarlen?" she demanded.

"Behind me," he replied, pointing towards her son's bedroom.

She brushed past the man to look for herself. There, in his bed where she'd last seen him four nights ago, her fair-haired boy lay sleeping. She threw herself to her knees at his bedside and hugged him, crying in relief. But her son didn't awaken at her caress.

She shook him gently. "Aarlen! Aarlen? Time to wake up now. Mama needs to talk to you."

No response.

Galicia rose from his bedside like a Paladin bent on avenging a heinous wrong.

"What have you done to my *son*?" she raged as she charged the young man with fingers extended into claws to choke the life out of him.

Startled, he stepped back and raised his hands, but she barrelled him into the hallway wall before he had a chance to cast anything. Hoarfrost, still on Galicia's back, tinkled anxiously at her. She paid it no mind.

"Wait!" the mage said in a panicked voice as her hands closed around his windpipe. "He's..." was all he could get out before her fingers cut off his air.

She choked him until he was unconscious despite him beating on her arms. It was only Hoarfrost's loud, sharp, and angry tinkles that broke through Galicia's rage and stopped her from killing him. She released her hands from around his neck and watched the man slump down the wall.

Galicia snarled at the sword, "All right, all right, I've stopped."

Hoarfrost went quiet. Galicia took a deep breath and fought to push the anger back down.

After a moment, Galicia said to Hoarfrost in a calmer voice, "Okay. Let's consider: this kidnapper is a mage. So maybe it's a spell Aarlen's under, and he can undo what he's done." She glared down at the man's unconscious body and said grimly, "He'd better be able to, or you won't be able to stop me a second time, sword."

Galicia dragged the young man to her kitchen and tied him to a chair, making very sure to wrap his hands up tight in separate dishcloths. Then she drew some water from the pump in the sink and threw it on him. Sputtering, he woke.

"Now, kidnapper, we will do this my way. Tell me what you have done to my son, undo it, and then we can discuss Hoarfrost," she informed him in clipped tones with her arms crossed.

The man shook the water out of his eyes, and then tested his bonds. She watched with no emotion as he struggled. The ex-Guild Master was too good at knot tying to be concerned at his efforts.

"With my hands tied, I can't cast the magics that will awaken your son. But just so you know, I've kept him safe these past four nights. I had no plans to hurt him, despite my note. He has no idea that anything has happened since he went to sleep," the mage finally croaked in a bruised-sounding voice.

Galicia sagged in relief. It was a spell that could be undone, her son would be fine, and he would not be traumatized by this whole experience. The mage eyed her and gave her a tentative smile as he cleared his throat. She almost smiled back until she caught herself, and frowned instead.

"You have a lot of explaining to do," she stated flatly.

He swallowed before speaking. "Err, yes, I guess I do. My name is Jorin, and the sword Hoarfrost is actually my fiancée, Sharel. Sharel and I are from Blythedale and are engaged to be married, but our old master Kaizan decided that he wanted to wed her instead. He challenged me to a wizard duel for her outside his house the day after she and I had graduated out from his apprenticeship."

Galicia raised her eyebrows. "Is that what's usually done?"

The mage shook his head. "No, because duels don't generally settle anything, as far as I'm concerned. I was going to tell him 'no' because I knew that no matter the outcome, Sharel would not leave me, but he launched straight into his attacks after the challenge. After the first spell I saw that he wasn't going to cast the usual non-lethal duelling spells, but killing ones instead. I needed to either defend myself, or die. I found out from his rantings during our battle that Sharel had already turned him down, and then he taunted me that he had turned her into an ice sword for her 'cold-hearted, back-biting ways,' as he put it."

Hoarfrost tinkled angrily on Galicia's back.

"I know, Sharel, I know," he said to the sword, "Believe me, I was shocked and horrified to learn what had happened to you. I had no idea that that was something which magic could even do! Anyway, Madame Galicia, I won the wizard duel more by default than anything else—Kaizan had a heart attack or something while casting a spell, and died. I immediately ran to his workshop, but discovered that Sharel wasn't there."

Galicia felt pity seeping into her heart, but squelched it.

The mage went on. "I found the notes on the unique magic he'd done to my fiancée, and then looked for her for months. Finally, I heard a rumor from a merchant caravan of a fabulous weapon made magical in the city of Ashbury. So I came here and paid the Thieves' Guild for information on it. They confirmed that a sword called Hoarfrost had been gifted to the Crown some months ago. From its description and name, I knew it had to be what Kaizan had called Sharel. But I had two problems in getting her back: the first was that I learned from the Guild that the treasury had been built in the middle of the castle with mages in mind. The second was that the Guild refused to help me rescue her."

Galicia nodded. "But how did you learn of me?"

"I happened to learn of your existence from a random street urchin willing to sell city information. You were perfect: someone with the skills I needed to get into the treasury who was not bound to the Guild that had denied me help. I scouted you out, made my plan, and the rest you know."

Galicia tapped her fingers on her arms. She was still angry at him, but now she felt a grudging admiration as well. She could respect someone willing to go to any lengths necessary to free the one he loved. Just like she had.

"You couldn't have just asked me?" she asked Jorin.

"I was afraid you'd say 'no' and then, having said 'no,' you would have taken precautions against me," he said straightforwardly.

She grimaced as she removed her dishtowels and freed him from the chair. He probably wasn't wrong.

"Thank you," he said with gratitude, shaking out his hands. "May I have her now?"

Galicia took Hoarfrost from the apron sling and handed it to Jorin without another word.

Hoarfrost tinkled happily in his arms. He cradled it for a minute with closed eyes. The sword lit up, and he released it to float away on a small contained whirlwind until it came to a stop mid-air about two feet in front of him. He waved his arms in intense concentration and intoned harsh sounding arcane words. Galicia felt a pressure grow in the air around them with each syllable he uttered. The tension burst at the end of his spell with a flash of silvery light and a brief, intense cold which blew open the wide kitchen window. Hoarfrost morphed into a pretty young ice mage with pale blond hair wearing a white robe.

"Jorin!" she squealed, and threw herself into his arms.

"Thank you again, Mistress Galicia!" Jorin exclaimed, casting a whirlwind about Sharel and himself and flying them out the window.

"Wait!" she shouted, running to grab at them; but spun around as she heard down the hall, "Mama? Mama? Where are you?"

She said with a relieved smile, "I'm coming, Aarlen!" As Galicia headed to his bedroom, she whispered, "I'll always come for you, my son."

The Curse of the Dwarven Necromancer
W. Adam Clarke

"Steady now, steady…"

My instructions were as much to myself as to anyone else in the room. In fact, as I was the only person in the lab, they were most assuredly to me. I couldn't remember exactly when I started speaking to myself, but I was pretty certain that it wasn't an altogether good sign. Still, these types of alchemical treatments were volatile to say the least. One drop too many into the solution, and the delicate precipice of combustibility would be thrown from "future" to "immediate" status. Five drops was all that was required. Five simple drops. I took a deep breath, then exhaled most of it. Holding your breath could make your hands shaky, and today wasn't exactly the day I wanted to burn alive. One… two… three… four…

"*Vaeallan*! Vaeallan, where are you, you weak-kneed fish codger?"

I jumped as the roar bellowed down the hallway. Five six seven eight went the drops of accelerant. I leapt for the door to my lab, pulling it shut behind me as I flew through the portal with a lack of grace only attainable by the incredibly old, the incredibly drunk, or the incredibly fearful of death. It just so happened that I landed at Duren's feet in the process.

I brushed his nearly-floor-length alabaster beard away from my face to speak. "My Lord," I responded with the feigned calm that comes with two centuries of practice. "You called for me?"

The lab answered before Duran could. A deep rumbling sound which made the heavy oak door bow outwards just slightly. A disturbingly teal smoke vented through the keyhole and the gap between door and frame.

"I did, lad! I did!" roared the impossibly old (and quite possible nearly deaf) dwarven champion. "I've received a messenger from King Kelanor himself!"

I couldn't help but be concerned with the ever-increasing cloud of smoke suspended in the rafters of the hallway.

"The messenger is a young fellow, probably not worth my time, but just in case there were any important details he might need to impart, I thought it best if you accompanied me, old boy!"

There were times where Duren's tenuous grasp on reality was enjoyable. My lab burning uncontrollably, however, did not make that list. I stood up and collected my appearance as best as possible, given the concern that our keep could explode at any moment. "An exceptionally sound idea as always, Master Duren. I shall be downstairs momentarily, so please refrain from any important discussions until I arrive to Chronicle them for you."

"Indeed I shall! Don't take long!" Duren paused, as if the bloated sheep's bladder he called a nose had finally detected something in the air. "Did you leave something in the oven, Vaeallan? Smells like you might have burned it! Right sloppy of you that is! Ah well, some day you'll learn, lad!" He turned on his heel and toddled off down the corridor, humming some ancient dwarven ballad to himself.

I nervously opened the door to my alchemy lab. Fortunately, the compound's reaction had not set alight anything else in the room. Equally fortunate, it seemed to not react with stone. Unfortunately, it seemed to melt glass and reduce wood to the consistency of overcooked noodles, as the mixing table and stool in front of it were both irrevocably destroyed. After opening the shutters, I hurried downstairs.

I wouldn't want anyone to think that, by means of this introduction, I did not travel with, Chronicle for, and play manservant to the Great Duren Ironoath by choice. Far to the contrary, assisting him gave me a means and standard of living far exceeding what I could have managed on my own. You see, I was born elven, which brought with it a certain number of expectations for those who wish to ascend to prosperity. In short, one is expected to be, at the very least, skilled in arms, versed in arcane knowledge, or trained in the fine arts. I, unfortunately, was none of those things. I am petrified by the sight of blood (most specifically my own), I lacked the ability to maintain even the simplest of magical cantrips, and my artistic expressions were once described as something approaching the level of a racial insult to my kind. What I did have, however, was a great love of money, a mind for alchemical measures, and a recognition of the fact that playing lackey to one of the living ancestral legends of the dwarven people afforded me a great many opportunities I might have never reached otherwise.

The matter at hand was in fact one of those. As I descended the stairs from my tower laboratory, I heard the voice of Captain Khondgan in the chamber below. Far from a messenger boy, Khondgan was a formidable warrior, and should he live another century or more might find himself in the hallowed ranks of the clan's greatest warriors. To Duren, however, everyone under the age of three centuries was simply a child—even an Elven Chronicler of two hundred and eighty-three years.

"Good morning, Captain Khondgan," I said in my most disarming and sincerest of tones. "What brings you to Ironoath Keep today? Surely this is a long travel for a mere social call."

Khondgan's beard was dark and coarse, resembling a wire bristled broom that had been dunked in pitch. His eyes burned as coals. Captain Khondgan was nothing if not severe in appearance and direct in approach. "His Majesty, King Kelanor, has requested the presence of Champion Ironoath to deal with a problem which not only threatens the Clanholds, but also the entire continent."

Duren never knew when his ego was being stroked. Sadly, it wasn't exactly ego… even in his advancing age, there were few who could neutralize problems as well as he.

Captain Khondgan changed his glance from Duren to myself as he continued. "I have a carriage waiting. I am to escort the two of you to His Majesty immediately."

I attempted to interject. "Immediately as in later this evening, perhaps tomorrow morning, yes? After all, Master Duren likely has other obliga—"

"Vaeallan, grab our travel satchels, further Glory awaits! *Haha!*"

I sighed. This was going to be a long afternoon.

The royal coach was quite comfortable, even if painfully dwarven. Leave it to these bearded non-sophisticates to not be able to comprehend the concept of a properly stuffed cushion, yet somehow master the art of designing and smithing a suspension system to smooth out the ride. The way their brains worked was truly an incredible, powerful, and terrifying feat of nature—not unlike an avalanche in many respects. The distance from the Ironoath Clanhold to Dwarvenholm was only a few hours. Be that as it may, practiced experience had warned me exactly what the conversation was likely to be. Practiced experience had not judged incorrectly.

"Vaeallan, did I ever tell you about the time I slayed three fire-breathing dragons to rescue the Duke of Ashbury's wife?"

"Yes, you have, Master Duren," I sighed heavily. "Further, you didn't need to, because I was there."

"Oh, it's such a good thing you weren't there, Vaeallan," he continued, oblivious to my commentary. "Vicious, massive beasts they were! Great snapping jaws, breathing gouts of flame! I had to constantly maneuver to keep them from being able to surround me!"

"My Lord… you do realize that it would be impossible for someone of either of our statures to outmaneuver a sixty-foot-long creature of profound intellect, don't you?"

"Ha! It would be had they not transformed themselves into humanoid forms! Lucky for me, they were much smaller!"

"That is because it wasn't three fire-breathing dragons, Master Duren. It was a trio of lizardmen with terrible breath."

"I slayed them all the same, you lanky, long-eared layabout!"

"If by 'slayed,' you mean were so drunk you threw up on them, you are impeccably correct, Master Duren."

"I slayed her captors and freed her!"

"Oh, for the love of… Master Duren, you got into a drunken brawl with her bodyguards, and we barely made it out of Ashbury City alive. Also, I'd refrain from discussing this particular escapade in front of His Majesty, as the Duke was a former drinking companion of King Kelanor's, and I'm not entirely certain that His Grace has forgiven us for the damage done to the city when your mighty weapon Honor's Wrath sundered one of their guard towers."

"I did no such thing! I toppled a stone effigy the vile dragons had erected to show their might!"

"You do realize that 'stone effigy' had a door in it, my Lord?"

"Of course! That's how big it was!"

"And that the door had a sign above it?"

"Which read *'Dragon Effigy'*!"

"Actually, it read 'Barracks,' my Lord."

"It couldn't have. How then would you explain the parade they threw us on the way out of town, Vaeallan?"

"The parade, Master Duren?"

"Yes, the parade."

"The one which proceeded at nearly a run, with torches and pickaxes in the air?"

"Yes! That one! Which parade did you think I meant, you blonde twig?"

"Ah, my apologies, I had forgotten that dwarven parades so often look like enraged hordes running someone out of town." I looked out the window of the coach, and could see Dwarvenholm quickly approaching. "My memory must have slipped, Master Duren. Thank you for reminding me. In any event… please refrain from discussing this in His Majesty's presence? Let us instead concentrate on this new future glory available to you, my Lord."

Duren bounced up and down in his chair like a schoolchild promised a sweet pastry. "Yes! New found glory! That's the thing to keep the old blood pumping! Let's go get the bast—"

"We are not starting a fight with the Dwarvenholm Honor Guard, Master Duren!" I screamed, suddenly terrified. He blinked, startled, and honestly appeared to pay attention. "We are here to have an audience with King Kelanor, to see what he needs done… remember?"

"Right! Quite right. I thought we had finished that part already and were up to the thrashing part."

"No, Master Duren. I'll inform you when we've gotten that far."

"Excellent! Good man, Vaeallan!" Duren regained his happy composure, and my heart settled down, confident that the old dwarf was not about to commit treason by attacking the palace single-handedly. Well, at least not today. Or right now. No telling where his mind might wander to if not kept busy.

Dwarvenholm was an impressive structure. While the majority of it would be found within the bowels of an ancient and mighty mountain, the entrance to the fortress was ostensibly at ground level outside. A forty-foot-tall wall protected the entrance to the Clanhold. Two towers hewn into the mountain itself produced the corners of the wall. A mighty portcullis nearly twenty feet tall sat in the center of the massive facade. The sheer size of the place was obviously intended as a statement: a dwarf may generally be a third the height of a door anywhere else in the world, but visitors were going to feel "dwarfed" when coming here as well. A full score of armed men and women (at least I assumed. When you can only see them from the shoulders up and they are bedecked in helmets, it's nearly impossible to tell the genders apart) stood at the ready behind exquisitely carved parapets along the ramparts. The wall itself had been quarried from the very spot, as proven by the ten-foot-wide and unfathomably deep pit that separated the Clanhold from the rest of the mountain.

The dwarven ingenuity of construction was evident: The drawbridge was counter-weighted in such a way that its natural position was closed rather than open. It could take twenty minutes to crank the portal to open, and mere seconds for it to slam shut if needed. The counterweights required to raise the foot and a half thick reinforced door were staggering, to say the least. Should an assailant manage to take the wall, the outer courtyard was nearly eighty yards long, and the ramparts aimed in on all faces.

The Honor Guard were the most effective non-elven fighting force I had ever seen, with most units holding hereditary positions passed down through generations of dwarves, meaning their pride in their unit was directly tied to their family honor. If I were to write a "Guide to the Top Five Hardest Places to Assault in Fortannis," Dwarvenholm would certainly make the list—which made the need to summon us to it all the more terrifying.

The carriage rolled through the outer and inner perimeters, continuing along streets of cut stone through the busy metropolis. Contrary to expectations, the inside of the Clanhold was brilliantly lit, and shops and homes were adorned with metals and gems of every kind, brilliantly reflecting light of sun, torch, and lamp. The city smelled of oils and incense doing their best to keep the air from becoming stale, and nearly succeeding. Perfumery, staleness, cooking, and the scents of livestock competed in a four-way conflict that quite frankly had me wishing for less of all parties, but Duren seemed to inhale it all with vigor.

The carriage made a final series of turns and approached the central hub of the Clanhold, the palace of King Kelanor. The heavily armored guards standing at the palace made the ones outside look like new recruits. Each one possessed a beard which must have taken centuries to grow, and held weapons of arcane nature enchanted so long ago that each one held a lineage of wielders.

The coach came to a stop, and Captain Khondgan held the door for us. The good Captain led us through the palace, which I was thankful for. Even though we had been here on a handful of occasions over the years, the fact that any number of rooms could hold state secrets which would cost me my life if seen left me with a healthy trepidation in regards to unguided meandering.

The throne room of the palace gleamed. I know that word is oft used poorly and in poetic fashion, so let me be clear. Every surface was polished to a mirrored finish, and the lamplight within cast shadows into the hallway and beyond. It was not difficult to keep one's view averted from the thrones. In fact, it was nearly a necessity. Looking up in that chamber was as staring into the sun itself.

Captain Khondgan led the way, and we followed down the long approach to the throne of King Kelanor. It was impossible to know how many long-bearded elder warriors stood at attention in the room, or if many of the heavy armor suits were simply racked there. One simply could not look up that long. After an approach nearly the length of a field, we respectfully took knees before the King of the Dwarves.

King Kelanor clapped heavily on the hand rest of his jeweled throne made pure mithril, his gauntlet slamming down like a gavel to cause a resounding echo through the chamber. "Duren Ironoath," the King began. "Lord Elder and Master of the Ironoath Clan, Champion of Champions, and my old friend," the King smiled, "it has been far too long." King Kelanor's beard had always been ebon black, much like the Captain's. However, where the Captain's was wiry and coarse, Kelanor's had a wave to it, which was emphasized by the very animated way he moved his head. It made the length of his beard always seem to be about a sentence or so behind the rest of his head.

Duren replied without ever looking up from the floor. "Your Majesty, Your victories are many, Your enemies with courage enough to threaten the Kingdom are few, and Your reign has been just and fair to all the Clans. Do not consider the years away as an insult, but as a compliment to Your rule." I was stunned. Was Duren just actually tactful of his own accord?

King Kelanor stood up, and walked down the short flight of stairs before the throne to clasp Duren on the shoulder. "I wish your words were as true as you believe them, my friend. Please rise, both of you. Join us in our private chambers." We stood as King Kelanor turned.

The king's private chambers were adjacent to the throne room, and something very few guests had ever seen in person. Fortunately, they were quite a bit dimmer. I could make out six armed guards, plus Captain

Khondgan and the King himself in the room. Kelanor was no lightweight when it came to martial prowess, either, although his studies of magic meant his sword work was somewhat less substantial than the Captain's.

Kelanor sat at the head of a large and heavy table of worked aged wood, and we collected ourselves appropriately in other chairs. "Guards, aren't you supposed to see to my health? I'm dying of thirst over here! So are my guests!" One of the Honor Guard moved from his position, and began to fill four goblets with a dwarven ale.

"So, Your Highness," Duren asked, "What is so dangerous that You have called me here to resolve it for You?"

King Kelanor glanced at Khondgan, who simply looked away. This was going to be big. I had no idea just how much the next three words he spoke would chill my spirit.

"Telchak... has returned."

Duren bolted upright, the large heavy chair clattering to the ground. "Impossible! I destroyed him myself!"

King Kelanor waved for Duren to take a seat again. "I know, old friend, but it is confirmed. Telchak once again walks."

There were famously few things that dwarves and elves agreed upon. Perhaps highest among them was that the raising of the dead by magical means was an affront to both cultures. For elves, the simple idea of necromancy was unacceptable. For dwarves, the puppeting of their ancestors was inexcusable.

Telchak was a necromancer of the highest order, having transformed himself into a lich many centuries ago. He had threatened dwarvenkind on several occasions, but had been finally put to rest by Duren quite some time ago, back when we had first begun traveling together.

"Your Highness," I began carefully, "could you please explain how Telchak could be alive? I witnessed Master Duren destroy the lich myself."

"It would appear that a new cult somehow managed to runebind his spirit, allowing him to return."

"Forgive my insolence, Your Majesty, but I thought that runebinding only worked on inanimate objects? And, also, was a magic limited to only high-ranking members of select clans?"

King Kelanor turned to face me. His sadness was apparent. "You are not wrong, Chronicler. Runebinding, we thought, could only work upon inanimate objects. It turns out that 'unliving' may be a more correct term. Also... that the cult that revived him is led by Our former Court Wizard, Balkas."

"I always hated that wand-toting wastrel!" bellowed Duren. "I'm going to smash him into pulp!"

Captain Khondgan interjected. "This is a delicate matter, Master Duren, and why we cannot use anyone from inside the Clanhold to resolve this. Balkas' involvement has been kept quiet, for now. Were it made public, it could cause political issues for Dwarvenholm. We need the two of you to infiltrate the Cult of Telchak's stronghold, destroy him again, and either capture or kill Balkas."

"Not that I don't want another shot at grinding Telchak's bones into powder, but why not send some of the elite palace guard? Or Captain Khondgan himself? This isn't something you need me for, you have more than a hundred able-bearded warriors who could handle this."

"True, all true," the King replied. "However, any of them could possibly be in allegiance with Balkas. Also, Balkas may have made runic protections against any of them. We know he would be less prepared against you, as he hasn't seen you in decades." Kelanor looked Duren in the eye. "I need this done by someone I can trust. I need the Bearer of Honor's Wrath to fulfill the task."

Duren scowled. Not because he wasn't going to do it, and not because he didn't want to do it, but because the King had left him no alternatives. Each Clan Champion has, at his or her disposal, an ancient artifact weapon dating back generations. In some cases, these weapons have been lost and needed to be reforged. Clan Ironoath's ancestral Clan Weapon was a two-handed cudgel of hardened oak, adorned with bands of mithril, and inscribed with the valiant deeds of its bearers. It was Clan Ironoath's pride and honor, and had never been replaced. It remained as powerful now as it had been a millennium, ago when it was first created by the earliest dwarven runesmiths. While each clan had a Champion which wielded a Clan Weapon, in theory all the Champions must answer directly to the King as well as their clans, as it was the ancient dwarven King Kelanor the First who sponsored the creation of the Champion Weapons. That bond has passed from King to King, and Champion to Champion. By stating that he needed the Bearer of Honor's Wrath, the King was calling on that bond.

Duren had no choice.

"Get me maps to their hideout, a cask of ale, and something to eat. I hate rampaging on an empty stomach."

The cultists had chosen to hold up in an old abandoned keep half a day's ride from the capital. There was not much surrounding it for cover, but that also made it easy to observe as well. Even in the middle of the night, it was a simple matter to track their movements. Keeping Duren from charging in headfirst without scouting the area was the hardest part.

"It doesn't matter how much you watch them," he'd complain. "They're still going to be in there, I'm still going to bash their skulls in, and you're still going to be a big wimp about it."

"Master Duren, please. For the last time, I need an accurate accounting of their forces, to make sure you don't miss any of them."

"Oh, come on, let's just go thrash them. It's not like it'll matter if we miss one."

"On the contrary, we still don't know how they managed to revive Telchak. I want to make certain none of them survive to do it again."

Duren fussed. "Vaeallan, I don't mind you being right so often, but why must your being right always cost me valuable thrashing time?"

"Because I don't stop you from thrashing things when it's appropriate. You notice me making you stop when it's inappropriate, my Lord." I continued trying to track movement, while relaying information to Duren. "There's about six or eight that I've seen, and neither Balkas nor Telchak have been with them." Balkas was fond of green robes adorned in gold, and Telchak would have stood out due to his dried leathery appearance. "If the above-ground numbers are half a dozen, the concealed numbers I'd expect to be at least that many, if not in fact much more."

"Good!" Duren boasted gleefully. "That means you can get the two on the left, and I'll take out the ten on the right! Filthy necromancers. Let's go, Vaeallan, it's time to bash some skulls in."

"For once, Master Duren, I cannot disagree with you." While I was not one prone to acts of violence—especially when I could myself be the victim of it—no pure-blooded elf could abide necromancy. It was the most abhorred of arcane skills. The issue was unlike most problems dwarves love to resolve with violence—troll infestations, orc attacks, and the like—necromancy was one that could not be resolved by simply waiting for it to die of old age. Not only would Telchak outlast even my own vast lifespan if left unchecked, but so would all the abominations he would create during that time. There was no reasonable course of action aside from his destruction, and experience had taught us that he would not retire quietly.

Duren and I snuck quietly along the underbrush towards the ruins. Duren had Honor's Wrath in both hands, striding forward as fast as his stunted legs would allow. For an old man, and a dwarf besides, he was able to keep his profile low and his movements silent. I had not yet drawn my sword, instead preferring a less direct form of conflict. From my pouch I had drawn three small glass globes filled with an exceptionally fine powder, which when inhaled immediately caused a tightening of the throat and difficulty breathing. Guards who cannot alert anyone are far less of a concern.

We continued to close the distance, and as fortune would have it, made it to within ten yards before we were spotted. I quickly took aim and hit the sentries in the chest with a globe apiece. The powder puffed into a cloud about their faces as the globes exploded on impact. As the guards drew in a breath to shout an alarm, they quickly found themselves unable to do so. Even their dwarven constitutions did not protect them from my concoctions. Somehow, however, Duren forgot that we were trying to be silent, and instead broke into war cries as soon as he was close enough to dispatch them.

"Filthy traitors!" Duren yelled as the two-handed cudgel struck the first guard in the ribs with a painful cracking sound. "I'll send you all to your ancestors, to get beaten by them as well!" The second guard's helmet met with Honor's Wrath in an unfortunate fashion, and gave under its weight. "You're not worth the beards you're wearing, you limp-armed codgers!" The third had managed to raise his shield in defense, so Duren swung low and swept his feet out from under him. As the sentry landed hard on his back, a downward overhand smash from Honor's Wrath resolved the encounter. I could hear alerts from within the ruins.

"Well, Master Durin, while it seems our approach did not go unnoticed, you have at least discovered where the entrance to the lower levels is."

"Quite right! Time to thrash the rest of the buggers!" Duren tore off into the keep, at speeds which seemed impossible for one of his advanced age. Which was the problem. They *were* impossible for one of his advanced age... at least to maintain for any reasonable length of time. Duren was going to pour himself headlong to the fight, and completely run out of energy by the time he reached it.

The entrance to the lower regions was simply an open staircase. Duren would be fighting at an extreme deficit on those stairs, without sufficient room to swing. As he reached the top of the stairs, I procured another handful of samples from my bag. These globes were different than the last. Instead of a coughing powder, they were filled with a potent hallucinatory. Dwarves were naturally resilient to such things (no doubt due to their near-constant drinking). I was willing to gamble that whomever was on the bottom of the stairs was not as resilient as Duren. After all, it was unlikely that anyone on the receiving end had lived with a master alchemist who had been slowly poisoning their food with it for the past two centuries. Purely to build up his resistance to it, of course... although the effects each time I raised his dosage were entertaining, I must admit.

Duren took to the stairs, and those coming up them were greeted by a wall of thick smoke. The first few he smashed his way through due to sheer confusion. The rest were having difficulties making out the actual invader from those that were simply herb-induced illusions. I allowed Duren a moment of exceptionally bawdy triumph at the bottom of the stairs as I waited for the gas to dissipate further. After all, I hadn't been lacing my own food. That stuff was dangerous.

"Will you hurry up, you yellow-bellied coward!" He barked to me, as he began walking further into the bowels of the keep.

"I'm doing my best, Master Duren," I declared. Which was true: my best to not inhale something that would take me out of the fight.

Duren had already begun to slow down. The Champion of Clan Ironoath would never admit it, but the age when he could engage in these activities without exhaustion had passed quite a long time ago. The more I held back, the more he could slow down and catch his breath. Once the fog had cleared sufficiently, I finished descending the stairs.

"Took you long enough, you soft-bellied buffoon." Duren pointed towards a door with his great maul. "Think you can manage to get your hands dirty long enough to unlock that bugger for me? Or should I just go ahead and hammer it to pieces?"

"Oh no, my Lord, I'll get it opened." I was suddenly swept up with confidence that we had managed to avoid further detection, and that once through the doorway we could continue on in relative stealth. All the more reason not to allow Duren to simply hit a hardened piece of wood with another hardened piece of wood rather loudly until one of them broke.

I examined the lock as I drew out my picks. I've always considered locks to be a lot like people: some are simple, some are complex, but once you know where their pressure points are, things generally go your way. The trick is finding those pressure points without snapping anything. A slight probe, a quick press of a few tumblers, and we were in. I smirked proudly as I stood up. Duren, I could see, did not approve.

"You know, a proper elf would have simply magicked it open."

"You are correct, Master Duren. However, a proper elf would not remain in your employ as your manservant, so one should be thankful for impropriety. Before we continue, are you injured, my Lord?"

"Of course not!" Duren balked. "Those scraggle-beards never laid a hand on me. Now let's hurry on. I'd like to be back to the capital before dawn."

I reached for the door, but it swung open of its own accord before I could grasp it. A familiar voice resonated from the chamber beyond.

"Come in, come in. It has truly been a while." Balkas' voice echoed through the portal. The room beyond was going to be large, but at least it was as far as we needed to go. I kept my hand upon the hilt of my sword, unsure for the moment if I should draw or not. Duren wasted no time in uncertainty, and swung the door wide to enter.

"Balkas! You thin-whiskered traitor! How could you turn on your clan and your King like this!" He took merely six steps through the doorway, and stopped.

The chamber was only forty feet long, with a large stone altar at the far end. Three large stone braziers burned coals to either side of the approach to the altar, giving just enough light to see shapes along the walls. There was a score of armored undead to either side of the chamber. In a large throne at the far end sat a figure in recognizable green robes. Balkas. He laughed as Duren's advance slowed.

"What's the matter, old friend? You used to boast that you were as good as twenty champions of any other clan. Here's your chance to prove yourself!" Balkas broke into a fit of laughter as he waved his hand. The ranks of undead along the walls began to move towards us.

Duren may be an insane old fighter, but he still had enough of his senses to know when charging would be certain death. He tactfully backed himself up to the doorway, where he could fight them one at a time. As an alchemist, there was little I could do against a foe who does not breathe.

The first to come through the door was an undead warrior fighting axe and shield. Duren braced both hands on the cudgel to block. The axe tried to chip into the ancestral weapon, but was unable to find purchase. With a wrench of his off hip and shoulder, Duren brought the massive two-handed club up into the creature's helmet. It crushed in the side of the skull. The bones crumpled to the ground. Even as it did, another with paired axes stepped over it. Duren wasted no time, and swung Honor's Wrath midbody like lumberjack's axe. The skeleton was propelled into the wall, the sound of snapped branches resounded from its chest. Duren howled in rage. The third and fourth fell just as quickly. The fifth in line clambered over the bodies, but lost its footing. Duren brought Honor's Wrath down in a spine-shattering overhand blow.

Although the defense of the doorway was holding, it was obvious that keeping a defensive position here was about to get as difficult for Duren to maintain as it was for the undead to traverse, even if the old champion could calm his battle rage enough.

Two more undead climbed the mountain of corpses. Duren took a stance, then summoned the arcane might of Honor's Wrath. A concussive blast of fire erupted from the head of the weapon, and the doorway was blown clear. The four abominations closest were engulfed by the flames and destroyed.

Duren charged forward before more could take their place. Down to under a dozen, they were something Duren felt he could handle. Four of the creatures surrounded him. I reached into one of my pouches, and then aimed for a skeletal champion wielding a two-handed axe. The globe shattered across his knuckles. Its contents leaked across the skeletal hands, and began to hiss. There were few things in an alchemist's repertoire that could affect the unliving, but acid made problems literally dissolve away. As his fingers eroded, so did his ability to clutch his weapon. It clattered to the stone floor. I closed and dispatched it with my sword as Duren swung in a wide arc, felling the four creatures that surrounded him. Another tried to move in quickly from Duren's blind side, but he rolled out of the way. A quick change of stance and a turn of the hips, and another skull had been removed from its former owner.

The six that remained engaged him in a circular fashion, trying to press for advantage. Fortunately, they did not regard me as a threat, and left me to the outside of the ring. I approached as close as I dared, as accuracy would be most important. Two more acid globes struck home, this time on the hips of the skeletons. The joints hissed and smoked as they closed in. The joints' ability to hold weight compromised, and the two animated corpses crashed to the ground. While not vanquished, they were also no more of a threat, and allowed Duren an escape route.

A quick glance towards Balkas showed he was not amused with this turn of events.

The four remaining undead champions regrouped. Duren again began to slow. The undead never tired, never fatigued. Duren was another matter, and each swing had less power to it that the one before.

I reached into another pouch, trying to buy my master some time. Three globes lobbed a few feet in front of the undead force, splattering upon the ground. Duren nodded in recognition and backed away, taking a breath. As they continued to advance, the front two found themselves unable to move further, the glue contained within the globes hardening around bones of their feet.

The last undead warrior circled around the immobilized ones. It advanced with shield held high. Duren swung low and from the opposing side. The creature's femur shattered on impact. As it fell, Duren followed up with a finishing blow which shattered its skull.

Balkas rose from his chair.

Duren charged the pair glued in place, diving to the ground at the last minute. His armored portly frame was too much stress for them to handle. Their knees snapped backwards like broken table legs.

Duren rose to a single knee, smiling. As he stood, he looked towards Balkas. "Boast proven, traitor." He snarled. "We have authority to bring you in alive. I really hope you're not going to disappoint me by letting that happen."

Balkas chuckled. "Oh, do not be concerned with that, Champion of Ironoath. You won't be bringing me in alive."

Duren had the look in his eyes that was normally reserved for a seventy-two ounce steak and a gallon of ale. "That's a good lad, Balkas. I was hoping you'd be understanding."

As Duren charged forward, Balkas began incanting a spell. Deciding that it was best to not see what it was, I pitched a choking globe at him as hard as possible. The cloud erupted in front of his face… and he kept speaking. I fired a second one with the same lack of effect. And a third. I had pulled back for a fourth volley when a screaming death's head appeared in his hand, and propelled itself into Duren.

The necromantic blast knocked him to the ground. Balkas began to laugh, but the laugh no longer belonged to Balkas. It was a coarse, cold voice, one that sounded like the wind crying through the tombstones. A voice of death itself.

As the smoke cloud began to clear, the eyes which were once Balkas' shone an evil green, and his pallor was that of a corpse.

"Did you forget who you were supposed to stop?" A black arc of lightning from Telchak's outstretched hand struck me in the shoulder. I collapsed, ducking behind the brazier for cover. "Did you think a mere wizard like Balkas would sit upon the throne in my chambers?" Another bolt of black lighting arced out, this time striking Duren. "This charade was pleasurable, but it's time for greater things." Another bolt arced towards me, cracking the stone brazier and spilling the coals to the ground. "I have little need of an elven alchemist in my undead legions. But you, Duren—" Another bolt streaked through my master's body. "You shall lead my armies."

More lightning coursed through Duren's frame, arcing across his armor as he writhed in pain. I tried to move to help him, and was blown back with another blast.

"You, Duren Ironoath, shall be my Agent of Death." Telchak began the death's head incant again, which would most assuredly kill Duren this time.

I screamed, and fired four more globes at Telchak in rapid succession. As they splattered in a harmless fashion against his robes, Telchak stopped his incant, simply to look in my direction.

"You half-witted fool! Did you expect staining these robes that had belonged to Balkas would halt me? Or did you think that there was some strange property to your toxins that would do me harm?"

"But there is," I said with confidence, as I scooped the fallen coals onto the flat of my blade, and hurled them at Telchak. As they struck, the robes immediately ignited. "They're incredibly flammable."

Telchak howled. Teal smoke erupted as the blue-green flames licked up his rotting body and across his face.

The moment's delay was all Duren had needed to get to his feet. The mighty war club struck Telchak with the force of an avalanche, and his necromantic frame let loose a cracking sound like roof timbers under the weight of too much snow. The avalanche struck again and again as the fiend screamed in pain from the flames. Each blow struck with the force to crush a stone wall.

Telchak dropped to all fours.

Duren summoned all his remaining strength, and with the might of his dwarven lineage, brought Honor's Wrath down on the length of Telchak's spine.

Each bone in the lich's back shattered as, one by one, they gave way, to force the next in line to hold back the power of the strike alone. Bone by bone, the spine shattered until only the head remained, which slammed to the ancient stone floor as if dropped from the tower itself. As magical energies escaped Telchak's vanquished corpse, Duren collapsed to the ground.

I slowly made my way to my master's side, and offered him what healing elixirs I had at the ready. "That was one for the ages, Vaeallan." He smiled, proudly.

"Yes, Master Duren."

"Not that you helped. Seriously, Vaeallan, could you have at least put your sword to him once? I'm not young enough to do this all by myself, you know. "

"Of course not. My apologies, my Lord."

Duren drank down the elixirs, and then coughed. "Vaeallan, did you give me poison by mistake?"

"No, Master Duren."

"Then what in blazes was that flavor?"

"Raspberry, my Lord. It was a new formula I had been experimenting with."

"It's horrible. Go home and throw out the batch. Make the next taste like something I'd want to drink."

"Yes, Master Duren," I sighed.

Well, I thought, *at least I wouldn't be making breakfast tomorrow.*

The Dragon in the Kettle
Christine L. Hardy

Callis raised her mallet, holding a chisel on edge against the rapidly cooling piece of metal on her scarred work table. She brought the mallet down, imprinting a vein into the leaf shape. Shifting the chisel slightly, she pressed another, then another, until the pattern was complete.

Darkness had tucked down around the corners of the building, hemming her in. She had worked since dawn on the hardware for Lord Garon's new house. With the money she earned from this job, she would put on a new roof and buy a new table and four new chairs for the parlor, replacing the battered ones that had been there since her childhood. Everyone had said that she couldn't work the forge alone, but she had done it. Her ironwork was the best in the province, but only she knew the secret that kept her forge so hot: a dragon's egg.

She wiped her hands on her leather apron, thrust the leaf into the fire just long enough to soften it, and hammered it down with three strokes of a larger mallet. Now it matched the leaf on the other end of the iron handle, lying flat for attachment to a door. Her arms, thick as a man's, ached with fatigue, and sweat poured down her face. She wiped it away with her sooty sleeve. Moving away from the forge, she thrust her hand deep into a bucket of clean water for the rag and wiped the blessed coolness over her face and neck.

"Callis, come out and kiss us!" The boys on their way to the tavern called to her from the street. It was later than she realized. "Let us feel your hot breasts."

She dropped the rag into the bucket, glared at them over the top half of the smithy door, and slammed it shut before they came closer. The raucous laughter moved down the street. She pulled off her leather apron and hung it on its peg. The front of her shirt was indeed hot and sweaty, but none of those boys would ever feel it. She was five years older than the oldest of them, and remembered how he had hidden behind his father's legs from the eyeball-cracking heat of the brick furnace.

They teased her because of her burly figure, reddened complexion, and because she was alone. It didn't matter, she told herself. She had a house, she had money, and she had the egg.

Callis went to the brick oven and stirred the bed of coals with the poker, revealing the smooth, oval shape buried deep in their center. After her parents moved to the sea because of the sickness in her father's lungs, she had struggled to earn enough to support herself and help them, too. Her father had been well-known, and some of his customers still came to her, but many scoffed at the girl who wanted to be a blacksmith. Her debts mounted.

She sat on a bench and recalled the day the curiosity dealer in Bordertown had approached her when she came into his shop on Market Day.

"You are Caden's daughter, aren't you?"

"Yes." Everyone knew that.

"I have something special for you." He gestured for her to follow him through the door in the back of his shop. She feared that he had a mind to take advantage of her, but he put his finger to his lips, eyes shining, face creased into a beneficent smile. She straightened her shoulders and followed. He shut the door behind them. Her heart skipped, but he moved past her to a basket sitting on a chair in the glow of an oil lantern. Something was wrapped in a shawl inside it. A baby?

He pulled the shawl aside to reveal a rough stone the shape and size of a round loaf.

She gave him a disbelieving look. "A stone?"

"No." He kept his voice low, leaning forward confidentially. "This is a dragon's egg. If you put it in your forge, it will make the coals so hot that iron will bend like copper. You will be the best blacksmith in the province."

She snorted a breath. "There are no dragons. I may be young, but I'm not a fool."

He drew back a little. "No, you are not, which is why I am offering it to you. I want to help you."

She narrowed her eyes. Help her? By giving her something the Mages' Guild would confiscate and throw her in prison for? More likely he was helping himself by getting rid of it. "How do I know it really is what you say?"

"See here." He lifted the stone and unwrapped it further. It was indeed shaped like an egg. The rough covering had chipped away at one end, revealing a smooth, milky surface with red specks that glowed like embers. "The covering is just for protection."

A shimmer of undeniable curiosity ran through her. "Where did you get it?"

"That I cannot tell you, but it is yours if you want it."

She thought for several minutes. It was a great risk, but no one would suspect her of having anything so fantastic, even if the stone was what he claimed. "How much do you want for it?"

"For you, ten pieces of gold."

She hissed a breath. That was all she had with her to purchase food and supplies. "I will give you eight."

His brows raised, but she didn't flinch.

"I must eat, too."

He considered, frowning, but she had the feeling he was just pretending to be annoyed. He had to know she hadn't much money. "Very well, eight."

He wrapped the egg up again and she shook the coin from her purse, wondering if she had just been taken for a fool. She hooked the basket over her arm. It was surprisingly light.

He led the way to the rear of the shop, but paused before opening it. "One important thing: You must not tell anyone about it or where it came from, and once it is put in the fire you have only six years before it hatches. You must destroy it before the sixth year passes. Promise me!"

Six years? That was a good long time. "I promise, and I won't say a word to anyone." She smiled wryly. "Even if it is nothing but a pretty rock."

It was more than a pretty rock. The outer coating crumbled and fell away, revealing a smooth, perfect, gleaming egg that kept her forge so hot she could easily work iron into beautiful shapes and fashion common objects twice as quickly as before.

Five years had passed, during which Callis made a name for herself, saw her parents comfortably provided for, and the shadow of the dragon she called Baby grew slowly inside its glowing shell. The sixth year flew by; there were so many things Callis still needed to buy before destroying the egg. Just one more job, she told herself over and over.

At the end of each day, she would uncover it and watch Baby's shadow move, mesmerized by the growing life in the midst of such cruel heat, and try to discern head from tail from curled foot, until the coals clouded over and Baby settled down to sleep.

Then she would clean herself up and go to the tavern. Mishel, the tavernkeeper, always saved some of whatever the supper had been that night, and gave her a table away from the fire. He made sure no one teased her, and gave her drinks. He was her friend and the only person in the village in whom she confided, but even he didn't know about Baby. If he did, he would certainly be angry. She jeopardized the whole village with her selfishness.

Tonight when Callis shoved the coals aside, the dark red blob of Baby's body blocked all of the yellow-orange glow that used to shine through the translucent shell. The dragon no longer had room to shift and turn inside. It had been Autumn when Callis first acquired it, and now the wheat was threshed and frost coated the stubble in the fields.

She should take the poker in her hand and drive it through the egg this very moment. When the dragon's innards had leaked out on the coals and burned to ash, she should plunge the egg into her bucket of cool water until it turned to stone. To do otherwise was to risk discovery and disaster.

Callis stood with the poker poised above the egg, willing herself to pierce its shell even as tight bands of sorrow compressed her chest. Baby was her only constant companion of these six long, lonely years. Baby had made it possible for her to make a name for herself and provide for Father and Mother.

She lowered the poker. She couldn't do it. Not tonight.

She pushed the coals over the egg and set the poker in its place against the wall. There were just six more handles to add to all the other handles, latches, hinges, hooks, pots, and utensils she had fashioned in the past weeks for Lord Garon. She was too tired to finish the handles now. They would come out badly if she tried.

She would destroy the egg tomorrow, when the order was complete. She gazed at the pile of glowing coals in the forge, her heart in a tight knot.

"Sleep well, little girl."

She locked up and crossed the yard to the house, the night wind stinging her face. She had not eaten, but she was too tired to go to the tavern tonight. Mishel would be worried. She had not been there for three nights. Tomorrow, when it was done, she would sit, eat, listen to the gossip she had missed, and ask his advice about selling the smithy.

Callis woke before the sun, shivering under the quilt in her bedroom. Her stomach gnawed at her. She should have eaten.

She lay alone in the darkness, thinking of Baby. It would be so lonely without her, and yet she had been fortunate that no one suspected a thing all these years. It all had been ridiculously easy. The very nobles who would seize the egg from her if they knew of it, paid good prices for her ironwork and praised her as an enterprising girl. Guilt and pain twined through her. She was being foolish and weak. It was a dragon, not a child.

Today was the day.

She dressed, cooked her last bit of porridge, and ate it with her toes right up to the fire in the kitchen. It would not take her long to finish the handles. She'd pack everything up in crates and have it ready to be picked up by Lord Garon's foreman tomorrow.

Dawn tinged the edge of the eastern sky with lavender as she crossed the yard to the forge and unlocked the door. All was as she had left it, the coals still glowing a dull orange in the heart of the forge pit. She stirred them so that flames licked their edges and scooped fresh black lumps of coal on top. She couldn't resist pushing them aside to see the egg one last time in its opaque morning state.

In the center of the pit where the egg should be, a gray head the size of a potato rested on a rippled gray body seamed with orange fire. Two yellow eyes opened and blinked. The hatchling's body was a lumpy oval without wings or spikes, just four curled stubby feet and a salamander's tail.

Baby opened her toothless mouth wide. A tiny curl of flame flicked out.

Callis froze with the poker in her hand. The dragon was the most marvelous, terrible, odd, beautiful, ugly, fragile thing she had ever seen. She wanted to keep her always, but knew with a sick certainty that she couldn't. The dragon would destroy the forge and the village with her need to fuel her fire. The bigger she grew, the more she would consume, and as soon as the mages found out they would capture her and force her to serve them. Callis couldn't let that happen.

Heat stung Callis's eyes as she picked up the poker. She thrust it at Baby's head. Baby grabbed the poker in her mouth and tugged. The iron turned red, bent, and broke off in the hatchling's mouth. Baby closed her eyes, making a low thrumming sound of pleasure. The seams of her skin glowed brighter.

Callis dropped the ruined poker, her heart racing.

Baby arched her back, rubbing it on the coals and exposing her bright, shimmering belly. She was a creature of fire that belonged deep in the earth.

"I have to hide you somewhere before anyone finds out. Someplace very far away."

Baby burped.

Callis looked around for something she could put the hatchling in. She had made a large kettle for Lord Garon, but she couldn't use that. She ran to fetch her own kettle from the house, and carried it back to the forge. She shoveled hot coals into it, then added more and waited for them to catch, trying to think past the pounding of her heart.

There was a sulphur spring at the foot of the southern hills. Fire from the earth heated the water. She would take Baby there. It was the only place hot enough for her, and no one lived near the boiling reek of the spring.

First she needed a wagon.

The fresh coals in the kettle lit. Callis eased her shovel into the forge underneath the dragon. Baby shuddered, curling into a tight ball. Callis lowered her into the kettle, then shoveled more coals around her as if she was tucking her in with a blanket. Baby looked up at her with adoring yellow eyes until she was completely covered. Callis put the heavy lid over the kettle.

"Stay there. I won't be long."

Throwing on her cloak and securing the door behind her, she dashed into the street. Her footsteps echoed on the cobbles in the stillness, and her breath made frosty puffs in the cold air. The houses were silent, their windows dark. She turned another corner, made her way to the back of the tavern and stared up at Mishel's window.

The tavern and the stable were locked up tight. She didn't dare call out and wake the neighbors. Instead, she took a handful of pebbles and tossed them against the panes. They clattered down over the cobblestones.

"Mishel," she hissed through chattering teeth. "Wake up."

She threw another handful. After a minute, a pale shape moved against the window. She waved her arms. "Mishel."

The window swung open a crack.

"What's wrong?" His voice was harsh from sleep.

"I need to borrow your wagon."

"What? Why?"

"Let me in and I'll explain."

She bounced from foot to foot, rubbing her arms, while she waited for him, hoping Baby wasn't too frightened in the kettle.

"Callis, what is this about?" Mishel opened the door and ushered her inside the little hallway between the kitchen and the stairs, holding a lantern in his hand. His long hair was disheveled, his kind, brown eyes worried. He had pulled on a pair of wool trousers and tucked the tail of his nightshirt into it, but the neck gaped open showing the curling hairs on his chest. Callis had never seen him in his nightshirt before. Something stirred inside her as the light glinted on his dark hair.

"Mishel, I need your wagon. Please."

"Right now?"

"Yes." She swallowed, willing him to understand. "There was a dragon's egg in the forge."

"A *dragon*?"

"I… I was hiding it in the forge. It hatched." She twisted the edge of her cloak in her hands. "I need to take it to the sulphur spring."

"Where is it now?"

"In a kettle. I just need to borrow the wagon. Please, Mishel."

Mishel blinked. "You have a dragon in a kettle and you want to borrow my wagon?"

"Yes."

"I. Well." He rubbed the back of his neck. "Of course, Callis. Wait here."

He started up the stairs, taking the light, then turned and came down again, handing it to her with an expression of mixed anger and sleep-fuddled concern. "Are you all right? It didn't hurt you?"

"Oh, no. It's just a tiny thing. It's harmless."

He nodded and went up again in his stocking feet. His shoulders were broad from lifting kegs, but his hips were pleasingly narrow. She heard him moving around upstairs, and the opening and shutting of furniture. Soon he came down again, properly dressed, his hair combed and tied back under a felt hat.

She helped him wake his cart horse, feed it, and hitch it to the wagon. Time stretched out as the lavender crept across the sky, changing to pink in the east. At last she was sitting beside him on the wagon seat, the horse clopping and empty barrels rattling in the back of the wagon.

Morning smoke curled on the air, smelling of fresh bread. Nearly every house had a lighted window. Old lady Yaris let her black dog into the yard and he barked at them. Callis pulled her cloak tight around her shoulders. How would they ever get out of the village without anyone knowing?

They pulled into the courtyard between her house and the forge. Callis jumped down, pushed open the door and gasped. The kettle lid was askew. The coal bucket had been tipped over, spilling its black contents across the floor. A half-moon had been bitten out of Lord Garon's kettle. The new railings were warped and gnawed.

Her stomach churned. She could never fix them before tonight. She cast her gaze back and forth, searching for Baby.

The hatchling lay huddled at the base of the forge, her skin glowing orange from every seam. She looked larger and lumpier than before, her body slack, eyes shut. Callis knelt and poked her with her finger, jerking it back at the sting of heat. Baby felt rocky hard underneath. It was the coal. She had lumps of coal in her stomach.

Baby blinked sleepily and squirmed.

"This is the dragon?" Mishel said from behind her. "We should kill it."

"I know. I tried but I just couldn't do it. Please help me take her to the spring."

Mishel stood looking down at her and Baby. Callis could feel his mind turning over all the possibilities. Mishel was a careful man and a wise one. He would know what to do.

"It will take all day. We won't get back until tomorrow. What about Lord Garon?"

"I can have everything ready if you help me pack it up." Worry attacked her even as she said this. She had never been late for a customer before. Garon might cut his payment if it wasn't ready when his man arrived, but it couldn't be helped. "Please, Mishel?"

He nodded curtly. "All right. We'll hide the kettle among the empty barrels. I have to return them to Bordertown today. It's on the way."

"Thank you." Her heart poured out in those two words. A slight smile flicked the corner of his mouth, but his eyes were grave.

They drew several curious stares as they left the village: the blacksmith and the tavernkeeper sitting side by side on a wagon seat in the frosty morning. Callis had learned long ago to keep her chin up and look ahead.

Mishel waved at their neighbors with an easy smile. "They will think we have run away together when we don't return tonight. It will give them something to talk about."

Heat crept up her neck to her cheeks. "I'm sorry."

"Don't be." He gave her a sideways glance. "I've wanted to run away with you for a long time."

"Don't tease me. This is awful." She glanced over her shoulder, but couldn't see the kettle among the barrels.

Mishel reached over and took her hand in his calloused one. "Not so awful. At least we can spend the day together."

Her nerves eased under his voice and hand. He was so strong and wise, Mishel.

The morning rolled on. The sun rose above the hills and warmed the air, but clouds built up on the northern horizon in great gray piles and the wind was brisk on their backs. It was market day and the roads were clogged with wagons and people eager to buy and sell. The two strangers with their half-empty wagon merged unnoticed into the crowd, but Callis watched anxiously for any sign of a passing mage or nobleman. Once she saw a purple cloak and feared discovery, but it was just a woman selling fine cloth, advertising her wares.

Callis pressed her hand to her chest and reminded herself to breathe.

"At last you have come with me on market day." There was gentle reproach in Mishel's voice as they slowed to pass through the clogged gates of the town.

He had invited her many times, but she had avoided Bordertown since purchasing the egg, without telling him why. When she did go to the big market out of necessity, it was at the last moment, rushing to find what she needed before the stalls closed, avoiding eye contact as much as possible.

She never saw the shop owner again, as if by tacit agreement each knew to pretend the other didn't exist, but surely he knew of her success. She expected him to come asking for more money, but he never did. She had learned recently that the shop had closed.

"Let's eat first, and then I'll return the barrels."

"All right."

He drove to the pub and as soon as he stopped, Callis climbed among the barrels, unwrapped the blanket she had placed around the kettle, loosened the hook of the chain securing the lid, and peered inside. Baby was sleeping, her skin gray on top of her head and back, but orange where the coals warmed her. Callis replaced the lid carefully and wrapped the kettle up again, hunching her body over it so no one passing by could see.

Mishel held out his hand and helped her down. "When was the last time you ate a whole meal?"

"This morning."

He gave her a doubtful look.

Inside, they sat at a long table, squeezed between other customers. It was too noisy to talk to each other. Callis found it odd to sit so close to him, their arms accidentally touching as they ate, surrounded by people neither of them knew.

A man walked up and nudged Mishel's shoulder. "Is that your wagon outside with the barrels in it?"

"Yes."

"It's on fire."

Mishel leapt up from the bench and ran to the door. Smoke billowed past the windows. The patrons surged as one body to protect their own conveyances. Callis shoved her way through them, using her strength to catch up to Mishel.

Flames leapt above the sides of the wagon. Two men with buckets tossed water on the fire and others ran to help refill them from the tavern's well. Callis helped Mishel unharness the wide-eyed, stomping horse, then peered among the charred barrels for the dragon.

Baby lay huddled like a pile of gray rags in a corner. Callis slid her gaze from one person to another, but apparently none had seen the dragon.

Praying the hatchling would remain still, she helped pass buckets until the fire was out. The back of the wagon was a pool of black water, with the smoking kettle in its center. The chain holding the lid had been bitten through.

The man who noticed the fire wrapped his hand in a scarf and lifted the lid to inspect it. "A kettle of coals? Are you mad?"

"It was to keep us warm on our journey."

"You'll be warm, for sure, when you're on fire." He scoffed and turned away. "Fool woman."

Callis's heart sank. Baby winked at her from the corner, her mouth widening in a lizard smile.

"Come." Mishel's voice made her jump. "I have hired another horse. Let's get out of here."

She climbed onto the wagon seat and stared straight ahead as they rode out of town. The clouds had moved further across the sky. When it was safe, they stopped and scooped Baby into the kettle again with the shovel.

Mishel, tight-lipped, stowed it under the wagon seat. They couldn't repair the chain, but the kettle fit snugly in the narrow space, tucked in with a spare blanket.

As they drove, Callis stared at the shadowed groove in the brownish-orange of the foothills where steam rose from the sulphur spring. They were incredibly lucky that no one had noticed Baby in the wagon. What if she hurt someone when she got bigger, or tried to find her way home? What if the mages found her and tortured her to do their bidding? Callis hugged her arms tightly around herself under her cloak. She had been so foolish. So weak. She should have crushed the egg months ago.

Mishel's face was as clouded as the sky, his shoulders hunched forward.

"I'm sorry, Mishel. I know it was dangerous, but I needed the money."

"You endangered yourself and the whole village. Why didn't you come to me? I would have helped you."

She huddled more tightly under her cloak. After a long silence, Mishel continued.

"All this time I thought you were refusing to acknowledge me because you were too shy. I wondered if your heart belonged elsewhere, but there was no sign that you loved anyone." His jaw tightened. "Now I find that it does belong elsewhere: to a damned dragon. You avoid me when it is convenient, but when you need me, you come in the dark to borrow my wagon. Did you never think to come just because of me, myself?"

He stared ahead as a cold wind blew at their backs, shifting Callis's world into new patterns.

"Mishel. I never thought—"

"Never thought what? That a tavernkeeper was good enough for you?"

"No! Oh, Mishel. I never thought anyone, least of all you, would want me to bother you." Her voice caught in her throat. "I thought you were just being kind because you felt sorry for me."

He turned to her, thick brows drawn in confusion. "Why should I be sorry for you?"

"Because I was never pretty or well-liked, and now…" She shrugged and pulled off her right glove. Along with the callouses and the soot that she could never completely scrub away, a red scar crossed her palm where she had burned it last winter.

"Callis, you are beautiful." Mishel's voice softened. "You are strong and kind. You are a girl a man could depend on. You. You."

He blinked back moisture from his eyes, shifted the reins and closed his own calloused hand around her scarred one. "You should not listen to the boys in the street."

Her heart surged, and she squeezed his strong fingers.

He held her hand for a while in silence. Warmth spread through Callis's chest despite the wind gusting around them.

As the day drew on, however, the wind bit more sharply, and snowflakes swirled around them. Mishel stopped to pull the blanket out from around the kettle and wrap it over her. It was warm from the coals.

"I want to check on her."

"No, it will only let the heat out."

"Do you think she will be all right?"

He smiled thinly. "She is a dragon."

This was true. Baby had kept the forge hot for six years. Surely she could keep herself warm for a few more hours.

Yet as the snow swirled thickly, obscuring the road, Callis found herself worrying. The wheels stuck and slipped and the horse's pace slowed. She huddled against Mishel's side, draping the blanket around them both, and drowsed.

Heat pressed against the backs of her legs. She blinked awake, shifting them away from the wagon seat. She must be so cold that she was prickling with false heat.

"Callis!" Mishel jerked the horse to a stop and grabbed her skirts, beating them. The smell of singed cloth cut through the air. She leapt down, threw herself onto the snow and rubbed her smoking skirts in it. Flames licked the seat of the wagon above her. The wood gave way as Baby's head and front feet pushed through it.

Mishel struggled with the panicked horse. Callis looked from him to the baby dragon biting the flaming edge of the hole, then up the road. No one was around; the air was a swirling mass of white.

Cold gripped her. They were at the edge of a pine wood, the lower branches brittle-dry. Callis broke off one with a cluster of cones and thrust it at the fire. They caught, flaring with a satisfying sizzle. Baby stared at the bright branch and crawled forward.

"Come on, little girl. Come." Callis choked on the words.

Baby slithered down from the wagon seat. When she hit the snow, she mewled and huddled into a ball.

Callis held the blazing cones just out of her reach. Mishel had freed the horse and was leading him away, stroking his neck and talking to him in tense, deep tones.

"Come, Baby."

The dragon snapped her mouth and darted forward. Callis scrambled to keep out of her way, leading her into the open field beside the woods. Snow hissed into steam under Baby's feet, but her back was gray with cold.

Step by step, Callis lured the hatchling away from Mishel and the wagon. The pine cones fizzled out, leaving just a small tongue of fire on the end of the stick. Baby grew grayer and stiffer, the light in her eyes dimming.

Callis's heart clenched as she watched, and her throat closed.

Baby wobbled, her eyes on the flame, then collapsed in the snow, half-buried. She opened her mouth to mewl again, but no sound came out, nor any flame. Her body curled around itself.

Callis sank to her knees. The wind gusted, extinguishing the stick. Flakes stuck to Callis's eyelashes and melted down her cheeks while Baby's body hardened.

Her yellow eyes were the last to gray out.

Callis touched her with a trembling hand. She was cool and firm as stone.

"No, no." Callis's eyes heated and her vision clouded. She stroked the round head and down the curled spine. "No."

Mishel's heavy steps approached from behind. He knelt and put his arms around her shoulders.

She pressed her face against his smoky sleeve, sobbing.

"Shh." He kissed her hair, his voice low and soft. "It's better this way. Come now."

The next evening, Callis sat alone at the forge. Lord Garon's man had collected his order and declared himself very pleased, despite the delay. He didn't seem to notice that the last half-dozen handles weren't as well made as the rest, nor that the kettle and railings had been repaired. She could replace Mishel's wagon and still buy her chairs and table, but the triumph was hollow with Baby buried beneath the pine trees on the lonely road.

Mishel, who spent all day talking to farmers about the weather, had surely known it would snow. Callis saw now that he had humored her rather than kill the dragon in front of her. He had left his ruined wagon on the side of the road, insisting that she ride the horse while he trudged through the snow. He was strong and wise, and he loved her.

She wished she knew what to do about it. All she felt was emptiness and uncertainty.

"Callis!" A deep voice called to her from the street, followed by shouts of laughter. "Callis, come out and kiss me."

She rose from her stool, went to the window, and opened the shutters. Mishel stood in the street with his arms spread wide. "I am waiting for you."

The weight inside her shifted a little. She leaned her elbows on the windowsill. "I thought you said not to listen to the boys in the street."

"I am not a boy."

The lads hooted with glee. The oldest one put his hands to his mouth. "Mishel wants you, Callis. Come out before he changes his mind."

She shook her head, suppressing a smile, and went to the door. "Are you sure? Once I come out it's too late."

Mishel stepped forward, holding his lantern high so that she could see his plain, sturdy face. "Only if you are sure, also."

Her heart lurched toward him, and her feet ran to keep up with it, carrying her to his side. His arm folded around her, and she lifted her face to his. She had lost Baby and nothing would be the same again, but Mishel was still here. He had always been here.

"I do wish it. I want you, yourself."

His mouth broke into a smile and his arm tightened around her. He pressed his lips to hers in a brief promise for later, when the cheering boys weren't present, but even so it sent her blood racing.

He shooed the lads ahead. "Go on, then, if you want drinks tonight. I am closing early."

She slid her arm around his waist and they walked together all the way to the tavern.

Bartleby Goes Adventuring
Jesse Hendrix

Five hideous creatures were the last thing between the hero and his goal. Rotting undead things grabbed for him with unnatural strength. To reach this chamber, Bart the Bold had defeated the hundred and one horrors of the dread necromancer's dungeon. It would take more than a mere five zombies to stop the savior of three duchies, two principalities, and a small village up the coast.

In the center of the damp stone chamber lay the object of his quest, chained on a skull-lined altar of jet black stone. The Lady Moonstar was known throughout the land for her beauty and her skill in magic. That beauty was in full display. She was clad in only a thin shift, her blond hair surprisingly perfect, her face defiant. The necromancer Zurnk the Foul stood cackling over her, glowing knife in hand. In mere moments he would slay her, and unleash a foul spell that would kill everyone for miles around. The hero leapt forward, decapitating a zombie. "Your schemes end today, fiend! Release the Lady and you may live to face trial!"

"How did you pull that off with a rapier?" Zurnk asked, dumbfounded.

"Like this!" Snicker-snack! With a few quick slashes he removed the "un" from the undead. Raising his sword, Bart charged just as the necromancer unleashed a spell…

"You can come in now, Bartelby."

Shaking loose of his daydream, Bartelby marched into the chamber. *Soon*, he thought.

The office of Lucas Lorik, Chief Bookkeeper of the Duke and Master of the Tax Collectors, was far too small and dank for a man with that many words in his job title. Every available surface was covered in distressingly overstuffed ledgers, and nobody knew quite how he managed to keep track of what went where. Bartleby found it appalling, and had penned several missives on the need for proper filing.

Bartleby had something important to say. He just needed to find the right words. "I quit!" Ah, there they were.

Lucas stared at Bartleby as if he had suddenly turned into an orc and begun singing bawdy songs about mermaids. "I'm sorry? You what?"

"I quit, I resign, I no longer wish to continue my employment with His Grace the Duke of Ashbury."

Bartleby had imagined several possible reactions to his announcement. His boss staring like he was trying to work out who was in his office had not been one of them. Perhaps he should have considered the possibility.

Bartleby was used to being forgotten. He had the kind of face you could lose in a couple, pale from too much time indoors, short dark hair, and eyes that failed to be piercing, soulful, or anything else notable. He was considered dull even by the other bookkeepers, who were world-class experts at it. Despite, or more likely because of this, Bartleby was excellent at his job.

A page seemed to rustle in the dusty ledgers of Lucas' memory. "Bartelby, if this is about your proposal for a new filing system—"

"No, it's not." Part of Bartelby was amazed at his own interruption. It was the kind of thing he would have never considered before he had made the big decision. "How long have I worked here?"

"Eight years, counting your apprenticeship."

"Ten actually. And in that ten years, has anything remotely exciting happened?"

"Well there was… er…"

"Exactly. And that is why I am going to become…" He stopped for a dramatic pause, went too long, and ended up with an awkward silence. "An adventurer!"

Lucas stared as if the bawdy song-belting orc had turned purple, grown a second head, and started harmonizing with itself. Then he started to laugh.

The problem started, as so many do, with magic. As a child, Bartelby wanted nothing more than to become a mage. Encouraged by his equally bookish parents, he spent hours each day reading about the theory and practice of magic, memorizing the words and gestures. His studious habits soon found him an apprenticeship.

The wizard's name was Malik. He lived in a large and well-decorated house on the edge of the city, rather than the traditional crumbling tower in the wilderness. He did have a pointy hat, rune-embroidered robe, and long white beard, because it pays to advertise.

"Now my boy," Malik said after the introductions, the tea, and the cake. "Your father tells me you've been studying all about magic."

"Yes, master Malik."

"Study is all well and good, but before I can accept you, you must prove to me that you can follow through with the practical applications."

They left the comfortable sitting room and headed into the Wizard's workspace. The room was large enough to hold a modest ball in, but to do so would have required cleaning away several oak worktables, multitudes of books, yards of oddly shaped glassware, and a large stuffed lizard. These items were arranged in way that either held deep occult significance, or were the mark of an indifferent housekeeper. Malik cleared a spot on one of the tables by the simple expedient of pushing everything non-breakable onto the floor. Then he placed a large half-melted candle into the newly empty space.

"We'll start with the basics." he said, "Do you know a spell for lighting small fires?"

Bartelby nodded, he had memorized several.

"Show me."

Bartelby focused on the candle, and spoke the words he had learned. The candle remained dark. He concentrated harder, tried a different spell. The candle stubbornly remained unlit. He essayed several more attempts, while the candle continued to do its impression of a particularly nonflammable damp rock.

"That's enough." Malik finally interrupted. "You know the technique, but you are not letting the magic flow through you. Stand by me and try to feel the power as I cast the spell." He gestured at the candle and said a magic word. Nothing continued to happen. Malik looked nonplussed, but quickly hid his reaction. Bartelby shared his confusion; a wizard of Malik's renown should have no trouble with such a basic spell. Malik rolled up his sleeves and tried again, a look of strained concentration on his face. There was a "woomph!" as the candle, candlestick, and a circular section of the table disappeared in a pillar of flame. Bartelby stared in awe.

"I meant to do that," the wizard said, unconvincingly.

They worked together for several weeks, with broadly similar outcomes, before Malik explained his theory. "As you've probably gathered from your reading, magic flows from the earth. Those of us who can reach into that flow can do magic, and those who can't, can't."

"And I'm one of the ones who can't?" Bartelby said, sadly.

"No." Replied the wizard, "You are something much rarer. Instead of drawing in magic, or ignoring it, you push it away. Not only can you not do magic, you actually make spell casting harder for those nearby."

"So I can't become a mage." An idea struck him. "Since I make magic more difficult, maybe I could help hunt necromancers and chaos mages."

"Well you could, but as this 'anti-magic' effect has a very short range you would basically have to run up to them and, well, give them hugs."

Bartelby did a passable impression of a kicked puppy.

"I know how you feel," Malik said kindly. "When I was your age, I wanted to be a bard. Turns out I can't carry a tune in a barrel." He chuckled at the memory. Bartleby managed to look even more downtrodden. "I have an idea. Bartelby, I can't take you as an apprentice, but since you are studious and precise, I would like to offer you a job as my research assistant."

Bartleby thought about this, but it seemed too hard to bear. To be so close to magic, but unable to learn it.

He forlornly left the wizard, and took the apprenticeship with the Duke's tax collectors which his father had arranged. And there he remained, a spring in the clockwork of bureaucracy. The thing to remember about springs is that when you wind them too tight, they snap.

Bartleby practiced his intimidating warrior stare on Lucas. "I'm serious. I'm going to be an adventurer."

The stare needed more practice, as it took Lucas several minutes to get his laughter under control. "But you don't know the first thing about adventuring."

"I've read all of the sword fighting manuals, and the records of our greatest heroes. Plus, I've already got my own armor and blade."

"How did you afford—"

"You know that dwarf blacksmith, Kazrac? I helped him figure out who was embezzling from his shop."

Lucas boggled. "Look, Bartleby…"

For the third time in his life, Bartleby interrupted a superior, "And I don't want to be called that any more. From now on, I'm Bart the Bold! Alliteration is very important. Makes things easier for the bards later on."

"Bartleby, you won't last a week adventuring."

"A week of adventure is better than another ten years of this," said Bart the Bold, and he stormed out to seek his destiny.

When people set out to seek their destiny, they rarely consider the paperwork. Bartleby had, of course, filled out all the necessary forms and gotten his licenses and travel papers. Now he just needed to find some adventuring to do. His studies suggested that he should hang out in taverns and wait for a mysterious stranger or a maiden in distress. After several days of this, he had succeeded in obtaining an improbably large bar tab, the names of several ladies who turned out not to be in distress (but would pretend to be for the right price), and the knowledge that no one ever wins the game with the ball and three cups.

It wasn't as if he didn't look the part. Kazrac had done his usual phenomenal work. Bart the Bold's sword was a rapier with a woven basket hilt, and his chain armor was gleaming. To complete the look, he had obtained tall black boots, a hunter green coat, and a wide brimmed black hat with a red feather. Years of ink-stained scribe's robes had not given him a chance to develop a fashion sense.

It took a week of bad food and worse drinks before an opportunity presented itself. As mysterious strangers went, he was a winner. He was dressed in head-to-toe black, topped with a hat similar to Bartelby's but somehow infinitely more stylish. He had a rapier and dagger in his belt, and walked in a way that insinuated that these weren't his only weapons. He tipped his hat to Bart, "You know how to use that thing?"

"I've learned from Spinoza, Montoya, and Flynn," Bart the Bold replied.

"That's a good trick, considering they've all been dead for a hundred years." The stranger laughed. "The name is Emrys Blacktalon."

"They call me Bart the Bold."

"They do, do they? Well, Mr. the Bold. What experience do you have?"

"For ten years I helped catch criminals for His Grace. First for Duke Aramis, and then for Duke Frost." It was mostly true, Bartleby reasoned. Tax fraud is against the law. "Duke Frost personally sent me a signed commendation." That was for finding a wine smuggler's money trail.

"I'm looking for sellswords to guard a caravan headed to some of our border towns. Interested?"

It wasn't princess rescuing, necromancer slaying, or gryphon hunting, but everyone had to start somewhere, right?

The caravan was smaller than Bartleby had assumed. Two wagons loaded with crates and barrels, and a third smaller wagon with the supplies and food for the journey. Emrys made the introductions. "Bart, this is the caravan master Rhyer Jolson. Rhyer, this is Bart the Bold, the swordsman I told you about."

"Pleased to meet you." Rhyer was a middle-aged man with salt and pepper hair and a sparse beard. He smiled brightly as he shook Bartelby's hand with not-quite bone-crushing force.

Emrys continued, "These are the drivers," he said indicating three large leather-clad men. "Aiden, Brandar, and Christopher." Bartleby shook hands with each and promptly forgot which was which. "And the last member is our cook and a healer. Phoebe, come out and meet the new guy."

A young woman came out from the supply wagon. Bartleby's reading had suggested that women on an adventure should be wearing either billowing robes or minimal chain mail, but she was sensibly dressed in dark wool pants and a tunic. She did have the apparently requisite long hair (red, not the gold of his daydreams), but it was tied up instead of flowing. No Lady Moonstar, but definitely a damsel he wouldn't mind undistressing.

"Phoebe, meet Bart the Bold." Rhyer said. "Bart this is my daughter Phoebe. So no funny stuff, my boy." He said the last with a laugh that said "just kidding" accompanied by a look that said "no, seriously."

Bart bowed slightly and kissed her hand. She blushed and said, "Pleased to meet you."

"The pleasure is all mine," Bart replied, thankful he had had that one prepared. Bartleby's experience with women was limited to what could be had on the job and a few celebratory evenings with Mary from the archives. So it was with great relief that he heard Rhyer say, "Enough chit chat, let's get rolling!"

The first day of travel passed without incident. That night after dinner, Phoebe asked Bart for a story of his adventures. "I suppose I should start with the time I helped capture the notorious smuggler Captain Childe."

There was an element of truth to this tale. Bartleby's part would have been told like this: "I was going through the records and realized the

Childe family merchant reported sales of five hundred barrels of Oldport wine, but only paid import taxes on half that number. The Duke sent men to investigate."

The way Bart the Bold told the story was much longer, included several swordfights, and ended with an explosion as the smuggled barrels of Alchemist's Fire caught alight.

Phoebe and her father had listened with rapt attention. Emrys gave him a slight nod, one storyteller to another. Aiden, Brandar, and Christopher drank beer and started singing a very bawdy song about a mermaid.

The thing about adventure stories, Bartleby thought, is that they always leave out how much traveling it takes to find an adventure. Several days had passed without excitement, unless you counted learning the amazing number of bawdy songs Aiden, Brandar, and Christopher knew. Bart was sitting up on watch, while Emrys snored in a bedroll beside him. The others had bunked down in the wagons.

There was a sound. It sounded almost, but not quite, exactly like someone trying not to make any noise. Bartleby nudged Emrys to wake him. "I think something's out there."

"It's probably just some animal." Emrys mumbled sleepily.

As if on cue, two men, or at least man-shaped things, burst from the trees. They were covered in mud, twigs, and leaves, and brandished huge wooden clubs. Bartleby desperately tried to remember if any of the fencing manuals he had read had included advice on defending against a thick piece of wood with a thin piece of metal.

Emrys leapt from his bedroll and engaged the left attacker. Bart lunged at the other with his sword, missing entirely but managing to avoid a crushing blow. They danced around each other, wild swings of the savage's club matched by equally wild sword swings. There was a crunch and Bartleby's left arm went numb. He looked to Emrys, who was busy with his own foe. No help there.

With desperate strength, Bart lunged forward. His sword drove into the savage's arm, causing him to yelp, drop his weapon and flee. His associate followed.

"We did it!" Bart exclaimed. He looked around, saw the spreading blood on his shoulder. "I spent five silver on this shirt," he said, and passed out.

When he awoke, Phoebe was standing over him, glowing. The soft pink light of a healing spell flowed from her hands into the wound. "Just relax. Sorry, usually this doesn't take this long."

"That's me," Bart explained. "A wizard told me I naturally resist magic."

"Never heard that one before." The pain in Bart's shoulder flared, then subsided completely. "That should do it. Emrys told me what happened. Thank you."

"Just doing my job."

She kissed him lightly on the cheek. Now it was Bartleby's turn to glow.

"Rest a bit," she said. "I need to take care of Brandar. Something got into the wagon and hurt his arm."

Bart rode in the wagon with Phoebe that day. She sat close and made small talk, he nodded and said as little as possible. *Bart the Bold is the strong, silent type*, he decided.

That night Aiden (or possibly Christopher) shared a bottle of a particularly strong whiskey with the heroes of the day. Bartleby fell asleep light-headed, and awoke heavy-bladdered. He noticed Emrys was missing from his place on watch as he hurried into the trees. As he looked for a private spot, he heard voices. Immediate concerns forgotten, he slipped closer to hear.

"You were supposed to scare him, not run away, you ass!" It was Emrys. Bartleby reeled with shock.

"You said he couldn't hit the broad side of a barn!" said Christopher. No wait, Brandar.

"Look," Emrys continued. "If we can't scare the little quill-pusher back to his old job, we won't get paid. We've got try something bigger." He stopped, and looked around. "Did you hear something?"

Bartleby slipped back to camp as quietly as he could manage, with one brief but necessary stop.

Bart the Bold spent the next several days on high alert, while Bartleby tried to figure out exactly how the others would try to scare him. Whatever it was would have to be a lot better than the wild barbarian act. Something flashy.

"Your money or your life!"

Well, that would do nicely. There were five of them visible. They had crossbows, dark green leather armor, crossbows, half masks styled to look like foxes, and crossbows.

"Stand and deliver!" shouted the leader, in the tone of a man who had always wanted to say that.

Bart was impressed. Whoever was behind the "Scare Bartleby" plan was putting a lot of time and effort into it. The important thing was not to look scared. What would Bart the Bold do?

"Well met, bold highwayman!" said Bart the Bold, also in the tone of a man who had always wanted to say that. "As you can well see, our small caravan is not a fitting prize for a renowned group of bandits…" Bart studied the masks and hazarded a guess, "…such as the Forest Foxes."

The leader looked nonplussed.

Please be right, thought Bartleby, *or close*. Close could work. He could explain close.

"You've heard of us. I'm not surprised!" said the leader, who clearly was.

"I've heard many tales of your derring-do," said Bart, who obviously hadn't. *This guy is some actor,* he thought. *Now to see how well he'll play the part.*

"I thought we were the Greenwood Wolves?" interrupted one of the bowmen. His closest companion nudged him. "Couldn't get the wolf masks, remember? The shop only had foxes left."

The leader smiled calmly at the members of the caravan while making frantic "shut up" motions behind his back. "Since you've heard of us, you know that no one passes through Forest Fox territory without paying tribute."

"I have heard tell, yes." Bart responded. "Is it also true then what they say? That the bold leader of the Foxes cannot resist a challenge?"

The bold leader raised an eyebrow and nodded slowly. "Very true, indeed."

"Then I propose a challenge. You and me, swords to first blood. I win, you let us go. You win, you take our goods and everyone leaves without further struggle."

"And why would I do that, when I can just have my men shoot you, and take the booty?" the leader replied, in the tone of a man second guessing his word choice.

"Two reasons. One, if you shoot, you won't get all of us, and our counterattack will certainly kill some of your men. Two, you seem like a fellow who cares about his reputation. Imagine what the bards will make of this."

The leader thought for a few moments. "Agreed. You stand over there by the tree line, I'll stand on the other side and we will cross swords in the center of the road. Now excuse me while I consult with my men so there are no misunderstandings"

"Of course." Bartleby tried to maintain his confident façade. *I can't believe this is working. Oh, bugger. What if they actually got a decent swordsman? Well, in for a copper…*

The other Foxes lowered their weapons and spread out. One of them made some kind of hand signal toward the woods. Apparently, there had been more bandits than the five visible.

"You seem like an honorable man," said the leader. "I wish to know your name."

"I am known as Bart the Bold."

"Well, Bart the Bold, they call me the Shadowfox, and I am very fond of honorable men. Would you like to know why?"

"Please enlighten me."

Suddenly Phoebe shouted, "Look behind you!"

Bart reacted too late, and something heavy struck him in the back of the head.

"I am fond of honorable men," said the Shadowfox as Bart sank into unconsciousness, "because they are so easy to fool."

Bartelby woke up. This was a good start, as he had not expected it to happen.

He took a moment to take an accounting of the situation. All of his major body parts seemed to be intact, if achy. That went in the credit column. He was tied to a tree. A debit. Phoebe was tied next to him, also in one piece. Credit. Emrys was on the other side. Call that break-even. The Shadowfox was sitting in front of him, sword drawn, and that put the whole business in the red.

"Finally awake, eh?" The bandit leader gloated. "You know, Bart, when I told my men to learn a hand signal for 'sneak up behind the talkative idiot and knock him out,' they thought we'd never need it." He chuckled. "Guess that's why I'm the leader. You just sit tight, while we figure out if any of you are worth ransoming." He walked away, still laughing.

Okay. This was bad. It was time for Bartleby to admit defeat. "Emrys. You win. Tell the master thespian over there to untie us."

"I have no idea what you are talking about." Emrys replied.

"I overheard you in the woods. I know you were hired to scare me back into accountancy. You win. A real adventurer wouldn't have fallen for a trick like that. I've got to admit, I didn't think I was worth all this trouble. It's way better than the Wildman act."

"Bartleby, it's true me and the boys pulled the Wildman routine to scare you. But we didn't set this up. That guy from the tax office isn't paying us nearly enough."

Phoebe chose this moment to interject. "Would either of you gentlemen please explain what in the blue buggering blazes is going on?!"

Bartleby sighed. "The truth is, I'm not an adventurer, at least not yet. I'm really a tax assessor. My former boss apparently hired these guys to scare me back to my old job. Wait, you weren't in on it?"

"I wasn't in on it," Phoebe replied.

"She really wasn't," said Emrys.

"Neither was I!" Rhyer chimed in from the other side of the tree.

"We were, sorry," said Aiden, Brandar and Christopher, who were tied to another tree nearby.

Phoebe pressed on. "So that story about the notorious smuggler?"

"Heavily exaggerated. I only found out about the smuggling from a discrepancy in the tax records. All the sword fighting happened to other people. And it was just untaxed wine, so no exploding alchemist fire. I got a nice letter of commendation from the Duke for finding out about the smuggling though…" He sighed. "I'm sorry I lied to you. You probably hate me for getting you into this."

"Look Bart, you seem like a pretty smart guy," Phoebe replied. "And that was a pretty good plan back when we first met Shadowfaux over there."

"Were you trying to make a pun just now? Because faux, meaning fake, is pronounced like 'foe' not 'fox'."

"Really? Huh, I've only ever seen it written down."

"Two things." Emrys interjected, "One, you both are terrible at heroic banter. Unless that was flirting, which you are also terrible at. Two, is this really relevant to getting us untied?"

"What do you mean terrible?" Phoebe protested.

"Well," Emrys elaborated, "You've been flirting with Bart the whole trip and he hasn't even noticed."

"You were?" Bart asked.

"She was?" Rhyer followed.

"She was," confirmed Aiden, or possibly Brandar.

"You're just mad I turned you down for a date when we first met," Phoebe huffed at Emrys.

"Can we get back to the other thing?" Rhys said, in a desperate attempt to change the subject. "The part where we get untied?"

"Right. I'm sure you can help me think of a way out of this mess, Bart." Phoebe gave him an encouraging smile. "Besides it's Emrys I'm really mad at."

"What did I do?" Emrys said incredulously.

"Lied about what you were doing when we hired you, lied about Bart the Bean Counter's qualifications, broke Bart's shoulder, got Brandar stabbed…"

"Nearly gave me a heart attack," Rhyer added.

"Nearly gave my dad a heart attack, need I continue? Now, Bart, got any bright ideas?"

Well then. Time to go to work. How would Bart the Bold get out of this situation?

Bart the Bold slipped the hidden knife from his sleeve and quickly cut his bonds. Grabbing his sword he rushed the bandit leader… and was immediately pin cushioned by crossbow bolts.

Right, that was a terrible plan. Besides, Bartleby didn't even have a hidden knife.

New plan. How would Bartleby get out of this situation?

"Excuse me, Mr. Shadowfox? I was just wondering, is all this really worth the effort?"

"What do you mean?" replied the bandit, coming uncomfortably close.

"Well, you've got what, a dozen men? And the road you ambushed us on doesn't seem that well-traveled. It seems to me you can't possibly be stealing enough to support an operation of this size."

"There's some truth in your observation, lad. But there is a very good reason we chose this particular bit of road. Our farms and businesses have been reduced to poverty by cruel and unfair taxes. We hunt these roads in order to rob the mayor's taxmen and return the money to the people."

"Well, as you can see, we aren't the mayor's men, so if you could just let us go.…"

"It's not that simple. After we caught one of the sheriff's wagons, they've taken precautions. Heavily armed precautions. So, it's become sort of a whatever-we-can-get situation. Bloody wagon wasn't even carrying any coin. Just a load of parchments."

Bartleby's eyes lit up. "Do you still have them?"

"Aye. Most of them. Used some for firelighters and… personal uses."

"I think I can help you then."

The Shadowfox stared at him a minute, then turned around, gathered up some of the documents, and held them before his prisoner.

It didn't take long for Bartleby's trained eye to realize that there were, to use the technical term, seriously shady shenanigans going on. "We are still in the Duchy of Ashbury, right?"

"Yes, on the outskirts, but the Lord Mayor calls the Duke liege," the Shadowfox replied.

"Then I can report, with the authority of experience, that there is no such thing as a sheep shearing tax. Nor a butchering tax, a baking tax, or any of a dozen others I see here. Your Lord has been skimming," he explained.

"So problem solved, right?" said Emrys. "We just need to send these ledgers back to the Duke and let him send some people to clean this up."

"You think we haven't thought of that?" the Shadowfox said, offended. "We've sent men to Ashbury city, but there's been no action. Blasted bloody bureaucrats."

"As a former blasted bloody bureaucrat," Bartleby added, "I can tell you that even if we got all this incriminating evidence to the right people, it could take months before they do anything about it."

"So what we need is a representative of the Duke closer to hand," Phoebe said, smiling at Bartleby in a way he did not like at all. "Bart, did you happen to bring that commendation with you?"

"**M**ake way for the Inspector General!" Emrys, in the role of herald, had been shouting that at everyone they had run into for the last mile. The plan was to make enough noise that someone in authority would come to investigate.

Bartleby was not comfortable with this plan. Nor was he comfortable riding the Shadowfox's second-best horse in borrowed finery. Phoebe had raided the bandit's wardrobe and put together a rough approximation of what a court official would wear. The hose was itchy, the doublet was tight, the shirt was an unflatteringly loud yellow, and Bartleby had managed to retain his hat only by holding onto it like a life preserver.

The Shadowfox, riding his best horse to Bartleby's left, played the role of bodyguard and looked worried. Phoebe, riding on the other side, had a very different response.

"You're enjoying this aren't you?" Bart asked her.

"Aren't you? This is an adventure, just like you said you wanted." She gave a smile.

"Impersonation and forgery weren't exactly what I had in mind. Besides, they might just decide to attack us."

"Attack a representative of the Duke? Nah. Try to bribe us, maybe."

"I wouldn't object to a decent bribe," the Shadowfox opined.

"Still, it could be dangerous," Bart objected. "Your dad would kill me if you get hurt."

"Which is why he gets to stay with the bandits. Now shush, these guys look important."

Three riders approached the band. The two in front were some sort of local guardsmen, dressed in well-used leather armor with short swords at their belts. Slightly behind them rode a thin older man. He was dressed in robes that might as well have had "Mage!" embroidered on the front, and had the kind of thin greasy mustache that Bartleby associated with the sort of merchant who needed his returns triple checked.

"Halt in the name of the Lord Mayor!" The left guard shouted enthusiastically. "Please present your identification and state your business!"

"I am Bartleby Scrivener, Tax Inspector for his Grace, Duke Frost!" He handed the guard his papers, who handed them to the mage. The forgery had been accomplished by adding the phrase "In recognition of your efforts, we are pleased to offer you the post of Tax Inspector General and charge you with discovering embezzlement and fraud in the outlying regions" in the blank space between "His grace commends your efforts in uncovering these smugglers" and the Duke's seal. The bandits had done a good job, since they were not immediately arrested.

"The gentleman is my bodyguard…" Crud, they had never learned the Shadowfox's actual name. "…guy… Guy Fox. And the lady is my personal secretary."

"Serena," Phoebe interjected, sparing Bart the need to invent another pseudonym.

"These seem to be in order," said the robed man. "My name is Jerrin Smithwick, assistant and chief mage to the Lord Mayor. How may I assist you?"

"We have received disturbing reports of illegal taxation from the farmers and tradesmen in your area. And while complaining about taxes is an old established tradition, His Grace feels that all such accusations must be taken seriously. We'd like to examine your records in order to put the complaints to rest." Bartleby had rehearsed that bit. The next part they'd need to play by ear.

"We would be happy to assist in your inquiries," Jerrin said, unsuccessfully concealing his unhappiness. "Perhaps you would like to refresh yourself at the inn, and then join the Mayor and I at dinner to discuss the issue."

Bartleby didn't want to give them the chance to hide evidence, but he didn't want to make them too suspicious either. He looked at Phoebe.

Phoebe took a journal from her bag and made a show of examining it. "We can fit that in, Inspector."

The local inn was called the Dancing Duck. It was small and shabby, but it gave them enough privacy to clean off the trail dust and discuss their next move.

"Okay, so they bought it. Now what?" Emrys asked.

"Well," Phoebe said, "first we go have dinner and let him try to bribe and/or threaten us. Then Bart looks at the books and gets the evidence we need. Then we give the Lord Mayor a chance to give the money back in exchange for a head start. Easy."

"And when he doesn't give it back?"

"Then we take the evidence to the Duke."

"Why would they listen?" Emrys asked. "They didn't send anybody when the people here complained."

"They like Bart here enough that they paid you to spook him into going back," Phoebe said. "Somebody is going to listen."

"Okay, and what happens when he decides to have his men get rid of us before we can get back? People disappearing on the road isn't exactly unheard of."

"I'm sure Mr. Fox's men will protect us."

Bartleby was only half listening to this conversation. His attention was focused on a small etiquette book. A small faux pas at the dinner might give away their deception.

"What do you think, Bart?" Emrys asked, yanking the book from Bartleby's grip. "Look, you don't need that. These Lord Mayor types don't actually know the difference between forks. He's either going to try to impress you with a 'man of wealth and taste' act, or he's going to try to show you he's a 'down to earth man of the people.' Believe me, I've done enough 'rescue the small town' quests to know how these things go. Don't worry about the dinner. Worry about the getaway."

Too soon for Bart's taste, a uniformed footman came to bring them to the Mayor's home. Not they would have had any trouble finding the place. It was the largest house in town, and perched at the top of a hill.

As soon as they stepped foot inside, Bartleby knew the mayor was going with the "Man of wealth and taste" option. Wealth was well on display. Taste not so much. Bart didn't know much about art, but he did know about audits and the signs of a person living beyond their reported means. The fine but haphazardly arranged furniture and blatant abuse of gilding all suggested wealth beyond what his position should provide.

Dinner was served in an overly large room, done in the same money-but-no-taste fashion as the rest of the house. The Lord Mayor, a stout, older man dressed in clothes that had been fashionable in the capitol ten years ago, sat at the head of the table along with Jerrin. Bartleby was seated at the other end with his "secretary" on one side and his "bodyguard" on the other.

"Welcome to my humble home, Inspector," the Mayor oozed. "It's an honor to have representatives of the Duke in our little town."

"The honor is all ours," Bart lied, "You certainly have a lovely home. Unfortunately, this is an official visit."

"You know how the common folk complain. They don't want to pay taxes, but they also want you to fix the roads." The road they had come in on was in dire need of repair, but mentioning that at this point seemed impolitic. "I'm sure you'll find no irregularities. Ah, the food is ready."

The dinner had been prepared by someone who had heard of what the nobility ate, but had never had a chance to experience it up close. What could have been a simple but filling repast of chicken and vegetables was nearly ruined by overuse of spices and odd decorative touches. Nevertheless, the Mayor tore into it like a man who hadn't had a decent meal in days. Bart and his companions, who actually hadn't, (Phoebe tried her best, but there was only so much one could do with preserved food and a campfire) soon followed suit. In between mouthfuls, Bartleby tried to inquire about the economic state of the town and local policy, only to have each question smoothly brushed aside by Jerrin.

When dessert was served, Phoebe spoke up. "This has been a lovely meal, but the Inspector has a very busy schedule, so we must insist on seeing your records right away."

"Just take a few moments to enjoy your pie. It's a local specialty," Jerrin said.

Bartleby put a fork in his pie. It went clink. Further investigation revealed several gold coins among the apples. "How dare you try to bribe me," he quickly counted the coins. "So cheaply."

"There must be some misunderstanding—"

"No, I don't think so. But I would be willing to not inform His Grace about this if you can show me your records. Now." *Wow*, Bart thought, *I'm getting really good at this assertiveness thing.*

After some apologies and bowing, Jerrin and his guards led Bartleby and Phoebe across the house to a small office. The room contained a small desk and a shelf groaning under the weight of the overstuffed ledgers.

"Just shout if you need anything." Jerrin said as he left them to their work.

It only took Bartleby fifteen minutes of reading to realize there was something amiss. After an hour, his suspicions were confirmed. "These records are too perfect."

"What do you mean?" Phoebe asked, peering over his shoulder.

"Even the best bookkeepers make mistakes. There should be crossouts, math errors. There's not even any quill splatter. I think I know what this is. Do you know a spell for detecting enchantment?"

"Of course."

Bart moved as far away as he could so she could cast.

"Yep, there's an enchantment on this."

"Thought so. We had to keep a full-time mage in the tax office because of this spell. I don't suppose you can break it."

"I have a few things in my bag back at the inn that might help. You'd be surprised how often people try to unload malfunctioning magic on a traveling trader."

"Get them. But be careful." He took her hand. "Before you go, just in case Emrys is right, there's something I'd like to—"

She took his other hand and kissed him, long and passionately.

"Was that it?" she asked.

"Very much so."

"I'll be right back. Be safe."

Bartleby couldn't believe what had happened. He tried to turn his attention back to the books, but couldn't focus. When the door opened, he nearly leapt from the chair. "Phoebe I—"

"Sorry," Jerrin said. "Just me. I wanted to make sure everything was going well."

"It's quite a lot to go through. I could use some more candles."

"Of course." Jerrin came in close and put his hand on Bart's shoulder. He muttered a few arcane words, frowned, muttered some more. "Why isn't this working?"

"You know that just broke any number of laws. Perhaps if you surrender and confess now, I can keep you from being hanged… hung?"

"Oh no. You have beaten me," Jerrin replied, deadpan. "Certainly that was the only trick up my sleeve and I can't just call for my guards!!" Jerrin stepped to the side as two armed men rushed into the room. Bartleby grabbed the heavy book and held it in front of him like a shield.

"You couldn't just succumb to the domination spell like that fool Mayor." Jerrin monologued, "You had to make this hard. Now I have to kill you, and your assistants, and fake a monster attack to cover the whole thing up. Bureaucrats. No respect for other people's schedules. Well, don't just stand there. Get him!"

Bartleby was considering leaping out the window when someone else came in the other way. Bartleby yelled and ducked as glass shattered into the room.

"I've always wanted to do that!" Emrys grinned as he stood up and brushed off the glass. "Also, ow." He drew a sword and tossed Bartleby his. "A bit fairer now, eh?"

Bartleby dropped the book and grabbed the sword. This was definitely a Bart the Bold moment.

The two guards advanced. They were unable to gain much advantage in the confined space, and Emrys easily held them off.

"I have to do everything myself, don't I?" Jerrin grumbled. He was beginning to prepare a magical assault when someone tapped him on the shoulder. "What?" As he turned to look, Phoebe shoved her hand in his face and said the magical incant.

At close range, the simple light spell was enough to blind. Phoebe followed up with an unladylike kick. As Jerrin doubled over, she grabbed the nearest ledger and gave him a solid whack to the head. The two guards, seeing this, decided that discretion was the better part of not getting paid, and retreated.

"That was quite impressive," Emrys opined, as he tied Jerrin's hands.

"That was amazing!" Bartleby said. "How'd you get back so quickly?"

"When I heard this guy coming, I hid in a closet. Then I followed him and waited for an opportunity."

Bartleby and Phoebe embraced. "I'm so happy you're safe." They both said.

"I hate to interrupt this touching, and slightly off-putting, moment," Emrys interjected, apparently irritated that no one seemed to care about the way he had snuck out and listened at the window, allowing him to leap to the rescue. "But what are we doing with him?"

Jerrin was shoved in a closet and one of the heaviest and most garish couches was pushed in front of the door. "We'll have to get a message to the nearest military outpost." Emrys said, "They'll take him off our hands."

"All right, nobody move!"

"Oh, now what?" Phoebe sighed.

The Mayor was shoved into the hall. The Shadowfox was right behind, holding a sword. "Everybody surrender, or the Mayor gets it!"

"Mr. Fox..." Bartleby tried to interject.

"I mean it! Weapons on the ground." The bandit chief finally paused to make a tactical assessment. "Oh, it's you. I've captured this blighter!"

"The Mayor's innocent," Bartleby explained. "Jerrin was using magic to control him."

"Well, that's just lovely," he grumbled "But where is my—I mean everyone's—money?"

"I don't have it," the Mayor sputtered. "It's—"

Before the Mayor could finish, he was interrupted by shouts from outside.

"To arms!" shouted a guard. "It's the Greenwood Foxes!"

"What are those halfwits trying now?" the Shadowfox grumbled.

"They better not have hurt my father," Phoebe threatened as she ran out.

Even with the mask, the figure at the head of the bandits was instantly recognizable. "Release my daughter, you villains, or there shall be violence!"

Rhyer was atop the gang's third best horse, wildly waving his sword in a manner that made injury very likely. Whether that injury would happen to one of the city guards, a bandit, or Rhyer himself was up for grabs.

"Daddy!"

"We shall burn your stupid fancy house to the ground… and… and… build a privy in the ashes!"

"Daddy!"

"Not now, darling, Daddy is rescuing you. We shall crush…" Rhyer's mouth finally received the frantic signal from his ears. "You're okay!"

"Yes. Thanks for noticing."

"Stand down, you scurvy dogs!" the Shadowfox yelled, ruining what could have been a tender reunion. "Your boss has already got this under control. His Lordship was just about explain how we get our money back."

"As I was trying to explain," the Mayor stammered, "Jerrin sent most of it out of town. He was investing in caravans and businesses. Said he'd never make enough just skimming taxes. It'll take months to go through the records and figure out where it all went."

Bart the Bold and Bartleby the bookkeeper had a brief discussion. "I can help you get that sorted out," he said, "It'll be something to do until my next adventure."

Phoebe took his hand. "*Our* next adventure."

Aiden nudged Emrys. "Does this mean we have to give the advance payment back?"

"Worry about that later," he replied, "Those two are new at this, let them enjoy a happy ending."

And they did.

Unscarred
Mike Strauss

"A knife? That's it? That's all you brought? Just a stupid dull knife?"

Cad cackled mockingly, in exactly the same way he had been laughing at me for almost a decade. It cut me as deeply as it had countless times before, leaving yet another scar.

"You should just stab it into your own heart. At least then you'll die quickly."

I didn't want to admit it, but he had a point. The knife was practically worthless, not because it was dull—it was in fact quite well sharpened—but because I was all but incapable of wielding it. I kept it sharp so that I could precisely cut ingredients, not so I could kill with it. I might as well have been unarmed.

Cad, on the other hand, was armed to the teeth. He had equal length short swords strapped to both legs, and a slightly curved broadsword in a sheath slung over his shoulder. He held a jagged polearm in his right hand almost like a walking stick, if walking sticks could eviscerate a person with a single, powerful slash. Finally, completing the picture of a seasoned warrior, he wore a hard leather jerkin intermittently covered with thick rings. The armor completely covered his black fur and limited his movement, but made up for it by being nearly impenetrable.

My own yellow spotted fur was uncomfortably uncovered except for a few straps from the multitude of pouches I wore. Made of soft leather, those straps wouldn't interfere with my movement at all, but they would also give to even the slightest pressure from all but the dullest of blades. Not only was I essentially unarmed, I was basically naked, too.

Cad wasn't the only reason I felt underdressed. Seventeen other gorbe stood around anxiously, double-checking equipment, securing their weapons, mentally reviewing their magical incantations, or otherwise preparing themselves for what lay ahead. And whether they were long haired, short haired, spotted, striped, pure breed, or mixed, every single one of them was better armed or better prepared than I was.

Tav, with her golden mane and beautifully tufted tail, seemed to be practically encased in steel and carried a massive great sword that she could swing with better skill than most of her instructors. Gah's black stripes and white fur were clearly visible from head to foot. He wore only bracers and leg guards and carried no weapons at all, relying on his reflexes to block or dodge and his natural claws to maim or kill. And then there was Jak. Her leather leggings and chain vest seemed to mark her as a warrior. But, in truth, it was her reputation for casting dark magic that sent a chill up my spine.

Every other kit in this brood had excelled in either martial skill or magical theory. Try as I might, though, I never succeeded at picking up even the basics of either. I struggled to understand both endeavors for three or four years before finally admitting it was a lost cause. Eventually I found my niche, the subtle arts of alchemy. Just by smell alone I could differentiate between the kaffa berry and the stego berry, despite the fact that they looked identical to eyes that had never seen color. My sense of proportions was such that I could easily mix powders, gasses, and liquids without needing to measure. I had crafted every single solvent, poison, unguent, reagent, and gel known to the tribe, and even invented a few of my own. I also brewed powerful liquor that my primary instructor, Adavos, loved.

It would have been a wonderful skill set in another land. But here, where survival of the fittest was the mantra that was drilled into every kit since birth, I might as well have spent my life learning to milk a bull.

A calloused hand on my shoulder interrupted my thoughts.

"Lam, I can give you one of my daggers if you'd like. I know it's not much, but it is all I can spare. It might help."

I just shook my head. It was a very nice offer, but I couldn't take it. Vaw only owned four daggers total, and he was only really skilled at fighting while holding one in each hand. There was no way he could afford to have only one spare with him. Also, while the rules might technically allow it, I felt like it broke the spirit of the rules. In this test of survival, we could bring anything we owned, but only that which we owned. I hadn't earned that dagger, even if he did give it to me, so I had no right to carry it today.

That, more than anything, was the problem with my lack of skill in combat. As a kit, you earned everything you owned through training. If you wanted a sword, you had to prove your worth with the weapon to one of your instructors, or if you could not, learn how to craft such a weapon with enough proficiency that your instructor let you keep one. I had earned a lifetime's supply of pouches and philters and pruning shears, but the closest thing I had earned to a weapon was the knife I used for my craft.

There was the crux of my problem. What was I to bring to the test if I didn't own any armor and no weapons to speak of? I could try cobbling together a few makeshift weapons, but I still wouldn't know how to use them. I considered attaching some belts and pouches to the heavy leather apron I used to protect myself from acidic ingredients I often worked with, but the encumbrance of that would hurt me more than any meager protection it gave. Thus, I had spent most of the last few weeks trying to decide what I should bring to the test.

I hadn't really put a lot of thought into this before then, but earlier this month Marigold and Drina each had triplets within a week of each other. Between the new kits, the three tribe members that had died in a recent illness, and the two that had been killed in a raid gone poorly, the tribe was clearly hurting for new adults. New adults meant the current brood of kits would need to be tested. I could no longer afford to put off planning for the test.

After a few weeks of careful thought, I had woken up this morning intending only to bring my knife, some water, and some food. Then the reality had sunk in, that I would likely die before the end of the day, and if there was even a remote possibility that one of my tools could save my life, I was going to bring it with me. Thus, that morning I had buckled in place over a dozen pouches and knapsacks with various perfumes, dyes, potions, flasks, lengths of rope, scraps of leather, and various craftsman tools squirreled away in them.

"Soon now. Are you ready?"

"Almost. Can you help me with the buckle on my shield?"

"Hush, you two. I am trying to meditate."

Impatience had begun to set in amongst most of the other kits. We had all seen four of the five adults that had been here when we first arrived, head out somewhere into the forest, preparing to kill us. Their departure signified the imminence of the event in a way that the moving sun couldn't quite. I also thought about the departure of Star Eyes, Lenora, Swift Claw, and Goran, but likely not in the same way as anyone else in my brood. Thinking of those four made me jealous, since they all had names, and unless the impossible occurred today, I never would. I would die as Lam, nothing more than a combination of letters that indicated my birth order in my brood. The main reason I wanted to survive the day was so that I could choose my name.

The one adult left, Lionroar, watched the shadow of a nearby tree. When it no longer touched a knothole near the bottom of the smithy wall, the kits could enter the woods. When the shadow no longer touched the wall at all, the test would begin. At that moment he, and every other adult in the woods—almost certainly more than the four we saw enter them—would be allowed to kill any of the kits taking the test. The test ended, for an individual kit, when that kit reached the ancient oak tree roughly two miles into the forest. That was how the tribe enforced survival of the fittest, and that is why kits didn't get real names. Adults simply didn't form attachments with kits, because there was a good chance they wouldn't survive to adulthood.

So, just like Lionroar, I watched that shadow too as it slowly moved towards my inevitable death.

"Watching it won't make it go any slower, Lam. You might as well watch the sun and expect it to move slower. At least if you do that you'll be blind when the test starts, and won't see it when Lionroar kills you."

Once again, Cad's arrogant, mocking cackle reverberated through my skull, cutting me like a knife. This was just one more in a long line of scars that Cad had given me. Even I can't explain exactly why, but at that moment I decided, no matter what it took, I wasn't going to die that day, and that this was the last time Cad would ever cut me.

I wasn't the only one who found his laugh grating. Lionroar's eyes narrowed as he turned furiously towards Cad.

"Enough already. I can't stop you, but you are getting on my nerves. I swear if you laugh one more time, I'm making it my mission to hunt you down and kill you!"

Suddenly not so sure of himself, Cad proceeded to unconvincingly apologize to Lionroar. The conversation finally distracted him from his diligent watch over the shadow. Taking advantage, I pulled a thick, dark dye from a belt pouch and smeared it on the bottom of the smithy, directly under the shadow. From where Lionroar was positioned, it would seem like the shadow was still touching the wall, at least for another few minutes. I hated giving Cad the extra time, but I needed it myself if I was to have a chance.

A few of the kits who saw me rubbing the dye on the wall gave me strange looks, but nobody said a word. Instead, we all watched the moving shadow in silence. That silence was only shattered when the dark edge of the shadow finally slipped below the knothole.

"Go!"

I didn't catch who yelled it, and didn't care. Nineteen pairs of feet broke into a run, including my own. As my fellow kits headed straight for the oak, I intentionally slowed my pace. After less than a minute, I had lost sight of all of them.

It had occurred to me that the majority of the adults in the forest would be waiting on the direct path between the starting point and the oak, probably waiting in ambush. Running straight ahead might work for some of the more powerful warriors, but most of the kits would be forced to retreat, and the adults were likely to follow.

A couple well-placed traps should winnow the threat notably. The adults wouldn't be expecting it. For the most part, nobody in the tribe used traps, mostly preferring to kill up close with spear or sword or teeth and claws. As far as I knew, I was one of only two or three gorbe in the whole tribe who even had a rudimentary knowledge of the art, and only because it was the most useful application for the poison gasses I occasionally mixed.

I didn't use poison this time, mostly because nearly every member of the tribe was highly resistant to both most natural poisons and the poisonous compounds I mixed in my lab. Instead, I used the rope in my knapsack to quickly construct a few net traps. The nets were just wide enough that any but the burliest of kits could slip out of them, while nearly all the adults, especially the big brute Lionroar, would struggle to escape. The traps were quite crude, but with any luck the surprise factor alone would be enough to delay some adults for a while.

As soon as the traps were set and hidden, I took off in a direction perpendicular to the direction towards the oak. About a minute later, Lionroar lived up to his name, giving the signal that started the test for real. Despite the new danger, again I moved at a slow jog, this time because I wanted to keep my senses focused on my surroundings and because, quite honestly, I was not in the best shape. Reaching an area of rocky ground, I stopped and rummaged through a pouch on my chest until I found a carefully sealed flask.

Basically incompetent when it came to most forms of wood lore, I was certain my path was visible to anyone with the slightest skill in tracking… but I also knew enough to know that the rocks would do what I normally didn't have the talent to perform.

That only dealt with half the problem, though. The other half was making sure my scent didn't give me away.

Quickly plugging my nose, I broke the seal on the flask and poured the contents all over the ground and trees in the nearby area, being very careful not to get any on me. The stench would nearly cripple anyone trying to follow me by scent, and would kill someone's sense of smell for a few hours at least.

Finally feeling like I had some real time to work with, I headed in a gentle spiral towards the oak. Occasionally, I heard the distinctive sounds of weapons clashing in the distance, always towards the direction of the oak. Listening intently, I kept my distance from those encounters.

Minutes later, frustration gnarled my fur. I had been so focused on listening for sounds of swordplay that I failed to notice the distinct inflections of someone chanting a spell incantation. I did not fail to notice the tiny bolt of lightning that nearly singed my whiskers.

Luckily for me, the spell hadn't actually been aimed at me. In fact, the caster of the spell, a tiger-striped female named Miru, didn't even seem to be aware of my presence. She stared into the eyes of Jak, who was completing the incantation of another spell. I couldn't identify the exact spell, but the result was obvious. A patch of Miru's fur and skin rotted away, exposing part of her intestines. I saw similar patches of rot on her left arm and where her right eye used to be.

Miru nearly collapsed, swaying precariously as she strained to remain standing. Yet she gritted her teeth and started to utter the first syllables of another spell. Jak's spellcasting was faster than the injured adult's, by a fair margin. This spell didn't just rot skin. It caused Miru's right leg to simply melt away completely. The vile necromantic curse was so powerful that I briefly felt like I was encased in ice, as the spell sapped a portion of all nearby life energy, including mine, to power the horrifying effect. The shock of cold was probably all that kept me from vomiting the last meal I had eaten.

Miru writhed about on the ground. Her wounds were far beyond anything I had ever seen before, and far beyond the healing capacity of the two herbal poultices that were in my bag. Jak was already walking away. She was not even slightly disturbed by the pain she had caused.

I couldn't even move at first. My mind was wrestling with the horror I had witnessed. I wanted nothing more than to run, but the next thing I knew, I found myself stepping closer to the fallen gorbe.

Her head whipped in my direction, though the action seemed to drain most of her remaining energy. Pleading eyes met mine.

"Please."

She didn't—couldn't—speak another word.

I am ashamed that I hesitated for almost a minute before I untied my bag and pulled out one of the herbal poultices. Using what little knowledge of first aid I had, I carefully applied the bandages to the stump of Miru's leg.

"It won't restore the limb, but it should numb the pain until help arrives."

Pounding footsteps alerted me to the fact that help was arriving sooner than I expected. I scrambled beneath a bush, putting only a thin wall of foliage between me and whoever had just burst into the clearing. Goran quickly knelt down beside Miru, facing away from me. I was certain he would hear my gasping breathing, but the older cheetah's hearing had been fading in recent years. My cover was now meaningless if he turned his head more than a fraction.

Leaning over the suffering woman, he calmly examined her wounds. In a practiced motion, he snapped open a belt pouch at his waist and withdrew about five philters. Goran returned four to his pouch and popped the cork on the last one. Almost the moment he pressed the philter to Miru's lips, flesh and fur miraculously grew out of the defiled stump, forming a perfectly healthy leg. The newly formed leg tore away the poultice I had placed on her and Goran instinctively caught it. His body tensed warily, and he held the poultice out towards Miru.

"Who did this?"

Miru sat up and locked eyes with me. That cold feeling of dread rippled through my bones once more.

"Jak. She just left."

Goran, with sharp eyes undiminished despite his age, must have realized that Miru wasn't looking at him. He started to turn his head to look at whatever she was looking at. Miru quickly grabbed his shoulder and pointed with her other hand.

"She went that way."

Goran jumped to his feet and sped off in the direction she had pointed, dropping the poultice in his hurry. The tiger-striped woman, still staring into my eyes, picked it up, and smiled briefly at me. She was stuffing it into a bandolier pouch as she lightly jogged out of the clearing in the same direction Goran had headed.

Sweat dripped from my whiskers and fur as I tried to still my panic. She hadn't killed me. She knew where I was and almost certainly had the means, but she didn't even try. I felt the same way I did the day I had accidentally inhaled the fumes coming from a batch of hallucination elixir. Only after double checking that none of my potion vials had cracked was I certain that the entire incident wasn't a figment of my imagination.

By the time I had finally calmed down, I had come to the conclusion that the longer I stayed in these woods, the more likely it was that I would encounter someone who would try to kill me. Slow and smart may have kept me safe for a while, but it was time to be a little daring. Jak and her pursuers weren't heading directly towards the tree. If there was ever going to be an opportunity to make a break for it, this was the time. Steeling myself, I plunged into the woods directly towards the objective.

I was not foolish enough to break into a headlong sprint, but I was moving much more recklessly than I had previously. In order to hinder any possible pursuit, I dripped a mild acid behind me. It wasn't strong enough to melt through boots, but most in my tribe went barefoot, and it was strong enough to itch and burn with prolonged exposure. I also palmed a few of my more volatile poison elixirs, hoping that if I did run into someone, it would be a rare member of the tribe who wasn't highly resistant to poisons. Or, failing that, I simply hoped the smoking fumes or glass shards of the makeshift bomb would be enough of a distraction that I could escape.

My planning completely failed to take into account my complete lack of combat reflexes. When the tip of a short sword cut a burning furrow into my cheek, not only didn't I throw a poison vial at my attacker, but I actually tightened my grip, causing the poison to soak my fur and even enter my bloodstream as the glass cut my hands. Years of contact with poisons and toxins had made me nearly immune to the substance in the vials, but I still experienced a momentary shock as my body reacted to the foreign substance.

"You?"

The obvious tone of resentment in Cad's voice shook me out of my stupor. Focusing my gaze on him, it was immediately obvious to me why he was so upset. He had either lost or dropped his polearm, his broadsword lay shattered on the ground near his feet, his left hand was mangled nearly beyond recognition, and he was freely bleeding from multiple contusions. The tattered leather and cracked rings hanging from his torso gave mute evidence that his armor had fortunately taken the brunt of many weapon blows.

I immediately recognized the irony of the situation. Even battered and broken, Cad had still cut me with ease.

I must admit, it was incredibly satisfying to see the envious way he looked at me, completely injury-free except for the shallow cut I had just received from his blade. We both knew that for all his bravado and combat skills, I had fared much better in getting to this point than he had. As tempted as I was to taunt him with the fact, getting him riled up wouldn't help me finish the test.

"What happened?"

I carefully kept my voice neutral while handing him my last poultice.

He looked at the poultice suspiciously at first, but was in no shape to turn down the gift. Finally, his pride gave way to necessity.

"The oak is only about a hundred feet away, but Stout is guarding it. He nearly killed me with that big sledge of his."

I groaned inwardly. Stout was the one member of our tribe who was not a gorbe. I never heard the exact details, but somehow the dwarf had joined our tribe when he was just a child. He had been made a kit just like anyone else born to the tribe, and had passed the test to adulthood.

The bigger problem, though, was that due to his race, Stout simply had a different approach to things than most of the rest of the tribe. Without a heightened sense of smell, he relied more on his hearing and eyesight, both of which were superior to any other in the tribe. Furthermore, he wielded a heavy sledge and fought with a powerful bludgeoning style that no gorbe had ever been able to learn or even fully comprehend. Finally, he could see colors that I and my kin could not.

I tried to think of any advantage that Cad and I might have over Stout, but I was lost for ideas. Stout had already bested Cad in combat and his dwarven blood made him nearly as resistant to most toxins as I was. Just as I was beginning to despair, I realized that there was a way to take advantage of his color vision.

"Cad, I have a way for both of us to reach the oak, but it doesn't involve fighting."

For the first time in his life, Cad actually seemed relieved to avoid combat. "Tell me."

"I have some dyes. I can apply them to your fur and armor to help you blend into the woods. I'll do the same for myself, and then we can sneak up to the tree without Stout noticing us."

"You sure it will work?"

"Yeah, it will work. But due to our different fur colors, I will have to use different dyes for each of us, and we'll have to take different paths."

"Whatever. I don't care about the details, just as long as it will work. You may be a weakling, but you are never wrong."

I was shocked for a moment. I never expected Cad to compliment me. It almost made me change my plan. But there wasn't time for a new plan. Even if Stout was content to simply wait by the tree, other adults might appear at any time.

I put on a pair of leather gloves, and then quickly applied a thick dye to Cad's fur and the remaining shreds of his armor. Covering him thoroughly enough took about ten minutes, mostly due to needing to be careful not to get any of the dye on me. As soon as I was done with him, I switched gloves and applied a second dye to myself. That process only took about five minutes.

As soon as I was done, Cad took off in the direction I pointed. I moved the opposite direction. Both of us were moving towards the oak tree, but stealthily amid trees and underbrush, so Stout wouldn't see us. We were both about twenty-five feet from the tree when Stout charged Cad.

I couldn't see Cad, but I was sure that Stout could. The dye I had applied to him was almost perfect camouflage to the limited color vision of gorbe. But I knew that the dye appeared much different to other races and would, in fact, make him stand out just as if he were waving a flag.

The moment Stout began to swing his sledge, I gave up all pretense of stealth and made a dash for the oak tree. At twenty feet away from the tree, I watched that dread sledge break Cad's good arm. The hammer broke both of Cad's kneecaps at fifteen feet away. I was only ten feet away when Stout stepped over the collapsed body, lifting the huge sledge over his head for a two-handed swing. Five feet later, without flinching, I watched Stout deliver a crushing, killing blow to Cad's head.

The cut on my cheek burned. I took one more last big step and touched the tree.

Twelve had survived. It was the highest survival rate in decades, and nearly the entire tribe was celebrating the success. I was in the laboratory, carefully putting all of my supplies back on the appropriate shelves.

"What's wrong?"

Adavos might not be my teacher anymore, but he knew me well enough to know when I was upset.

"I don't deserve to be alive. An adult saw me, but chose to let me live simply because I helped her out. And I sacrificed Cad in order to complete the test. He was much more skilled in combat than I was. All of the other kits were."

"I've spoken to both Miru and Stout already. Best I can tell, there was absolutely no way you both were going to make it past Stout. If you tried together, you would almost certainly have both died. Instead, you tricked Cad into sacrificing himself so you could survive. That certainly sounds like you were the fittest to me. And as for Miru, I'm a little disappointed in you."

"I know."

"No, not for the reason you think. Never once during your training did you ever ask me how I passed my test. Have you ever in your life seen me holding a weapon?"

He didn't give me time to answer.

"I survived the test by bribing my way past every single adult I met with mint liquor, aphrodisiacs, and silver pieces. You may not have directly bribed Miru, but your aid earned her approval that you were fit enough to be a full member of the tribe. Survival of the fittest means you prove yourself as capable of surviving with your chosen skill set. You did just that. Now choose a name."

For years, I had been thinking about this moment. About half the tribe chose descriptive names that highlighted their skills or something important in their lives. Most of the rest chose names that they liked for some reason, but had no meaning beyond being a name. There was no stigma for one choice or the other.

I thought about my life to this point and my chosen profession. I thought about the test, my interactions with Cad, Vaw's generous offer, Jak's dark magic, and watching Stout mercilessly kill another kit, knowing it could have been me.

Looking at Adavos, I thought about all he had taught me, including this final lesson. Finally, I thought about the cut on my cheek which I had yet to find healing for, which still burned, and would almost certainly turn into a scar without the care of a medic.

"I've made my choice."

The Otherside Alliance
Jon Cory

The sound of my bedroom door banging against the wall shattered my dream. Only one friend would arrive with such a disregard for my privacy—Mumblepeg, the spotted dwarf.

"You act like you own every stone in my cottage," I said.

"I do," Mumblepeg agreed. "Remember, we are business partners."

"But the mortar, land and roof are now mine." Buying my cottage bit by bit from the spotted dwarf had seemed the only way to gain my own home. A life of living in tents or sleeping in some cramped room at a noisy lodging house had lost its appeal, even for someone as footloose as a hired knight.

"King Bellabond demands your immediate attendance in his private chambers."

Mumblepeg hopped around the room gathering the clothing I had strewn about last night. He presented the pile of garments to me and urged me to hurry.

"In two turns of the hourglass," the spotted dwarf said, "he will send his gryphons to fetch you in a most unpleasant manner."

"What does fat old Bellybump want now?" I asked. "Is he not pleased with the three-bladed sword of Cameron that I snatched from the heart of Goosland Castle? The same trophy he now proudly displays above the Kingdom of Otherside's throne, upon which he plunks his royal bottom."

Mumblepeg held open my scarlet jacket while I groped my arms around, trying to find the sleeve openings. A twinge of pain in my chest reminded me the knife wound, a token from my recent battle at Goosland, had not fully healed. Perhaps women would admire my new battle scar and trace their fingers around it, as they often did with the old mark on my shoulder.

My parade helmet—had I stored it under the bed? I got on my knees to investigate. Boobay, my six-legged pet cat, greeted me with a playful swipe of a forward paw.

"Here's your helmet," Mumblepeg said. "I brushed the plume and buffed the silver. Now hurry before the king imposes another fine upon you. Then you will never be able to pay me for the building stones."

"True. Belly has me deep in his debt hole." I sat on the bed and tugged on my leather boots. "Why do you think I keep agreeing to go on dangerous missions for him? Risking my very life."

"If you wouldn't keep refusing to marry his sister's daughter," the dwarf said, "all would be forgiven."

"That shrew?" I said. "There are better ways to die." I gave Mumblepeg a playful tap on his forehead with the flat of my sword blade as I went out the cottage door. "Off to see Uncle King."

The entrance to the king's private chamber was situated at the end of a long hallway. My brisk steps echoed off the stone walls as I approached the two beefy guards stationed in front of the door. The soldiers crossed their ax-headed pikes to bar my entrance. It happened every time. Even though they knew me, these dullards would pretend they didn't. The burly mountain men were paid to protect Bellabond, not to think. I had to state my name and purpose.

"I am Sarlon," I said in a bored voice. "The king has summoned me. I live in a cottage at the edge of village Moorside. His Majesty sends for me when he needs a knave to undertake an impossible mission."

"Leave your sword and dagger with us," the older guard ordered. He scowled, protruding his lips, pulling his hairy brows taut.

"Then how can I protect the king if someone attacks him?" I cocked my head and tapped my foot, impatient for a proper answer.

"Well, all right, I guess." The man signaled his partner to stand aside.

I grasped the large iron ring mounted on the door and struck the thick oak planks. The king had sent for me, so one loud knock should be sufficient. I put my shoulder to the heavy door and pushed it open.

"I was going to say 'come in,'" King Bellabond said, "but you already have."

The king's unbuttoned jacket accommodated his oversized stomach. Bellabond sat in a carved, high-backed chair behind a massive desk made from the planks of the captured pirate vessel he had seized when he first came to power.

Bellabond had had the pirate chief beheaded and the man's skull made into an inkwell. I watched the king dip a quill pen into the black ink and sign a scroll laid out in front of him. He rolled the vellum, tied a red ribbon around the document, then tossed it onto a pile of papers stacked on his desk.

Sunlight from the arched windows behind him cast a glow around the king's head. He rested his elbows on the desk and propped his chin on the knuckles of one hand.

"Never become a king unless you like paperwork." Bellabond made a sour face. "Once I fought battles, conquered lands, plundered villages, ravaged damsels, and did other manly tasks. Now I just argue with my ministers, read stacks of boring reports, and listen to useless chatter from my courtiers."

"Well, sire," I said, "you could always round up the army, pick a fight somewhere and march off for gold and glory." I removed my helmet, tucked it under one arm and sat in a large wooden chair whose leather back was secured by bronze nails. Why were chairs never as comfortable as a saddle? I twisted in the seat and dangled one leg over its arm.

"Costs too much in coin, men and time," the king said. "The days of easy conquest are over. The ruling class and the merchants have found they are better off figuring out schemes to make money than fighting each other. Even the eastern barbarians have stopped raiding and are now content with their farms and cattle."

"Sire, am I to assume you called me here for reasons other than to discuss the nagging problems of running your kingdom?"

I turned forward and extended my legs to admire my polished boots. Women in the palace seemed to notice such details.

"Sarlon, I consider you an irresponsible and callow youth more interested in adventure and partying than a serious life." The king stood, scratched his ample stomach, and plucked an apple from a plate of fruit sitting on one side of his desk. "However, I must admit you are a skilled warrior, have a clever mind, and have a way with words when it suits your purpose."

Bellabond chewed on a bit of the apple while rummaging among the papers on his desk. He pulled a thick ledger from the mess of documents, inserted a bejeweled finger into the space marked by a black ribbon, and opened the pages.

"This is a ledger of all the money my subjects owe me. Taxes, fines, levies, debts of all sorts, borrowed money, pawned items, pledges, and unpaid commissions." The king ran a finger down the page and landed on a name. Still holding the apple, he pointed at me. "You owe me a great sum, nephew." He held up one palm. "Before you ask, no, I do not have any new foe or monster threatening me that you can slay. By the way, thanks for the Cameron sword. It looks impressive mounted above my throne."

The king wouldn't be pleased if he knew I had considered selling the sword to a traveling merchant. My better judgment had overcome my temptation to refill my empty purse.

"Is there no way I can settle my debt?" I asked. "Other than agreeing to marry your sister's daughter."

"I have more important things to discuss than making my sister happy." Bellabond rejected my protest with a dismissive wave of his hand. "The information I now reveal to you is known only to my most trusted inner circle. My spies report that the Kingdom of Otherside is threatened by a pending secret alliance between Gonderland and Warla."

"But those lands are traditional enemies," I said. "They hate each other."

"Yes, but they are preparing to unite against us. They are coming together under the falcon flag of Zarror, a caster who revels in chaos magic."

"Together, they could overwhelm us," I said. "It would be a bloody battle. We might win. We might not. How do you propose to stop this pending alliance?"

"I will sign a mutual defense alliance with the kingdom of Icenia," the king said.

"Icenia? Do they even know we exist?"

"In truth, a distant land, but powerful and potentially a strong ally," Bellabond said. "They are aware of our Otherside Kingdom, but we have had minimal contact with them—a few merchant traders on rare occasions. Icenia is a young kingdom that has not yet ventured far beyond its shores. Icenians rarely sail past the Vaccaran Isles."

I weighed the idea. While Otherside was on friendly terms with Icenia, I doubted they would get involved in our politics. The prosperous kingdom used its army to defend the homeland. Bellabond's idea was really dumb. How should I respond in diplomatic terms?

"Their knights would resist any foreign involvement."

"True," Bellabond said. "But I have conceived a brilliant plan."

"Do share with me, sire," I said. "And I will poke holes in your plan—just to be helpful." I cupped my chin as if I were contemplating serious thoughts, and hid a smile behind my hand.

"The key to my alliance is convincing Duke Frost Vardik of Ashbury to agree to my proposal, to put the weight of his authority behind the idea. If the Duke champions our cause, the others will fall into line."

"His barons would reject such a proposal." The king's plan was folly.

"True again," the king said. "No one single thing will do the trick. But a combination of bribery and guile might pull it off."

"An impossible task for any man." I brushed a fallen lock of dark hair away from my forehead. So much for watching my words.

"How would you like to be debt free and have enough money to live the life you wish?" The king showed a toothy smile. "Own the stones in your cottage. Marry whomever you please. Maybe that healer you seem so friendly with."

"You are not seriously considering asking me to undertake such a task in Ashbury?" I said. "I am the last person you should pick." I raised my hand as if taking an oath. "I officially refuse any such offer. I am young, inexperienced, and irresponsible." Also, I valued my life too much. Ashbury was a dangerous place. There were other humans there, but also many biata, elves, ogres, and the cat-like gorbe. Even the dwarves living there were not the spotted kind.

"I have made my choice." The king walked around the desk and stood in front of me. He placed a heavy hand on my shoulder.

"What if I refuse?"

"One nice thing about being king is that people can't refuse and still live." Bellabond sliced a finger across his own throat.

The king roared with laughter; his head thrown back with his mouth open. I choked back my anger. Did the king want me to fail or get killed? Such a result would remove a troublesome nephew of embarrassing lineage from his court.

"There are three possible outcomes," Bellabond said. "First, you may be killed carrying out the task or for refusing to accept it. Second, you may succeed and receive the rewards I have promised. Or third—I tell this true—if you fail and live, I will banish you from the Kingdom of Otherside. You will never see your little cottage, your friends, or your homeland again."

"I don't know what to say." Hands behind my back, I paced around the room trying to conjure up arguments for rejecting Uncle Bellybump's demand. "Since childhood I have reconciled myself to being an outsider. My sword is my only trusted companion."

"Poor little orphan," Bellabond said. "Spare me your sad tale. You somehow managed to become a feared warrior." The king paused for dramatic effect. "Besides, you will get something that has been denied you all your life: a title, recognizing you as a legitimate member of Otherside royalty. How about being a Count? No. Count Sarlon sounds like an activity rather than a title. I will name you as Duke of Umpelen and give you all the holdings that go with the title."

A title would be nice, but I needed more than mere honors. I needed a fresh start, free of debt. Without merchants hounding me for payment. Out from under the King's thumb.

"Sire, I am certain you will confirm your words with a signed document forgiving all my debt," I said. "Your risk is small. I may be killed in this mission—before, during or after."

"Some day, young Sarlon, you will push me too far." King Bellabond, a scowl darkening his face, took pen in hand, wrote, then sealed the document.

"You mentioned money." Without resources, I had no chance of carrying out the king's orders.

The king walked to the oversized cabinet standing in the corner of his private chamber. He took a key from his coat pocket and unlocked the door.

"Here is a sack of gold coins," Bellabond said. "To be spent as needed. Bribes, clothing, transportation, entertainment—as you alone deem fit. Take it. I only demand results—a mutual protection alliance between Ashbury and Otherside. A war on one would be war on the other."

I hefted the heavy sack. Coins clicked against each other. Never in my life had I held so much money.

"I am appointing a special ambassador from the Kingdom of Otherside to plead my cause in Ashbury." The king retreated to his desk and grunted as he lowered his bulk into the chair.

"Well, I wish him good luck, whoever he is," I said.

"Oh, did I forget to give you this?" The king tossed me the rolled document tied with a red ribbon. "Your appointment as my new ambassador to Ashbury. A copy of your official credentials has been dispatched by courier to Duke Frost of Ashbury. Now, go view your new holdings in Umpelen. I have arranged for a Captain LeForge, sailing the

Revenge, to meet you there and take you to Ashbury. I want you on your way before the new moon."

"I see from the set of your jaw there is no way to escape this quest and live." I grasped the scroll. "I ask only one favor."

"Name it," the king said, "and if it is within my power, I will grant it."

"Mumblepeg, the spotted dwarf, goes with me disguised as my servant."

"That muscle-bound stoneworker?" King Bellabond protested, then shrugged his shoulders. "Granted, if you are foolish enough to stake your life on one of those devious troublemakers."

The narrow, raised road meandered around the marshes before descending toward the fishing village of Oldport. Weeds grew between the two rutted wheel tracks. Dragonflies flitted over the reeds. Here and there ripples moved the floating green algae when creatures slid into the water as our horses approached.

"Now that King Bellabond has declared you Duke of Umpelen," Mumblepeg said, "you can pay me for your cottage's building stones." The dwarf would tilt to one side of the saddle, then the other. His short legs were a poor fit for gripping the horse's broad back. "I am not pleased with the small amount of money you have paid me to accompany you on this doomed quest."

"I too am disappointed," I said. "The other nobles smirked and offered faint praise on my elevation to Duke of Umpelen. Apparently, the duchy is as small and impoverished as such property can be here in the Kingdom of Otherside. Umpelen is more an afterthought than an estate, containing neither castle nor farms."

"We can't arrive soon enough for me." Mumblepeg grabbed a handful of the horse's thick mane and raised his bottom off the saddle. After a few moments, the dwarf settled back down with a grimace. "Any income from tax levies? Or perhaps a rich widow?"

"Neither one," I said. "Uncle Bellybump giveth and taketh at the same time. Me being a duke sounds nice, but the entire duchy of Umpelen consists of the fishing village of Oldport and a few surrounding acres of swampy land."

"I seem to recall that the cove was once a smuggler's landing." Mumblepeg tugged on the reins to detour his horse around a wide patch of mud in the road.

"The village had a brief moment of glory during the Ten Years War when the main Otherside ports were blockaded," I said. "Now Oldport is neglected and forlorn."

"He also made you Ambassador to Ashbury," Mumblepeg said. "That must amount to something."

"The only good thing about being appointed ambassador is that Duke Frost of Ashbury has agreed to meet with me." I patted the saddlebag. "I have in here a document, already signed by King Bellabond, declaring an alliance between Ashbury and Otherside. I will present it to the duke for his consideration and signature."

"Fat chance," Mumblepeg said.

"In two days, a ship will arrive for us at Oldport," I said. "From there we set sail for Ashbury."

A freshening breeze stirred the reeds and ruffled the standing water. The horses raised their heads, turned their ears forward, and quickened their pace without urging.

"We must be close to the village," Mumblepeg said. "I can smell the sea."

The horses topped a rise in the road. Below lay the coastline. A gentle swell rocked the waves before spilling them onto the shore. Oldport huddled against the shoreline in the cove. A broad street started at the pier, ran through the village, and ended at a large, windowless building. Everything in town appeared dirty brown or faded gray, without a hint of bright colors. The weather-beaten houses leaned against one another like drunken men after a victory feast.

As my horse dutifully started down the sloping road toward the village, the sudden clopping of hooves against cobblestones surprised me. I leaned forward from my saddle for a better view of the ground.

"Guess what, Mumblepeg! My village has a paved street," I said. So far, my fortune had improved by one short street and one small village. Not much to boast about yet.

Mumblepeg decided to examine the large, windowless building. He flicked the reins, dug in his heels, and bounced in the saddle as his horse trotted ahead.

"You are also the owner of a storage warehouse." Mumblepeg trotted around the structure. The dwarf's laughter carried back to me. "A rundown building with half a roof, missing doors, and sagging timbers."

"Let's see the rest of the bad news," I said.

We eased our mounts past the houses and shacks situated on both sides of the cobblestone street. Shutters were open on the few windows facing the street. Doors were shut. There were no cross-streets or corners. Houses lined up like ducks in a row, down to the sea. The closer to the water, the more ramshackle the dwellings seemed to be. Three men wearing faded and ragged clothes stood in huddled conversation in front of a store that, according to the faded sign dangling above, housed the Lost Anchor Tavern.

A prune-faced woman, her hair a tangled pile of wispy grey, leaned her arms on a second-story windowsill. She hunched forward for a better look at us, then ducked back inside when I smiled at her.

Suspicious eyes followed our every movement as our horses stepped down the street. No one offered a greeting or said a word. One man arced his load of spit to the ground just off to the side so that he couldn't be accused of aiming at us. Mumblepeg leaned toward me.

"I'm used to being stared at and made unwelcome," Mumblepeg said. "Some people think dwarves are mischief-makers who bring bad luck. But you, Duke of Nothing, might be offended by such lack of warmth from your subjects."

"I may have tenants, serfs, and workers, but only the king has subjects," I said. "I will introduce myself later. First, I want to inspect the port. If you can call this collection of hovels a seaside village, then I must lower my expectations for the shipping dock."

The last house on either side of the street was indeed the most decrepit. Years of taking the full brunt of the wind and waves had hammered boards and framing into submission. The decks facing the water had collapsed and sagged precariously. I doubted that people dared stand upon them.

Mismatched oars leaned against the side of one house. Fishing nets were strung out to dry. Two small rowboats were overturned on the slope leading to the shoreline. Nothing I saw impressed me. To be more accurate, it depressed me.

Mumblepeg and I dismounted at the water's edge and walked onto the pier. The wood beneath my boots yielded to my steps. Rotted planking made each step perilous. Pilings leaned at awkward angles or were broken at the waterline. I had often journeyed from one port to another in my warrior quests, and I had stood on good docks and bad. Oldport's pier was worse than bad.

"The jetty stones have shifted and fallen into the water," Mumblepeg said. He stood with his hands akimbo. "Such a condition saddens my stonemason's heart."

I studied the port, looking for signs of activity. There were neither anchored ships nor sails on the horizon. No dockworkers lounged about. Even more discouraging, I could see no goods piled on the dock, nothing stacked for shipment.

"Worse than what I do see is what I do not," I said. "This place should be called Noport rather than Oldport."

"May I be of service to you gentlemen?" an earnest voice asked.

I turned to find a white-bearded man clutching a formless woolen cap between his hands. The top of the man's balding head glistened with perspiration. Wisps of white hair stuck out from the sides. He offered a slight bow of respect to me, and even nodded a greeting to Mumblepeg.

"And who are you?" My hand rested on the hilt of my sword, as was my habit when meeting a stranger.

"I am the most important man in Oldport," the man said. His bony ankles showed beneath his too short trousers. "First, because I am the oldest, and second, because I have a title and position."

"And I am Sarlon, the new Duke of Umpelen," I said. "Recently appointed by King Bellabond." I started to explain the purpose of my visit, then decided I should at least pretend to be in charge. "What is your name?"

"Walter of Umpelen." His eyes were deeply set, yet clear, in a wrinkled face darkened by years of exposure to the sun. "I am the last surviving Umpelen. My family owned Oldport since before it was old." Walter stretched his thin frame to its fullest height. "Our lands stretched a day's ride in all directions."

"Your current title and position are?" Mumblepeg eyed the bearded man with suspicion. He only trusted other dwarves, and very few of them.

"Harbormaster," Walter said. "Nothing moves in or out of Oldport without my approval." He squared his shoulders for a moment, then let them sag. "But I must confess, nothing moves in or out nowadays even with my approval. Business isn't just bad, it doesn't exist."

"According to the king's appointment," I said, "title to all lands, buildings and the workers within my duchy are mine."

"We poor folks of Oldport don't much care who owns the land," the harbormaster said. "None of us own anything of value. Not our houses, nor any field. There are no jobs. We do a little fishing to put food on the table. Each family tends a tiny garden patch to feed themselves. Barely does that. Mostly potatoes."

"Implying that if I want a meal," Mumblepeg said, "I must eat fish stew made with potatoes."

"We call it Makedo Stew. It is quite tasty," Walter insisted, "once you get used to it. We add seaweed for color and flavor."

Mumblepeg made a face. He hitched up the wide leather belt fastened loosely around his waist and held one hand over his stomach as if having a bout of gas. I knew if he had a choice, Mumblepeg would avoid eating anything green. The dwarf and I had often dined together. He relished his meat: boar, venison, pig, or cow.

A great idea came to my mind. At least, it had the potential to be great. Right now, the thought peered in the window of my brain, waiting to be welcomed.

"Walter, what would the villagers think of Oldport being owned by one of the nobles of Ashbury?" I floated my idea, half-formed, to the harbormaster for his reaction.

"Oldport and its people are naught but a bit of jetsam cast on the seashore, ignored by King and country," Walter said. "If the Ashbury man brought money and jobs, I see no harm."

"Well, then," I said. "My new mission is to convince the Duke of Ashbury to accept my gift of Umpelen and all of its shipping trade in exchange for a document that I need him to sign."

I flung out my arms and circled, my cloak swirling, in a grand gesture taking in all of Oldport and its harbor. My audacious idea had been born.

"I will convince the Duke to send a commissioner to approve my gift of Umpelen to Ashbury."

Mumblepeg stomped his foot on one of the rotting planks. The board broke with a cracking sound, and the splintered piece splashed into the water below.

"One look at this miserable seaport," the dwarf said, "and the commissioner will laugh at your proposal."

"I must agree, sir," Walter said. "No thinking person wants our sorry port." A seagull swooped low over the pier looking for food and, finding none, squawked in rebuke before flying away. "We used to have skills of value. But there is no call for tradesmen around here."

"I got it." I punched the air. My new idea had taken flight. "The villagers will clean up the town, fill the dock with boxes and barrels—empty of course—and pretend to be a busy port."

"We will?" Walter said.

"And, Mumblepeg, you will restore the fallen jetty and the pier. Then put a stone facade on the warehouse to make it appear sturdy."

"I will?" the dwarf said.

Walter and Mumblepeg exchanged puzzled glances. The spotted dwarf circled his finger around his temple to indicate what he thought of my scheme.

"Duke Sarlon," Walter said. "As much as I would revel in a ploy to convince Ashbury to sign your document, such efforts would take money. I doubt there are three silver coins in the whole of Oldport."

I threw one arm around Walter's drooping shoulders and another around Mumblepeg's thick neck. I pulled the unlikely duo close to my chest.

"Leave those concerns to me," I said. "Enough coins are in my purse to buy supplies and pay each man a modest amount for his work. Two weeks is all the time we have. We either succeed together or fail together."

"I suggest we gather at the tavern and discuss your mad plan over ale," Mumblepeg said. The dwarf left me and stomped off to gather the horses. Walter squirmed a bit, so I released him.

The dwarf and the harbormaster would hear part of my plan. The rest would stay safe within me. I intended to spend some of the King's coins dressing up Oldport, then exchange my worthless village to Duke Frost for his alliance with Otherside. Lest my ruse be discovered, His Majesty would have to rebuild Oldport or risk war with Ashbury.

I would also drop a few more gold coins into Mumblepeg's hands, thus purchasing the whole of my cottage from him. After all, when Uncle Bellybump gave me the money he did say, "to be spent as you alone see fit."

The space inside of the Lost Anchor Tavern had fared no better than the faded sign that dangled above the entrance. And no customers cluttered the empty room. I selected the least wobbly of the four tables. Walter slid three chairs across the uneven flooring, and waited for Mumblepeg and me to take our place at the table.

"There is but one choice of ale," Walter said. "I brew it myself. My Bilge Ale is the finest in all of Oldport—since it is the only one." He went behind the dusty plank set between upright wooden boxes to collect three fired-clay tankards and fill them with beer.

"Walter," I said. "Do I gather that, in addition to your harbormaster duties, you own this excuse for a tavern?"

"Occupy would be more precise," Walter said. "In the eyes of the king's law, the whole place belongs to you."

I chewed on the implications of Walter's statement. Ownership of anything beyond my personal needs—my weapons, war-horse and little cottage—had never stirred feelings in me. Rich trappings seemed more a burden than a prize. Yet, now I hesitated to risk gambling away my newly acquired duchy, even though it was diminutive and impoverished.

The harbormaster opened the shuttered windows. Fresh air arrived with a strong breeze that stirred the dust on the plank flooring. He joined Mumblepeg and me at our table.

"Walter, take this gold piece." I plucked a coin from the sack purse on my belt and laid the gleaming piece on the tabletop. "Do as I command. Build a sturdy bar with a place to hold a barrel of ale. Get some people to give the building a proper scrubbing. Find a woodcarver to make a new sign renaming this place the New Oldport Tavern."

Clever ideas were bubbling up in my mind. As quickly as one rose to the top, my tongue spoke it. From the looks on their faces, Walter and Mumblepeg struggled to remember my stream of orders—as did I, for that matter.

"Send someone with a wagon to fetch a barrel of the best beer from around these parts," I said. "Borrow old artisan items from locals. Mount them on the wall and call them antiques."

"Certainly, my Duke," Walter said. "But what you call antiques are villagers' everyday possessions that are still in use."

"Temporary loans." I dismissed Walter's protest. Didn't he understand my commands were tactics necessary to carry out my grand strategy? "And hire the village's most beautiful maiden to be the serving wench here at the tavern."

"Could be a problem, sir." Walter scratched his bald head while searching for a proper response. "I doubt if Oldport has a maiden. And certainly not one deemed pretty by inland standards."

Must I solve every problem myself? Perhaps I should broaden my definition of maiden.

"Go find a busty young woman at another village inn and import her along with the new beer. Her job will be brief but well paid. And have her dress fetchingly, so as to entice a foreign dignitary."

I turned my attention to Mumblepeg, who had been listening with an amused grin. The dwarf drained his tankard, leaving a ring of foam around his lips. He twisted the ends of his mustache and scratched his thick mutton-chop sideburns. Then he pulled my untouched beer to himself. His other arm rested outstretched on the table. "I feel that whatever you are going to ask me to do requires two brews."

I held my hand above the dwarf's empty hand, waiting for Mumblepeg to turn his palm upwards. When he complied, I dropped a fistful of gold coins into his open hand. Even in the dim light of the tavern, they glittered. The dwarf arranged the coins into two equal stacks on the tabletop.

"Mumblepeg, you have just been appointed overseer of the Oldport reclamation project. Send word to your fellow stonemasons. Offer hard work with extra money for quick completion. Your word will be law. I trust you will repair the pier and make the town appear busy and prosperous."

The dwarf tented his spotted fingers, then blew into them while contemplating my offer. After a long pause he pocketed the coins.

"I will apply bright paint to the side of the houses that face the street." As new thoughts occurred, Mumblepeg opened his eyes and mouth wide like he had sat on a thorn bush. "And sweep the weeds and clutter off the street." He smacked his palm on the table to emphasize his latest idea. "I will transplant some trees along the cobblestones at the edge of the village to hide the dirt road beyond the warehouse."

"According to my instructions from the king, Captain LeForge should arrive in Oldport tomorrow," I said. "I will sail on the *Revenge* to Ashbury without you. I know LeForge, a red-headed rogue, whose loyalty shifts with any winds that favor him. The captain behaves himself while sailing in Otherside waters, but pursues the pirate's trade along Gonderland's coast."

A bribe might entice LeForge to play my game, as long as he did not know the whole of my plan. He would sell me out without a qualm. And smile while he did it.

I shook off thoughts of treachery. Mumblepeg and Walter appeared eager, but continued to loll about the tavern.

"Why do you sit on your arses while work awaits?" I said. "Go, get busy. I depend on you. If my efforts in Ashbury bear fruit, I will return with the Duke's representative in two weeks."

Many times I had risked my life in battle, but now I was betting my whole future on one throw of the dice. The laughter came from deep within my chest—such an audacious gamble. The stuff the bards would sing about for years to come. I struck my fist across my heart, pledging to wager all to win all.

To prepare me to carry out his orders, King Bellabond had informed me of recent happenings in Ashbury. Baron Frost had been named Duke upon the death of Duke Aramis in a battle with barbarians. Bellabond warned me to keep my mind alert when standing close to the Duke. Frost was a biata, a race known for mental skills.

My journey to Ashbury had been uneventful. For all his faults, LeForge captained the *Revenge* with masterful sailing skills.

My feet had no sooner left the gangplank than a scar-faced, muscular man blocked my path and demanded my name and purpose. I had been instructed to present my ambassadorial credentials to Arrack of Hillcroft, one of the Duke's advisors, a man reported to be more comfortable in his prior role as a knight than in his current position as a diplomat. This stern man standing in front of me had to be Arrack.

"I am Arrack," he said. "Give me your identification." The richness of his cloak contrasted with the plainness of his breastplate armor and the roughness of his demeanor.

I handed him my official document, accompanied by a serious, authoritarian smile. Arrack glanced at my credentials, paying close attention only to King Bellabond's signature and seal.

"Follow me," Arrack said. "You will spend the night as Duke Frost's guest." He turned on his heels and thrust his arm forward like an officer ordering a charge of mounted knights. "You have a private meeting with the duke, tomorrow, mid-morning."

I had better be careful around Arrack. The battle-scarred knight would take grim delight in spoiling my plan.

The rising sun made an early intrusion through the window of my room. My sleep had been a restless one. I could not still a parade of dire thoughts. What if Duke Frost laughed at my proposal? Or held me for ransom? Bellabond would not spend a single copper coin to gain my release.

With cupped hands, I splashed cold water from the basin over my face, washing away all such negative thoughts. My fingers combed my unruly locks into a semblance of order.

I dressed in my finest uniform, buffed the buttons bright, and cinched my belt tight. My fur-trimmed cloak fit snug around my shoulders. The polish on my leather boots could not be finer. I studied myself in the looking glass.

"I am as handsome and elegant as I can be."

Observing court protocol, I left my sword scabbard empty as a symbol that I posed no threat to the Duke's safety. For the third time, I opened the pouch strapped around my waist to make certain the king's proposed mutual defense document was secure. Four sharp raps on the chamber door summoned me for my audience with Duke Frost.

I expected the bottom-numbing wait on the hard bench outside the Duke's private meeting room—the usual treatment for a foreign visitor. A ploy to show who held the superior position. I used the time to rehearse my speech, rearranging and rephrasing my words.

The chamber door opened and a moon-shaped face appeared. A plumpish hand wiggled a beckoning finger at me. The gaudily dressed courtier ushered me into the room, then left and closed the door behind him.

I looked into the penetrating brown eyes of Frost, the Duke of Ashbury. The sight of his large, upturned red-feathered eyebrows unsettled me. I had never stood this close to a biata. A scowl rather than a smile was his greeting. The intensity of his scrutiny carried across the room. I must discipline my mind.

The baldheaded Duke stood tall behind a thick oaken table. While King Bellabond's desk always held jumbles of papers, scrolls, and documents piled high in stacks, the Duke's table was devoid of any item, as if the man wanted to focus on one and only one thing at a time.

I looked for a chair, only to discover there were none. I surmised the Duke kept visitors standing to send a message that he was a busy man, with no time for pleasantries. Forget the diplomatic speech. I would state my proposition in precise words. Press him for an immediate answer.

"Sire, I will not waste your time." Speaking rapidly, I rushed through the formalities. "King Bellabond sends his greeting, wishes you good health, prosperity, and death to your enemies. I am here to present a treaty for your signature. My king has already affixed his name and seal."

To give the appearance of confidence, I set my feet apart, folded my arms in front of my chest and dared the Duke to respond with equal directness. "Your first response should be to ask me why you should care about King Bellabond's problems."

Frost, who had been leaning forward, fists clenched, with his knuckles pressed against the tabletop in an aggressive stance, now pulled back a bit.

"Sarlon, your reputation as a warrior and man of action is well-founded for so young a man." A sharp edge overlaid his words. The Duke pointed to the table. "Come forward and lay your proposal before of me."

My fingers undid the flap on the pouch and fetched the proposed alliance agreement from within. I stepped boldly forward, unfolded the vellum and laid it on the Duke's desktop.

"Speak. I shall determine if you are as smart as your words," the Duke said, "or an impertinent pup."

"I would ask, if I were you, 'What is in it for me?'"

Frost nodded, feathered eyebrows moving with the motion. I forced my gaze away. I must act like a man of experience. I deepened my voice as best I could to sound more noble, and spaced my words to make my sentences more authoritative.

"Speaking officially as the Duke of Umpelen and Ambassador appointed by Bellabond, King of Otherside," I said, "I present my harbor village of Oldport, the surrounding lands, and all trading rights to you in exchange for your signature on the proposed mutual defense alliance. Before you decide to accept my generous offer, I recommend that you send a commissioner to verify the worth of my gift. You might also want to consult someone in your duchy who knows the story of Otherside's battles known as the Ten Years War. The important role of Oldport is well documented."

My claim about the value of Oldport had been true at that precise time in history. But what if the Duke talked to LeForge, or some traveler recently arriving from Oldport? He would be angry at my failure to mention the port's current rundown status. No sane person chanced a biata's anger. My scalp begin to prickle with perspiration.

Frost studied me in silence. He turned his face toward a heavy red drapery that covered the center of one wall.

"Come forth, Lord Alan."

The curtain moved. A walking stick poked beyond one edge of the fabric, then pushed it aside. A man stepped out. Had he been listening the whole time? Was this the renowned Lord Alan, Master of Numbers, in whose name accounts are judged correct and accurate throughout the kingdom of Icenia?

Lord Alan was true to the stories of his image. A mousy man with squinty eyes, dressed in a long black coat that covered his knees. His shoulder-length hair, dark with stands of gray, was neatly parted in the middle. A reading stone, held by a braided loop attached to a wooden handle, dangled from his belt. Its round convex glass was said to magnify anything held beneath it, exposing the smallest detail to scrutiny. Alan was famous for poring over account books, searching for clerical errors no matter how trivial. He crossed the room towards me, walking with a disjointed hitch in his gait.

Lord Alan's walking stick was like no other I had ever seen. The wooden staff was carved from bottom to top with figures of acrobats standing one upon the others' shoulders. The very top figure, with hands extended above his head, held a large bronze ball. The end of the carved walking stick was protected by an iron base that thudded against the stone flooring to announce the owner's arrival. Alan capped his hand over the bronze ball as he walked towards me. He stopped in front of me, held the reading stone in front of one eye, and examined my face.

"I shall see what you really offer in exchange for the Duke's signature."

"Sarlon, Ambassador from Otherside, meet my commissioner. Lord Alan is my Seneschal. In addition to running my castle, he makes certain every iota of taxes due me is collected and recorded." The Duke suppressed a faint smile. "He accompanies you to Oldport. No one sneaks anything past my Lord Alan. Upon his word alone will I sign King Bellabond's alliance."

Sails billowed as the steady wind drove the *Revenge* through the choppy sea toward Oldport. The commissioner's stomach had protested the entire journey. The Duke's representative had seen more of the ship's head than the cloud-laced blue sky. On the second day of our voyage, I decided to visit Lord Alan in his quarters to offer him some winebark tea to settle his queasy guts—and perhaps gain favor with him for my caring gesture.

My fist was raised, ready to knock on Lord Alan's cabin door, when I heard muffled conversation within. Two voices, one gruff, the other more refined. Much to my frustration, I could not make out what they were saying—only a scattered word or two: ..."pay me"... "discover the truth"...

A chair scraped against wood planking. I retreated down the narrow hallway and hid in the dim corridor. I had no sooner positioned myself in the darkness than I heard the cabin door squeak open. LeForge stepped out, with his jaw firmly set, and climbed the steps to the upper deck.

LeForge knew full well the sad condition of Oldport. He had made several cutting remarks about the town and the pier when I boarded the *Revenge* to start my journey to Ashbury. We had negotiated a deal that would position his fleet around Oldport to give the impression of a busy port. Had he sold me out? I must keep a keen eye on LeForge.

I stood on the deck and watched Captain LeForge bark orders to his crew to reposition the sails, adjust ropes, and correct steering. The *Revenge* responded like a trained war stallion to a rider's commands. The Captain, once satisfied with the ship's course, caught hold of my sleeve and pulled me aside.

"We will make Oldport harbor tomorrow, around midday," LeForge said. He lowered his voice and turned his back to the crew lest they overhear our conversation.

"My fleet of ships should have arrived today, as we agreed. They wait for our arrival to carry out your pretense. Four ships will tie up at the pier, three others will be stationed outside the harbor entrance."

"I trust they will have lowered their pirate flags and stored their weapons," I said. "Remember, your fleet poses as peaceful merchants."

"It will be difficult for them to behave, but in truth, we need provisioning before launching our raids along the Gonderland coast. This way, we will skirt the Vaccaran Islands to avoid tangling with the

Vaccaran Corsairs." LeForge tilted his hat to a rakish angle. "Besides, I am a peaceful merchant—when I want to be, as long as my ventures reap fat profits."

I stepped close to LeForge and pulled my sword far enough from its scabbard to show its blade. If it came to a fight, even if I bested him, his crew would cut me down. I had no place to escape. But I am a warrior.

"Any man that betrays me does not live," I said.

"Put your heart to rest, Sarlon." LeForge put his hand over mine and pushed my sword back into its scabbard. "You are a most fortunate young man. I have provided Lord Alan with secret maps of the dangerous shoals and the shipping lanes used by Gonderland's traders. He has already paid me well. I do not need to expose your ruse." LeForge leaned forward and added with a twisted grin. "Besides, the boldness of your plan to fool the arrogant Duke appeals to my rebel spirit."

Le Forge was a rogue, but for now he was my rogue.

The *Revenge* entered Oldport harbor, gliding on the currents paralleling the jetty. Anxious for my first view, I leaned far over the railing. A soft breath of relief escaped my mouth. Mumplepeg's stonemasons had replaced the breakwater's fallen stones.

"Duke Sarlon," a voice behind me said, "even with my weak eyes I can see the pier that marks the end of our journey." One hand shading his eyes from the sun's overhead rays, Lord Alan steadied himself against the ship's railing. "My, what a small but busy port. I count seven ships about."

The crew secured the ship against the dock, lowered the gangplank and stood at attention as Lord Alan and I disembarked. Walter of Umpelen, wearing a blue coat with a red sash, greeted the Duke of Ashbury's commissioner with a deep bow.

"I am Walter of Umpelen, harbormaster," he said. "Please be so kind as to follow me." He raised a cautioning palm as he back-stepped in front of Alan. "Walk straight down the middle so you don't trip over any stray merchandise lying on the pier." The harbormaster stepped aside and waved the commissioner past him before leaning close to me to whisper, "We only replaced the center planks. Step to either side and you might fall through."

I had taken half a dozen steps before I stopped short. Something new had been added where the pier ended and the cobblestone street began. A tall stone archway had been erected. Chiseled into the keystone was the greeting: WELCOME TO OLDPORT. GATEWAY TO LOWER OTHERSIDE. Mumblepeg had outdone himself.

Walter strutted about pretending to fulfill his duties as harbormaster. He ordered three workers, all wearing the same bright blue coats, to stack crates. Another two dock-men, dressed in the same colors, rolled barrels along the shore. The ease with which they accomplished their tasks caused me to suspect the containers held nothing but air.

"It is an Oldport tradition to offer first-time visitors a free tankard of ale," Walter said to Lord Alan. "Our Inn is small but quaint. And the beer is the finest for miles around." Walter kept a serious face, but winked at me behind the commissioner's back.

All the homes along the street had been freshly whitewashed. Doorframes and shutters were painted bright yellow. The village women all wore the same red aprons, the men blue coats. The scene was a riot of vivid colors.

Several brazen women called out to Lord Alan, making suggestive remarks and offering the favor of their company. The commissioner blushed and quickened his steps, hastening toward Walter. I slowed my pace and fell behind. One woman approached me with a wicked grin and linked her arm around mine.

"Mumblepeg said we should hassle the Ashbury man to hurry him along, so he could not examine our houses too closely. So, my handsome young man, how did we do?"

"Lovely, my dear." I patted her hand before disengaging my arm. "You almost fooled me. As much as I am tempted to dally, I must keep Walter from misspeaking to our foreign visitor."

I jogged ahead and caught up with Walter and Alan as they entered the New Oldport Tavern. Lord Alan mopped his brow with his linen handkerchief. Walter shoved a chair under the back of the commissioner's legs, forcing him to sit. Then the harbormaster and I took our seats. The dowdy little tavern now sparkled. The waist-high bar was solidly built and richly carved. A beer barrel rested on an "X" frame.

An alluring serving wench delivered three large ale tankards. The dark-golden brew gave off an enticing aroma. Alan squinted his eyes as he lifted his tankard. He focused on the server's tight bodice.

"Thank you, my dear," Lord Alan said. "Everything I see here in Oldport is lovely." He took a sip of beer and set the tankard aside.

"However, I am here to inspect, not enjoy. I must certify the suitability of Oldport for shipping and trade." He slid one hand inside his coat and extracted a slip of paper. After placing it on the table, the commissioner removed the reading stone from his belt, held it over the paper and read out loud.

"My list of items verified: merchant ships in harbor, dock workers, merchandise stacked ready for shipment, friendly villagers." Lord Alan added a sheepish aside. "I might say, some too friendly." He punctuated each item with a tap of his finger on the list. "My remaining task is to inspect the storage and warehouse facilities. Very important."

"High time we move along." I motioned for Walter and Alan to join me. The three of us gathered outside the New Oldport Inn.

"Harbormaster," Lord Alan said, "lead me to the warehouse."

"Certainly, follow me," Walter said. "I will introduce you to the Warehouse Master. I should warn you that all the workers are spotted dwarves. They are the only ones willing to haul heavy loads and work long hours in the stifling heat."

"Spotted dwarves? Dangerous troublemakers, each and every one." Lord Alan pulled the collar of his coat around his neck. "I never associate with them. They are, well, well… *different*. You do know, they sweat a lot and are easily agitated."

I held back my retort. You would sweat a lot too if you had to carry large building stones all day.

If there ever was a time for *me* to sweat, it was now. Mumblepeg had to keep the Duke's commissioner from entering the warehouse doors. Once inside, a glance at the holes in the roof and the sagging timbers would reveal our trick.

The cobblestone street ended at the warehouse. Alan took a tight grip on his walking stick as we approached the entrance. I was honor-bound as a knight to defend the Duke's representative. I hoped Mumblepeg could control his gang of hot-tempered spotted dwarves.

The front of the warehouse had been transformed. Large blocks of stone now covered the front of the building. White mortar gleamed between the cut blocks. Two pillars adorned the outer edges of the warehouse, giving it a touch of grandeur.

I recognized Mumblepeg standing at the bottom of the ramp leading to the entrance. He wore a rimmed-leather hat and had a vivid green-colored leather apron tied around his waist. Behind him, just inside the warehouse, a gang of spotted dwarves stacked boxes and rolled barrels to and fro. Their shouts, curses, and orders generated a cacophony of noises.

"Mumblepeg," Walter shouted, "I present Lord Alan, commissioner from Ashbury. He wants to inspect your warehouse."

The dwarf wiped his hand across his sweating brow then offered to shake hands with the reluctant commissioner. Alan put both hands behind his back and responded with a terse, thin-lipped grimace.

"I would be happy to show you around," Mumblepeg yelled in a loud voice, a spray of spittle accompanying his words. "I must warn you to stay close. Lots of accidents and injuries lately. Even worse, the workers are demanding more food and coins for their labors. They are easily riled."

"Lord Alan, if trouble happens, I will try to defend you." I pulled a dagger from my belt and held it by my side. "Walter, best you remain here to summon help if need be."

Alan darted his eyes from side to side nervously at my warning.

Mumblepeg turned his back on the visitors and started up the ramp. As if on signal, two dwarves got into a shouting match and threw punches at each other. A third dwarf dropped a wooden crate, which crashed to the floor and broke apart. Rotten fruit, accompanied by a foul odor, rolled down the ramp towards Alan's feet. Another dwarf hopped about on one leg, holding his foot and screaming that he was bleeding.

Lord Alan turned and retreated down the cobblestone street. Walter and I hurried to join him. Looking neither right nor left, the commissioner made haste toward the dock. He focused on placing his feet carefully on the cobblestones so as not to trip. The sound of his walking stick striking the stones echoed down the street.

"We must catch up with Alan and discover his judgment on my gift of Oldport," I said to Walter. "The dwarves put on quite a show. Hurry, the commissioner is waiting for us by the gangplank."

Captain LeForge and Lord Alan stood at the end of the pier. The hubbub of activity around the ship had quieted. Most of the workers had gone home for the day. LeForge, his red hair fashioned into a ponytail, was listening to the animated words of the Ashbury commissioner. Alan, bent forward at the waist, was gesturing wildly.

"Ah, there you are, Sarlon," LeForge said. "The commissioner has been telling me all about his experiences here in Oldport. He is not feeling well. He has decided he will dine alone tonight and seek the comfort of his cabin."

Lord Alan rested a hand on top of his walking stick, fiddling his fingers over the bronze ball. He dismissed Walter with a perfunctory thank you. The harbormaster made a hasty retreat.

"Duke Sarlon of Umpelen, today has been a most unique experience," Alan said. "I feel I have done my duty to the Duke. I am anxious to return home. Travel is a tiring adventure I would gladly leave to younger people."

"Is there anything more I can do to help you make your report?" I kept a tight rein on my emotions. I dared not grovel or appear anxious. LeForge stood by and said nothing. It was not his problem.

Alan rested his walking stick on my shoulder. The Duke's commissioner twitched his nose as he studied my face.

"It will not do," Lord Alan said. "While there is much to recommend about Oldport, the incident at the warehouse persuades me to reject the alliance. Troublesome dwarves would provoke Duke Frost."

I started to object, but Alan motioned me to be silent. My wonderful plan had fallen apart. Mumblepeg's antics had worked all too well. My stomach felt as if someone had rammed a fist into it.

"Young Sarlon, you are not experienced in matters of diplomacy," Lord Alan said. "Here is some advice. A wise man will consider not only the current facts, but will look ahead to see the consequences of his acts."

I had failed. The king would banish me from Otherside. I might have gained wisdom, but I had lost my home—a sorry trade.

"Suppose I approved your offer to exchange Oldport for the mutual defense agreement, and then trouble broke out with the dwarves?" Alan said. "Duke Frost would take it as a personal insult. He would send Arrack to quell the dwarves with force. Perhaps hang Mumblepeg or throw him into prison. Such stern action on Otherside territory could lead to war between your King Bellabond and my Duke. I cannot risk such troubles."

"Speaking of trouble," LeForge said, "here it comes in the person of a spotted dwarf."

Hand upon my shoulder, LeForge turned me around. Mumblepeg limped towards the three of us on the dock. In his hands he held his rimmed hat. The green apron he wore was streaked with red blotches. Blood?

Walter, hurrying along the street behind Mumblepeg, soon caught up with him. Mouth turned down and forehead wrinkled, the harbormaster's face was most unhappy. The two of them faced Alan, LeForge and me.

"Now you have done it." Mumblepeg threw his hat on the ground at Lord Alan's feet. "All your fault, Alan. Your contempt of spotted dwarves riled my workers beyond repair. You ran away from a little, everyday bickering." Mumblepeg stomped off the pier and up the cobblestone street yelling and gesturing at bystanders.

"All the warehouse dwarves have quit," Walter said. He took the end of his red sash and blew his nose with it. "Now we will have to replace them with new workers at higher wages. Once the agreement with Ashbury is signed, I will send word out for new workers. Should be no problem since Oldport is such a lovely village."

I bit my lip. Mumblepeg's rant was a bluff. All the spotted dwarves were his fellow stonemasons. Their jobs were finished in any case.

"Well, Lord Alan, that removes your reason for rejection," I said. "You advised me to look ahead. Will you be responsible for Duke Frost losing a prosperous port and the opportunity to expand his duchy in a peaceful way?"

Gulls cried as they circled, accenting the murmur of the waves washing the shore. Alan pulled his coat tight around his body like a child with a favorite blanket. Wisps of his long hair fluttered in the breeze.

"I know what I have seen. I checked every item on my list," Alan said. "Yet, there remains a nagging suspicion that I have overlooked something." He tapped his forehead.

I swallowed and tried not to look nervous.

"But, the agreement does provide Ashbury with a foreign trading port. Duke Frost has given me final authority to decide on the Alliance." He pulled a scrolled document from his black coat and rested it against his chin. He cleared his throat, and handed the scroll to me.

"I present you with the official agreement. Duke Frost of Ashbury's signature is on the document. The seals have been affixed."

The commissioner turned to Captain LeForge. "Take me home. I have had enough of Otherside and its rather strange people."

The reins sagged in my hand. My horse plodded along with steps as lazy as the warm day. The scattering of early morning clouds had drifted away. Behind me, gentle hills hid Oldport from view. As the sounds of the surf faded, I distanced myself from Umpelen.

The Duke of Ashbury's signed agreement lay tucked inside my saddlebag, ready for me to present to King Bellabond. The bards would sing of my great triumph. But for a moment I regretted trading my duchy for the Otherside Alliance.

A whinny sounded from somewhere ahead. My horse returned the greeting. I pressed my feet hard in the stirrups and stood straight-legged for a better view. There, by the thick grove, Mumblepeg sat with his back against a smooth-barked tree. When last I had seen the spotted dwarf, he had been storming up Oldport's cobblestone street hurling curses at Lord Alan. I spurred my horse and galloped to greet Mumblepeg.

"King Bellabond will be pleased with the Otherside Alliance." I said. I grasped Mumblepeg's arm and helped the dwarf onto his horse's saddle.

"No, he won't," Mumblepeg said. "You solved one problem but created a bigger one. When Duke Frost discovers your trick, he will tear up the treaty." The dwarf twisted in his saddle. "And blame King Bellabond."

"When the king gave me Umpelen he gave me nothing," I said. "He sent me on a dangerous mission knowing there was scant chance of success. He cared not a fig if I was killed or failed."

I rode in silence for a distance, not wanting to burden Mumblepeg with the whole of my plan and how it had worked out.

"I see that there is a solution," Mumblepeg said, "but King Bellabond will not like it." The dwarf reined his horse to a stop and leaned toward me, jabbing a finger at me to show the certainty of his conclusion. "He must rebuild all of Oldport."

"Then the village will be as we had pretended to Frost," I said. "The King will rage over the building cost, but saving the Otherside Alliance is more important than any extra money spent."

"Bellabond will take back your title and kick you out of his kingdom." Mumblepeg made a sour face. "Or behead you."

"Well," I said with an uncomfortable grin, "the first two I can live with."

Chalric Hill
Henry "The Mad" Hart

Recruit Edmund Boyd, a soldier of fourteen years of age, had drawn the short straw.

Grumbling about his early morning watch duty, he stared as the scout on horseback galloped up to the encampment of the Alpha Company, Western Regiment, Icenian Royal Army in the pre-dawn gloom. A cool fog had slowly settled over the valley and as the moon had long ago slipped beneath the horizon, the only light was from Boyd's lantern.

The rider drew his horse to a halt and slid from the saddle with a practiced ease. He strode purposefully towards Boyd's lantern with palms outstretched. Boyd could see he was armed but had left his shield attached to his saddle.

"Who goes?" Boyd called out, as he nervously grasped his spear.

The rider identified himself as a scout for the Western Regiment and in addition wore the red belt of a squire, marking him "Knight in Training" and one of the King's men. "I have a message of great importance to deliver to the commanding officer of this Company."

Boyd led the man to the large tent of the Company Commander, then timidly called out. "Hello? Anyone awake?"

The scout looked at Boyd. Boyd felt as if he was being sized up and then judged to be inadequate. "I know Dame Catherine," he said. "I will awaken her. Come inside or stand guard if you will, but I can bear no delays." With that, the Scout slipped into the tent.

Boyd stood sullenly outside. He had never really wanted to join the Army, never really had much ambition to anything that most considered "great," and yet he had always felt diminished and ashamed when his superiors snubbed him. He felt like a child who got a pat on the head for not spilling his food.

From inside the tent, he overheard tense, concerned whispers and low voices—only fragments of a conversation, but enough that he was able to put together something big was going on.

"The Galanthians... and that's certain?" It sounded to Boyd as if Dame Catherine was truly worried, not something he was used to hearing coming from the confident pillar of decisiveness. "And King Thrombolis wishes for us to expose ourselves to see if it provokes them?"

"His Majesty was clear. He does not wish to start a war, and we are not to strike first, but if the Galanthians are in this territory to cause mischief, he must know their intentions."

The voices quieted down, and Boyd leaned in to try to overhear more, causing the scout to nearly collide with him on his way out of the tent. He looked at Boyd—really looked him over this time—and placed his hand on Boyd's shoulder. Boyd saw that the man was pained; in his deep brown eyes he bore the look of one who was deeply mournful for just a moment, and then seemed to get control of his emotions by force of will. "What is your name, son?"

"Recruit Edmund Boyd, sir."

"From where do you hail?"

"Descante, sir."

"My family has lands near there." He took a deep breath and nodded to himself. "Boyd. I'm sure your family is proud of you." The scout turned away quickly and returned to his horse.

Dame Catherine stepped out of her tent, not quite fully dressed. Her chestnut face was serious and bore no trace of the sleep she had been pulled from. Boyd dropped to one knee immediately, the customary show of respect to a knight of the land.

"Rise," she commanded. "Boyd, isn't it? Call for reveille. We are bugging out. Now."

By his reckoning, this was the seventeenth latrine Boyd had dug since he had joined the Icenian Royal army the day after his birthday last spring. He had helped set up and broken down eight camps for Alpha Company. He had marched ninety-four miles. When he had begun digging this afternoon, his legs were tired from the march. His arms had still been heavy from the fighting practice the day prior with his Sergeant, a daily training session mandated for all of the younger soldiers by Dame Catherine.

After a hasty packing, the Company had marched six hours through wooded and hilly terrain and arrived at Chalric Hill. There had been a peculiar urgency amongst the troops. No one understood exactly why, but they had all known that the situation was serious. There had been no songs, no banter.

There were those among his comrades who had been in the service for years who spoke at length about the glory of victory and the pride they felt in defending their kingdom. There were also recruits like Boyd who were seen as too young for combat, and thus did most of the rest of the work needed to keep an army camp maintained. He was among a handful of youths who sharpened weapons, cooked meals, cleaned laundry, fed horses, and yes, dug latrines. His youthful compatriots bemoaned their fate and longed for their first engagement. They dreamed of honor and valor. Some had even snuck off to fight against the goblins in the last skirmish.

Personally, Boyd had fought in zero battles, and this suited him fine.

A year ago, a Royal Decree had been issued. "Those of disciplined minds, able bodies, and the desire to serve the Kingdom" were called upon to join the Icenian Army. Boyd's father had wanted to answer the call himself, but an old injury had limited his mobility. Though he could putter around the farm well enough, long journeys were physically impossible for him, and he was forced to sleep in a specially built bed lest he awaken in near-paralytic pain. His father had felt greatly shamed because his older brother, Edmund's uncle and namesake, had served and died in the Army many years before Edmund was born.

Boyd's father was a very patriotic man and talked frequently about how, when he was a boy, every family was expected to offer one member to serve in the military. Boyd had been disappointed that his older brother had gone in his place. The day the Decree reached their farmstead, he had worked himself up into a near frenzy. Boyd was afraid that his father was going to join up even with his injury, and that he would be left to tend the farm alone while even his friends would go off to join. So Boyd offered to go in his place.

He was worried that his father would have trouble running things without him, but the recruiter said that soldiers his age could return at harvest time.

Boyd recalled how proud his father had been of him while he dug a pit in the mud that would serve to catch excrement. At the time, Boyd thought he would get to be with his friends from town and that he would be stationed near Descantes, deep in the heart of the kingdom. Instead, he had been almost immediately transferred to fill in this company, a hundred miles from home, on the western border of Icenia.

"Recruit!" shouted Boyd's sergeant, which startled Boyd out of his daydream.

"Sir!" Boyd responded as he snapped to attention. Boyd prepared to be chewed out for slacking off.

"C.O. is giving us a mission briefing," the sergeant said, and then dropped her customary barking shout. "Best that you muster outside of the command tent, Boyd."

"Do you know what's going on?"

The sergeant paused and looked forlornly at Boyd. "I do, yes. Dame Catherine will explain it all."

Boyd trotted up to the command tent and stood as the rest of Alpha Company filed in from their various duties around the new camp. He wondered why his sergeant, who to Boyd's recollection had never spoken to him in anything other than a shout whether she had been teaching him to fight, to march, or to correct him for his numerous mistakes, had suddenly been almost nice to him. And that squire… he had looked so sad.

"What do you suppose this is about?" Boyd asked the soldier next to him.

"Don't know. Something serious, though. Officers have been in that tent for the past hour."

"Do you think we're going into battle?"

"Could be. Doubt they'll let you come along, though. Whatever it is, it's going to be much more serious than a goblin skirmish. They usually don't let people fight until they're sixteen."

"Why is that?"

The soldier glanced sideways at Boyd. "Pick your reason. Unreliable when faced with death, not strong enough or skilled enough or mentally able to kill an enemy, haven't seen enough of the world to risk being taken out of it…" The man's gaze fell away. "Too young," he whispered wistfully.

"Dame Catherine Deenan!" shouted the sergeant.

The Company knelt in unison. Dame Catherine stepped out into the warm autumn afternoon sun.

"You may rise," Dame Catherine responded. "We have received word that a full Regiment of Galanthian soldiers has entered this territory."

The soldiers murmured to each other, and one veteran audibly gasped.

"Quiet down!" The sergeant commanded immediate silence.

Dame Catherine continued. "Their intentions are unclear, but their presence here is in violation of the non-aggression accord that has been in place for the past decade. It is believed that the new Emperor, Glantri, is probing Icenian responses. He is testing Icenian courage. And if he thinks that we will not rise to this threat with measured diplomacy, followed by the full might of the Icenian Royal Army, then he is questioning our honor!"

Alpha Company roared.

"Our spies tell us that Glantri was made Emperor via their ancient art of prophecy. He has since replaced many of the senators and leaders in the government with superstitious so-called prophets. The people of Galanthia are judged by prophecy. That means that they do not choose their paths in life. If they should establish control of this area, then they would judge our people. They would take away our freedom to choose!"

Again, the Company expressed its unified displeasure.

"Would you let them?"

"No!"

"Will you stand idly by while they take our freedoms?"

"*No!*"

"Within the next two days, the Galanthians will be within striking distance of this hill. There is no way that they can miss our campfires, especially because we'll be making three times the usual amount. They may peacefully approach and bring us information about a threat in the area that they are responding to. They may attack with no formal declaration of war. Either way, we expect them to arrive tomorrow. And we must be ready for either."

Dame Catherine nodded at the sergeant, who then said, "Everyone get some chow and get some shut eye. The officers will be keeping watch."

The mess tent was always the largest structure in the camp. Boyd numbly entered the familiar dining pavilion and smelled stew. Usually, the Company only got stew once a month. He also spotted a table with cakes, and the officers were passing out ale as well. There was little chatter.

Boyd walked past a table of veterans who spoke in hushed tones as he approached the chow line. He lingered near enough and eavesdropped.

"Do you think this is the start of another war?"

"Dunno."

"The last one was bloody and went on for years."

"Ayup."

"Well, we'll stop 'em here. None of them fools are getting past us!"

"Nope."

"Meal like this, you know that they don't expect many of us to make it through…" The man looked around the mess tent, and Boyd quickly feigned interest in a different part of the tent to hide his attentiveness.

"Ayup."

"If we don't make it, I sure do hope my daughter and her wife can manage the mill. They know what they are doing, but harvest is coming up and that's a really busy time."

"Hope so."

"Well, you're just a scintillating conversationalist, aren't you?"

The second man chucked into his cup and smiled warmly at his friend. Boyd slipped out of the tent.

All Boyd had heard was that he was going to die and that his father would need to manage the farm on his own. He panicked. It took every measure of his control not to sprint across the camp to his bedding area. Once there, he grabbed his rucksack and frantically jammed his bedding and clothing into it.

Boyd muttered to himself. "Gotta get home. There's a town a couple days from here. I can trade for some provisions, maybe borrow a horse. I gotta get home. Father and I can defend the farmstead together if the Galanthians make it that far."

He threw his bag over his shoulder and nearly ran out of the tent. He crashed headlong into Dame Catherine Deenan and fell to the ground.

The knight barely flinched and stood stoically with her arms folded across her chest. "The penalty for abandoning your post is a court martial with a dishonorable discharge, prison, and in some cases execution. So where are you going in such a hurry, Recruit Boyd?"

Boyd stammered as he clambered to his feet. His mind raced to come up with some plausible lie as Dame Catherine watched him placidly, her eyebrow arched.

"Go back into your tent, Boyd."

Boyd's shoulders dropped and he slouched back into the tent. Dame Catherine followed.

"Sit down."

"Dame Catherine, er, my Lady, I was just going to move to a different tent and…"

"Quiet please. I cannot bear being lied to."

"I wasn't lying, I—"

"Be quiet." She spoke with a certain timbre in her voice that demanded compliance. "Sit."

Boyd sat sullenly and stared at the floor of the tent. His heart hammered away at the inside of his chest. Dame Catherine stood over him like a tower of strength and authority.

"Icenia is a free kingdom. You chose to join the army, just as your father chose to be a farmer. Just as I chose to follow the path of chivalry and become a knight. Our fates are our own." She paused. "Boyd, I get it. I'm afraid, too."

"No, no, Dame Catherine! I mean, I *am* afraid, but it's not that. It's just, my father… he has an old injury. He can't get around as well as he used to, so he needs help on the farm. He almost joined up himself. He's so brave. If I don't go to him, I think he'll do something foolish and fight the Galanthians. Then he'll die and it will be my fault. Together he and I can defend the farm! But now I'm stuck here! I've never felt so un-free in my life!" Boyd said this all in one breath. He clamped his jaw down hard and fought back his tears.

"You signed up for a term of service. You pledged, on your honor, that you would perform the duties of a soldier for the length of your enlistment term. You've learned to fight, and we've fed and housed you, and taught you, because you agreed to fight for Icenia. If you didn't want to join we would have kept searching for another, and that person would have had the benefits—and the risks—of being in the Royal Icenian Army. Were you pressured to join?"

Boyd considered lying but there was earnestness in the Knight's eyes which compelled him. He whispered, "No, Dame Catherine. I chose this."

"Oh, Boyd." Dame Catherine's demeanor softened and she exhaled slowly. She sat down next to him on the cot. "Suppose for a moment I release you from service. I have the authority to write you a missive excusing you. Do I do the same for everyone who wants to leave? Most of the soldiers have families to go home to, that need them, and would miss them if they were gone. Those who remain—how would they fare against the Galanthians here on this hill? If we do not stand against them, won't they roll right into the heart of Icenia?

"You and your father, and these soldiers and their families, may fight well. You may even battle a goblin or two that attack your farm. But as individual family units how would you fare against an organized invasion force bent on total dominance? It is through unity that we stand against evil.

"Glantri's prophets would use the 'power of prophecy' to decipher the fate of Icenia's citizens. Do you really think that they would value our people as anything other than slaves to their ideals? According to our Ambassador from Lempur, this is exactly what they are doing to conquered lands. I don't have to experience it for myself to believe our allies. 'Coincidentally,' any who oppose the rule of the Galanthians are 'judged' to be the lowest caste in their society. Those who welcome their regard for prophecy are 'fated to higher purpose.'

"Make no mistake, the Galanthians seek to control the lives of us all and will use their superstitious beliefs to justify it."

Boyd stared at the floor as tears welled up in his eyes.

"Boyd," she continued, "this place, Chalric Hill, is named for an Icenian King who gave his life for his people. That may be my destiny as well and if so, I gladly stand against evil in defense of the innocent. If I must die, I shall choose the hill on which to do so."

The warm tears began to roll down Boyd's cheeks and Dame Catherine put her arm around his shoulders.

"You are young. There will be many other fights, many other hills. Take this writ and go. Stop at the provisioning tent and take a few days' worth of supplies. Live and make your own fate." Dame Catherine stood, handed him a folded piece of paper, and then left him alone in the tent.

Boyd opened the writ. He saw that the ink was not wet. She must have written the letter hours ago. By her hand, Dame Catherine had released him with full honors.

Boyd was not challenged by any of the officers as he packed food. With only a few of the officers milling about, the camp seemed deserted. Much of the company was either at dinner or trying to catch a few hours of sleep before the expected activity of the evening. Boyd wondered how they could sleep with a threat looming. He imagined most of the soldiers tossed and turned.

Boyd thought for a long moment about leaving his sword behind in case it was needed. He decided to keep it. After all, he thought, no one could use two long swords at once, and a brigand would think twice about attacking an armed individual. He left the camp, again unchallenged, and walked into the disappearing sunlight.

The autumn evening was warm, but Boyd felt cold inside. His pack seemed heavier even though it bore less gear than it had just that morning. He had never fully enjoyed marching with the group, with their cadence and the sounds of a hundred stomping feet. The sounds of nature were much more welcome. He was too distracted by his own terrible feelings of inadequacy to bother about being afraid or feeling alone.

Boyd had initially felt sure that he remembered the way back towards the last village Alpha Company had come by, but as each step fell, he became less sure.

The minutes turned into an hour.

He started to feel lost.

Up ahead, he saw a crossroads he felt sure that he would have recognized had he passed it before. A huge old oak tree sat at the corner with a dark eye-shaped hollow near the roots large enough that a full-grown person could easily stand inside. The weather-beaten signpost was illegible in the gloom of the overcast and moonless night; nevertheless, Boyd peered intently at it as he tried to make out the letters.

The slightest whisper of a footfall was all the warning Boyd received—fortunately, it was enough. He spun on the spot and drew his sword in one deft movement just as a shadowy figure lunged at him. Their blades clashed in the darkness and Boyd staggered back.

Again, the dark-clothed assailant's blade slashed out and again Boyd's constant training bore his blade up to deflect the attack.

The combatants broke apart and circled each other.

"Who are you?" Boyd cried out.

"I am your fate, Icenian. And I *will* kill you."

The attacker lunged again and Boyd deflected the thrust, but the blade nicked his sword arm. Boyd's blade followed the momentum of his attacker's blade, and he spun around and slashed out at his foe's head. His attacker was too swift, however, and sprang back from the attack unwounded.

"You have some skill with a blade, Icenian, but it is all for naught." Boyd's assailant hissed and drew a dagger. "His Radiance's High Prophets have foreseen our victory."

Boyd adjusted his stance to better deal with the Galanthian's Florentine. The shock had worn off and he was worried. This scout could block and attack simultaneously and Boyd didn't know if he could deal with both. He calmed down enough to wonder if he would survive. "So, the Galanthians mean to invade us then. Don't you care about the years of peace your people are throwing away?"

"Only those on the losing side seek peace!" The Galanthian attacked and the two figures exchanged swings. Steel clashed on steel in the darkness on the dusty road.

Time seemed to slow for Boyd. He saw the swings coming from his opponent's long sword and swatted them aside with relative ease. The dagger Boyd found to be the main challenge. It was faster, for one, and the Galanthian varied the angle of attack. Sometimes the blade slashed, sometimes it stabbed. Boyd found that the only way he could defend was to twist out of the way and step back, but he was running out of road and he knew it. He tried to circle around but the Galanthian cut the angle and closed the distance.

The dagger bit into Boyd's leg. White hot pain, like nothing Boyd had ever felt before, shot like lightning through his body.

Boyd dropped all pretense of defense and shouted in rage, "No! You won't kill me!"

He lashed out again and again with his long sword. The first blow knocked the Galanthian's long sword outwards, the second came crashing down on the Galanthian's sword wrist, knocking the blade to the ground. The third, an overhead strike, was one the Galanthian managed to block just barely with the dagger. Boyd's final strike shattered the defender's dagger and buried the long sword blade through the Galanthian's collar bone and into his enemy's chest.

They both fell to the ground and gasped for air. The labored breathing of the Galanthian become wet-sounding, like porridge slowly boiling. He crawled over to his assailant.

"Come to finish me off?" The Galanthian coughed but could not draw enough breath to clear the mucus and blood pooling at the back of the throat. "It matters little. His Radiance's forces will be here soon. They will make a swift end of you and your comrades at your encampment."

Boyd tried to stem the Galanthian's bleeding and put pressure on the wound.

Confused, the Galanthian asked, "Do you intend on taking me prisoner? Your leg is injured. You can't carry me. And it doesn't matter. I won't talk." Even in the dim light Boyd could see how glassy the Galanthian's eyes had become.

"No, I'm just trying... just trying to save your life."

"Why?"

"Why save your life? Because I won but I still want peace. Because I believe in mercy. You don't?"

"It is not..." The Galanthian had a fit of weak coughing. "...for me to decide. I am... fate's instrument."

"You make your own choices on how you achieve your fate!"

"Fate... provides opportunities. I came here to kill, and if I cannot kill, then I came here to die."

"If I can stop your bleeding, perhaps your unit can pick you up."

"They... shall... be here... soon." There was a haggard breath between each word.

Boyd worked in silence as he desperately tried to stop the blood from flowing. After a few silent moments of effort, Boyd noticed that the blood flow had stopped.

"What's your name, Galanthian?"

There was no response. No movement, no indication that his query had been heard. Boyd listened for a few seconds and could no longer hear the Galanthian breathing.

"No... no. Please, don't... die. I am so sorry." Boyd, bathed in the blood of his foe, quietly cried.

In the darkness, he heard the distant sound of marching.

He knew that Alpha Company expected the Galanthians to arrive tomorrow, and Dame Catherine didn't know that their intentions were purely hostile.

"I have to go back," he mumbled to himself. "I have to warn them."

Boyd bound his leg wound as quickly as he could. He grasped around in the darkness and picked up the hilt of the Galanthian's broken dagger. A long moment passed as he looked at it in the gloom before he tucked it into his belt. He stood and winced as a shooting burst of pain radiated from his thigh. Though his leg bore his weight and all of his muscles still worked, Boyd knew his movement would be hampered. He dragged the Galanthian's corpse into the hollow of the giant tree near the crossroads. Inside, he saw a light backpack with provisions similar to his own. He dropped his pack into the hollow after he removed his blanket.

Using the blanket, Boyd swept the road where they had fought. It wasn't perfect, but in the dark it was hard to see that anything had transpired. He laid the long sword lengthwise over the Galanthian's body and covered the body with the blanket. With any luck, the approaching army wouldn't know that their scout had been slain.

The marching sounds were closer now, and in the far distance he could see torches.

Grabbing his own long sword, he headed back towards the encampment as swiftly as his injured leg would allow. Even his hobble was marginally faster than a column of troops, thus, in half an hour he had out-distanced the sound of the marching. Each step he took with his injured leg brought a burst of pain. It was odd, he thought—the pain didn't seem to diminish, and yet it freshened with each step. His foot squelched in his blood-soaked boot.

Boyd felt light headed. He was sweating profusely and was nauseated. He thought for a moment he could hear the soldiers marching behind him, until he realized it was his own pulse, ragged, light yet fast, rushing in his ears. He stumbled in the dark and fell. The ground felt cool and comfortable despite the stones sticking into his body.

He imagined the camp. He saw his fellow soldiers talking and laughing, trading stories by the fires of the camp. Shadowy figures leapt from the darkness fully surrounding the warriors. Caught unaware, they were all slaughtered. One of the figures was the Galanthian that he had killed, who looked right at Boyd and said, "This shall be your fate." Boyd saw the small village they had passed through days before, crushed under the might of the Galanthian forces. He saw his friends in chains before the High Prophet, having their fates handed out. They were all to be made slaves. His father was there, too. "I refuse your judgment! I refute your prophecy! I choose the manner of my living. Failing that, then I shall choose the manner of my dying!" His father stood up and raised his sword.

"Father!"

Boyd snapped out of his delusion. The stomping sound of marching feet sounded so close. How long had he been unconscious? He stumbled to his feet and nearly passed out again from the explosion of agony in his leg. He tightened the make-shift bandage.

"I will not die on this road!"

Boyd ran.

The campfires of Chalric Hill came into view. The pain in his leg had dulled and he could not feel his foot. A further few minutes of his stumbling jog and a familiar voice called out of the shadows as a lantern was uncovered, "Who goes?"

"Recruit Edmund Boyd! Ma'am, you must sound the alarm immediately! The Galanthian army is on their way right now and they mean to attack."

"Boyd? You're hurt. Let me help."

The soldier threw her shoulder under the pit of Boyd's arm and half-carried him into the command tent. "Dame Catherine! Boyd has returned with news!"

The tent was warm and well-lit by hanging lanterns. Many of the officers were present and gathered around a table with a map of the area. Some of them winced when they saw him, others became wide eyed. Boyd slowly attempted to kneel and was cut short by Dame Catherine.

"Given the circumstances, please do not kneel. Boyd, what happened to you?"

Boyd looked down at himself. He was covered in blood as if he had been swimming in it. As best as he could, Boyd explained he has been attacked by a scout and though he tried to render first aid, the scout died. He told them that he had seen and heard the army coming this way.

"And you have no reason to doubt what this Galanthian said?"

"No, my Lady. He spoke with a conviction as strong as your own."

Dame Catherine nodded and gave out orders to her officers, who began scrambling as soon as she spoke, "Go around to the tents. Don't sound the alarm but get everyone out of bed and ready to fight. Get a messenger and get them on horseback. Get them out of here and alert the regiment command."

She paused.

"Recruit Boyd. Good work. Go and get yourself a horse and get out of here."

"My Lady, is that an order?"

"Why?"

"Because if it isn't, I want to stay."

Dame Catherine looked Boyd over and said, "You can barely stand. Would you be of any use to us, or is this just some pointless last stand? Why the change of heart?"

"With all due respect, my Lady, I can use a long spear. I wouldn't have to move too much. I could stay in formation and lean on my comrades. My thigh isn't strong enough to manage to gallop on a horse and I might get caught on the road. Every moment we keep the Galanthians here is one more moment for our messenger to get the word to prepare Icenia for invasion.

"I may die on the road running, or I may die on this hill defending Icenia. Defending my family and countless other families." Boyd's eyes again filled with warm tears.

Dame Catherine nodded. "Or you might actually live." She smiled warmly. "Who knows? With an attitude like that, you might even become a knight. I know someone who thinks you'd make a pretty good squire."

Boyd beamed as his heart leaped in his chest.

"But first, let's get you cleaned up and properly dress those wounds."

Recruit Boyd stood in formation with his unit as he grasped his spear. Dame Catherine stood ahead of the line and faced down the wall of Galanthian troops. She had dressed in the formal Icenian Royal colors of blue, yellow, and white. Her white belt, a badge of office for her knighthood and a beacon of hope to her soldiers, gleamed in the light from the camp.

A figure emerged from behind the Galanthian line, flanked by two other soldiers. All were dressed in brilliant silver-and-blue tabards which shimmered in the torchlight.

"I am Colonel Pontius Throxis, Sword of Lore and commander of the Galanthian Third Regiment. I am the Voice of His Radiance, Glantri, Emperor of Galanthia. Our High Prophets and His Radiance himself have read the omens and have seen portends of what is to come. Icenia is destined by the Prophecy of Glantri to fall and shall vanish from

Fortannis. To resist fate is folly. Prevent the needless suffering of your people during this time and allow them to be judged by the fates peacefully. We are the instruments of Prophecy and we will guide you to your fate. You are commanded to surrender."

"I am Dame Catherine Deenan, Knight of the Realm and upholder of the Code of Chivalry. Servant to my people. None commands me but my liege, the good King Thrombolis, long may he reign! I am tasked with defending Icenia's freedom everywhere and always. You may use whatever justification you choose, be it your so-called prophecy or a simple desire to control our territory and enslave our people, but if you mean to persist you provoke war with Icenia. We will not back down. We will fight you until our dying breath. We choose our own destiny. Take your soldiers now and leave, or be prepared for battle!"

"As it is written in the Prophecy so shall it come to pass. Leave no survivors! Attack!"

The battle lasted throughout the night, all the next day, and into the next night. The Icenians dug in and held their own, but casualties were massive. The Galanthians had brought an entire regiment into the area. They outnumbered the Icenian defenders five to one, and had swiftly surrounded Chalric Hill. There had been little time to eat, and no time to sleep.

At times throughout the day, the Galanthians had shouted out offers to allow the Icenians to surrender, but Alpha Company's resolve had only grown deeper.

Boyd's unit was targeted multiple times and had lost a few good soldiers, but so far was holding. Dame Catherine had stayed near the unit. Boyd thought it might have been because of him, but he heard that she always stayed near the spear brigades. The unit was arranged so that shield wielders were positioned around the outside of the unit, then spear users, then the pikes. The knight was a "high value target" most of the time, so she easily could draw enemies into the waiting points of the pikes. This had happened a few times during the past day with devastating results. Boyd had seen more than his fair share of Galanthians struck down.

Midnight drew close and the battle quieted down. Dame Catherine addressed Boyd's unit again. "How are you holding up? Are you ready to quit?"

"No, Dame Catherine!" the unit roared back.

Her smile lingered, "Excellent. Any questions?"

One of the soldiers called out. "Once we beat these Galanthians, are we going to invade them?"

The unit cheered again.

"That depends on a number of factors, and the will of His Royal Majesty."

Another called out. "Well, we should! Get them to stop following that prophecy stuff and mind their own business!"

Again, the unit shouted its approval. One of the veteran soldiers, the same soldier who gave single word responses to his friend at dinner the other night it so happened, clasped the man on the shoulder and gave him a heartfelt, "Ayup!"

"Perhaps," Dame Catherine said. "In my view, if we try to force the Galanthians to give up their belief in their prophecy, then we become tyrants. They can believe whatever silly thing they want, just as long as they don't try to make us follow those beliefs." There were thoughtful nods to Dame Catherine's words.

"A person's life is their own, their beliefs are their own, and their choices are their own—right up until they start forcing others to follow them. This is the freedom that we are all fighting to defend."

There was a bustle in the tree line to the north of their position. Boyd shouted a warning, and the air was filled with the twanging buzz of dozens of crossbows. He watched in horror as Dame Catherine fell to the ground, along with many of her soldiers. Many of the shields of the front line and the edges of the formation stayed up, but many others fell and did not rise.

The spear brigade roared into action and charged forward. The crossbows fired again. And again. Boyd stumbled along with his brigade, but he caught a crossbow bolt to his shoulder and fell backwards. He hit his head when he hit the ground, and saw flashes of light. He forced his eyes to stay open as he looked around for Dame Catherine. She was close. He had fallen near her. The eyes that gazed back at him were unblinking and cold. He tried to crawl closer, but something heavy dragged him down and his vision swam. He could hold on to consciousness no longer.

It was years later. Boyd stood in the Icenian Royal Castle of Cil Cilurion. He had heard rumor of the Castle's incredible beauty but was not prepared for how breathtaking it was. Everything was amazing, from the wooden carvings of the tables and chairs, to the tapestries depicting historical figures and battles, to the plush blue rugs which were works of art. The high ceilings were hung with glimmering chandeliers and the whole of each room was bathed in white light.

He stood outside of the throne room with Dame Catherine, waiting to be called.

"Now Boyd, when they call your name, don't be nervous. All of the tests are over and you've passed. The reason that we've held off on your knighting ceremony is because the king wishes to confer this honor upon you himself. He wants to hear of the Battle of Chalric Hill from its hero!" She smiled warmly at him.

"Dame Catherine Deenan!" a beautiful voice called out from within.

"I must go and take my place. Wait a moment, and you'll be called."

Dame Catherine embraced Boyd, and the doors to the throne room were opened for her. She entered the chamber and the doors closed behind her. A moment passed in which Boyd basked alone in the warmth of the anti-chamber. A roaring fire was lit and the smell of wood smoke made him smile. He looked at a beautiful tapestry hanging on the wall depicting the knights of the past in a serene sunny grove. None of the figures bore arms or armor and they all had faces of peace. Atop the tapestry was woven the words "The Land of Hallowed Deeds."

"Recruit Edmund Boyd!" the voice called for him.

Boyd entered the throne room. There were two lines of knights dressed in glimmering silver plate armor, and the room was awash in a golden light. On a great raised platform was the figure of the king with a blue cloak, and standing next to the king was Boyd's father. Boyd beamed with pride as he walked, as if in a dream, towards the dais turning his gaze left and right as he walked. Many of the knights had their helmets closed and he could not see their faces, but he saw many he recognized amidst all the gleaming armor.

His sergeant was among them, and nodded at him as he walked past. On his left, the two soldiers from dinner. He smiled. He never thought that they would make it through their trials, but here they were. He moved further down the corridor of heroes, stopping to turn to Dame Catherine.

"Thank you, Dame Catherine. Without your wisdom, I would never have found my courage."

She nodded and smiled at him.

Boyd returned to his path towards the king and there on the left, was the Royal Scout—the squire on horseback that had warned them all about the Galanthians. Boyd noted that the man was still a squire, and for some reason he was dressed in his dark scouting clothes, caked in dirt and sweat.

"Don't worry," Boyd said. "You'll soon be a knight if you keep following the path. Especially if you keep working so hard! It takes some longer than others but the journey is no less worthwhile."

"Boyd," the Scout said with deep concern in his voice.

"I mean no insult. I can see that you have just come from an important errand, and yet you still find the time to perform your duty here. It is really quite commendable."

"It is my duty and I honor it. Boyd, what happened?"

"At Chalric Hill?"

"Yes. Chalric Hill."

"For my part, I did no more than any soldier would, less perhaps. I could have left. Dame Catherine gave me leave to go, but I met a Galanthian Scout at the crossroads and I had to kill him. I tried to save him. I was injured and yet I got back to Chalric Hill and gave warning, and we fought. We fought the Galanthians for a day and a night. There were archers near the end that shot us down. I watched Dame Catherine get shot down. But she is here, right next to me."

For a moment Boyd felt that he was still there, on Chalric Hill, still lying in the mud pierced with crossbow bolts. He could still vaguely feel the pressure from where he had been stabbed and shot, but not quite the pain.

"Yes. I see her, now," said the Scout. He seemed so sad. "You showed such bravery, Edmund Boyd from Descante. You stood against evil unflinchingly. You saved countless lives by holding the line. Your father could not be more proud of you. You served with honor and distinction."

"Honor and distinction," Boyd whispered through his smile.

An Icenian Royal Scout, a squire in service to the King, gently closed Edmund Boyd's eyes and wept over the young man's body in the dark of the pre-dawn on Chalric Hill. "May your spirit with great haste make to the Land of Hallowed Deeds, child. I shall carry news of your honor to your father." He crawled over several corpses to Dame Catherine's body and recovered her sword and her knight's belt.

"First, though, I must warn our people. I must tell King Thrombolis that war has come to Icenia."

A Matter of Death and Life
Mark Mensch

"I thought zombies only came out at night," Nigel said to the milling mass of corpses.

Every story he had heard about the undead had always been that they come out of graves at night and roam the darkness looking for the living to feed upon; or at least wait until there was a thick fog to hide within. So he was quite unprepared, when walking through the woods one afternoon, to run into a group of three of the lumbering creatures.

Once the initial shock of seeing them wore off, he figured he wouldn't have any difficulty with them. After all, they were "lumbering." What turned out to be difficult for him though was the forest. He was quite adept at moving through a city. Throw drunks, cut purses, fenced off areas and dead-end alleys at him, and he could navigate it like a sailor with a magical sextant. But apparently trees, roots, loose dirt and other woodland debris was not the same thing. He found himself stumbling as he ran, cursing at the brambles snagging his clothes and quickly losing his sense of direction.

In addition, the dead had brought friends. Before he knew it, over a dozen of the rotting corpses had him surrounded, and his only choice was to climb up a very large tree. Luckily, hand-eye coordination and balance are not in a zombie's repertoire. Nigel was treed, but safe.

That was three days ago.

Nigel began to realize why it was better that zombies only came out at night. The sun, even through the canopy of the trees, was doing its best to accelerate their decomposition, and the stench had removed all sounds of wildlife from the area. Nigel had hoped that maybe he could wait them out until they rotted away, but watching flesh sluice off of an arm while it continued to claw at the tree told him that that wait would not bode well for him.

Not that he was in a bad place at the moment, though. Apparently, his bad luck in the forest ended with being treed by slow moving undead. His sanctuary was thick in the bough, giving him a pleasant place to perch himself, and the fruit he plucked from the branches was something akin to a pear. A bit rounder and slightly browner in color, but definitely sweet, albeit with a strange texture. Nigel preferred apples, but he realized beggars and all of that. Occasionally he'd move from branch to branch to ensure that his muscles didn't get tight, but he also used a type of muscle tense-and-release technique that was useful when having to sit, lie or hang slightly upside down while motionless for extended periods of time.

The zombies weren't going anywhere. During the first day, he had joked and even told a couple of stories for his capturing audience, not only to keep himself entertained but also hoping that someone might hear him and come to the rescue.

His voice was raw and hoarse a couple hours after sunset that first day, and no rescue had occurred. On the beginning of the second, he climbed high into the tree to see what he could see, and saw he was screwed. No one was in sight, but from the way the treetops made a furrow a hundred feet away, he figured the road wasn't too far off.

Taking some of the jewelry he wore and some objects of metal, glass and twine from various pockets and pouches, Nigel made a few crude wind chimes. They weren't a church bell's knell, but with the sudden absence of the wildlife in the area, he was pretty sure they could be heard from the roadway.

As the third day's sun approached its apex, Nigel decided he wasn't going to stay there a fourth. He had hoped for a passerby to at least yell a hello, distracting the monsters so he could make his escape and yelling a warning to his unwitting savior. As this hope faded, however, he had worked out a path along a series of neighboring trees that could be reached with slightly risky jumps, getting lower to the ground and—he hoped—hit it running before his worshipers got close enough to hook him for a meal. Nigel figured he'd implement this new plan at first light on the morrow, after some stretching and ensuring that he would be running in the right direction for the road.

That all changed when he heard the first blast of magic.

Hitting one of the corpses below him, a ball of green energy burst it into a small rain of dust with a modest "pop." Nigel and his dead audience turned in the direction from which the blast had come and stared blankly as a well-dressed man, rapier in hand, entered the area. Dancing.

At first Nigel thought he was simply moving gracefully around the forest floor, but when the man actually gave a slight pirouette, he knew better. "What in the names of the Dragons are…" Nigel started to shout at him when the dancer finished with a flourish and another blast of that silver energy leapt from his outstretched hand; and another dusting of ex-zombie graced the trunk of Nigel's vacation home.

A spell… dancer? Nigel thought. He had heard of spell singers—mages who drew forth and culminated their energy through verse and song before releasing it. But he'd never seen a spell dancer before. It was definitely a sight to behold. Sword fighting—heck, *all* combat—is in itself a type of dance. To see someone go above and beyond that, to make it into an actual form of flowing function, was quite mesmerizing. At least for Nigel. The zombies, however, didn't care about the performance. They turned towards the interloper and shambled in his direction.

Between ballet moves, the stranger's sword would whip out, slicing at the shambling corpses. They might not die from blood loss or massive damage to their soft parts, but a hamstrung zombie would fall just like any other person requiring feet to move about. Lost fingers meant there was nothing for them to grab with, and slashed eyes left them quite blind. And this gentleman knew what he was doing.

"Thank you, kind sir," Nigel said from the tree, gathering his makeshift wind chimes. "I've been here for some time and appreciate the assistance. I was wondering if…"

"I'm executing a rescue here," the stranger said with a bit of annoyance in his tone. The man slew through two more bodies, cursing in concentration.

"Of course, of course," Nigel commented, tucking away the last of his dangling items and looking at the ground. The zombies were leaving the tree and falling fast to the spell dancer. Nigel could pop down and probably get clear, but he figured it would be slightly rude—leaving his hero alone and such. So he sat on the lowest bough and watched while the dancer dispatched the rest of the dead. It took less than a minute.

Nigel shimmied down the trunk while his savior wiped his sword clean before sheathing it. The man had fair skin, slightly angular facial features, and wore a wide hat over long, dark hair. He was dressed in black trousers and white shirt, a leather jerkin his only form of armor against zombie claws and teeth. Nigel approached him, his gloved hand out. "Thank you for your help," he said. "The name's Nigel."

The man clasped wrists with Nigel. "Kintar," he replied, "And no thanks are necessary. I have been tracking these creatures and the man who made them for a week now. It's just part of the job."

"Oh? Is that so?" Nigel asked with a smile. "Well then," he continued, brushing off his vest and realizing that he probably didn't smell much better than the zombies after being in that tree for three days, "I will not delay you any longer. Good luck in your hunt." Nigel turned to leave.

"Wait a moment," Kintar said before Nigel got more than two steps away. Nigel turned back to face him. It isn't wise to run from a mage and even less wise when he would probably brain himself with a low hanging branch before he made it ten yards. "I was hoping that you might be able to help. I didn't realize the number of graves that this man has dug up and…"

Nigel raised a hand, interrupting him. "Sir," he said with a polite, stern voice. "I can appreciate your situation. But as you said, this 'rescue' was part of your current plan. I did not cause you to go out of your way nor, as I see it, did I incur any debt with you. In fact, I'd imagine that my chimes helped you find this group quicker. You'd have dispatched them either way, with or without me being in that tree."

Kintar tilted his head to one side, giving Nigel a half confused, half barely tolerating look. Nigel seemed not to take notice as he continued talking.

"The only thing I feel I owe a debt to is this tree which kept me out of harm's way for three days. And fed me as well. However, as the only way I could possibly thank it I have done a few times already, as the wet ground on the other side will prove, I don't believe there's any more need for me to be here."

Kintar brought his head back to the upright. "Is that so?" he said, a grin playing across his lips.

That unnerved Nigel a bit. A mage and swordsman smiling could not be good. He brushed his vest again, palming a small, glass sphere of orange dust from it as he did so. "Yes," he stated. "That is so."

"In that case, I accept your debt," said a soft, musical voice from behind Nigel.

The squeak that Nigel produced was less than manly, and the jump and spin he did was clumsy compared to his savior's grace, but he did come down in a crouch, his hand pulled back to throw. However, the beauty before him stayed his throw.

She was willowy, half a head taller than him and quite lovely. Her pale skin reflected the light in an almost luminous sheen. Her green eyes reminded Nigel of a summer's meadow, and her high cheek bones only added to her allure. The dress she wore was made of some diaphanous material that was the same pale green color as her long, curling locks. Small vines wrapped themselves through that hair and around her throat as well. Oh, and she was currently walking out of the tree. Her left leg was still inside, slowly pulling itself free as if from a placid pond.

Nigel swallowed and then stuttered, "And… and you are?"

She gave him a smile that made him want nothing more than to walk to her and see if her skin was as soft as it looked. Of course, a chance encounter with a beautiful woman in the woods never came to anything good. He stayed his ground.

"I am the guardian of these woods," she said. Her smile then fell into a look of dismay. "And these woods have a blight within them. There has been a sickness growing northeast of here, at the location of a mine that I had allowed some humans to work. Their damage to the woods was minimal, nothing more than the scratch of a thorn would be upon you. But now a darkness grows there, and it is of the same ilk as that which surrounded my tree."

She then gave Nigel's savior a slight bow, "That is until master Kintar removed them from my realm. The rot is gone from here and I thank him for it."

Kintar's response was to take off his hat and give her a rather graceful bow with a flourish. That's when Nigel noticed his tapered ear tips. *Great*, Nigel thought to himself, *an elf.*

Nigel had known many good elves as well as bad ones. The trait that he found in most of them though was a lack of any alacrity. When one can live centuries, if not millennia, there's usually no great hurry to get a job done. That can be frustrating to humans who have, say, only three or four decades left in their lifespan. But Kintar seemed eager to take down these dead things, so Nigel was willing to give him the benefit of the doubt. At least until he gave Nigel a reason otherwise.

It also explained to Nigel both his almost unearthly grace as well as his ability to fight and cast spells simultaneously. Elves had a slightly better affinity towards magic, and if they have been practicing for two hundred years or so, they could dance through a chicken coop and not disturb a feather.

Nigel shook his head a bit, clearing it of his musings as well as of the distracting beauty of the wood nymph before him. "So, if I understand this correctly, you are transferring my debt of three days of protection from yourself to him," he said, hooking a thumb over his shoulder.

She tilted her head a bit to one side. "Better to say that I am tasking you to help him with his current quest as payment for the safety and sustenance I provided."

"But what good will I be?" Nigel all but pleaded. "You saw me up in that tree. I'm about as effective against zombies as a spark on a serpent's scale."

Kintar looked at him gravely. "The necromancer is human."

Nigel mumbled to himself as he threw his arms up in futility. "Great. Wonderful. I'm boned." He let out an exasperated sigh. He picked up his pack he had discarded nearby when he needed his hands free to climb the tree three days ago. "All right, Kintar, let's get this over with." Nigel shouldered his pack and began walking off into the woods.

"Milady," Kintar said, this time with a shorter bow, donning his hat and giving the spirit a smile. "Do not worry. Your forest shall soon be free of this darkness."

She smiled back to Kintar as Nigel stomped back into the area, scowling. "Hey!" he growled at the elf, "Pretty boy. Let's get going." He then added in a lower voice, "I need you to show me which way is northeast."

Kintar took the lead. There wasn't really a path, but the trees were spaced somewhat apart. It didn't require a lot of pushing through underbrush or squeezing through spaces, so travel was rather unimpeded. Still, Nigel was surprised his companion wasn't more of the "forest ghost" that all the tales have about elves. He was quieter and more sure-footed than Nigel, but his steps could be heard, albeit somewhat muted compared to Nigel's.

That's when Nigel noticed that Kintar's gait was not regular. He seemed to be taking steps in time with the sounds of the forest: the breeze that blew through the trees, a slight cawing of a few birds and the rustle of some animal. It wasn't so much as his steps were silent but that they simply blended in with all the rest of the background noise of the forest.

Nigel mentally slapped a hand to his forehead. It should have dawned on him sooner. It was the same when Nigel was working in a city. Waiting for the ambient noises so that his sounds blended with them. Kintar's steps while the trees moan in the wind were the same as Nigel's scurrying sounds of climbing a drainpipe while a coach went by.

Nigel smirked as he heard Kayleigh's voice in his head: "Same recipe, different ingredients."

After the mental voice faded, so did his smirk; fading into a frown. Since that thought brought more thoughts that Nigel didn't want to think about, he decided to occupy his mind with idle chatter instead. "So why are you after this necromancer?" he asked.

Kintar looked over his shoulder, a surprised look on his face. "Do you have to ask?"

Nigel shrugged. "I guess so since I just. I mean, I know that necromancy is against all natural laws as well as those throughout the known kingdoms. But what I meant is why are *you* after *this* necromancer." Nigel put emphasis on the words so that hopefully Kintar would get the hint.

He did. "Ah. There's been a series of raids on various crypts and graveyards in the area. They were small at first but have been increasing exponentially. Obviously, someone was gathering the bodies, animating them, and using them to help dig and haul back fresh subjects."

"Obviously," Nigel agreed without commitment.

Kintar gave him a slight grin. "I had been following the desecration in the area and came across a village who had most of their graveyard dug up. Nearly a hundred graves emptied. The townsfolk had formed a mob to go after the culprits. As you can imagine, zombies aren't really good at covering their tracks. So the townsfolk ran into a group of them on the road and had to flee. That was the group under the tree."

Nigel gulped a little. "Those things at the tree were the townsfolk?"

Kintar barked out a low laugh. "No, the zombies were set there to cover the necromancer's withdrawal. I followed the townsfolk's directions and then I heard your unique chimes. And now you're caught up."

Nigel paused for a moment and then asked, "Are you going to kill him when we find him?"

"No," Kintar replied. "I'm going to bring him to Garrenshaw for judgment. Where he will be tried, found guilty and executed."

Nigel began chuckling. "So it's an open and shut case," he said.

"Yes."

"Why bother then?"

"What?" Kintar asked.

"Why bother bringing him back? If he's just going to die anyways, kill him now. Take his head or whatever with you and head back. Easier to carry and it's all done."

"That's not the way we do things," Kintar said sternly.

"Not the way *you* do things," Nigel intoned. "Let me ask you a question. If this necromancer gets a chance—either when we meet him or on the way back to the city—to kill you, you'll try to stop him, right?"

"Yes."

"And you'll use deadly force to do it. I mean there isn't a non-bleedy way to use that rapier."

"Yes," Kintar admitted, "I would kill in self-defense."

Nigel then asked, "So why not just preemptively counter attack him when we see him? I've got this thunder stick and—"

"Because it's wrong," Kintar interrupted, then stopped in mid stride. "Thunder stick?"

Nigel nodded and pulled out of his pack a leather tube four inches long and half that wide. The ends were capped with pewter. "This will blow just about anything to bits. I'd need some time to set it up, but if we get near the necromancer, he'll be just a sanguine spray that we'd—"

"It's wrong," Kintar interrupted again and then restarted their journey.

Nigel threw up his hands, "May the Serpent save me from the hypocrisy of heroes." Kintar gave him a glare and Nigel showed his palms in a placating manner. "It's your show; your rules."

Kintar gave him a genuine smile. "Thank you."

Nigel nodded to himself, committed to that task, and stumbled over some piece of flora that he would never have to worry about in a street. "But why you? Are you part of the law in the area? A special warrior trained to hunt down this specific evil?"

The elf stopped and turned around with a bemused smile on his face. "Me?" he said, crossing his arms and leaning up against a nearby tree, a heel of one boot over the ankle of the other. It was obviously a practiced stance of his. "I'm just a wandering elf who likes to do good. A knight-errant, if you will."

Nigel snorted. "Everyone has a selfish reason—even if it is simply to make oneself feel good by helping people. So why hunt necromancers?"

Kintar remained silent for a moment, his fingers idly sliding a charm of an emerald leaf back and forth along a thin chain around his neck. Then his posture changed. His shoulders tensed and drooped at the same time, his leg slowly uncrossed the other and he let the charm drop back against his shirt. He gave Nigel a hard yet regretting look. "I have my reasons." He then turned and continued walking.

Nigel didn't press, and fell in behind him. He didn't need Kintar to say what his reason was. He recognized the posture, the look, the slow gait that he now walked. He remembered it on himself quite well. In the end, there's only one thing that will spur a man on to put himself in harm's way, into mortal danger when it is so easily avoided.

Love lost.

After an uncomfortable silence, Kintar asked, "So what about you?"

"Huh?" Nigel replied. Sometimes he was too witty for his own good.

"Why were you on the road?"

"Oh," Nigel shrugged, "I'm on my way to Garrenshaw."

"For what?"

This time Nigel stopped. Kintar turned around again, his eyebrows raised once more.

"You can't be that naive," Nigel said.

Kintar's expression went from questioning to one of polite tolerance. "About?" he prompted.

Nigel gave a soft smile and shook his head. "I don't believe it. Someone like you who travels all around the place doesn't know about the rules of the road?"

Kintar blinked. "Rules of the road?"

Nigel nodded. "The polite societal interactions when meeting someone while traveling. If you're going to be sharing any time with them, the one thing you don't ask them is why specifically they're traveling."

"Why not?"

"Because," Nigel began, then stopped, searching for the right words. "Look. Let us say that you tell me you are on the road hunting the necromancer. And as it turns out, I am on the road going to offer aid to said necromancer. Suddenly there's a whole new conflict that you have to deal with."

Kintar cocked his head a bit. "But I told you that I'm hunting a necromancer."

"Yes," Nigel said, exasperated. "But that was after I incurred a debt with you. Not to mention that, if I was working with him, I'd probably not be treed by his minions. But if we had just happened to meet on the roadway, we'd both have to keep one eye on the other."

"But not if we don't reveal our final goals?"

"No. There is safety in numbers—if those numbers aren't against one another. Oh sure, there's the odd highwayman here and there, but they often don't bother with such guile as it takes them away from their hunting grounds and takes longer to get what they really want."

"But at the end of the journey..." Kintar began.

"At the end, if there arises a conflict with one another, at least you've arrived at the final destination intact. And who knows, maybe you'll have learned a bit about the person in the time you've been together and maybe find a resolution other than dirking one another."

Kintar turned on his heels and began walking again. "Humans have strange customs."

Nigel got a little irritated. "Actually, it's common sense. I guess you don't travel with people all that often, eh?"

Kintar shook his head. "No," he replied, his steps slowing for a moment again. "I don't."

Nigel nodded, more of the story of Kintar unfolding in his mind. The elf probably had lost friends in the past on his knight-errant missions— maybe even had to put them down after a necromancer had turned them against him. Perhaps even his unrevealed love. Nigel didn't have close friends because he didn't want them to be used against him. Kintar didn't want them as he didn't want to lose them. Nigel understood the reasoning but found it flawed. In his profession, loss was part of the trade. And you should appreciate the value of it while you have it, as everything is transitory.

Nigel's thoughts then went on a tangent. If that was true, then why was he, Nigel Peaks, professional opportunist, heading to Garrenshaw? A man had set him up to take the fall for a theft. Well, he *had* committed the theft, but still he could have simply chalked it up to a loss and moved on. Fortannis was a huge world, and even if one city of dark elves wanted his head, he could easily avoid them. He'd done so with other groups for a couple of decades now. Why was he heading back to a place that probably remembered "transgressions" of his and would look to have him pay for them? Was he going to exact revenge? Was he just going to steal the item and run? Or was he heading there for another reason his subconscious had yet to clue him in on? It was definitely something that required further thought.

However, that thought would have to wait for Nigel as Kintar said, "We're getting close."

"How can you tell?" Nigel asked.

"There are no animals in the area. It's silent."

Nigel stopped and listened. He was right. Like at the tree, there was no bird song, no slight crashing of bushes as a rabbit or squirrel avoided them. But there was something else on the wind.

"Forget about being silent," Nigel gagged out, bringing a kerchief to his face. "What about that smell?"

The two stopped moving, both of them going statue still. There was yet no noise, but the scent of rotten meat and unwashed bodies was definitely on the wind. They quickly exchanged a look and then silently agreed to head forward, quiet and slow. Nigel followed Kintar, mimicking his steps, trying his best to be as part of the arbor ambience as the elf. They stopped a short time later in the tree line of a small clearing.

The clearing was man-made—literally. If elves had made it, well it wouldn't be a clearing but a communal area adapting the forest to their needs. Dwarves would have tunneled out dwellings in the hillside located on the opposite side of the clearing. Only man would cut down the trees, turning the lumber into a large lodge and a rounded stack of firewood.

Stumps dotted the thousand square yards of clearing. The ground was muddied with only a few areas showing any green growing. Along the back hill, a log lodge stood—perhaps fifty yards long and a third of that wide. Big, but depending upon the size of the mining crew that lived there, it could be rather close quarters. There were a couple of doors on the front of it, another on the left side, and half a dozen windows. All closed and shuttered tight. No smoke was rising from either of the two chimneys. No signs of life from the cabin at all.

Then again, there were no signs of life in the clearing—only the two dozen corpses standing up, swaying slightly, and smelling horribly. They seemed to be in a lot worse shape than the ones at the tree. Their facial features were all but gone—either by simple time and exposure or by the quick land and snag off a morsel of flesh that a raven aptly demonstrated while Nigel and Kintar looked on.

"Only two dozen?" Nigel whispered. "I thought you said that there were over a hundred corpses missing."

"There are," Kintar whispered back. "But it takes time to turn them into zombies. He must have them stored somewhere. Probably in the cabin."

"I doubt it," Nigel said.

"Why?"

"The place is sealed up. You said that he's human—or at least a living being. Imagine being stuffed up with a hundred corpses in that amount of room. You couldn't breathe."

"True. Maybe they're in back."

"Maybe," Nigel hedged. Cocking his head inquisitively towards Kintar, he asked, "How does one make a zombie, anyways?"

"Ritual magic," Kintar replied offhandedly, commenting as if one was reciting a recipe for making muffins. "Although a necromancer can make zombies singularly as easily as casting any other spell, it is taxing. Even a master of such magic could only do perhaps a dozen before he passed out from exhaustion.

"However," Kintar continued, "Using ritual magic, the caster can create zombies by the dozens without becoming too winded."

Nigel gulped again. "You think he's a master necromancer?" Nigel couldn't contain the quiver in his voice.

"Doubt it. If he is that strong, he'd be using something less… rottable to guard his place. He's going to lose those bodies in another day or three."

"Can you take them?"

Kintar gave a wolfish grin and began to draw his rapier from his hip. "It will be a bit of a fight, but they aren't the best of dance partners."

"Wait!" Nigel hissed, putting his hand onto Kintar's, staying his draw. Kintar raised an eyebrow. "Look at the way they're dressed."

Kintar did. Besides the rotted and moldering clothes, he could make out some shiny bits. There were pieces of silverware hanging from their wrists, empty pans tied to their ankles and even bells balanced on their shoulders. "What the—" he began.

"Alarm bells," Nigel supplied. "Once they move, they'll make a racket. My guess is that your guy is sleeping during the day since he has to pull his rituals at night. If someone approaches, the din begins and he's awakened." He looked at the elf, "Is he dangerous?"

Kintar nodded. "They prefer to fight with zombies since it keeps them safe, but someone who can do this can rip the life right from a person if he's prepared. Can't do it too often as it's actually harder than raising the dead, but definitely a couple of times. And as we are a couple—"

"You have to buy me dinner first," Nigel mused and Kintar choked back a laugh. They both quickly shot a look at the mob in front of them, making sure they weren't heard.

"So," Kintar said, "What should we do about the alarm?"

Nigel grinned. "We should wake him up."

Fifteen minutes passed while they made their plans and preparations. Nigel had made his way around to the left side of the clearing, where a worn, wide trail left the area. He took a steadying breath, tugging his vest down a bit and adjusting his sash—thereby making sure that all of his tricks were where they were supposed to be. Kintar was just waiting for his signal.

"Signal… signal…" Nigel said to himself, now patting his chest. He had told Kintar to look for his signal, but he never said what it would be.

"For the love of dragons…" he growled to himself, and then opted to take his kerchief and tie a rock in it. Then he began tossing it up high into the air over the smaller treetops along the path, hoping that Kintar would see it. After the fifth toss, there came the faint sound of a familiar popping noise, followed by a clangor of the metal junk jewelry that the zombies wore. The elf was beginning to cut into the horde. "Good," Nigel said, "good, good, good." He then retreated to his hiding spot along the trail.

Kintar would be hitting the zombies hard at first, then leading them back into the woods. He told Nigel that they would pursue him, some sort of pre-existing instructions to kill anyone they saw. Kintar would have an easier time in the woods fighting them than Nigel would, in part due to his elven heritage but also due to the various trip lines the two of them had put up. Zombies shuffled, they didn't hop.

It wasn't long before Nigel heard rapid footfalls heading in his direction. He peered from his vantage point and saw a man wearing dark, dirty clothes and carrying a staff running up the trail. He seemed to be around fifty and thin but in good shape from the speed he was maintaining with only a little heavy breathing. His head was shaven, with some twisting tattoo design encircling the top. He was cursing under his breath as he ran.

It hadn't been hard to deduce that the necromancer needed someplace to store his zombies. Someplace cool and out of the sun. And since this was the only path heading out of the clearing, it was a good bet that it was a road to the mine—a perfect place to keep corpses, animated or otherwise.

The necromancer was looking back over his shoulder, but even if he had been looking at the ground, he would have been hard pressed to find the thin but strong silk threads Nigel stung across the path. A single one wouldn't have really stopped someone, but a half dozen had the same effect as a moth hitting a web. The man tripped up and threw out his arms to break his fall, dropping his staff in the process.

Nigel hopped out onto the trail and hurled his glass globe at the man. It hit him in the head, a hissing of orange vapor escaping from the shattered orb and forming a cloud around his target.

Nigel's triumphant shout stuck in his throat as he watched a cascading flicker of argent sparks interact with that cloud. The necromancer, instead of falling asleep like any normal person would have, glared at Nigel from the ground and began to get up. The necromancer's eyes widened in fear as Nigel leaned harder on his knee.

"Damn magic," Nigel growled as he began to move. He should have realized that anyone who was working with dead bodies all the time would take precautions. The shaved head, for instance, was probably more to keep any sort of vermin from making his hair their home than an evil overlord fashion statement. And like that, he'd probably have some ward to protect him against all sorts of sickening mold and dust that can be found on and around corpses; and it would work just as well against Nigel's poisons, too.

All of this went through Nigel's head in less than a heartbeat. As he took two bounding steps towards the necromancer, the caster stood up and raised his hand with his fingers in a strange position—pale, sickly white light forming around them.

Nigel dove forward towards the ground, hurling his baton at the necromancer's chest. Two feet of oak haft with a studded iron head spun towards the spell caster. In that instant, something that Nigel could only describe as a freezing crocodile slithered past his back. The sensation of the magic that clawed over him froze his breath in his lungs and set his stomach into spasms. The overwhelming wrongness of that power literally caused Nigel's mind to go blank with disbelief.

But luckily, momentum as well as a couple of decades of inborn muscle memory worked without his conscious thoughts. He finished the dive in a forward roll and came up just in time to see his baton bounce off of some invisible barrier around the necromancer, the magic discharging in another silver flash an inch away from his body. Nigel would have cursed magic again, but he was still trying to fight over the fact that his death just passed over him. His forward roll reflexively turned into a spring to his feet, and he slammed into the necromancer, taking them both to the ground.

The impact snapped Nigel's mind back into the area of dirty hand-to-hand fighting just in time to use his left hand to seize the wrist of the necromancer, who was trying to pull a long knife from his belt. Nigel's other hand joined the first, and his right elbow hit the man hard in the chin as it passed by.

The necromancer glared up at Nigel, who replied by slamming his forehead against the spell caster's nose. A sickening yet satisfying crunch could be heard. It wasn't any party for Nigel's forehead, but he used that pain to clear his mind of any lingering effects of the death magic.

Using the fraction of a second's pause the broken nose caused his opponent, Nigel twisted on top of him, pinning the wrist with the dagger down against the ground and putting one of his knees against the man's throat. Nigel leaned forward, adding weight, and said sharply, "Stop!"

The man continued to struggle, so he put more weight on the man's throat and repeated his command. The man's free arm clawed at the offending leg, but it didn't accomplish anything. He was wheezing and his struggles began to ease. "Good," Nigel said continuing the pressure.

"When I get up," the necromancer croaked, "I'm going to kill you. Then bring you back, pull off your arms and legs and leave you to rot in the sun."

"Really?" Nigel said with a hint of amusement in his voice.

The man tried to nod, but finding that Nigel's knee prevented that, he rasped out a yes.

"In that case," Nigel said as he began to lean more into the man's throat, "You're never going to get up."

Kintar found Nigel and the necromancer ten minutes later. The elf had dispatched all of the zombies and came jogging up the path. Nigel kneeled next to the necromancer's still form. Kintar's jog turned into a slow pace forward. "Nigel?" he asked hesitantly.

Nigel gave a long sigh. "You sure you don't want to preemptively counterattack this idiot?"

Kintar let out a breath.

"He's fine," Nigel continued. "Out cold, and he'll have one hell of a headache in an hour, but he'll live." He then looked up at Kintar. "That is, until you get him back to town and kill him there."

"Thank you," Kintar said as he kneeled over the necromancer. He slid his hand into the man's shirt and gave a tug. Nigel saw as he withdrew a silver leaf charm.

Nigel looked closely at Kintar's face. Unfortunately, his ability to read expressions failed him. Nigel couldn't tell if the man was the killer of Kintar's love, or if he himself was actually Kintar's love. But whatever the case, Nigel could tell it was now closed.

Kintar secured some interesting restraints onto the necromancer's wrists. The shackles had runes and sigils carved into them, and when they were locked, they flared for a moment with azure light. The shackles were then locked about the man's waist by a chain. "This will keep him from casting any further spells."

Nigel nodded. "Well then, I say we head up to the mine, use my thunder stick, and seal those poor spirits up. Not sure if you could handle a hundred, no matter how pretty you look while you dance."

Kintar grinned. "Thank you. And yes, we should do that." He stood up, dusting the dirt off of his knees. "And your plans after that?" he asked.

Nigel mirrored his mannerisms, including the grin. "I'll help you get this guy back to Garrenshaw." Working on a hunch, Nigel asked Kintar, "He may need to return alive, but what about unharmed?"

Kintar shook his head and turned towards the path heading towards the mines, "I don't want to see you doing anything like that," he said.

A sudden, meaty thump and a grunt caused Kintar to turn around quickly. The necromancer's head had turned to the opposite side, a reddish area beginning to form, which was sure to soon turn into a lovely bruise.

Nigel gave a look of innocence and shrug as he said, "What? You said you didn't want to see it."

As the corner of Kintar's mouth turned up into a slight smirk, Nigel realized his guess was right about the necromancer being the murderer and not the victim. He didn't think the elf would be smiling if he had just put a boot to the head of his ex-lover. "I did," Kintar said. "And I mean it."

Nigel nodded and followed his friend up the path.

The Mutiny of Broken Things
Beth W. Patterson

The morning started like any other day, complete with Ollie hanging upside down in my doorway so that I accidentally rammed him with my handcart in my haste to get out of my home.

He did this to me every now and again, and always when I least expected it. The impact never hurt him—in fact, he seemed to enjoy the trajectory. The diminutive young man would get knocked a good five feet away before spreading his wings, doing a midair flip like a dry leaf, and landing on his feet, as batkin always seemed to do.

I was always in a hurry, and Ollie was constantly trying to teach me how to slow down and enjoy life more. My best friend was a homely fellow, but he had a heart of gold—which went unappreciated at that moment.

"Ollie!" I snorted. "What are you up to now?"

The batkin scampered around the perimeter of my cart, flapping his wings and shedding little sparkling flakes, leaving a glimmering trail like a firefly with dandruff. "I found mica at an old quarry deep inside a cave today!" he announced, his voice carrying overtones of near-sonar pitch just audible enough for my wolf senses. "It's only about an hour's walk from here, near the sandstone formations where no one bothers to hunt or farm. I made some sounds in the grotto, and the echo goes on forever and ever… no telling how big this thing is! *Churkee*! And there's evidence of some *very* interesting activity!"

I shook my head in wonder at his boundless energy. "Ollie, you look ridiculous." I lightly chided him. "No one will be interested in a sparkly bloodsucker. What's going on at the quarry? Why has no one else discovered it? Maybe I can find some crystals or semiprecious stones for my art."

Ollie extended one long twiggy digit, connected to a membrane as delicate as a soap bubble. He tried to lay it alongside his leaf-shaped nose in a conspiratorial gesture, succeeding only in poking himself in one large elliptical nostril. Wincing, he did away with theatrics. He persisted, "It's so well hidden, I think that vines were deliberately planted there, because once you sneak in, it's like a whole labyrinth of tunnels and dugouts. And some sort of secret society that meets there… some sort of cult of human babies!"

"What would human babies be doing wandering around Synvia?" I parried. "What would any sort of babies be doing in a group, for that matter?"

"I'm telling you, I saw evidence!"

"Does it have to be today?" I snarled. "I'm late for the market, and I want to get first dibs on glass. I think this mosaic I'm working on is going to be my best yet."

"I would be in favor of your craft, dear Kylix, if you weren't so caught up in trying to be productive! You are a workaholic. You act like a *human*! The process of creating mosaics is supposed to make you fall into a meditative bliss—not tory-rory productivity frenzy! One of these days I am going to abduct you and show you that there is a great big world outside of this little island of Synvia."

"I have a good life here. I can choose my hours, work my fingers to the bone, and still run free and howl under the full moon without fear of persecution."

"That moon is your only emotional outlet. Don't you think I understand? I feel its phases just as strongly as you do. You know, I could very well be one of those fabled vampires of Tar'Navaria."

"Nice try, boyo. You are not a vampire. You are a living wylderkin who has features of a vampire *bat*. You are an animal person through and through, as am I. As is…"

The words died in my throat, because the door to my neighbor Ardyn's house opened. He lived on the opposite side of the thicket that separated us, just down the dirt road. I forgot all about the market, my career, or even my best friend Ollie standing right before me. My neighbor greeted me with an impassive wave of his hand before heading into the forest with his lute slung over his shoulder, for some reason I would never be privy to. Because he was a bard, he was unconcerned with the mundane, or so I concluded. Denial usually wears a cheap mask of hope.

I had always tried to initiate conversation with Ardyn, just so that I could gaze into those cornflower-blue eyes, silver stars radiating outward from their depths. His creamy skin was a stark contrast to the jet-black mane that he always pulled into a long ponytail. My eyes often traced the contours of those full pouty lips of his that were almost a shame to waste on a man. Even the most casual onlooker with no imagination might think him to be a black swan turned human by some wicked fairy's spell. But he was werewolf to the core, just like me.

Ardyn never ceased to take my breath away, and I hated myself for it. I may have been a master mosaicist and a fearsome hunter, but I was still a woman hopelessly in love. I was an artist, I justified in my mind, and I needed to see beauty if I wanted to keep creating.

When I shook myself to, my pint-sized friend's sanguine demeanor had changed. "Let me walk you to the market," he said tightly. "Shapeshifter that you are, whenever you see that guy you shift into a third form altogether that will either get you killed or break your heart. If I cannot talk some sense into you, I will nag you until you agree to come out and play with me tonight. *Churkee*! You can't come up with your genius ideas if you don't get out and see something new, can you?"

He had a point, and I silently agreed. Ollie might not have understood the ferocity of my ambitions, but he was a loyal friend and he kept me balanced.

"All right," I finally conceded. "First the market, then I want to work awhile. And then I will come out tonight."

The cool afternoon was when I could finally manifest my sanctuary. Having interacted with enough people in choosing some cheery cracked vessels, I was glad to be back in the sanctuary that was my little studio. The market had been a fruitful endeavor, but now it was time to create. Mixing the plaster to set my fragments was part of my ritual, and it helped me to go into a mental mode of creation. I glanced at my sketches for reference, but my hands seemed to work of their own accord.

As a mosaicist, I could almost fancy myself a healer. People brought me broken things, and I transformed them into something beautiful. Shards of glass and pottery, seashells and pebbles, things unwanted or unnoticed would be brought together to make a person stare in admiration. Certain stones or fragments would sometimes catch the light just right, twinkling like stars. I sometimes also fancied myself a bit of an ambassador in how the tessellations brought together the products of glass blowers, potters, and miners—all laid out in order and harmony.

My current work was stunning, and I was wondering how I could somehow get Ardyn to see it. I don't know why I thought that he might fall for me simply by seeing what I could do. But this picture was intended to seduce the viewer… somehow. That was my goal, anyway, and I was still trying.

I had once tried to win Ardyn's approval by showing him my work. I had had an excuse to draw him into my studio under the subterfuge that I knew someone who needed a bard for a clan gathering. He had glanced once at my studio and said, "Very pretty. How much money do you get for those?" And so then I was further motivated to increase the value of my creations, in hopes of somehow proving my worth.

Most artists try to depict a single scene from an outsider's point of view. Too many times I'd seen maidens and unicorns, regal lions, and depictions of luxury and beauty that I could never be a part of. My mosaics were different. They all strove to bring the viewer into a werewolf's world. I wanted people to wonder what it was like to be streamlined nose to tail. I wanted them to feel the earth beneath my pads, smell the musks and pollens on the wind, to notice every detail of an animal's heightened senses through a sentient mind. How a creature allegedly designed for killing really only wants to play.

This particular piece was my finest to date, and captured many transitions at once. It was a forest scene of a winding path. The vibrant hues of the night sky, stars, and the tops of trees were assiduously placed shards of the finest glass and flakes of sliver. They gradually faded to duller sepia made from old pottery at ground level where a lycan's vision becomes sharper but less brightly colored as he drops to all fours and shades become duller. The point of focus was a spiral of brightness at the edge of the horizon: mystery, things unknown. Whether people found it forbidding or inviting was entirely up to them. I privately chose to pretend that the luminous, swirling unknown was my eventual happily ever after with my neighbor. It was my own shameful secret.

I lifted my head to a tiny sound that only someone with very sharp hearing would notice, such as a wolf or a bat. It might have been a tiny bell, but I knew it was Ollie here to rescue me from myself. Fine. I needed to stretch my legs anyway. Looking outside to see the setting sun, I hadn't realized how long I'd been working. I doffed my cloak and in one fluid motion dropped to the floor onto all four paws. A long, languid stretch from nose to tail, an unapologetic yawn ending in a high squeak, and I was ready.

"A cult of babies," I muttered through my long muzzle. "This I have to see."

We chose an overgrown path away from any normal commuter routes and followed the first stars appearing. I decided that it would be safest to investigate the cave as an animal, and Ollie couldn't have been fussed with his own appearance. Ollie was naturally heat-sensitive, but with my heightened sense of smell I could detect the congregation of creatures just as quickly as he could.

Outside the entrance of the overgrown cave, there were easily thirty of them, not babies, and definitely not human. The sea of fully-grown people stretching out as far as the eye could see was unnatural, even with the familiar sounds of growling and squalling amongst themselves. I had never seen so many raccoonkin in one place before. They looked like mortal men and women save their bushy tails, pointed ears, long snouts, and heavily dark-rimmed eyes. The sly-faced people donned robes like those of a holy order, although they remained barefoot, as if wishing to remain connected to the earth.

My furry companion hid his face behind his wing a little too late, and even though I lacked heat sensors, my night vision was good enough for me to tell that he was blushing furiously. "Human babies?" I grilled him in amusement. "How did you mistake these raccoonkin for *babies*?" I was mildly exasperated to have been torn away from my work.

"Cut me some slack, Kylix! I only saw their tracks! *Churkee*! They look like… you know… little hands and… feet…" he trailed off.

Just then the raccoonkin stopped squabbling amongst themselves and began walking clumsily towards the cave in eerie unison. Their bipedal gait made them shamble like zombies, and even though I was a formidable predator, it made my flesh crawl. A small member with a limp moved along the walls, lighting torches one by one that had been set into the stone. Some people carried pickaxes, some carried buckets made of some kind of hide.

Ollie and I had no trouble eavesdropping.

"No jokes, folks, it's got to be here!" said a gruff male voice.

"We've searched every surface, so we have!" contradicted another. "We've been mining here so often, this cave might as well be a clubhouse, and I keep saying that we've been wasting our time!"

"Unless," said a third, "the inscription is etched into the halls-to-the-walls of the cave itself. Think about it. A petroglyph would last longer than a parchment scroll, so it would. If the map of Icenia's veins of ore were to withstand the elements, someone might have carved it and merely concealed it, such as behind that pile of boulders."

"Brouhaha, balderdash, ballyhoo! If someone wanted it hidden, do you think I could roll this rock so easily…?"

The sudden rumbling tremors commenced before I could bark a warning. Mighty earthen bulls turned loose from a holding pen might have made less noise than the ensuing rockslide. It was deafening to Ollie's and my sensitive ears, and I slid into my human form in order to endure the sound—on an island ruled by wylderkin, I cared very little for my own modesty.

Not only were we truly afraid, but the earth itself also shook with terror. The flickering torches illuminated a giant cloud of dust rising from the wreckage and the backlit shapes of panic-stricken raccoonkin.

The horrified wails that carried overtones of confusion and the scent of animalistic fear led us right to the scene of the disaster. I tried to wrap my head around the tangle of arms, legs, and stone. One of the men was frantically trying to dislodge himself from between two rocks in spite of the fact that his leg was obviously crushed and pinned. A swarm of surrounding people were trying to dislodge him, calling encouraging words of "Stay calm, Pobblebonk!" Others formed a protective circle, and a woman bared her teeth at our arrival.

"Intruders!"

"My friends, peace," I tried to reassure them. "My companions and I heard the commotion. No time to explain, just let us help this man!"

"*Wisssssht*! You smell like predators!" accused another.

"It's true that I am werewolf and my friend is vampire batkin. But we do not hunt fellow sentient beings. Now if you would please… I'm going to ask you to back away and give me some room." They melted away, either from fear of me or desperation of the crisis.

Drawing myself upright, I went into an in-between phase of metamorphosis. Wolf-headed, I still had opposable thumbs and tremendous upper body strength. Even still, the largest boulder atop the unfortunate man's leg would not budge when I grabbed it, and he let out a howl of pain. I was afraid that if he went into shock, he would revert to his more animalistic nature, panic, and be further injured.

Time to rethink this. My long claws were not sharp enough to dig into the solid stone floor of the cave, but I could use them to pry up smaller rocks, and I perused the rubble until I found a flat slab of stone and a second chunk of rock I could carry with the other hand. Using the two as a lever and fulcrum—and my brute strength—I was able to finally roll away the offending piece of debris while Ollie in his human form helped with the other stones and checked for injuries among the raccoon-kin. Someone else began to bind Pobblebonk's leg. Adrenaline rolled off of me in waves.

The urgency passed, their leader turned to face us. Even in human form his eyes had a wild glint, and his mouth gaped in an animalistic rictus. "I'm not going to lie to you," he told us gravely. "We normally don't allow outsiders into our circle, so we don't, but I suppose we are in your debt." He extended a bony hand. "I am Gribble." He introduced me to the wounded Pobblebonk and his advisors Yulara, Grot, and Thimberoo.

I smiled. "A pleasure to meet you, Gribble. My name is Kylix, and my little friend here is Ollie. If I may ask, what brings you all to such a treacherous place?"

Gribble's eyes were bright with passion. "We have tired of living paw to mouth every day here on this little island. My clan and I are craftspeople of metals—miners, blacksmiths, bladesmiths, jewelers, and wheelwrights. It definitely helps that we have the most dexterous hands of all the animal kin, so we do! Opposable thumbs, stewed plums!" I nodded my assent. Raccoonkin handiwork of any sort was the finest in all of Synvia.

"We have been searching for raw materials, mostly ores and minerals, but anything that can be traded is on our radar, wattle-bottle. We are soon embarking on a journey to further our skills through swapping lore and apprentices, so we are, away from this isolated island of Synvia. There is so much to be seen in world beyond—all of Icenia, Imladar, maybe even the Plains of Rage! No more of this bog, dog!" His words caused my heart to beat a little faster. Ollie had always tried to stir my imagination with tales of exotic places outside of Synvia, but this was my first time meeting someone who was planning to embark on such a journey.

But what if Ardyn suddenly took interest in me someday? Could I risk missing that chance? My thoughts were met with a pang, hot razors in my heart.

Gribble snapped me out of my musings. "There has been a rumor of some sort of guide to the best raw materials all of Icenia, which is what brought us to this rubbly-grubbly cave in the first place. We've made special efforts to keep it a secret, so we have." There was more than a hint in his tone.

"I have no interest in your quarry," I reassured him. "I am an artist, and my companion and I were on a stroll in hopes of relieving some of my... creative malaise. Rest assured we want no piece of your enterprise. But if I may? I would love to see this inscription you are seeking, as I'm always trying to get new ideas for my mosaics." I was excited, wondering what sort of messages I might be able to encode in hopes of furthering my legacy.

Someone brought a torch, and Gribble examined the surface where the rock pile had been. With his bushy tail he cleared away the dust to reveal a winding pattern divided into segments, each of which bore a rune. The odd inscription appeared to wriggle in the flickering firelight, and I blinked my eyes hard.

"*Churkee*! It looks like a snake, but it doubles as some sort of map," whispered Ollie.

"You are correct, mad respect, it's what we've been seeking," whispered Gribble. "It's a pathway to all the veins of ore and seams of stone in Icenia! *Wissssht*! Some very powerful magician must have created it for future empires, so he did. The runes along its segments don't seem to make any sense, however."

"I know this writing," I suddenly brightened. "This is the work of trolls! Let's see... *Malevolent Udrun calls forth your destruction.* That's an odd thing to inscr—"

Once again the explosion of sound sent my friend and me reeling. It was no picnic for the raccoonkin either, and they clapped their clawlike hands over their ears, yowling. But all sonic assaults were soon forgotten when the zombie troll materialized before us in a hail of rocks, just behind a fanglike barricade of stalactites. I had never known what it was like to be truly afraid before.

Sightless eggshell-white eyes trained on us, the gigantic corpse burst through the rocky teeth, sending rock splinters raining down on us. I automatically protected my eyes, but had the good sense to open them in time to see the zombie troll raise a club as long as I was tall, the weapon imbedded with everything from sharpened bone to… werewolf teeth. My mouth went dry even as I tried to stand my ground, and Ollie tucked himself against my side, quivering but still trying to shield me with a webbed arm. The undead abomination cleared a path for itself with its weapon and shambled toward our party. Undiscerning in its destructiveness, it smashed its weapon against the side of the cave, loosening a hail of fist-sized stones.

I'd never heard a meteor strike the earth, but I imagined that it wouldn't be unlike the collision of stone on stone resonating through the cave. The guttural roar was no force of nature, however, and the stench of rotten flesh and chaos magic was a heavy assault on my oversensitive nose. The top of its head grazed the roof of the cave, sending patches of dead scalp and bristly hair enveloping us in a crumbling cloud. Holding my breath, I tried not to think of what particles might be settling on my skin, let alone what I might be breathing into my lungs. I hoped that the creature would fall to bits before it could do any more damage, but the boarlike lower tusks jutting upward from its decaying jaw still looked sharp. Tales came to mind of how trolls tend to just scour the earth looking for something to bash even while they lived. I had to remind myself that it was no longer sentient, nothing more than a tool that targeted our party.

Several torches guttered and died, plunging us into near-darkness. The raccoonkin were in a panic, some scaling the walls of stone with their bare hands and feet. Others clustered around the wounded Pobblebonk, and some made a defensive formation behind Ollie and me.

Okay, that was too easy, I thought. *A map to all of the richest veins of ore, and it happens to be guarded by an undead troll, lying dormant until some explorer opens her big, fat mouth and utters the words on the rune sheet…*

I don't know if anyone else saw the door in the cave wall that appeared behind the zombie troll, one that I knew somehow should not be kept open. It led to things warped, chaos magic.

"It's the work of the troll warlord Fangthorn!" someone yelped.

"Nonsense, the Fangity-thorn has been dead for years, his bones long shattered-scattered. Any necromancer could have—"

"Would you stop playing wobbly gob and get the backpack?" snarled Gribble. "There's a trawling net in there, so there is!"

The belly of the sack was ripped open in panic, spilling the net like woven entrails onto the cave floor. Gribble snatched up the unassuming looking trap and tossed it with surprisingly fluid grace at the monster. The net dropped into a perfect circle around the zombie troll. Magnetized weights kept the woven web wrapped around our attacker, and Gribble twisted a clamp attached to a pole on it, binding the abomination as tightly as a spider would a fly.

The grid-like fibers detained the zombie troll for only so long before they began to snap. Designed to hold living prey, the net began to loosen as chunks of the zombie's flesh fell away, and the nightmare was soon able to move its arms again. The raccoonkin were able to halt the progress, but the troll still kept bashing people through the net.

Brave little Ollie flapped his wings menacingly, emitted a series of audible shrieks and ran circles the monster, managing to distract it somewhat. I was at a loss as to what to do. Human, wolf, or in between, I would be no match for a zombie troll.

This broken creature was attempting to destroy everything in its path. But I was damaged as well, and I knew a thing or two about the mutiny of broken things.

Flowing back into my wolf shape, I threw back my head and tried to howl. Choking on fresh dust and gagging on the stench of rot, I coughed, sneezed, and finally managed to launch a true note. And as I did, something within me unlocked. I attuned myself to a pulse I could feel within the cave, as if its chambers were a living, beating heart. My song drew up an energy that I had never channeled before, as if it were coming up from the very earth. I poured out all of my sorrow for the things I had never known, all of my love for my friends old and new, and my yearning for a greater destiny. I imagined each facet of the perversion slowly dislodged. I held the terrible thing in my sight, and I willed this image to unbind. Plaster broken, chaos reassembled into a pattern, and made new to tell a different story. The undead troll froze in its tracks, as if it could comprehend my wild music somehow.

We now we had another invader, this time attacking from the entrance of the cave, swinging a weapon and hurling threats in deep, melodic tones.

My attention wavered for an instant, and the troll began to solidify again. I snarled at the figure until I realized that it was Ardyn who had tried to come to the rescue, sword drawn, too late to take down the enemy.

No time to admire him, I was not to be steered off course this time. I resumed my wordless soliloquy, feeling the vibrations resonate down my spine to the tip of my tail. A strong current of energy shot through me, and I imagined it sparking off of the tips of my fur. The cave was so sweetly resonant, with its natural apses and wylderkin-made dugouts. The reverberations and overtones enveloped me as I poured out my sadness: for myself that I might never have a mate, for the innocent raccoonkin, for the corpse of this troll that had once been an innocent child, and even for this long-gone necromancer who was tormented enough to choose such a dark path of reanimating the dead.

The outline of the zombie troll began to blur. The door to the world of chaos beyond melted back into the solid stone wall. I closed my eyes and continued singing, tones rising and falling from my throat as if from some other world.

Sometimes emotion overcomes even death. I didn't know if the thought was my own or some ancient echo, but it didn't really matter.

I saw Ardyn out of the corner of my eye react to my wolfsong magic, watched his face as my song still echoed around the cave walls, resonating with magic long after any sound should have naturally died out.

At last only the sound of heartbeats remained. All things magical still decay. Nothing remained of the troll except a glimmering pile of brightly colored stones.

By this time, I was so lightheaded I couldn't even stand. I dropped to the floor of the cave with an undignified *woof*.

Ollie was the first one to swish to my side, with Gribble coming in a close second. "Giddysnickers! You never told me that you could do magic!" the bushy-tailed man exclaimed.

"Magic? What do you mean?" I was drained, disoriented, and too weak to do much but lie on the cool floor of the cave like a dusty gray rug.

"You drew upon the power of the earth with your song, so you did!" he went on. "That's a skill that requires rigorous training in most magicians, and you just accessed it naturally! Dumb lucky, duckie? You should come with us. We could use your skills for thrills! Somehow your howl has a healing pattern to it. How did you—"

And then Ardyn was pushing through, shooing my companions away until he was kneeling beside me. As he turned his face to study me, his brow smoothed. "That was magnificent," he admitted.

I tried to raise my head to see what he was talking about. "It was?" I mumbled hopefully.

He idly stroked my muzzle. "Yes, of course! Amazing that I should arrive on the scene just in time to bear witness. My song about this will be passed down along the ages!" Strong body pulling me into an awkward sitting position onto my haunches, he coaxed me to drink from his water skin. "It's Kyra, isn't it?"

"Kylix," I corrected him, thumping my tail in agitation. I hadn't realized that he had never bothered to learn my name.

"You have quite a voice. It might be quite a compliment to my own. Such a waste of talent, with you sitting in front of that painting!"

"*Mosaic*," I chided, but he was spellbound by his own speech.

"You could enjoy a more glamorous life as my backup singer and assistant," he continued. "You and I could potentially make a lot of money."

So I finally had his undivided attention. Well, sort of. He droned on and on about show business, and I had a hard time remaining focused on him. Possibly because I had just brought down a zombie war troll with some sort of howl music magic that I didn't know was within me, and I was exhausted. Or possibly it was because Ardyn was actually quite self-absorbed and boring.

"I am actually composing a ballad in my head *right now*. Did you know that I could do that?" He broke into song:

"*Zombies gathered in their masses*
Moving slower than molasses
No more war trolls have the power
When they hear my song, they cower
Yeah!"

And I wondered why in the world I had wasted so much of my talent paying tribute to him.

Stretching, expanding, muzzle retracting, fur fading, paws become hands, and I was back to human form. All of these metamorphoses in the span of one day were making me sore, and I groaned. A quick flex of my fingers, and on hands and knees I gathered the stones that had once been the troll—for a piece of art, or for a simple reminder of my newly discovered talents for singing magic, I did not know. I rose painfully to my feet, unassisted, while Ardyn continued to yammer away about glory and fame. Judging by the way the cave seemed to spin, I think I may have rolled my eyes in exasperation.

"*Churkee*! You're bound to be the most celebrated bard in all of Synvia," called out Ollie, not even bothering to hide his sarcasm regarding our tiny island.

Ignoring the batkin, Ardyn turned his gaze back on me. "Shall I call upon you when you recover?" he asked. "The full moon is in three days, and I would enjoy your company. We werewolves only find strength when we run together under the lunar spell, when we sing together."

It appeared that my song had broken more than one spell. In the unbinding of magic that does not heal, I had ripped away the glamour he had cast upon himself. His features dulled right before my eyes, this homely narcissist. His eyes were actually small and conniving, his mouth crooked like a dry riverbed. Skilled as I was, I lacked the talent to transform some broken things into true beauty. My best friend Ollie's face may have been plain and unremarkable, but there was something outright gruesome about Ardyn's spirit by comparison that I could not ignore.

As I glanced at Ollie, a quiet revelation nearly brought me back to my knees. Perhaps either my friend had been transformed, or else some sort of blindness within me had been healed. For I no longer saw Ollie's face. Instead, his sweetness was flooding so strongly from his infectious smile, I had to catch my breath. It was the most beautiful thing I'd even seen, and I knew I'd never capture it in jewels and glass. This was art that was meant for me alone. My friend threw me a wink and drew a bony, webbed finger across his lips before sneaking up behind Ardyn. I managed to suppress a chortle, pretending not to notice what he was about to do. A long trek to a cave and fighting a zombie troll made for a very hungry vampire batkin.

Ollie had a hidden talent as well, I realized. He was able to lend his strength to others, and wanted no credit for it, either. And he too could see the beauty in broken things, broken things like me.

I looked at the sea of raccoonkin faces, dark-rimmed eyes eager for unchartered territory. Ready for combat, ready for adventure. And these people needed me, they valued me for more than my art, and I hazarded a guess that they would even come to like me.

I had not even begun to know myself yet, I realized. There was more to life than my career or trying to win the affection of a man who lacked kindness. There was so much out there to capture in plaster and shards. And there were so many broken things to be found and loved and resurrected, simply for the sake of the beauty, of the process, the journey... not the final outcome.

I was the only one who noticed Ollie belch, lick a trace of blood from his lips, and roll his large eyes innocently before casually strolling away from Ardyn. The oblivious bard would most likely have a headache in the morning, and an inexplicable scratch on his neck.

We headed out for the coast in three days with the raccoonkin, where a chartered boat awaited us. It would take a full day on foot, but I had plenty of spring in my step. I wasn't sure yet if we were going to go straight to the Ash Forest or sail along the coastline, but I didn't care. It was time to lay out my greatest mosaic ever: the rest of my life. I would press into the eager plaster the facets of events yet to come: new places, new people, battles, trails, and joy.

One last glance at my now-empty house, and I set my jaw in determination to experience a wider world. I pretended not to see Ollie stick out his long tongue at Ardyn's door as we headed past it and off towards the coast and into the unknown. As I tried to keep a straight face Ollie chuckled, and I wondered how I'd never noticed before how musical his laugh was.

And the final shard slid into place, gleaming deeply within me.

Greenpool
Sarah Stegall

By the time she found the pool, Yllaria was nearly dead. She had run for days and nights and more days, from the seacoast to the marshes to the farmlands to the desert. Her feet were cut to ribbons, swollen and bleeding, but she ran on, pursued by the screams in her memories. After an eternity of running, she felt coolness on her face, under her feet. She knelt in the shade of a pine tree, no longer caring where she was, only dimly remembering that she must run, run, run. Once, she looked back, but saw only a tower of black smoke.

Wind through the pine. No, pines. More than one. She had reached the foot of the mountains. Here, the woods were thick and dark, with pine, beech and white-leaf intermingled. It was night, but bright moonlight had lit her path up the mountain scarp.

A cool breeze, and now the scent of water. She thrashed through a tangle of brush and tripped over a fallen branch. A great cliff loomed before her, its face a green curtain of elf-ivy and rain vines. She heard the drip of water. She pushed through a hedge of iron-thorn, and stopped. A wide green pool spread out at the base of the cliff, flowing from a horizontal crack in the base of the rock wall. She leaned forward to look, but her feet slipped on moss and she fell in.

Cold water grabbed her, pulling her under. Up and down disappeared, light and dark reversed themselves. Then her feet touched stone. She stood up, and found herself neck-deep in water. Pale light flickered all around her; she was inside a cave. Yllaria realized that the pool extended under the cliff overhang. On either side of the pool, a narrow shelf led out into the open. The light slanting in from outside showed her a shelf to her right. She climbed onto it slowly, feeling rough stone on her abraded feet. She dangled them in the cool water, and lay down. In two heartbeats she was asleep.

Fever woke her, and shivering that had nothing to do with the chill in the air. The light was stronger; it was morning outside the cave. She drank again from the pool. Hunger woke in her and her belly cramped. She had no food, and did not have the strength to forage. She lay down and slept again.

Nightmares screamed through her sleep, of blood and fire and battle. She saw her father's face as he swung his two-handed sword, heard her mother's fierce war cry as she charged with her spear. And then her brother, Ongro, bringing his axe down on the arm of a barbarian. And then a new horror—the face of an old ally and friend turned foe, Berne...

She jerked awake, screaming. But waking was as bad as sleep: she was alone, in a strange land, and her feet hurt. She lay down again. All that mattered now was water, sleep, and the moonlight shimmering in the pool.

There came a day when she woke with a clear head and agonizing hunger. She ducked under the overhang and waded outside. The late-summer sky hung clear, without clouds, and the wind smelled of pine and oak.

She spotted wild radishes at the edge of the pond and dug them up with muddy hands, forcing them into her mouth as fast as she could. They tasted of earth and water. There were other plants there: a bush with golden berries, a patch of flowers nodding white bells over the pond. She feasted on the berries, then dug up and ate raw tubers. When she had eaten all she could, she slipped back into the water, letting its cold clarity wake her, center her, heal her. Then she pulled herself out onto the bank and found a patch of sunlight. She let the warmth of the sun seep through her, and grew drowsy. Through heavy lidded eyes, she watched the sun go down and saw the moon rise. The moonlight threw silver rays across the pool's surface. Yllaria slept.

She dreamed of green water and black sky, of tendrils of glowing light twining round her, of the smell of earth and flowers weaving itself into her soul. And the unspoken whisper in her mind: *home*.

When she woke, a cat-face hung above her, black nose against red fur, with whiskers as long as her hand. Yllaria sat up, stifling a scream.

A gorbe—one of the wylderkin cat-creatures—crouched on haunches over her, body lithe and strong, half hidden in the moonlit shadows. It held up a hand. "Be quiet!" it commanded in a low growl. "Do not scare my prey."

Yllaria held her hand over her mouth and watched as the gorbe withdrew silently into the brush. She tried to watch its passage, but saw only the twitch of one leaf. Then there was a rushing noise, a loud growl, and the squeal of a small animal. Heart pounding, Yllaria moved quietly back towards the edge of the pond. Perhaps she could hide in the cave.

The saar emerged from a thicket, blood on its cheeks. "You have been in a fire. And come from… salt water?" It looked her up and down, and suddenly Yllaria was aware of her tangled hair, her ragged dress, her naked feet.

She pushed a hand through her brown hair. "I'm from Ocean Keep. My… my family has kept it for half a thousand years."

"What are you doing here?"

"I was running away."

The saar sat down. Yllaria spotted the sway of heavy breasts and decided the saar was female. "You ran away?" She snorted. "Humans have no honor. I would die before I ran from battle."

"There were so many of them." The horror of it thickened her throat with fear. "Berne Volnarsson, our own Oath-brother, attacked us without warning. My mother, my father… they fought. I saw them fall. My brother stood over their bodies, defending the keep."

"Yet you honor his courage by running away."

"He *ordered* me to run." Yllaria swallowed. "Who are you?"

The felinoid stopped licking her fingers and stared. "I live here. Who are *you*?"

"Yllaria."

"I do not like it that you are here." She drew in a deep breath, her tail twitching. "But since the Greenpool has accepted you, I must accept your presence."

"The Greenpool?"

The gorbe snorted. "You *are* an outlander. The Greenpool is this." She swiped at the still surface of the water, her claws sending up a spray of water to sprinkle on Yllaria's face. "And now you are the Greenpool."

"I don't understand."

The gorbe stood and turned around several times, then settled into a crouch. Her fur was tawny, striped with dark red on her body and muzzle. Her jerkin and trews were leather. The dagger at her hilt looked worn, and her claws were sharp and black. She snicked them back and forth as she studied Yllaria.

"I can smell the magic on you," she said, "but you are human, and have no sense of smell. I have been told this, but it is hard to understand."

She reached out, and with one deft stroke of her paw unearthed a tuber of the white bell-flowers. "Do you recognize this?"

"No."

Another swipe, and this time a branch holding golden berries landed in Yllaria's lap. "You ate these."

"Yes." Yllaria's hand crept to her midsection. "Are they poison?"

The gorbe laughed, a high mewling sound. "In a way. Human, you have eaten of the feyander and bathed in the Greenpool in starlight. You are bound to it forever now."

"Bound?"

The gorbe shrugged. "If you journey more than half a day's distance from this pool, it will bring you back."

"You mean, I'm *trapped* here?"

The gorbe shrugged. "Until you die, or find another to take your place. But that has never happened."

Horrified, Yllaria hunched into a ball, hugging her knees. "But how…" Shock spooled through her, and she felt tears creeping down her cheeks. "This is not right. I did not choose this."

"Few of us choose our fates, human. However, it is not a bad life. The last servant of the Greenpool lived a hundred years past her normal lifespan, before dying last moon-dark." She yawned widely, exposing sharp fangs and a rough tongue. "I must sleep. I will come see you again."

"But wait!" Yllaria cried. "I don't know what to do! And what is your name?"

The gorbe got to her feet. "My name? I thought I told you. I am Strixxa, of the clan Smilodon." And with that she turned, stepped past the golden-berry bush, and vanished into the forest.

Left alone, Yllaria let her tears flow. Could it be true? Was she now enslaved to this… this spring? She pushed the golden-berry branch away from her with a gesture of repugnance.

She wanted to go home.

The moon waxed, then waned. Yllaria gathered plants along the Greenpool's edge, pounded roots and tubers. She healed, slowly. The gorbe, Strixxa, did not return, and as time passed, Yllaria decided she did not believe the gorbe's tale of being bound to the Greenpool. Her feet had healed, and it was time to return and find out what had happened to her people. Even if her family was all dead, she was of Ocean Keep, and it was her duty to lead the people. She could not leave them in the clutches of barbarians.

In her head, she heard Strixxa's voice: *If you journey more than half a day's distance from this pool, it will bring you back.* Surely the gorbe was wrong. She had to be.

Yllaria's dreams continued to alternate between nightmares of blood and fire, and strange dreams of plants and water and starry skies.

One morning, she braided a bundle of tubers together, slung it over her shoulder, and set off down the mountain side. It had taken her only a few days to run here from Ocean Keep, but she knew it would take many more days to walk back, keeping out of sight of any roving barbarians. She had to know why Berne had broken his oath, why he had killed her family.

And when she had those answers, she would kill him. She didn't have a weapon, but she was sure she would be able to find one between here and the keep, even if she had to rob one of the Old Ones' tombs to get one. If all of her family was dead, she still had the duty to lead her people. She must get home.

The day grew warm. She wished she had figured out a way to bring water, but walked on with determination. Surely there would be a spring or a ditch between here and her home.

Home. What awaited her there? Death and ruin, she was sure. Anger curdled in her as she thought of Berne's treachery. Revenge burned hot in her, as hot as the sun above her head, as hot as the stone under her feet.

Hot stone? Yllaria stopped and looked down. She had emerged from the forest into a glade with exposed slabs of rock. Standing on one, she felt the burn and tingle burning through her leather shoes, climbing up her legs. It grew more intense, until she had to lift one foot and then the other, dancing in place to avoid the heat. It grew hotter, a searing heat like walking on coals. Bewildered, she backed into the woods, until her feet left the rock and were on cool earth again. What could have caused the rock to become so hot? There was no sign of a fire, and the sun was too weak to heat it up so much. Puzzled, Yllaria detoured around the glade and set off downslope again.

Another glade, another slab of rock, this time even hotter. She detoured around this one, and the next one, aware of the sun rising higher, of time lost in these repeated diversions. The sun had reached the zenith when she finally came to a stop on the edge of a cliff, with no way down. Disappointed, she realized she would have to backtrack and find another way. Yllaria sat down on a log in the shade of the wood; in the noon warmth, she lay back to rest and fell into a deep sleep.

She floated below the surface of the Greenpool, looking up through the shifting surface at blue sky and white clouds. The gorbe called Strixxa peered into the pool, shook her head and went away. Yllaria didn't care, she was relaxed and whole. She drifted down, sinking deeper into the green, but it wasn't scary, it was welcoming. She didn't fear drowning, she knew the water would lift her up for air when she needed it. As she drifted in its embrace, she heard the sounds of fish swimming, heard the roots of the forest drinking deep, heard the whispers of plant to plant.

When Yllaria woke, it was late afternoon and the sun was setting. Sitting up, she rubbed her eyes, blinked, and then gasped.

She was sitting beside the Greenpool.

She looked around, seeing the plants and water and cave just as she had left them this morning. Had she been sleepwalking? Had she gotten turned around somehow? But to return here she would have had to walk uphill, and surely that would have told her she was going in the wrong direction.

She shivered, hugging herself.

Over the course of the next few days, she stubbornly would set out, only to encounter hot rocks, downed trees across paths that had been clear the day before, and paths that twisted and turned but brought her back, inevitably, to the Greenpool. Sometimes she fell into a deep sleep, even as she was walking, only to wake at the edge of the Greenpool. There was never a sense of menace or danger, but do what she would, her feet led her back to the Greenpool. Every time.

She stopped trying to leave when the first snow fell, burying the forest in two feet of icy fluff. She knew the paths would be closed to her.

For days, as world turned colder and winter settled in, she sat in a dark stupor beside the Greenpool, watching its ever-changing surface, cursing the day she had arrived. Hunger broke her out of her depression. Winter had arrived, and she would have to make ready for it. Resigned to spending more weeks at the Greenpool, she got to work.

Yllaria gathered in the last fruits of the year: apples, nuts, wild onion and garlic. Other plants she gathered as well, not knowing what they were or whether she should eat them, but driven by some impulse she could not explain. She tied together a drying rack, and then another, and soon the inside of the cave was festooned with bunches of herbs and plants hung up to dry. She gathered firewood, too, and stacked it along one wall of the cave, resigned to the fact that she was not going anywhere until spring. From clay at the pool's edge she fashioned a crude cup and plate, firing them in her cave at the little fire she kept going. The reeds along the edge of the pool she made into baskets, or split and soaked the stems to make a linen-like plat she could weave into a kind of cloth. It wasn't much, but it was all she had.

Once or twice, she wondered where she got the knowledge to make linen, or weave a basket; it was not a skill much in use in the ruling family of Ocean Keep. But Yllaria found that when she needed the knowledge, it was there in her mind. She was too busy most of the time to wonder where it came from.

By Yllaria's reckoning, it was a half-moon before Midwinter Day when she met the wood-woman. Emerging from the cave one morning, Yllaria knelt beside the frozen-over pool and pounded on the ice to crack it. It splintered, ice floes bobbing away from her, and Yllaria drank deep of the icy water. When she straightened up, a woman with leaves in her hair was staring at her from across the pool.

Yllaria jumped to her feet. "Who are you?"

The woman's large, dark eyes held hers, not moving or blinking. She was tall, slender, and upon closer inspection, much younger than her gray hair would suggest. Her simple tunic hung past her knees. It was patterned in the colors of clouds and snow. They gazed at one another for some moments, until the woman looked away and grimaced. Yllaria saw the festering wound in her side then, weeping and red.

Something strong and deep in her reacted to the sight of the woman in pain. "What happened to you? Are you hurt?" Yllaria strode quickly around the pool.

The woman took a step, then another, then stumbled and fell. Yllaria knelt next to her, looking at the wound. "Have you been burned? This looks several days old," she said.

The woman shook her head weakly, and a shudder went through her. "Iron… burned me."

Yllaria laid the back of her hand on her forehead. Sure enough, the woman was burning with fever. "Come, let me help you into my cave," Yllaria said. She grasped the woman under the arms and helped her to her feet; the woman was as light as a milk thistle. Yllaria draped the woman's arm over her shoulder, and together they limped into the cave.

Once inside, Yllaria laid the woman down on her own pallet next to the fire. She built up the fire with a few sticks and laid her blanket over the woman.

"Would you like some water?" Yllaria asked.

The woman nodded weakly, and Yllaria gave her water to drink from her clay cup. The woman drank thirstily, and then her head fell back. "I seek the healing... of the Greenpool," she said, her voice faint and weak.

"I don't know what to do for you."

The woman waved her hand feebly. "Dream it. The Greenpool will tell you." And with that she fell into a deep sleep. Her breath came so slowly Yllaria feared she was dying.

Dream it? The Greenpool would tell her? What was it supposed to tell her? Yllaria felt frustrated and angry, resentful at her situation. She was chained to this cursed pool, and it was supposed to tell her something?

Deciding that there was nothing more she could do for the woman, Yllaria went out into the day. For a moment, Yllaria was back in the kitchen garden outside the door to the pantry at Ocean Keep, hearing Cook tell her assistant which herbs to winter over and which ones to pull and dry.

The winter sun shone dimly through the overcast, but it was enough for Yllaria to find her way to the ferry-bark grove a half-hour's walk to the west. She filled a basket with thin red strips of the bark, which peeled off easily this time of year. On her way back, she found a tuft of late mullein thrusting through the snow and gathered that. A whortleberry bush still clung to a few handfuls of fruit. She found herself irresistibly drawn off her path, and rather than fighting it she went deep into the woods, pulled by some force she didn't understand but did not fear. And there in a clearing grew a stand of fever leaf. Carefully, Yllaria gathered the flat brown leaves into her basket, then turned and hurried up the path to the cave.

Inside, she shivered and held out her hands to the fire. The gray woman slumbered on, moaning in her sleep and tossing fitfully. Squatting down, Yllaria closed her eyes and held out her hands to the fire.

The Greenpool will tell you.

In the darkness behind her eyes, she saw a grinding stone, leaves, earth. She smelled water and felt the heat of the fire. Without words, through image and taste and the glow of heat, the process came together in her mind. When she opened her eyes, she had it clear.

Taking handfuls of ferry-bark, she pounded them into dust on a flat rock. Scooping ash from the fire, she scattered it over the dust, then crushed whortleberry and fever leaf into a paste, moistened with heated water. Finally she wrapped the entire concoction in flat mullein leaves, to make a packet twice the size of her hand. When she was finished, Yllaria knelt beside the ailing woman and laid the poultice against her side. The woman moaned, but did not wake. Yllaria sat back on her heels, wiped her forehead with the back of her hand, and waited.

Without her blanket, Yllaria shivered. She piled more branches on the fire, and arranged her basket to block a draft. She munched on apples and nuts while she watched the forest woman. The stars came out. Yllaria put her hand on the poultice, realized it was cool, and made another hot poultice. This time the wound looked a little better, not the angry red it had been.

Dozing by the fire, Yllaria felt a song in her mind, tying together her thoughts like twine around a bunch of flowers:

Fire and water, earth and stone
Star and moon, blood and bone
Alone they thrive, together heal
By Greenpool magic, wound and weal.
Thistle of white, mullein green,
Whortleberry yellow, thin bark red,
Pull the iron from out the sheen,
Mend the skin and mend the head.

Yllaria woke in the early morning hours. The fire was nearly out; she rebuilt it into a warm blaze. Only then did she check on the woman; lifting the poultice, she gasped. The angry burn had faded to a healthy pink, and the edges were drawing together. As she sat marveling, the woman opened her eyes.

"The poison is leaving me. Thank you." She coughed. Yllaria gave her more water to drink, and the woman said, "I am grateful. You have saved my life. I and my kin are your friends forever."

"I'm not sure it was really me. I was sort of guessing as I went along."

The woman nodded. "Yes. The Greenpool is your teacher. It is usually the way."

Yllaria wanted to ask more questions, but the woman was clearly tired. She tugged the blanket up around the woman's shoulders. She noticed a faint tracery of vines on the woman's skin. "My name is Yllaria," she said. "Tell me if you need anything."

The woman smiled a very small smile. "My name is Frond. I am of the dryad folk, and we are forest-kin."

Yllaria blinked. "I've heard of your people, but only in songs and stories. I didn't know you were real."

"We are real," Frond said sleepily. "Most of the time...." And she slept.

Frond healed very quickly. She lay quietly the first couple of days, sleeping and drinking and watching Yllaria out of her large eyes. One night they sat together at moonrise, and Yllaria told her the story of her family's massacre.

"If you were not here, would you be back there, fighting?" Frond asked.

"Yes." Yllaria hugged her knees. "I would kill Berne Volnarsson and all his evil kin."

"To avenge your family's honor." Frond shook her head. "You would die."

"It's not only about honor," Yllaria said. "If my family is dead, then Berne rules in Ocean Keep, and our people are suffering."

Frond tilted her head. "You care so much for them?"

Yllaria looked at her, astonished. "Of course. I am responsible for them."

Frond waved her hand, indicating the Greenpool. "Now you have different responsibilities."

After five days, Frond was strong again. Yllaria woke one cold morning to find the wood-woman gone, but a pile of rare cloudberries lay on the pallet.

At night her dreams were either nightmares of terror and anger and burning grief, or strange fantasies where the woods spoke to her, the water of the Greenpool sang to her.

A week after Midwinter Day, Yllaria found a human woman with a feverish baby waiting for her beside the pool. This time Yllaria knew what herbs to brew for the child. She gave the woman instructions and a packet of herbs. A week later the woman reappeared and shyly presented her with a goose; Strixxa had to show Yllaria how to dress and cook it.

From then on, a steady stream of patients showed up at the Greenpool, bringing broken bones, fevers, and wounds. She rarely was at a loss for healing knowledge, which amazed her at first. But she came to realize that whenever she lacked the skill to heal a wound or cure a cough, a night's dreaming would reveal it to her. Always, the medicine she prepared was made with the waters of the Greenpool. Soon she knew that the pool itself was the source of most of the healing, supported by the chants she dreamed and the herbs she added to it. Now and then Frond would appear, seemingly emerging from the bark of a tree, to sit quietly by the pool as Yllaria worked, in friendly and companionable silence. Strixxa occasionally came by with a kill to share, or climbed a nearby tree and sat all day watching Yllaria at work. They were friends, of a sort. Still, Yllaria mourned her family and missed her home.

By spring, Yllaria was known throughout the forest for her healing prowess. Fruits, game, furs, and other goods appeared regularly at the edge of her pool, as the people of the forest expressed their gratitude. Yllaria did not forget, however, the tower of black smoke over her home, or the cries of her people slaughtered in her father's halls. Revenge burned in her, and she hoarded to herself the knowledge of herbs and concoctions with the power to kill as well as heal.

On the spring equinox, she tried again to leave the Greenpool, but was herded back to it by intertwining hedges, paths that twisted. This time she stumbled, exhausted, to the edge of the Greenpool and found Strixxa waiting, chewing on a rabbit bone.

"Why do you continue this foolishness?" the gorbe asked. She tossed the bone into the brush. "You know you cannot leave. This is your fate. The magic of the Greenpool has bound you."

Yllaria slumped to her knees at the edge of the pond and splashed water on her face. "I know. But can you blame me? What would you do if you could not go home?"

The gorbe shrugged. "My kin are my home. Yours are dead. This is your only home."

Yllaria nodded, but in her heart rebelled.

Spring turned to summer, dry and hot, with crackle-berry bushes bursting in the heat to reveal oozing red fruit, juicy and sweet. Yllaria gathered and harvested, tended and watered, led always by the dreams and half-dreams the Greenpool visited on her in her sleep. At night she slept in moonlight, near the water, knowing nothing would harm her. In the day, the dwellers in the forest brought her their broken arms, sprained wrists, bruises, coughs and agues. She cured them all, glad to be helping them, but feeling more lost and estranged from Ocean Keep every day.

She wondered what had happened to Cook, to the guards, to the tanner who lived outside Eastgate and the old woman who sold spices in the market square. She mourned her family and ached for her people. Only her growing friendship with Frond and Strixxa eased the ache of memory and home-longing.

Yllaria was pounding young tangle weed roots in her mortar one morning, when Frond dropped into a squat beside her. Her dress had turned green for summer. Frond's eyes were greener, and her hands and arms were painted in green, twining lines like ivy.

"Man coming," she said, reaching for a root.

Yllaria pushed her hand away. "That's for sick babies. Who's coming? Is Keran the farmer sick again?"

Frond shook her head and twisted her hair around her finger. She pointed southwest. "Coming up the deer trail. He's limping." Frond stood. "He's a stranger. I don't like strangers in my forest. I will be in the beech tree over there." Without waiting for an answer, she strode off, nearly disappearing in the yellow-green bushes.

Yllaria jumped when a lithe figure fell from the cliff face to land on four feet. "Strixxa! Are you trying to drive me into an apoplexy?"

The gorbe faced southwest, the fur over her shoulders twitching. "I don't like this one coming. He smells bad."

"A lot of the sick people who come here smell bad," Yllaria said. "Don't be rude."

Strixxa wrinkled her nose. "No, I mean his spirit is bad." She lifted her face into the breeze, her claws half-extended. "I will stay near. Be wary of this one." She slid into the shadow of the cliff and curled into a hunting crouch.

Uneasy, Yllaria realized that her only weapon was her belt knife. She was sharpening it on a whetstone when the sound of approaching footsteps reached her. She got to her feet and stood facing downslope, her knife clutched in her fist. Overhead the leaves of the beech rustled.

"He comes," whispered Frond.

Berne Volnarsson limped out of the tree line, as big and menacing as she remembered. His tangled blond hair was full of leaves. His tunic was torn and bloodied. He carried his war axe in one hand and a leather bag in another. When he saw her, he stopped and stared.

"You!"

Yllaria gripped her woefully inadequate knife tightly. "Oath-breaker." Her voice was hard as stone.

"You're dead."

"You must be so disappointed."

"How did you get here?"

"I rode on the back of a dragon. What do you want, Oath-Breaker?"

"Don't call me that!" His face went red.

"Why not? It's the truth," Yllaria said. "You swore a pact of friendship on the Oath-ring of your tribe. Do they know you dishonored it?"

Behind her in the shadows, she heard an ominous growl from the gorbe. "Kill him."

Berne's face went white, then red. "You lie!"

"I was there," Yllaria said. "At my father's table, at Midwinter Feast three years ago. You swore on the Oath-ring, with my father and my brother. My mother witnessed it, too."

Berne half-raised his axe. "You—"

"You attacked an Oath-friend, you have shamed not only yourself but all your kin." She cocked her head to one side. "Ah. So that's why you have come now, to kill the last witness. Me."

The beech above the pool rustled; Berne paid no attention.

"I didn't know you were here," he said roughly. "I came because they said there was a healer here." He raised the arm holding the bag. Yllaria saw the deep red gash, the edges puffy and dark with infection. Berne tossed the bag to the ground; it chinked faintly. "I was waylaid by bandits. I killed them, but not before they slashed me a few times. There is gold. If you are a healer, heal me, and keep the gold."

"I will not."

"Then your brother dies," he said, and now he almost smirked.

She stared. "Ongro is alive?"

"He lives in the cellars of Ocean Keep, as a hostage for your people's good behavior. I have the only key. If I do not return in a few days, he will starve."

Yllaria felt her whole body shudder. Ongro, trapped in the cold and dark, alone.

"And my parents?"

Berne shrugged. "I fed their corpses to the ravens."

Yllaria felt blackness fill her head.

Another soft growl from the shadows behind her. Yllaria made a slight "stay there" motion with her hand. "Why did you attack us?"

The man snorted. "I am a younger son. There was nothing for me, but there you were, fat and rich, with a good port and a stone keep. Why should you have it and not me? But I don't expect a woman to understand these things."

She stared hard at him. "I understand honor. Which you do not."

Berne's face contorted. "You will help me, daughter of the Keep. You will heal my wounds. You will not hurt me, because your brother will die if I do not return."

Even as the last syllable hung on the air, Frond dropped from the tree above him onto Berne's back. With a howl of rage, Strixxa leaped from her hiding place, claws out. The three of them snarled and howled, rolling around on the ground.

Yllaria ran around the pond, screaming, "Stop!"

Frond rolled away from the thrashing berserker, blood welling from below her eye. Strixxa yowled and slashed, her razor talons shredding Berne's boiled leather tunic, ripping through the chain mail around his waist.

Yllaria caught Strixxa's foot and yanked. "Stop! Let him go!"

Strixxa spun to face her, fangs white and sharp in her mouth, with death in her eye. But then she slowed, stepping away from Berne, who had curled into a ball on the ground. "Of course. His death is for you, not me. He is without honor, and does not deserve life."

"He holds my brother's life in his hands."

"If he tries to harm you, I will rip his skin off."

Slowly, Berne got to his feet, holding a hand to his bleeding face. He glared at Strixxa. "Wild cat! Bitch!"

Strixxa laughed at him. "*Human*," she said, and her voice dripped with contempt.

Yllaria looked at the man who had killed her mother and father, anger black in her heart. She wanted to plunge her dagger into him, to pick up his own axe and brain him with it. She remembered her mother charging her enemy with a spear, her father going down under the axe, the blood and fire and terror.

No one would know if she killed him now. She didn't even have to do it herself; Strixxa would do it gladly and without remorse. She would be rid of the nightmares and the fear, and she could go home.

Home.

Berne took a step, gasped as blood welled from his side and his knee buckled under him. He could barely keep his feet, but his glare was unabated. "Heal me, and your brother will live. And so will you."

She didn't want more nightmares. Honor demanded vengeance.

Her brother's life depended on her not taking her revenge.

Yllaria slumped. "Come to the cave," she said to Berne, and turned towards the Greenpool.

Strixxa stepped in front of her. "No!" She hissed. "You will not avenge your dead? You will not reclaim your honor?"

"I will deal with this."

Berne sneered. "I am not a fool. You will poison me. Or put your knife in me."

Yllaria met his gaze without flinching. "Do you have your Oath-Ring?"

Startled, he nodded.

Yllaria held out her hand. "Give it to me."

"What do you want with it?"

"I will swear an oath on it, not to harm you."

"No!" Strixxa hissed, but Yllaria ignored her.

"An oath?" Berne stared.

"I will honor an oath, even if you do not."

The barbarian put a hand into his tunic and brought out a bronze arm-ring, green with age and inscribed with runes. Scowling, he handed it to her reluctantly. "You know what this means."

"Better than you do, Oath-Breaker." Yllaria took hold of one edge of the ring; Berne held onto his side of it. Looking him straight in the eye, Yllaria said, "Berne Volnarsson, on this Oath-Ring I swear that I will not kill you. I will tend your wounds. I swear by my name, by the honor of my people, and of my House. If I break this oath, may my life be forfeit." She released the ring.

Berne stared at her, dumbfounded. Slowly, he put the Oath-Ring back into his tunic. "This is some trick."

"Unlike you, I do not seek ways to break an oath. Come to the pool and sit. I will tend your wound."

Frond drifted along behind Berne as the big man lurched around the Greenpool. He sat cross-legged at the edge of the pool, his war axe in his fist.

"Take off your jerkin and shirt," Yllaria said. At his look, she said, "I must stitch your wound and bandage it."

"Remember that I can kill you as fast as I killed your mother."

"And I can kill you just as fast," Strixxa growled.

Silently, Frond helped Yllaria gather her ingredients: thistlewort, mullein, and ferry-bark. Frond built up the fire while Yllaria and crushed the herbs with honey and oil of thora-root. Finally, Yllaria dipped water out of the Greenpool and poured it into the concoction.

Frond laid golden-berries and white bell flowers before her, looking meaningfully into Yllaria's eyes. "You don't have to do this. I can kill him from behind, while he isn't looking."

Yllaria shook her head.

"You fear him so much? Let me do it."

"What are you whispering there?" Berne bellowed.

Yllaria settled her clay pot close to the fire. "You must clean your wounds. Get into the pool."

Berne stared from her to the water, and absently scratched at his arm. The wound there was red and angry-looking. "You swore."

"I will not come near the pool. And it is shallow enough on your end that you need not fear drowning."

"I am not afraid of water!"

Without taking off his heavy trousers, the big man rose and then stepped gingerly into the pool. He held his war axe out of the water, muscles flexed. The water rose around his thighs, and he stopped. Still staring at her with deep suspicion, he scooped water onto his arm, his chest. He hissed when the cold water touched his skin. Finally he crawled out of the pool. "Get on with it," he said.

Yllaria smeared the poultice on a strip of cloth and stepped closer. "Raise your arm."

Quickly, efficiently, she bound the poultice around his chest, covering the wound. She stitched and bandaged the gash on his arm. She did not look at him, forcing herself to pay attention to what she was doing, not to think of the tower of black smoke over Ocean Keep, of his face when Berne attacked her father, her mother.

"That feels better," Berne said.

"You must change that every day," she said. "Get some sleep."

"You will kill me in my sleep."

"*She* won't," purred Strixxa. "I, however, have sworn no oath."

"But I have, Strixxa." Yllaria looked coldly at Berne. "Perhaps you remember what that means to persons of honor."

When he looked away, she entered the cave and returned with her arms full of bedding. She dumped it unceremoniously at Berne's feet, then walked to the other side of the pool.

"I'm hungry," he said. "Would you starve me?"

"Yes," said Strixxa, with no hesitation.

Frond dumped a double handful of golden berries and white bell flower tubers at his feet. "Eat," she said, contempt in her voice. "Fear not, they are not poisonous. I honor my friend's oath."

Slowly, he tasted a berry, then another, and then crammed the berries and tubers into his mouth, smearing his beard with juice. He scowled, fidgeted with the bedding, and finally lay down next to the fire. Soon he was snoring.

Yllaria could not sleep. The moon rose, full and white, and shone on the surface. Yllaria sat beside the Greenpool, hugging her knees, half-dozing. Frond curled against her side, and Strixxa sat staring at Berne, her eyes narrowed to slits.

"You don't have to stay," Yllaria said.

"I will not leave you with that killer," Frond said.

Strixxa didn't bother to answer.

The moon's reflection rippled in the surface of the Greenpool. A curl of mist rose from its surface. A deep feeling of peace stole over Yllaria, a greeting and a farewell, both. She felt an... *ebbing*.

Strixxa rose, went to the sleeping man and picked up his axe. She carried it to Yllaria and laid it at her feet. Frond shifted away from the iron weapon.

With loathing, Yllaria stared at the weapon that had killed her parents. Slowly, she lifted the heavy axe in her hands. She could kill Berne in his sleep with it, avenge her parents. But she had sworn an oath. She would not stoop to his level.

Yllaria opened her hands, and the axe fell into the pool with a quiet splash.

"Cold water to drown cold iron." Frond nodded her approval. She held out Berne's tattered tunic. "What you seek is in here. I will not touch it."

Yllaria rummaged in the tunic and drew out an iron key.

Strixxa came up beside the dryad. "Dawn is coming." The cliff wall above the pool showed a band of gold from the rising sun.

The ashes of the little fire were cold. Yllaria took her knife from the clay pot and stuck it in her belt.

"I'm ready."

"We will miss you," Frond said.

Berne woke and stretched. "I am hungry. Fix me something to eat," he said.

Yllaria faced him. "I am leaving now."

"What? No, you are not. You must stay and heal me!"

Yllaria turned and walked away.

"Stop! Come back!"

Yllaria kept walking. Nothing would stop her. The morning breeze was cool on her cheek.

"Stop!" A heavy tread behind her. "Stop right there! If you leave me, Ongro dies!"

Yllaria turned to face him. "Who stays and who goes from the Greenpool is not up to you, or to me." She gestured at the pool lying quiet in the sun. "You have bathed in the water, you have eaten feyander—plants infused with magic. You have slept in moonlight. Now you are bound to the Greenpool."

"What? You lie, woman!"

Yllaria shrugged. "I do not."

"I will follow you."

"You cannot. You are bound to the Greenpool."

Frond stepped forward. "She speaks the truth. You cannot leave the Greenpool now. It will call you back if you try to go."

Berne cursed. "You swore an oath! Do you break it now?"

Yllaria looked at him calmly. "I swore to heal you and not to kill you. I have kept my oath."

Frond nodded. "In fact, you will live longer than any other of your kind, here at the Greenpool. She has done you a favor."

Strixxa sat on her haunches. Her tongue lolled between her fangs. "Human, you will be here the rest of your life."

"No!"

"Forever," Frond whispered. "Unless, of course, you choose to end your miserable life."

"I can help with that," Strixxa said.

Berne fell to his knees. Yllaria knew he was already feeling it, the pull and tug of magic, the Greenpool's call in his blood. "No."

Yllaria lifted her face, felt the sun warm on it. "Forever," she murmured. "Never to roam free again, never to wage war again, never to break your oath of honor again." Yllaria drew forth the key. "But my brother, and our people, will be free."

"No!" Berne slammed his fists on the ground, howling his rage.

Strixxa watched him, a feral grin on her face. "This will be amusing," she said. Glancing at Yllaria, she waved a hand. "Go, my friend. He cannot follow."

Yllaria knew she could turn and go, knew that nothing would stop her. But she paused. A year spent as a healer had changed her. And there were people who depended on her now, not just the folk of Ocean Keep, but the forest dwellers as well.

"There is one chance for you," she said. Berne raised his eyes, anger and fear naked on his face. "You can starve here when the berries are all gone, or you can become the healer in this forest, and the people will feed you."

"A healer?" Berne spat. "I am a warrior. Where is my axe?"

"You will never lift it again. But if you change your ways, if you let the Greenpool make you into a healer, you may live a long, long time here. It is up to you."

Frond raised an eyebrow. "He does not have the courage to change."

Berne stared at her, despair in his face.

Strixxa laughed. "Yllaria, this is a fine revenge." And turning so that Berne could not hear her, she whispered, "We won't tell him the part about finding someone to take his place."

Frond grinned. "Not a word."

Yllaria turned. Ahead of her lay the paths that would take her back to her brother, to her people.

"It is time to go home," she said.

Garg the Good
Dominic Bowers-Mason

I am Garg. I am strong. I am strong because I am ogre. No one in the forest is stronger than me. When I was young, the old ogres make the rules, hit me when I don't follow. Now I am older. I make rules. I go where I want. I eat what I want. I take what I want.

One day, I find something I want. Pretty pink-skin sharpclub. Bright stones on short round end, and long sharp end shimmers like pond water. I want, so I take. Little hard-shelled pink-skins have come to my forest with sharpclubs before, long time ago. They smarter than others. They know that they can't hit stronger, so they need to hit better. I am going to use pretty sharpclub to hit stronger *and* better. I am looking forward to using sharpclub to hit.

I am not expecting sharpclub to hit me.

Sharpclub is alive. Sharpclub is angry. It does not want what I want, and so it hits me. I have been hit before. I am strong so I can take hits. But it hits my mind, and I do not know how to hit back. For the first time in long, long time, I submit. Sharpclub is strong. Sharpclub makes rules now.

Sharpclub tells me what to do. Sharpclub makes me stop fighting others in forest. Makes me give up land. I do not want to, but Sharpclub makes rules now. I am not strong now. Eventually, Sharpclub stops being angry at me and starts being curious.

Sharpclub tells me her name. She is Moonslicer, made by pink-skin shamans for pink-skin warriors. I understand this. She was made to kill pink-skin enemies. But I am pink-skin enemy. She does not kill me. I do not understand this.

One day, while eating dinner, I ask Moonslicer. "Why do you not kill me?"

"I don't understand your question," Moonslicer replies.

"You are pink-skin sharpclub—"

"Greatsword," Moonslicer interrupts.

"—and you are made to fight pink-skin enemies."

"I was made to destroy evil," Moonslicer answers. She always talks in strange riddles. I have become used to this.

"Yes, evil. I know this word. It means pink-skin enemy. I am pink-skin enemy. I am evil. Why do you not destroy me?"

Moonslicer does not answer for long time.

"You are… 'pink-skin enemy,' yes. And most people would say you are evil. But I am not sure. I expected you to fight me, but you didn't. I expected you to resist when I told you to stop bullying the other creatures of the forest, but you didn't."

"Moonslicer is stronger than Garg, so Moonslicer makes rules."

"All the same, I think there might be some good in you, somewhere."

"What is Good?" I ask.

"Good is…" Moonslicer stops talking. I can feel she is confused. "Good is… how to describe it? It is…" She stops again. She is quiet for long time. "You know, I believe the best way to explain it is to show you. Go to sleep, Garg. Tomorrow, we will start doing Good."

Next day, Moonslicer leads me to pink-skin home, in the middle of fields. No pink-skins there right now. She shows me broken walls. Tells me to take stones and fix walls. Then we leave. I do not understand.

"Why do we fix walls?" I ask.

"Those walls protect the humans from harm," Moonslicer says. "They have been torn down by raiders over the years. By repairing the walls, you have made the humans more safe. More strong."

"Why do I make them safe?" I ask. "I am pink-skin enemy. I do not want them to be strong."

"Patience, Garg," Moonslicer says. "Have patience and faith. You will understand eventually."

I do not believe her, but I say nothing. This does not make sense. This is pink-skin strangeness.

For the next two seasons, Moonslicer keeps sending me out to pink-skin lands. Fixing walls. Catching cows and taking them back to paddocks without eating them. Sometimes she makes me scare humans on roads. Sometimes she makes me hide from humans on roads. She calls the ones I scare "bandits" and the ones I hide from "merchants." I do not understand the difference.

"The merchants are weaker humans," Moonslicer says. "The bandits are stronger, and want to take from the merchants. You are driving them away from the roads so that they do not take from the merchants anymore."

"This makes sense," I say. "They are stronger, they take what they want. But why do you make me scare them so they cannot?"

"Because it is not good for the strong to take what they want from the weak."

"This Good does not make sense. I will never understand."

"You will understand," Moonslicer says. "Have faith."

For many more seasons, Moonslicer makes me do many things I do not understand. Eventually pink-skins—humans—start to see me. At first they are afraid. I understand this. But they slowly become less afraid. They no longer run when they see me. I do not understand this. I dig long ditches from the river to their farms. I build walls along their roads. I bring large sacks of food to their towns and leave them there.

One season, there is a great storm. Moonslicer wakes me during the night, urges me to leave the cave and go to the human lands. There is a town I have been near many times before. The river that flows through the village is flooding. The humans are splashing, shouting, drowning. They are scared. Moonslicer sends me through the flood to their homes. I lift humans from the water and put them at the top of the homes. I do this again, and again. I am tired, but Moonslicer pushes me on. I save more humans. I wade through the water that is up to my chest. I save the male humans, the female humans, the young humans, the old humans. I save all of them. When the dawn comes and the water goes down, I am more tired than I have ever been. I sink to my knees. I know the humans will kill me while I am asleep but I am too tired to get away. I fall asleep.

I wake up. I am not wet, cold or tired. I am warm, dry, resting on something soft and comfortable. I recognize it as a human barn—I have brought escaped horses to these before. I am covered in many skins. I am lying in dried grass—the humans call it hay.

A male human comes in. He sees I am awake. He does not run or look scared. Instead he smiles. He brings a large bundle up to me. The bundle has meat in it. Good, cooked meat. Better than I have ever tasted. I watch him carefully, but I am hungry and I concentrate on eating. Once I am done, he takes the bones and the bundle away.

The day goes by, and many humans come to the barn. Some hide by the door and only stare at me. Others come in. I recognize many of them as the humans I saved last night. I am still tired, so I lie in the barn. I feel… I do not know how to describe it. The humans do not threaten me, but not because I am stronger. Finally, in the evening, many humans come to the barn. They bring Moonslicer with them.

"I have been negotiating with the humans on your behalf," she says. "They are going to give you this barn to live in as a new home. They will give you food, while you keep the roads safe from bandits and help them tend their flocks and fix their buildings. I will stay with you to guide you."

I am quiet for long time.

"I do not understand." I say. "If I was strong, and I came to take these things, they would not give them to me. They would run, or fight."

"But you didn't come to take them," Moonslicer replied. "And that is what makes the difference. You have made the humans' homes safe. You have protected their merchants. You have rescued their animals. And now you have saved their lives. And because you gave and gave and did not take, they now want to give to you, freely. And as long as you do not wish to take, you will receive. By serving them, you are now more free than you ever were in the forest. Not because you are strong. But because you are a friend. They are your strength now, and you are theirs. This is what Good is."

And I understand.

About the Authors

Derek Beebe's first novel, *It's a Wonderful Death*, takes place in the world of Fortannis. His "Dynasty" fantasy trilogy was released in 2024. He was also published in the *Baker Street Irregulars* anthology series. He is a co-host on the *Sci-Fi Pubcast* podcast and once spent an agonizingly long period as a high school history teacher (three whole months!) before settling into a boring career in banking. He lives in Pennsylvania and his web page is www.DerekBeebe.com.

Susan Bianculli, a happily married mother of two, has loved to read all her life. Fairy tales from collections like *The Yellow Fairy* took her to magical places when she was young; and Fantasy and Sci-fi stories took her to places such as Middle Earth and Dune in her teens. A graduate of Emerson College with a Minor in Writing, she is the author of the four-book Young Adult e-series The Mist Gate Crossings: *Prisoners of the Keep*; *Bascom's Revenge*; *Descent Underearth*; and *The Long, Dark Road*—all published by CBAY Books. She has also written three prequel novellas to it, and has appeared in other anthologies. To see what else she's written, check out her website: www.susanbianculli.wix.com/home.

Dominic Bowers-Mason lives under the hole in the ozone layer in New Zealand, where his Scottish/Scandinavian ancestry ensures that summer is his least favorite season. He stumbled into professional writing quite by accident, when he failed to end a heartwarming short story with the standard, internet mandated fake-out. His interests include science fantasy, choice-driven story games, and repeatedly failing to get cast as the villain in amateur theatre productions.

When not writing, **W. Adam Clarke** plays saxophone, streams Live Plays of six different role playing campaigns on Twitch under SingleStepGaming, and produces materials with Single Step Gaming for home use. His first book series should be available in early 2025. He hopes to soon be able to afford first person pronouns.

Jon Cory comes from a family of readers and writers. His humorous writing has won awards in the Foster City International Writing Contest and the London Book Festival. His debut novel, *A Plague of Scoundrels*, received an IPPY silver medal for popular fiction. The second novel, *Roly's Relic* is a humorous caper about an ancient Celtic cross with a bad attitude. He has had stories in all the earlier *Tales of Fortannis* collections, and is currently creating new Sarlon The Sellsword adventures.

Jon lives with his wife in the San Francisco Bay Area. An amateur archaeologist, Jon has participated as a team member on expeditions in seven countries. He enjoys being an active member of the California Writers Club.

In **Tera Fulbright**'s world, she is dedicated to driving stronger engagement at her place of work, creates innovative programming for SF conventions—including her own (ConGregate), and writes short stories that tug on the emotional heartstrings of her readers. She is also the author of several short stories including her first, "History in the Making," published in the anthology *Rum and Runestones* in 2010. Her stories have continued to be published in various other anthologies, including *Athena's Daughters, Dark Fairy Tales Revisited, Urban Fantasy, Spells and Swashbucklers*, and in the original *Tales of Fortannis* collections. When not writing, working or running cons, you can find Tera with her family and friends playing Pathfinder, coming up with a new costume idea or curled up with a good book.

Jesse Grabowski is a former veteran high school English teacher, track coach, drama director, and set designer. He now enjoys his days doing leather work, restoring old furniture, and writing fiction. He enjoys video games, reading, writing, directing plays, going to sporting events, concerts, conventions, and live action role-playing games.

Christine L. Hardy analyzes data by day and writes fantasy by night. Her stories have appeared in the anthologies *Tall Tales and Short Stories from South Jersey, Reading Glasses: Stories Through an Unpredictable Lens*, and *Different Dragons Vol. II*. A proud member of the South Jersey Writer's Group, she lives with her son Jeff, her cat Koko, and an escape beagle named Zeke. Their escapades can be found on Facebook as well as at "Write First, Blog Later," aka ChristineLHardy.com.

Henry "the Mad" Hart lives with his wife in Boston and is, at the moment, drinking a cup of tea and watching the rain. He enjoys telling stories with his friends and making music. His Fortannis tales have appeared in previous collections, and his horror novella will soon be available.

Jesse Hendrix has written blogs, short films, plays, and short stories for small but appreciative audiences. His short film "Hypothetical Dilemma" was accepted into the Union City Film Festival and can be seen on YouTube. "Bartleby Goes Adventuring" is his first published short story. Jesse lives in Bayonne, New Jersey, with his wife and two sons. He is very involved with the fan community and has helped run Lunacon since 2007.

For **Miles Lizak**, Fortannis was the setting of Miles' first LARP experiences, the start of the path that would lead him to writing for over a dozen LARPs, including some of his own. Miles comes from the salt marshes of southern New Jersey and resides in Barcelona, Spain. When he isn't writing fiction, Miles works as a freelance science journalist, produces and hosts multilingual storytelling events (*StoryMachine BCN*), and creates theater. His short fiction has appeared in *Nature Careers*, *Society for Misfit Stories*, *Five2One Magazine*, and others.

Mark Mensch has always been interested in telling stories—whether it was from his BA in both Theatrical Arts and English or running tabletop games since he was twelve. His passion for both has given him an eclectic resume—from working at a virtual reality theme park to directing computer and online games as well as helping to build the Ex'pression College for Digital Arts. His current way to pay the bills is working as a scene tech at Zellerbach Hall at UC Berkeley. He continues to create various props, masks and other items for multiple Live Action games (https://www.etsy.com/shop/LARPGear) as well as consulting on the creation and running of them. He has had stories in each of the original *Tales of Fortannis* collections. And for fun, Mark is a magician as well as a fire eater/breather.

Much to his embarrassment, **Bernie Mojzes** has outlived Lord Byron, Percy Shelley, Janice Joplin, and the Red Baron, without even once having been shot down over Morlancourt Ridge. Having failed to achieve a glorious martyrdom, he has instead turned his hand to the written word, in the pathetic hope that he shall here find the notoriety that has thus far proven elusive. His work has appeared in a number of anthologies and magazines, including *Bad-Ass Faeries II* and *III*, *Gaslight & Grimm*, *Betwixt Magazine*, *Daily Science Fiction*, and *What Lies Beneath*. In his copious free time, he published and co-edited *Unlikely Story* (www.unlikely-story.com) and the ever-timely *Clowns: The Unlikely Coulrophobia Remix*, as well as editing *The Flesh Made Word* for Circlet Press. Should Pity or perhaps a Perverse Curiosity move you to seek him out, he can be found at the rarely updated and grossly outdated website: www.kappamaki.com.

Beth W. Patterson was a full-time musician for over two decades before diving into the world of writing, a process she describes as "fleeing the circus to join the zoo." She is the author of the books *Mongrels and Misfits* and *The Wild Harmonic*, and a contributing writer to over ninety anthologies. Patterson has performed in over twenty countries, collecting lore. Her playing appears on over two hundred albums, singles, soundtracks, commercials, and voice-overs (including nine solo albums of her own). She frequently tours with fiddler Seán Heely and occasionally performs comedy as Bad Beth and Beyond. Her web page is www.bethpattersonmusic.com.

Sarah Stegall writes science fiction, mystery and horror. Sarah's most recent short story, "Hungry," appeared in the anthology *Hot Iron and Cold Blood* from Death's Head Press in Fall 2023, under the nom de cowboy of Jesse Allen Champion. Her novel *Outcasts: A Novel of Mary Shelley*, about the writing of *Frankenstein*, was released in May 2016, in time for the 200th anniversary of the book. Her horror story "Rearguard" was a finalist for the Scribe Award given by the International

Association of Media Tie-In Writers. She got her start researching and co-writing the first three Official Guides to *The X-Files*, which spent fourteen weeks on the *New York Times* best-seller list. She has also written murder mysteries (the Phantom Partners series) and science fiction. Sarah lives in California. Her website is at www.munchkyn.com.

Mike Strauss discovered his love for fantasy in a homebrew Dungeons & Dragons game when he was only six years old. Eventually, that passion led to telling his own stories at the table with his friends and then at a campground for dozens of like-minded people living out dreams of fantasy. When the opportunity came to put some of his stories in writing, he jumped at it. He has been writing ever since, hoping to help future six-year-olds someday find a fantasy to love.

Individual Story Copyrights
(this page is a continuation of the copyright page)

"The Mystery of the Dead Cat in the Darkness" by Bernie Mojzes. Originally published in *A Bard Day's Knight*, copyright 2015.

"Hidden Bouquet" by Derek Beebe. Originally published in *No Holds Bard*, copyright 2018.

"The Lost" by Miles Lizak. Originally published in *No Holds Bard*, copyright 2018.

"The Vacarran Corsair" by Jesse Grabowski. Originally published in *A Bard in the Hand*, copyright 2013.

"A Charming Encounter" by Tera Fulbright. Originally published in *A Bard Act to Follow*, copyright 2016.

"Hoarfrost" by Susan Bianculli. Originally published in *No Holds Bard*, copyright 2018.

"The Curse of the Dwarven Necromancer" by W. Adam Clarke. Originally published in *A Bard Act to Follow*, copyright 2016.

"The Dragon in the Kettle" by Christine L. Hardy. Originally published in *A Bard Day's Knight*, copyright 2015.

"Bartleby Goes Adventuring" by Jesse Hendrix. Originally published in *No Holds Bard*, copyright 2018.

"Unscarred" by Mike Strauss. Originally published in *A Bard Day's Knight*, copyright 2015.

"The Otherside Alliance" by Jon Cory. Originally published in *A Bard's Eye View*, copyright 2011.

"Chalric Hill" by Henry "The Mad" Hart. Originally published in *No Holds Bard*, copyright 2018.

"A Matter of Death and Life" by Mark Mensch. Originally published in *A Bard Day's Knight*, copyright 2015.

"The Mutiny of Broken Things" by Beth Patterson. Originally published in *A Bard Act to Follow*, copyright 2016.

"Greenpool" by Sarah Stegall. Originally published in *No Holds Bard*, copyright 2018.

"Garg the Good" by Dominic Bowers-Mason. Originally published in *A Bard Act to Follow*, copyright 2016.

Milton Keynes UK
Ingram Content Group UK Ltd.
UKHW042037031224
452078UK00001B/194